Lord of War

Peter Darman

Formatted by Jo Harrison

Contents

List of characters

Those marked with an asterisk * are Companions – individuals who fought with Spartacus in Italy and who travelled back to Parthia with Pacorus.
Those marked with a dagger † are known to history.

The Kingdom of Dura
Aaron: Jew, royal treasurer at Dura Europos
*Alcaeus: Greek, chief physician in Dura's army
Azad: commander of Dura's cataphracts
Chrestus: commander of Dura's army
Claudia: daughter of Pacorus and Gallia, princess of Dura, Scythian Sister, now adviser to King of Kings Phraates
Eszter: daughter of Pacorus and Gallia, princess of Dura
*Gallia: Gaul, Queen of Dura Europos
Kalet: chief lord of Dura Europos
Klietas: squire to King Pacorus
Lucius Varsas: Roman, quartermaster general of Dura's army
*Pacorus: Parthian, King of Dura Europos
Rsan: Parthian, governor of Dura Europos
Sporaces: commander of Dura's horse archers
Talib: Agraci, chief scout in Dura's army
Zenobia: commander of the Amazons

The Kingdom of Hatra
*Diana: former Roman slave, now the wife of Gafarn and Queen of Hatra
*Gafarn: former Bedouin slave of Pacorus, now King of Hatra

Other Parthians
Akmon: King of Media, son of King Spartacus
Castus: son of Spartacus, heir to the throne of Gordyene
Haytham: son of Spartacus, prince of Gordyene
†Phraates: King of Kings of the Parthian Empire
Spartacus: adopted son of Gafarn and Diana, King of Gordyene

Non-Parthians
†Amyntas: King of Galatia
†Artaxias: King of Armenia
†Glaphyra: mother to King Archelaus of Cappadocia
Karys: Jew, Satrap of Mesene

Kewab: Egyptian, Satrap of Aria
Lusin: Armenian, Queen of Media
†Polemon: King of Pontus
Spadines: Sarmatian, close ally of King Spartacus

Chapter 1

The atmosphere in the throne room was oppressive, beads of sweat appearing on the foreheads of those I was circling in a menacing fashion. Or at least I was attempting to be threatening as I limped up and down in front of the four individuals drawn up in a line, saying nothing at first to increase the tension. I was probably fooling myself and the truth was my leg was aching like fury, which made me wince, thus spoiling the façade of intimidation. Nevertheless, I was far from happy and wanted answers, though the one who could provide them was not present. Not yet.

I walked slowly behind the four, all much younger and fitter than me, though all nervous in the presence of an angry King of Dura. I took a few more paces to stand before them, folding my arms across my chest prior to speaking, the overall effect being ruined as a sharp pain shot through my leg, which felt as though a red-hot branding iron had been pressed into the flesh. I grimaced in pain.

'Are you hurt, highborn?' asked Klietas, concern etched on his face.

'Silence!' I shouted. 'You will speak when spoken to.'

It was warm in the throne room, the morning dry and hot, the doors to the chamber having been shut and the guards instructed to leave so I could be alone with the transgressors, though I was feeling more breathless and tired than they. I walked back to my throne, though hobbled would be a more accurate description, lowering myself slowly on to the wooden seat. My leg continued to throb, and I cursed the archer that had put an arrow into my limb all those years ago.

I stared at each of the accused in turn. Talib, the Agraci leader of the army's scouts stood next to his wife Minu, the deputy commander of the Amazons, whose name meant 'paradise' in Persian but who was an accomplished killer, her lithe frame and full lips belying her deadly skills. Next to her stood another Amazon, Haya, taller, her hair slightly lighter and her heart-shaped face giving her a most charming appearance. But my eyes were drawn to the small scar on her neck, the result of an arrow wound at Irbil, which had killed her. Yet here she was. Hale and hearty. The last member of the group was my squire Klietas – the scrawny, threadbare orphan from Media who had returned with me from Irbil to be trained to eventually become a cataphract, though he had of late been absent from the palace. I continued to stare at the scar on Haya's neck. I wondered if she knew she was a walking miracle? Probably not. I decided to break the silence.

'Imagine my surprise when a former Roman slave, a man who worked in the kitchens of a villa in Zeugma, presented himself to me outside the Citadel yesterday morning, throwing himself to the ground in front of my horse and thanking me for releasing him and his family from a life of bondage.'

Klietas, innocent that he was, smiled in recognition of his achievement. The other three stood like statues, unblinking.

'General Chrestus riding beside me nearly killed the man on the spot, fearing it was an assassination attempt. Either that or due to his extreme annoyance at nearly being thrown from his horse. But I was intrigued and after I had calmed the general down, I got talking with the cook, who told me an interesting tale. Of how he and the other slaves in the household of a rich, fat Parthian and his wife had all been freed by four individuals, two men, one young, one older, and two women, again one older than the other, who had all entered the villa as slaves.'

I nodded when I saw furtive glances between Talib and Minu.

'I will not ask you to betray your mistress, for after speaking with the cook some more I learned he was the property of a man named Cookes and his wife Hanita. He was so grateful for him and his family being freed that he and they walked all the way to Dura from Hatran territory, though he informed me he and the other freed slaves had all been given money to start new lives. But he wanted to thank the King of Dura personally for sending his servants to Zeugma to free him.

'You can imagine my astonishment at this declaration, having had no knowledge of any mission to Zeugma.'

At that moment the doors to the chamber were opened by the guards outside and in swept Gallia, nostrils flaring, and eyes narrowed to slits, her face a mask of steely determination. I sat back and smiled as she marched to the dais, turning to look at her co-conspirators.

'You may all leave,' she barked.

Talib gave Minu a sideways smile, Haya looked relieved and Klietas was grinning like a mischievous teenager, which, despite his now sinewy, toned frame, he was. Caught between their queen and king and unsure what to do, I flicked my hand to indicate they all should leave. They did so, in haste.

'Close the doors behind you,' I called after them, Talib, bowing his head as he did so.

Gallia drew herself up in front of me, eyeing me icily before speaking.

'I hope you have not meted out any punishments to my loyal servants.'

'*Your* servants? I thought I was king at Dura. As to punishing them, in view of the fact they were acting under your orders, they are blameless of any infractions, though I do not endorse using this kingdom's soldiers as assassins.'

She touched her necklace, from which hung a lock of Rasha's hair. She pulled out the lock from under her tunic and examined it.

'You remember Rasha, Pacorus? The child we first met in this palace over forty years ago? Perhaps you have forgotten her already.'

The chamber was hot and airless, my leg was aflame, and I was in no mood for my wife's sarcasm. I rose from my seat.

'How dare you! I loved Rasha as much as you did. But I have not sunk so low as to use her death as an excuse to send assassins to indulge your base instincts.'

'You have gone soft, Pacorus,' she sneered.

'Soft!' I raged. 'I will not have the Kingdom of Dura become an abode of murderers, and I tell you this now, if I find out about any other Amazons carrying out assassinations in foreign kingdoms, they will be banished from Dura.'

'That is not your decision to make,' she replied with Gallia fury. 'The Amazons answer to me and me alone.'

'Not when they bring the Kingdom of Dura into disrepute.'

She threw back her head and laughed mockingly.

'The only thing the world respects, Pacorus, is strength. If Dura's enemies know they are always in danger, that they can never rest easy, then they will think twice before instigating wars against us.'

She pointed at me accusingly. 'You made a mistake allowing Atrax and his sisters to leave Irbil and the result was a fresh invasion of Parthia and the death of Rasha. It pains me to say so…'

'But you are going to do so anyway,' I interrupted.

She suddenly changed her demeanour, took her seat beside me and laid a hand on my arm.

'You are an honourable man, Pacorus, but we must deal with the world as we find it, not as we want it to be. Do you really lament the death of that fat traitor Cookes?'

'No, but I object to being treated like a fool. You told me it would be good for his education if Klietas accompanied Talib and Minu to Palmyra, but instead I discover he was part of a mission to Zeugma to assassinate Cookes and his wife.'

She removed her hand.

'Klietas did go to Palmyra, and then on to Syria and Zeugma.'

'The point is I should have been told of your plan beforehand, not kept in the dark to learn of it from a freed Roman slave.'

'Ah, so you are angry because your pride has been hurt.'

'I am angry because members of Dura's army are being sent on secret missions without my permission,' I shot back, 'and for your information, the Amazons are not your private army but are under my command.'

'They are not,' she hissed, putting the emphasis on the last word.

I decided to try another tactic. 'All our actions have repercussions, Gallia. Cast your mind back to when Cleopatra sent assassins to Dura to kill Kewab.'

'They were caught and executed.'

I smiled. 'Exactly, and that might be the fate of your Amazons if you continue to use them as assassins.'

'Menkhaf and his band of Egyptians were caught because they were careless,' she said. 'They did not prepare for their task thoroughly and paid the price.'

'Which brings me neatly to The Sanctuary.'

Her eyes narrowed once more.

'What about it?'

The brothel where Roxanne and Peroz had first met all those years ago had fallen into disrepair and was brought to the verge of bankruptcy following the death of the fearsome Samhat, the madam who became head of Dura's guild of prostitutes. When it closed its cracked doors for the last time, Gallia purchased the premises and paid off the not inconsiderable debts the whorehouse had incurred. She then set about having it renovated, after which it became a residence exclusive to the Amazons.

'The clue is in the name, Pacorus,' she elucidated further. 'It is a place where the Amazons can relax in an all-female environment, free from the prying eyes of men.'

'I have heard otherwise. That it is a place where poisoners impart their wisdom and other dark arts are practised.'

'Street gossip,' she sneered.

'Do you deny it?'

'I am not on trial,' she responded indignantly. 'I would have thought you had more pressing things to attend to rather than pestering me about inconsequential matters.'

'What more pressing things?'

'Parthia's enemies are still at large and no doubt plotting to return to the empire to wreak more mischief.'

'What enemies?'

'Has age dimmed your memory, Pacorus? Have you forgotten Atrax, Titus Tullus, Laodice and Tiridates so quickly?'

'Of course not,' I snapped at her. 'But as they are not *in* the empire there is little I can do about them.'

I saw a glint in her blue eyes.

'No one is out of reach.'

'No! I will hear no more of assassination. Henceforth, you are forbidden to send any Amazons on clandestine murder missions, and neither my scouts nor my squire are at your disposal.'

I stood and stormed from the throne room, though limped in a rapid fashion would be a more accurate description. How I wanted to taste again the magical elixir that had restored our physiques during the time of trial at Irbil. That said, now I had officially retired from military campaigning, my daily exertions had been reduced considerably. Gallia still thirsted for revenge against those who had wronged Dura, or rather her, but I had had my fill of bloodshed. And by all accounts so had the enemies of Parthia.

It had been twenty-seven years since I had fought Marcus Licinius Crassus at Carrhae and in the years afterwards I never dreamed that there would be a lasting peace between Rome and Parthia. And yet the Euphrates, once watched and guarded closely by Hatra and Dura, both kingdoms forming the western shield of the empire against Roman aggression, had become nothing more than the waterway that delineated the boundary between Parthia and Rome. The bitterness that existed between Rome and Ctesiphon had dissipated to such an extent that negotiations regarding the return of the eagles captured at Carrhae and Lake Urmia had formally commenced, Phraates and Octavian corresponding with each other on a regular basis regarding their repatriation to Rome and reuniting the young son of Phraates with his father. By all accounts, Octavian himself, who ensured the son of the high king enjoyed a privileged life, doted on the baby that had been captured by Tiridates and taken to Syria, thence to Rome. I wondered if the young Phraates would wish to return to a land he had never known after being 'Romanised'? But that was a matter to be resolved later. Having fought Romans on and off for forty years, I was delighted the legions no longer cast a long shadow over Parthia.

There was also peace in the east.

While Gallia and I had been fighting for our lives at Irbil, King Ali of Atropaiene, Lord High General and the commander of a great army that had been mustered in the west of the empire to assist the kingdoms of the east in their fight against the Kushans, had brought the Kushan emperor Kujula to heel. After defeating one of his generals near the Indus, Ali, ably assisted by Satrap Kewab, had laid waste to large swathes of Kushan territory. Faced by the Parthian threat and the outbreak of war with the Satavahana Empire to the south, Kujula had agreed a perpetual peace with the Parthian Empire, formally recognising the Indus River as the boundary between the two empires. Ali was returning to his home in triumph, as were the horsemen of Dura.

The horse archers and cataphracts had been away for eighteen months and when they returned the Durans, Exiles and whole city turned out to welcome them back. Azad and Sporaces had sent casualty lists ahead before their arrival and though our losses had been mercifully light, there were still women made widows who had to be cared for out of treasury funds, in addition to the children of the fallen that Dura would have to provide for. The route from the pontoon bridges to the Palmyrene Gate and on to the Citadel was lined with the Durans and Exiles, behind them cheering crowds throwing flowers and applauding the returning heroes. Cataphracts sweltered in full-scale armour, their heads covered in full-face helmets as they trotted into the city and back to their barracks, Sporaces and his horse archers doing likewise. Azad, Sporaces and their senior officers rode on to the Citadel where their king and queen waited to greet them, being joined by the uncouth and bad-tempered commander of the ammunition train, Farid.

A colour party of Durans and Exiles stood to attention in the courtyard when they rode through the gates, trumpeters playing a fanfare, Chrestus saluting the horsemen and the colour party presenting the golden griffin and silver lion standards. Opposite them, Zenobia and a detachment of Amazons drew their swords and raised them in salute, their commander lowering the griffin banner as they did so.

Stable hands came forward when the salutes had ended to take the new arrivals' horses, Azad tossing his helmet to a servant and handing his *kontus* to another as he marched up the steps to bow to me and Gallia. Alcaeus stood between us, which the commander of my cataphracts noticed. Our Greek friend had tried to act as mediator between husband and wife to affect a reconciliation, to no avail. I was still annoyed at her and she was livid with me, a situation that showed no sign of changing.

'Welcome, welcome,' I gushed, 'and you, too, Sporaces.'

They were both tall, but Azad had a powerful frame whereas Sporaces was spindly and far slimmer in comparison, accentuated by the scale, leg and arm armour worn by Azad. Horse archers rode agile horses and tended to replicate their mounts, whereas cataphracts were big, strong men riding sturdy horses.

'It's good to be back,' grinned Azad, his square face beaded with sweat.

'The air in Dura is sweeter than in the east,' said Sporaces.

'Can't argue with that,' agreed Azad, who had made the journey to the eastern edges of the empire twice, 'though the Kushan lands offer rich pickings.'

'When you have both changed and rested,' I said, 'I want to hear all about your great adventure. How are you, Farid?'

His robes covered in dust, his hair and beard wild affairs, how Sporaces and indeed Chrestus would have liked to submit him to military law. But Farid was a civilian, as were the men who rode and maintained the fifteen hundred camels that made up Dura's ammunition train. Farid himself had been a camel driver at the Battle of Carrhae and knew all there was to know about camels and how to manage them on the battlefield. He also had a keen eye when it came to recruiting camel drivers who would not panic on the battlefield. He loved his camels and attended to their needs most diligently, but he was like the beasts he spent his life around: gruff, obstinate and bad-tempered.

He gave a nod of the head. 'Eighteen months spent surrounded by horse and camel shit and eating dust produced by over one hundred thousand horses and camels, how do you think I am?'

Rsan and Aaron standing behind us gasped in astonishment and Alcaeus allowed himself a wry smile.

Farid sniffed. 'Meant no offence, majesty.'

'If you were in the army I would sentence you to a hundred lashes,' seethed Sporaces.

Farid winked at me. 'Good job I ain't, isn't it? You never ran out of arrows, though, did you? Not like those useless eastern goatherds who went on campaign without any ammunition. I was saying to my men…'

'Thank you, Farid,' Chrestus interrupted him, 'I'm sure the king does not want to be bored by your idle gossip.'

'I will hear all your stories,' I assured them, 'for you have all covered yourselves in glory and increased the prestige of Dura immeasurably.'

Alcaeus laughed, and Gallia rolled her eyes, but both Rsan and Aaron nodded in agreement. The latter had been delighted to see Dura's professional horsemen depart for the east, not because he disliked Azad or Sporaces, but rather because the upkeep of the men they led had been borne by the eastern kingdoms for the duration of the campaign rather than Dura.

Our returning heroes were feasted in the banqueting hall that night, the chamber reverberating to the babble of raised voices as men who had been on campaign for months finally relaxed and enjoyed the lavish occasion laid on for them. Many drank too much and got drunk, though both Sporaces and Azad, invited to sit at the top table with their king, queen and General Chrestus, imbibed only in moderation.

'We heard about what happened at Irbil, majesty,' Azad told me, tearing at the rack of ribs on the platter before him.

'Heard from whom?' asked Gallia, sipping at her wine.

'General Hovik, majesty, just before he and the horsemen from Gordyene departed for their homeland, on the express orders of King Spartacus.'

'Did that affect the campaign?' I queried.

Sporaces, finishing off a chicken kebab, shook his head.

'No, majesty, by the time the message reached the army we were on our way back to Parthian territory.'

'General Herneus was also instructed to make his way back to Hatra,' added Azad.

'Due to the scheming of Phraates, we and the army's legions nearly met with disaster at a place called the Gird-I Dasht,' said Gallia bitterly, finishing her wine and holding out her cup for it to be refilled. 'It is just as well you are back because Dura has unfinished business to attend to.'

Chrestus, Azad and Sporaces exchanged glances but none spoke.

'How is Kewab faring?' I asked, eager to change the topic.

'He has been the bulwark preventing the Kushans from breaking into the empire,' reported Azad, 'and hopefully now Kujula has agreed a fresh truce, he can enjoy a period of rest.'

'Without him, King Ali would not have achieved what he did,' added Sporaces.

I beamed with delight. I was immensely proud of Kewab's progress, and his achievements both at Dura and in the east had earmarked him out for greatness.

'I am hopeful he will make the transition from satrap to king very soon,' I said. 'Aria needs a ruler.'

Azad nodded. 'He could not do any worse than Tiridates. Is he still in Syria, majesty?'

'He is indeed,' said Gallia, 'where he continues to plot against Parthia. While he still lives, there will be no peace with Rome.'

'There will be no war with Rome,' I said, 'Octavian and Phraates are in advanced negotiations regarding agreeing a lasting peace between Parthia and Rome.'

Gallia took another sip of wine. 'And we all know how trustworthy those two are. The king forgets that we, having been abandoned by Phraates, were recently fighting for our lives in Irbil, against an army financed by Octavian.'

All three commanders stared into their drinking vessels, squirming with embarrassment as their king and queen argued.

'There will be no war between Rome and Parthia,' I said again, 'regardless of what Tiridates may or may not want.'

'That remains to be seen,' she sneered.

Both of us sunk into sullen silences and the atmosphere on the top table became noticeably cooler as the evening progressed. All three commanders made their excuses and left the event early, the hall still filled with raucous chatter and laughter as they sloped off. Alcaeus, who followed soon after, stopped off at our table to berate us both. His beard and wiry hair were now heavily streaked with grey, but his mind was as keen as ever.

'I see you have both managed to make this evening about yourselves rather than our returning soldiers.'

'I don't know what you mean,' I replied innocently.

He looked down his nose at me.

'Heard of Socrates, Pacorus?'

'No.'

'And you, Gallia?'

She shrugged. 'Is he a Greek?'

He raised his eyes to the roof.

'He was one of history's great thinkers, not that I expect such individuals to be recognised in Dura. But you two remind me of one of his sayings. That children have bad manners, contempt for authority, show disrespect for their elders and love chatter in place of exercise.

'Whatever the cause of the discord between you, try to remember you are king and queen as opposed to an old, bickering couple living in a less salubrious part of the city. As such, you have a responsibility to act in a dignified manner and be an example to others.'

He departed before either of us had a chance to reply, though Gallia was bristling at his brusque manner, mumbling something under her breath that I could not discern. But his words were wasted on her because that night I was banished to a guest bedroom in the palace until I agreed not to interfere with the activities of the Amazons.

She was all smiles and affection, none directed at me, when Alcaeus took his leave to embark on his trip to Athens a few days later. Byrd had arranged for him to join a caravan journeying to Palmyra and on to Syria for the first part of his tour, after which a ship would take him first to Cyprus and then on to Greece.

Our friend, Companion and former head of the army's medical corps stood at the foot of the palace steps, around him his friends and colleagues to bid him farewell. Rsan, his closest friend, was most unhappy he was leaving Dura while Scelias, a fellow Greek and head of the Sons of the Citadel, was giving him advice on what to do when he arrived in Athens.

'Avoid at all costs the Sceptics, my friend; they are an abomination. Any school of thought that believes true knowledge is unobtainable deserves to be closed down and its tutors banished.'

Alcaeus laughed. 'I will do my best to avoid them.'

There were tears in Gallia's eyes when she embraced her old friend.

'You should have an escort, let me organise a party of Amazons, or a company of horse archers.'

'A company?' he exclaimed. 'A hundred armed men, now that would arouse suspicion.'

She gripped his arms. 'Greece is occupied by the Romans and you are still a wanted man. If they learn the physician of Spartacus is in Athens, they will seize you and take you back to Rome.'

Scelias frowned. 'Majesty, the Servile War ended forty-five years ago. It is highly unlikely Alcaeus would be in any danger. Besides, knowing the Roman appetite for rewriting history and nostalgia, if they learned he was in Athens they would probably lay on a banquet for him. They might even invite him to Rome itself, so he could entertain Octavian with stories about Spartacus, his flight to Parthia and subsequent service in the army of King Pacorus.'

'I could organise an escort if Alcaeus desires it,' confirmed Chrestus.

'Excellent idea,' agreed Rsan.

Alcaeus held up his hands. 'All I desire is to be left in peace, so I can begin my journey. As for the Romans, if they wish to punish an old man then so be it, but either way I am determined to see Athens again before I die. And now, if you will all excuse me, a caravan is waiting for me.'

Klietas placed a footstool beside the horse I had gifted Alcaeus, enabling him to gain the saddle more easily. Before he did so I embraced him.

'Just make sure you return,' I told him.

'And you heal your rift with Gallia. At our age life is too short to waste on petty bickering.'

'I will do as you say, my old friend.'

None of us wanted him to go, not because we suspected Roman subterfuge but rather we desired him to remain at Dura to live out the rest of his life in peace. It was entirely selfish and in truth he was still sprightly for his age as opposed to being an invalid. But the thought of him wandering around the eastern Mediterranean alone filled me with trepidation, though for Alcaeus the prospect of the trip had given him a new lease of life.

The departure of Alcaeus signalled the beginning of many changes in the running of the kingdom, which became apparent when Aaron and Rsan first brought their deputies to a weekly council meeting.

They were not strangers because I had seen them around the Citadel many times, though the meeting was the first time they were formally inducted into the small group that directed the affairs of the kingdom. Both Rsan and Aaron still had many years left in them, or at least I hoped they did, but like all of us they were not getting any younger and to ensure the kingdom continued to run as efficiently as possible, both recognised the need for their deputies to step up to assume more responsibilities, and Alcaeus' replacement also attended.

The styluses of the two clerks worked feverishly as I rose and addressed those present.

'I would like to officially welcome three new members of the council who will be attending meetings from now on.'

I smiled at the short, dark-haired individual seated next to Aaron.

'Welcome Ira.'

For years he had worked in the Treasury before becoming Aaron's deputy. He rose and bowed his head.

'Thank you, majesty.'

His grey-green eyes briefly scanned all those present before retaking his seat. He had sharp features and unlike many Jewish males had a small, pointed beard. His skin was also quite pale; a result of his aversion to the sun, or so Aaron had informed me. Of the newcomers, he was the stranger as the other two were well known to the others present. I turned to the elder of the three, a man with a stump where his left hand should have been.

'Welcome, Almas, former dragon commander of horse archers and veteran of many years' service in Dura's army.'

Chrestus, Azad and Sporaces, the latter two invited following their return from the east, rapped their knuckles on the table in acknowledgement of a fellow soldier.

Almas, whose name meant 'diamond' in Persian, rose and bowed his head to me, blushing slightly at the applause.

'Thank you, majesty, I hope to serve Dura as diligently sitting behind a desk as I did when in the saddle.'

'Try not to lose the other hand in the process,' said Chrestus.

Almas had lost his hand during the Battle of the Araxes when we had tried to prevent Mark Antony from leaving Parthia after his failure at Phraaspa. Alcaeus and his medics had saved his life, but the wound had ended his army career. Some men would have buckled under such a calamity, turning to drink or even contemplating suicide. But Almas instead turned his mind to commerce; using the knowledge he had gleaned during his years with the army, chiefly talking to Dura's desert lords and Malik's Agraci warlords about the vast desert that surrounded Dura and Palmyra. Many had thought his wits had deserted him when he used his severance pension from the army to purchase an area of land in the desert some fifty miles south of the city of Dura and thirty miles west of the Euphrates, a stretch of land significant only for its barrenness and population of snakes and scorpions. But the area was also rich in a mineral that when ground down and mixed with olive oil, became antimony eye makeup. In a short space of time, Almas became extremely rich and purchased a mansion in the city. By chance it happened to be next to the home of Rsan and the two struck up an unlikely friendship, leading to Almas taking a keen interest in civil affairs, eventually leading to a seat on the city council.

The last new member was also well known to the soldiers at the table, having been a member of the army's medical corps for many years. Like Alcaeus, Sophus was one of Dura's Greek citizens, though unlike most of them he had blue eyes like my wife's. They studied him closely as I spoke.

'Last but not least, welcome Sophus, who has replaced Alcaeus as commander of the army's medical corps.'

'No one can replace Alcaeus,' said Gallia sternly, staring unblinking at the Greek.

Sophus, whose name meant 'clever' in his native language, rose and bowed his head to the queen.

'And I would never attempt to fill the boots of the man who is a legend in Dura and beyond. I consider my role to be more of a mission to keep his legacy alive and continue his work.'

That pleased Gallia for she flashed him a beautiful smile.

'Then you are most welcome among us, young Sophus.'

He was not really young, being in his mid-thirties, or thereabouts, but Gallia and I were now in our early sixties and so most people appeared young to us. It was all very demoralising.

'Perhaps we may commence the meeting, majesty,' said Rsan, studying a papyrus sheet before him.

Almas pointed to it and Rsan nodded.

'Please proceed,' I instructed.

The shutters to the room were open but the spring morning was overcast and mild and so the temperature in the room was pleasant enough. Though it dropped markedly when Rsan began speaking.

'Yesterday, I received word from the chief of court at Ctesiphon enquiring if the King and Queen of Dura had received the several messages sent to them by King of Kings Phraates over the past few weeks.'

'Write back and inform Phraates' sycophant the King and Queen of Dura have no time for men who abandon those who saved his neck,' sneered Gallia.

Chrestus laughed and banged the table, Azad and Sporaces slapping him on the back, but Rsan was appalled.

'I would never use such intemperate language when addressing the high king of the empire, majesty.'

'And we would not expect you to, Rsan,' I said, 'but at this present juncture we have nothing to say to the high king, not until he apologises for inciting an invasion of the empire he is supposed to protect, anyway.'

'I must send some sort of reply, majesty,' pleaded Rsan.

I looked at Gallia expectantly, waiting for a witty retort, but she merely stared out of the window.

'Inform the chief of court, Dura's king and queen are still recovering from their trial at Irbil,' I told him, 'and subsequent near-death experience at the Battle of Diyana, where they faced a combined army of Parthian rebels and Armenians.'

The clerks were recording every word but worry lines appeared on Rsan's forehead.

'I had no idea you were wounded, majesty. Have you seen a physician?'

'Alcaeus did not mention you were injured, majesty,' said Sophus. 'I have to say you do not look ill.'

'That is because I am not,' I assured him, 'but Ctesiphon's chief of court does not know that. You understand, Rsan?'

'I am not in favour of deceiving the high king's officials, majesty…'

'Just send the letter,' snapped Gallia, 'and let's have no more talk of Phraates and his wretched courtiers.'

There was an uncomfortable silence before my wife turned her ire on Klietas who was filling cups with water, my squire-cum-part-time assassin staring wide-eyed at the queen.

'Refill my cup,' she ordered.

Klietas snapped out of his daze. 'Yes, highborn.'

Gallia gave him an evil leer.

'And remember, Klietas, it is death to speak of what goes on in council meetings. You remember the street of crosses at Irbil?'

He gulped. 'Yes, highborn.'

'Then you know what your fate will be if you betray the king's confidence. Now put the jug on the table and leave us.'

He did so hurriedly, bowing deeply to her and then me before shutting the door behind him.

'What is next on the agenda?' I asked, shaking my head at Gallia.

'Centurion Bullus has refused his promotion,' announced Chrestus.

I was determined to promote the hero of Irbil after our return to Dura, but it appeared he did not want any extra responsibility.

'He says he cannot rise any higher than a centurion,' grinned Chrestus, 'because he can't count higher than a hundred.'

Ira stopped perusing a ledger sheet and looked up at the general.

'If he does not have a command of numeracy, how is it he is a centurion, general, for surely the army has certain standards when it comes to holding positions of command?'

The veins on Chrestus' thick neck began to bulge.

'It was a joke, book-keeper.'

'Not a very funny one,' retorted Ira.

'That is a shame about Centurion Bullus,' I said quickly before Chrestus' short-temper manifested itself. 'What are those notes before you, Ira?'

Aaron's deputy looked at his master who nodded. Ira held up the sheet.

'An inventory, majesty, a projection of this year's crop yield.'

Chrestus sighed and the eyes of Azad and Sporaces glazed over, but Ira was undeterred.

'God willing, when the crops are gathered in the kingdom will have a great surplus of flour, dates, honey, flax, olives and wine.'

I was surprised by the latter commodity. 'Wine?'

Ira looked surprised. 'Have you not visited the vineyards to the south of the city, majesty?'

I had not. 'I rarely get a chance to journey the length and breadth of the kingdom, I regret to say.'

'That is a pity, majesty,' said Ira. 'The southern lands have been expanded greatly and there are now dozens of medium- and large-sized farms extending south from the city for a distance of two hundred and fifty miles, all watered by a complex system of irrigation systems financed by the city treasury, which means we benefit from taxes paid to the treasury by those farms benefiting from said systems.'

' *We?*' queried Gallia.

'Meaning the city treasury, majesty,' smiled Ira.

'Ira has a plan to increase revenues substantially, majesty,' Aaron informed me.

'We would like to hear it,' I said, Chrestus sighing again.

'Media had traditionally exported commodities to surrounding kingdoms,' reported Ira, 'especially Mesene, Atropaiene, Babylon and Susiana, though its goods have also found their way to Persis further south. However, the recent invasions of Media have had a detrimental effect on the kingdom's agricultural output, resulting in exports falling drastically.'

'And so, Dura will step in to fill the gap,' said Chrestus.

Ira nodded. 'As it is currently a sellers' market, our exports will be priced with a thirty percent mark-up across the board.'

'More revenue means more money for the army,' added Aaron.

'At the expense of Mesene, Atropaiene, Babylon and Susiana,' I said.

Ira shrugged. 'Market conditions are what they are, majesty. It would be foolish not to take advantage of the happy position Dura finds itself in.'

Gallia was unhappy, or rather unhappier than when she had entered the room.

'We should not take advantage of our allies.'

She was thinking of Atropaiene and Mesene, the latter formerly ruled by Nergal and Praxima, Nergal always a loyal supporter of Dura and Hatra.

'I agree with the queen,' I said, 'export produce to foreign kingdoms by all means, Aaron, but only increase the price for goods going to Babylon and Susiana. They can afford it.'

It was perhaps churlish, but those kingdoms were ruled directly by Phraates and it would be a way of sending a message to the high king that Dura's rulers were displeased with him. My ignoring his messages had probably already intimated that he was no longer welcome in the kingdom, but it would do no harm to emphasise the point.

The rest of the meeting consisted of Rsan reporting on renovations to the caravan park immediately north of the city, Aaron listing revenues earned from trade caravans, and Chrestus briefing us on army recruitment.

'Most new recruits now come from within the kingdom,' he informed us. 'The days when the army was composed mostly of foreigners are long gone.'

The Exiles had always been composed almost exclusively of non-Parthians: men who had travelled from foreign lands, usually under the control of Rome, to fight for Dura, hence their name. In the early days, many harboured dreams of returning to their homelands as soldiers of Dura's army, though I had always made it plain the kingdom's army was for the defence of Dura and Parthia only. The Durans were initially composed of men recruited from within the Parthian Empire, mostly runaway slaves eager to escape their masters, criminals with a price on their heads, and poor commoners who were technically free but were actually slaves to a life that was slowly grinding them into the earth.

I was slightly alarmed. 'Does Dura have a large enough pool of potential recruits to maintain the army's strength?'

Ira gave me a quizzical look. 'Have you seen the latest population census, majesty?'

'No.'

'There are more people living outside the city than there are in it,' he reported.

'When I first came to Dura,' I reminisced, 'the only people living outside the city were lords and their retainers inhabiting walled strongholds. The land south of the city was a wasteland.'

Rsan was smiling as he too remembered the dark days when most of the desert had belonged to the Agraci, at the time sworn enemies of Parthia. But that had been forty years ago. Now the desert bloomed with crops and settlements. If I had achieved nothing else, that was a fine legacy to leave: peace and prosperity.

'Peace and prosperity,' I said absentmindedly.

They all looked at me, but Aaron seized upon my words.

'Happily, majesty, we appear to be entering a new age for Dura, an age, as you say, of peace and prosperity. We now have permanent peace with Rome, the Agraci have been friends of Dura for many years and King of Kings Phraates is a young man with hopefully many years of life ahead of him.

'As Ira has alluded to, the kingdom's population is expanding, which in turn means an increase in agricultural produce, leading to a further expansion of the kingdom's population.'

'The gods shine on Dura,' agreed Almas.

An image came into my mind of a camp with no camels or horses where Gallia and I had been entertained one evening, where the hosts were not of this earth. The blessing of the immortals could be a double-edged sword, however. Aaron's voice interrupted my daydream. He took one of Ira's papyrus sheets and perused it before speaking.

'Ten thousand foot soldiers, one thousand cataphracts, five thousand horse archers and two thousand squires, to say nothing of the queen's bodyguard, Farid's fifteen hundred camels and their drivers, and the muleteers who service the legions, all of which impose a considerable burden on the treasury, majesty.'

'The army safeguards the kingdom,' growled Chrestus.

'Indeed, general,' said Aaron, 'but as the kingdom no longer appears to be in any great danger, one wonders if that army has outlived its usefulness.'

'What!' roared Chrestus, pointing at the window. 'Why don't you and your clerks take a trip outside the city to visit the legionary camp, in the centre of which is a tent housing the Staff of Victory. It is decorated with silver discs commemorating the army's victories during four decades of service. The newest disc, recently cast, celebrates the Battle of Diyana, fought only a few months ago and only two hundred miles from this city.'

'There will be no change in the army's numbers,' I said to calm Chrestus' rage, much to the disappointment of Aaron.

'But do not forward the results of your census to Ctesiphon, Ira,' commanded Gallia. 'There is no need to broadcast Dura's prosperity to the whole world. It will only encourage envy and place the kingdom in jeopardy.'

Ira was delighted. 'Yes, majesty, you can rely on my discretion.'

Aaron began drumming his fingers on the table top, much to the amusement of the three commanders present. Sophus, more attune to the workings of the treasury, allowed himself a wry smile. The annual tribute that all kingdoms paid to Ctesiphon was calculated according to the number of soldiers each kingdom could put into the field, the figure loosely based on the population figures for each realm. Dura's population increase would result in a commensurate increase in the amount paid to the high king's coffers, something neither Aaron nor the king and queen desired.

Immediately after the meeting I caught up with Gallia as she marched to the stables, prior to riding from the Citadel, where to I had no idea.

'Did you have to threaten Klietas like that? Having involved him in your nefarious scheme, I would have thought you realised he is reliable.'

She stopped to face me. 'He is a useful idiot, there is a difference.'

'Explain.'

She gave me a malicious leer. 'He is in love with Haya, which means he is like a red-hot piece of iron – easily malleable. He would walk over hot coals for her.'

'You should not take advantage of his affections.'

'Why not?' she scoffed. 'That is what men do to women all the time.'

'There is no need for this, you know, this bitterness and resentment. We are both on the same side.'

She continued pacing towards the stables.

'War is coming, Pacorus, any fool can see it.'

'What war?' I said loudly, causing stable hands within earshot to stop what they were doing to stare at us.

She turned to face me. 'You want peace and a happy retirement? The only way to ensure both is to eradicate our enemies before they have time to mobilise. I have the interests of Dura at heart. Do you?'

At the time I thought her attitude preposterous, but I had reckoned without her feminine intuition and had allowed my desire for peace to blind me to what was happening beyond Dura's borders.

The first sign of gathering storm clouds was the visit of Claudia to Dura.

Chapter 2

Determined to see for myself what took place within the walls of 'The Sanctuary', I walked with Klietas from the Citadel the next morning after riding out to the training fields to watch my squire being put through his paces by a company of horse archers, and afterwards eating breakfast alone on the palace terrace. Gallia was still maintaining her resentful demeanour and decided to eat breakfast with the Amazons, at least those who were not guarding their secretive headquarters. The duty centurion allotted a score of Exiles to provide an escort for the trip into the city. The streets were heaving with people, carts, camels and donkeys, making the going slow as we left the main street to head towards the city's central square, leading off of which were side streets where the majority of Dura's brothels were located.

The Exiles used the non-lethal end of their javelins to usher people out of the way, who tended to stop and stare when their commander shouted, 'make way for the king'. Klietas, sling tucked in his belt and a wicked knife in a sheath next to it, looked around nervously.

'Is someone after you?' I asked.

'No, highborn.'

'Then why do you look like a rabbit frightened of being seized by an eagle?'

He shook his head. 'You should not wander the streets, highborn, there are dangerous people about.'

'I am not wandering the streets, as you quaintly put it. I am taking a stroll in the city I rule. Any king who cannot walk around his own city is either a fool or a tyrant. Have you been to this Sanctuary?'

'No, highborn, men are not allowed inside.'

'Is that what Haya told you? I hear you are fond of her.'

He beamed with delight. 'Yes, highborn, she would make a fine wife.'

I laughed. 'I have no doubt, and I assume you are the one who wishes to marry her?'

'If I prove worthy, highborn, yes.'

I wondered if she had told him about the mortal wound she had suffered at Irbil and her miraculous recovery afterwards.

'I am informed your horsemanship and archery skills are improving by the day,' I said, changing the subject. 'You are doing well, Klietas, but you must not let distractions interfere with your training.'

'Distractions, highborn?'

'Thoughts of marriage and getting involved in the schemes of the Amazons,' I told him. 'If the queen approaches you again about anything, you must inform me immediately.'

'Yes, highborn.'

'We are here, majesty.'

I turned to see the commander of the party of Exiles pointing his javelin at the former brothel now den of the Amazons. I was surprised at its spruced-up appearance. The last time I had seen it was when Salar, my son-in-law, was in the city and had wished to see the place where his now dead mother and father had first met. It had always been an impressive two-storey building, with twin oak doors fronting the street it was located in, though when I had seen it last the plaster on the walls was peeling and the doors were cracked and in need of a new coat of paint. There was also a sign over the door depicting a scantily clad buxom woman reclining on a couch. But the sign had gone, the doors were freshly painted, and the plaster was new. The roof tiles, formerly cracked and aged, had also been replaced. The motto of the Amazons – *behind every strong man there is a stronger woman* – had been chiselled into a dark-grey marble plaque mounted above the doors. Adjacent to the building was a wide alley that led to stables at the rear of the establishment, formerly for the convenience of wealthy clients visiting their favourite whores, but now used for the comings and goings of Amazons. Two of them stood guard either side of the alley's entrance, another two outside the closed doors of The Sanctuary.

We were spotted immediately, one of the guards at the doors disappearing inside the building and the other taking up position in front of them. The street was empty, which was surprising because when the building had been a brothel it was always bustling with customers at all hours. I told the Exiles to stay where they were and walked up to the doors, Klietas beside me.

The Amazon bowed her head. 'Majesty.'

'Who is in charge here?'

Before she could answer one of the doors opened and Minu appeared, wearing mail armour, sheathed sword at her hip. The Amazon who had disappeared into the building followed and assumed her prior position. Klietas smiled at Minu but she ignored him, bowing and focusing her attention on me.

'How can I help you, majesty?'

'I wish to see inside The Sanctuary.'

'Men are forbidden to enter,' she told me.

'On whose orders?'

'The queen's, majesty.'

I jerked a thumb behind me.

'You see those soldiers behind me?'

'Yes, majesty.'

'I could order them to force an entry if you continue to bar my way.'

'That would be unfortunate, majesty.'

I lost my temper. 'Unfortunate! I could have you executed for your insubordination. How dare you speak to me as though we are equals. I am your king and commander and I order you to stand aside.'

'What's going on here?'

The sound of horses' hooves on the dirt and the jangling of harnesses and bits averted my gaze from the rock-like Minu to see Gallia at the head of a score of Amazons, the queen dismounting and striding towards me. She interposed herself between me and Minu, speaking in a low tone.

'So, poking your nose where it is not wanted. Men are not allowed to enter The Sanctuary, which is called thus because it is a place of refuge from male boorishness.'

'I am not just any man,' I retorted. 'I am the king and as such I may go where I will.'

'You will not enter The Sanctuary,' she growled in a low tone.

I could sense her rising temper and saw her nostrils flare. But my own disposition was confrontational, and a loud argument was now inevitable. Or at least would have been had not a runner arrived to divert our attention. The man, sweating and panting, went down on one knee before us.

'Speak,' I said.

'The Princess Claudia has arrived at the Citadel, majesty.'

Gallia was shocked, 'Claudia, here?'

Instantly her anger and confrontational attitude disappeared, to be replaced by concern. I too forgot about The Sanctuary and thought not of my daughter but rather of a high-ranking Scythian Sister and adviser to King of Kings Phraates. Something must have happened to prise her away from Ctesiphon, something calamitous, perhaps.

'I will meet you in the Citadel,' said Gallia, returning to her horse to regain the saddle before leading the mounted Amazons away.

I followed, my leg beginning to ache as I retraced my steps hurriedly, the commander of the Exiles slowing down his men so as not to embarrass their king. Like the runner who had sprinted back to the Citadel to keep pace with the queen, I arrived sweating and panting at the palace. In the courtyard Claudia's escort – two score of Babylonian mounted spearmen superbly equipped in dragon-skin armour and burnished helmets adorned with purple plumes – were leading their horses to the stables. The Amazons had also dismounted, a stable hand leading the queen's mare away.

'Fetch me a towel,' I told a remarkably fresh-looking Klietas, my squire bounding up the palace steps to disappear into the porch. Ashk, the palace steward, frowned at him as he passed, bowing to me as I walked slowly up the stone steps.

'I showed the princess to the terrace, majesty, where she and the queen are waiting. Refreshments have been ordered.'

'Thank you,' I panted.

'It is good to see the princess back at Dura, majesty,' he smiled.

'Indeed.'

A sharp pain suddenly shot up my leg, causing me to collapse on the stone slabs. The guards standing next to the pillars supporting the porch roof rushed to me, but I waved them back, taking a few seconds to regain my dignity before standing, Ashk lending a hand. A towel was thrust at me.

'The leg, highborn?'

Klietas was wearing an impious grin.

'Do you want a walking stick, highborn?'

'What I want is for you to attend to your duties. Go the stables and assist the staff unsaddling the Babylonians' horses.'

'Why can't they do it?' he asked.

'Just go, damn your hide.'

He bowed, turned on his heels and sprinted away. How I envied his young mind and limbs. Ashk, who was no young man himself, assisted me from the porch to the entrance hall and into the throne room, the pain in my leg diminishing to allow me to walk unaided past the dais to the door to the rear of the chamber that led to the palace's private quarters.

'Perhaps walking around the city is inadvisable, majesty,' he suggested, 'bearing in mind your age.'

I was going to scold him but realised he was right.

'I will take your advice, Ashk.'

There was a time when Claudia was a striking young woman, with a mischievous smile, a keen mind and her mother's high cheekbones. She was not beautiful like Gallia but nor was she plain. Once her thick light brown hair tumbled to her shoulders and she wore leggings that hugged her womanly figure and light-coloured tunics and dresses that accentuated her feminine qualities. But that was before her terrible ordeal at the hands of Prince Alexander's soldiers, her subsequent healing and induction into the Scythian Sisters, the secretive, powerful sect of sorceresses that was a force to be reckoned with in Parthia.

When I walked on to the terrace to greet our oldest daughter the young, carefree woman was long gone, just a fading memory. In her place was a formidable woman clothed entirely in black, with black hair and cold eyes. She smiled at me, but it was in a purely obligatory fashion, planting a kiss on my scarred cheek and noticing my limp.

'The hero of Irbil,' she remarked mockingly, 'alas, father, the reality before me is far removed from the myth currently circulating within the empire.'

I hobbled to my chair beneath the awning and eased myself into it.

'Have you come to Dura just to mock your father?'

Gallia, who had remained seated during my entrance, sipped at her fruit juice. A servant offered me a cup of the same beverage and I took it gratefully. Others placed small silver plates containing pastries, sweet meats, grapes, pomegranates, figs, apples, raisins and almonds on the low tables between our cushioned seats.

I picked up a pastry. 'Is your journey one of pleasure or business?'

Claudia sat and nibbled on a grape. 'The high king wonders why you have been ignoring his letters, father, especially after he was so concerned to hear of your trial at Irbil.'

'A trial he orchestrated,' remarked Gallia coolly. 'Did you also have a hand in encouraging Atrax and the Armenians to invade Parthia, which led to the death of Rasha?'

Claudia's eyes darted between us. She finished eating the grape and picked up another.

'I grieved deeply when I learned she had died. And to answer your question, no, I had no hand in Phraates' encouragement of Atrax.'

'I thought Phraates was a puppet of the Scythian Sisters, a man who is high king but answers to your sisterhood.'

Claudia rolled her eyes.

'I am merely an adviser to the high king, father, not his jailer.'

'More's the pity,' remarked Gallia. 'Thanks to his plotting, Rasha is dead. That will not be forgotten.'

'Phraates did not kill Rasha, mother; rather, it was Spartacus who brought about Atrax's invasion of Media.'

I laughed mockingly. 'I saw the letter signed by Phraates himself, which encouraged Atrax to invade Media.'

Claudia turned a third grape in her fingers.

'If Spartacus had not invaded Armenia, King Artaxias would never have allowed Atrax to march his army through his kingdom, notwithstanding any letter that Phraates may have signed.'

' *Did* sign,' I said.

'His scheming nearly cost Akmon and Lusin their lives,' added Gallia, 'though we have taken measures to safeguard both their lives and their reign.'

Claudia stopped toying with the grape.

'Oh?'

I had to admit I enjoyed revealing to her the details of the alliance between Media, Hatra and Dura, partly to remind Phraates that he was not the only one who could plot, but also to remind

Claudia and her black-robed sisters they did not rule the Parthian Empire.

'You should tell your master,' I said with relish, 'that our three kingdoms can easily put one hundred thousand men into the field.'

'More than enough to send the Armenians fleeing back to their homeland should they be tempted to cross the Araxes again,' added Gallia.

Claudia sipped at her fruit juice. 'My congratulations, I am glad to discover you still remain diligent concerning the defence of the empire.'

'Which is more than can be said for Phraates,' sniffed Gallia.

I raised my cup to her, but Claudia's temper was beginning to fray.

'Phraates *is* concerned with safeguarding the empire. It is Spartacus who acts like a brigand and in so doing places Parthia in danger. However, with regard to Media, it seems it was never in danger and nor were its rulers.'

She rose and walked to the balustrade, placing her hands on the stone to stare at the blue waters of the Euphrates below. I looked at Gallia who shook her head.

Claudia turned to face us. 'Curious is it not?'

'What is?' I asked, eating a second pastry.

'That the King and Queen of Dura happened to find themselves in Irbil just before Atrax and his army appeared before its walls.'

I shrugged, avoiding her eyes. 'Mere coincidence.'

'Mere coincidence,' she repeated. 'Let us accept for the moment it was so. That you just happened to find yourselves in Irbil, though who informed you the city was in peril remains a mystery.'

'Lucky for Parthia we were there to aid Akmon and Lusin,' said Gallia.

Claudia walked back to her seat.

'At Ctesiphon we heard stories of the King and Queen of Dura wearing magical armour, against which the weapons of the enemy were useless. And you can imagine my surprise when I heard other tales of King Pacorus and Queen Gallia having more vigour and stamina than people half their age, like demi-gods, if the anecdotes are to be believed.'

'Back-street tittle-tattle,' I retorted, 'I am surprised you listen to such idle gossip.'

'Can I see it?' asked Claudia.

'What?'

'The armour you wore at Irbil.'

I had had enough. 'I am not here to be interrogated, Claudia. You forget who you are talking to.'

'You should have more respect for your parents,' said Gallia sternly.

Claudia leaned back and stared up at the awning.

'A while ago, Phraates told me of a troubling dream he had experienced, though nightmare would be a more accurate description. He disclosed to me that Shamash himself appeared to him and revealed he had offered the high crown to the King of Dura.'

'Are you an adviser or fortune teller?' Gallia taunted her.

Claudia ignored her. 'The dream alarmed Phraates greatly, and consequently he is taking measures to curtail the man he believes has for too long cast a shadow over Parthia, and indeed his own reign.'

She fixed me with her cold eyes.

'Me?' I exclaimed.

'You, father. It is not lost on Phraates, or indeed the empire, that you are an influential figure in Parthia.'

'If he is,' said Gallia, 'it is because your father has dedicated his life to serving Parthia.'

'And Phraates is grateful for that service,' smiled Claudia, 'but try to see things from his point of view. Dura, Hatra and Media have an alliance; Kewab, a protégé of Dura, is a powerful satrap in the east of the empire; Karys, the Jew, rules Mesene; and Salar, King of Sakastan, is married to your daughter, Isabella.'

I had to admit the list was impressive, though I had never considered it a power bloc to challenge the authority of the high king.

'Phraates should remember those who came to his aid when Tiridates deposed him,' growled Gallia.

Claudia smiled at her mother but did not reply to her.

'Phraates believes a realignment of power within the empire is long overdue,' she continued. 'He has decided to replace Karys with Sanabares and to abolish Kewab's rank of Satrap of the East.'

'Who?' I asked.

'Another one of Phraates' sycophantic courtiers?' sneered Gallia.

'He is the satrap of Susiana, mother, and is a loyal and conscientious ruler, if a little dour. But more to the point, he is not a Jew.'

'What does than matter?' I said. 'I have never questioned a man's faith or judged him on his race or parentage.'

'But you follow our gods, father, and have always prayed to Shamash, the Sun King, the God of Truth, Justice and Right. You also honour Ishtar, Marduk, Erra and Girra.'

Gallia laughed and gave me a knowing look. If only Claudia knew of our shared experience. What would she make of it; what would she make of us? I too chuckled. She would probably think we were mad.

'It is no laughing matter,' she rebuked us. 'The Jews are loyal above all to Yahweh.'

'Who?' I asked.

'How ignorant you are, father. Yahweh, also called Tzur Yisrael, Avinu Malkeinu and Melech ha-M'lachim, is the god the Jews worship, pledging their loyalty to him alone, irrespective of whether they are ruled by a pharaoh, king of kings or the Roman senate. No Parthian kingdom should be ruled by a Jew because they are unreliable.'

I raised my eyes to the heavens. 'I used to hear the same rubbish from Dobbai all those years ago.'

'Sage advice,' said Claudia.

'Karys was trusted by Nergal and Praxima and that is good enough for me,' stated Gallia.

'Me too,' I agreed.

'Nergal and Praxima are dead,' replied Claudia.

Gallia erupted, jumping from her chair and pointing accusingly at her daughter.

'Dead because of that pompous jackass who sits on Ctesiphon's throne, who now seeks to eradicate their legacy by appointing his own lackey to rule Mesene. And he is going to dismiss Kewab, the man who saved the eastern half of the empire? That's ingratitude of the highest order.'

Taken aback, Claudia sought to soothe her mother's anger.

'Kewab's appointment was always a temporary measure, mother. Surely, you did not think he would be made King of Aria?'

'Then who will be?' I asked.

'Altan,' she said softly.

Her answer did nothing to calm my wife down.

'Altan? The snake who helped Tiridates forge the alliance that toppled Phraates.'

She looked at me. 'You should have killed him when you had the chance.'

I nodded. 'I am apt to agree.'

Claudia threw up her arms. 'How easy it is to criticise from the safety of Dura, a thousand miles from the empire's eastern border. You think Phraates wishes to appoint Altan, a man whose life you argued should be saved, father? No. But he recognises that Altan comes from an old and influential Arian family, one that holds great power in his kingdom. Of all the surviving lords of Aria, he is the logical choice to be crowned king to unite those lords in the face of the Kushan threat.'

'The Kushan threat has diminished greatly,' said Gallia.

'But it still exists, mother, and will no doubt flare up again in the future, which is why Phraates needs to plant the seeds of loyalty on his eastern frontier.'

'I did not know you had become a poet, Claudia,' I said sarcastically.

She raised an eyebrow at me. 'The kingdoms of the east are in a weakened position following their defeat at the Battle of Ctesiphon.'

'Are we supposed to feel sorry for traitors?' hissed Gallia.

'You and father defeated the army of Tiridates and in so doing butchered thousands of the eastern kings' best soldiers.'

'That is the nature of defeat,' I remarked smugly. 'The losing side suffers high losses.'

She ignored me. 'And let us not forget the kings of Anauon and Yueh-Chih also fell at Ctesiphon, which meant of the six kingdoms guarding the empire's eastern frontier, only Antiochus of Drangiana and Salar of Sakastan are left alive to provide leadership against the Kushans.'

'Your arithmetic is faulty,' I told her, 'for you forgot about Phanes who rules Carmania.'

Now it was her turn to laugh.

'Phanes is a drunken fool who spends his days raging against the world, though by all accounts he is quite mad. He is fortunate to have a capable son, Babak, to keep the kingdom in some sort of order. Rumour is civil war is about to break out in Carmania.'

'Can't you send one of your witches to cast a spell of harmony over the kingdom?' I jested.

She gave me a condescending stare.

'How childish you can be at times, father. If Carmania descends into civil strife, Phraates will request King Salar to assist Prince Babak, as the two have been in correspondence for many months. I am hopeful they will form an alliance, which will secure the southern sector of the eastern frontier.'

'So, the only obstacle to your little plan is Phanes,' I said. I looked at Gallia. 'Expect him to be poisoned in the coming months.'

I could see Claudia's expression harden but she did not let anger get the better of her. Instead, she picked up an apple and bit into it, chewing for a few seconds before speaking.

'Phraates considers the recent campaign led by King Ali to have been a success, though not a triumph. He believes another expedition led by Ali would…'

'No,' I said firmly. 'No more of Dura's soldiers will be riding east, and I can state with some certainty that you will receive the same answer in Hatra and Vanadzor.'

Claudia was shocked. 'The Kushans are the enemies of Parthia, father, and you have always been the first to defend the empire.'

'Not any more,' I stressed, 'I am retiring.'

'*We* are retiring,' said Gallia, conveniently forgetting about her ambition to assassinate Dura's surviving enemies.

I smiled at Claudia. 'There you have it. For forty years we have ridden hither and thither in the defence of Parthia, fighting battles too numerous to mention and in the process losing thousands of soldiers. Dura's soldiers will no longer be falling on foreign soil; they will exist purely to defend the interests of this kingdom.'

Claudia was shocked and for a split-second I detected fear in her cold, calculating eyes. She took another bite of her apple, placed the core on a dish and brought her hands together.

'I was not born when you marched against Porus and defeated him on the other side of the Euphrates, before assisting the current high king's grandfather in defeating Narses at the Battle of Surkh. As you say, since that time Dura's army has been at the heart of efforts to defend the empire. Today, that army is a living legend and I have heard its mere presence on the battlefield is enough to cower an enemy.'

'Not in my experience,' I said bluntly.

'Be that as it may, father,' she snapped, 'if you retire from the empire's affairs then Parthia will be weakened, for it is known that

Hatra follows Dura's lead. At a stroke, the two most formidable armies in the empire will no longer be available to the high king.'

I stood and walked to the balustrade, the ache in my leg having finally subsided.

'The high king has relied on Dura for too long, Claudia, and in any case, he has a new lord high general to fight his wars.'

'King Ali is not Pacorus of Dura,' she replied.

'That's true,' I agreed, 'he's younger, fitter and full of energy. I am old, Claudia, and have no desire to see the face of battle again.'

I used my fingers to count the number of kingdoms Ali could call upon to form a very large army.

'Babylon, Persis, Atropaiene, Susiana and Gordyene, all able to put at least twenty thousand men into the field, which totals one hundred thousand soldiers. More than enough to fight the Kushans and reinforce the armies of the eastern kings.'

'And I daresay Media, once it has recovered, will be more than willing to contribute to the defence of the empire,' added Gallia.

Claudia sank into a sullen silence, eating an almond cake, her honeyed words having failed to win us over. Ashk appeared on the terrace, bowing to me, smiling at a now miserable-looking Claudia and then bowing to Gallia before whispering in my ear.

'Show him in,' I said.

When he disappeared, I leaned in closer to Claudia.

'Elymais is also part of our self-defence league, just in case Phraates, in a moment of vindictiveness, decides to murder Cia and her infant son.'

My daughter frowned. 'You are forgetting the demi-god Prince Pacorus of Hatra is her guardian, father. The irony being Cia is in more danger from him than Phraates.'

'Impossible,' I insisted.

'It's no use uttering a bad word about your father's namesake,' said Gallia, 'he won't hear of it.'

'Well, you can be assured that Phraates has no ill intentions towards the infant or his mother,' Claudia assured us.

Ashk escorted Almas onto the terrace, the former commander of horse archers bowing to us as I rose from my seat. Despite his great wealth, he wore a simple white tunic and tan leggings, a pair of brown leather boots completing his appearance. In fact, he looked like an ordinary horse archer and I wondered if he deliberately dressed in such a manner to preserve the memory of his time in Dura's army. A simple leather cover strapped around the wrist concealed the stump on the end of his left arm.

'Claudia, this is Almas, the city's deputy governor.'

He bowed to her and she in turn fixed her stare on his stump.

'Almas is a veteran of the army,' I told her to save any awkward silences.

She stood and walked over to the tall former army officer.

'You lost your hand in battle, sir?'

'Yes, highness, at the Araxes River during the Phraaspa campaign, nearly ten years ago now.'

She reached inside her robe and pulled out a chain at her neck, hanging from which was a lock of hair.

'We all lost precious things during that campaign.'

Her eyes were suddenly pools of sadness and her face momentarily showed an expression of utter despair, before the cold Scythian Sister returned. I looked at Gallia and both of us remembered Valak, the dashing commander of King Silaces' bodyguard, whom Claudia had fallen in love with. Only for their love to be cruelly ended by his murder.

'You bring news of the new irrigation system, Almas?' I asked, eager to change the subject.

'Yes, majesty,' he beamed. 'Work will be complete in a month and in addition to reducing the damage caused by the spring melt waters, will hopefully lead to increased crop yields.'

'You have become a farmer, father?' said Claudia mockingly.

'I have done with fighting, and you know what? Dirt is easier to wash off your hands than blood. For years I took Dura for granted. It was the city from which I planned military campaigns. After we had made peace with the Agraci, I gave little thought to the farmers that toiled in the fields, thinking the caravans of the Silk Road provided the wealth that enabled me to build and maintain the army.'

'They are,' said Claudia.

'They provide money, nothing more,' I replied, 'but the real wealth of this kingdom resides in the thousands of men and woman who toil in the fields under an unforgiving sun.'

Claudia rolled her eyes. 'You are spending too much time with Greeks, father. You remind me of Plato.'

I wracked my brains, in vain, trying to work out when I had met him.

Claudia looked at me expectantly. 'One of the Greek philosophers that Alcaeus is so keen on dredging up. Where is he, by the way?'

'Gone on a trip to Greece,' Gallia informed her, 'he wants to see Athens again before he dies.'

Another roll of the eyes. 'I assume Athens is like any other city, being filled with noxious fumes, cripples, beggars, prostitutes and politicians. So, the army has no head of its medical corps. How remiss of you, father.'

'On the contrary,' I replied smugly, 'it has a rather excellent replacement chosen by Alcaeus himself, a fellow Greek named Sophus.'

Claudia was silent for a few seconds. 'If I am right, which I invariably am, his name means "skilled" and "clever". I wonder if there is a Greek word for "humble"?'

'Who is this Plato,' I demanded to know.

She pointed at me. 'He was like you, father, a man who grew disgusted with the bloodshed and rank incompetence of his times. He turned his back on politics to devote his life to philosophy.'

'Not like me at all, then,' I said.

'You *are* quite like him, father, in as much as you pursue wisdom, understand that wisdom requires understanding of the world, and are determined to remain entirely apart from politics, that is, the affairs of the empire.'

'I am determined to devote my remaining years to my kingdom, Claudia, which means improving the lives of its citizens, the same citizens who serve in the army and produce the food, weapons, clothing and animals that enable that army to operate effectively. To which end, for months now Almas has overseen the renovation and expansion of the kingdom's irrigation systems to take full advantage of the waters of the Euphrates.'

'Most noble,' said Claudia. 'But here's the thing. You may have finished with politics, father, but has politics finished with you?'

'As I told you, I have retired. And as Phraates is realigning the empire, he will be delighted I have done so.'

I ordered a chair to be brought for Almas and when it arrived, asked him to sit in it, pouring him a cup of fruit juice as Claudia engaged in her favourite pastime: lecturing others.

'Interesting philosophical point, is it not?'

'What is?' I asked, handing Almas a platter of pastries.

'Can a man who has devoted his whole life to war suddenly become a man of peace?'

I held out a hand to Almas. 'Here is the living proof he can.'

'You will forgive my bluntness, Almas,' said Claudia, 'but your change of profession was forced upon you when you lost your hand, though you must be a man of remarkable talents to go from being a lowly officer of horse archers to deputy governor of Dura.'

'Your tongue is too sharp, Claudia,' Gallia scolded her.

'You must forgive my daughter, Almas,' I said.

'Not at all, majesty,' he said, finishing a pastry, 'normally, I would be enjoying a modest living on the pension your majesty has kindly established for wounded veterans. But the gods have been kind.'

'Which gods?' demanded Claudia.

'I pray to Shamash, highness,' he told her, 'who has been most generous to an old soldier.'

'The gods always reward those who pay homage to them, Almas,' she smiled

'Contrary to the high king,' I lamented, 'who has seen fit to dismiss the man who held his eastern frontier together.'

Almas was surprised. 'Kewab has been dismissed?'

'Phraates cannot dismiss his lord high general,' said Gallia, 'so instead he has made a scapegoat of Kewab.'

'His appointment was only temporary,' insisted Claudia irritably.

'If only the same could be said of Phraates,' remarked Gallia.

I laughed and Almas smiled but Claudia was far from amused. Her mission was failing but I was determined that no soldier of Dura would again be fighting in a high king's wars. The kingdom deserved peace, its people deserved peace and their king and queen deserved peace.

'Tell me about irrigation, Almas,' smiled Claudia.

That night I penned a letter to Kewab telling him he would always have a home and position at Dura.

Claudia left two days later, after first visiting The Sanctuary and spending many hours inside its walls. In my quest for a quiet life I forgot about forcing my way past its doors and told Gallia as much the evening prior to our daughter's departure for Ctesiphon.

'I have no wish to argue with you,' I said, 'I have not the energy. So I surrender to your wishes.'

We were in the corridor of the palace's private quarters, Claudia having already retired to her old bedroom to get a good night's sleep before her journey on the morrow. The palace was quiet, the corridor being cast in a pale-yellow light produced by oil lamps flickering in recesses in the walls.

She embraced me. 'You are right, we should not bicker, especially at our age.'

I made to go to the guest bedroom where I had been sleeping, but she pulled me back.

'Where are you going?'

'I thought....'

She pressed a finger to my lips. 'Allow me to be a generous victor.'

With that she led me towards our bedroom, a sultry glint in her eye. I felt a tingle of excitement in my loins.

Careful Pacorus, your lust might be making demands your tired old body cannot fulfil.

We said farewell to Claudia in the courtyard the next day, the sky cloudy and grey to match the mood of our daughter, which had darkened when both Gallia and I had told her we would not be visiting Ctesiphon in the near future, if at all.

'Phraates is welcome to come to Dura any time,' I told her as her richly uniformed Babylonian escort waited in line behind her, 'but I have little inclination to leave Dura.'

'Me neither,' added Gallia.

Claudia looked around the courtyard. 'He will be disappointed.'

'An emotion I have experienced many times,' I said, 'mainly due to men like Phraates.'

She suddenly looked at me. 'Dura must remain a loyal ally of the high king, father.'

'Dura has always been loyal,' I replied, 'but loyalty cuts both ways. Try to keep a muzzle on Phraates, especially his scheming against Spartacus, which almost cost the lives of your mother and father.'

She smiled. 'It is not your destinies to die in Irbil, or any other city of the empire. I have arranged a present for you, mother. Farewell.'

She turned her horse and rode from the Citadel, her Babylonian escort forming two files behind her.

Life at Dura continued as normal, Claudia keeping us abreast of developments from her privileged position as the high king's adviser. If Phraates had been angered or disappointed by our decision to absent Dura from the politics of the empire she did not say so, but she did report that Sanabares had been made King of Mesene and the former ambassador Altan became King of Aria. We received happy news from Sigal that Isabella was pregnant with a second child, both she and Salar begging us to visit Sakastan to meet our first grandchild and hopefully our second. We replied that we would make the journey in the autumn when the heat of summer had abated. In truth neither of us looked forward to a thousand-mile journey that would take upwards of five weeks, but it was advisable to undertake it before either one or both of us was unable to ride.

In a vision of the future, I rode in a cart with Gallia to the opening of the new irrigation system a month to the day after Almas had visited the palace to announce the date of its completion. It was not because we had suddenly become unable to ride in a saddle, but rather to keep Rsan and Aaron company. Both rarely left the city and Rsan had suddenly become very frail, his wrists alarmingly thin and his steps short and faltering. We were all very concerned about him and even Chrestus, who had been his sparring partner in council meetings for years, no longer shot his curt barbs at the governor. Indeed, on the day we left the Citadel to visit the irrigation works five miles south of the city, he assisted Rsan into the back of the cart before gaining his saddle.

As if to herald a new dawn for Dura, the sun shone from a cloudless sky and there was a slight northerly breeze to prevent the temperature from becoming too uncomfortable. Almas rode a magnificent brown stallion beside the cart, explaining the technology behind a successful irrigation system. The wagon was covered to shelter us from the sun, though the canvas sides had been raised to give us a view as the cart trundled down the city's main street towards the Palmyrene Gate, a score of Amazons led by Zenobia following and a score of male horse archers trotting ahead.

Farmers had always used the Euphrates to water their crops, but in Dura it had been a relatively recent practice. Before I came to the kingdom there were no villages north or south of the city because of the on-going war with the Agraci. There were the walled strongholds of the kingdom's lords positioned close to the river, around which crops grew to feed the lord and his retainers, plus their horses. But these were islands in a literal desert, a desert that was moreover filled with enemy raiders. But peace with the Agraci had meant settlements could be established the length and breadth of the kingdom. But these required safe and reliable supplies of water if they were to flourish.

'Having spent many hours in the company of the guild of farmers,' Almas began, 'I can safely say that Dura will have one of the most up-to-date irrigation systems in the Parthian Empire, if not the world.'

'A system that has absorbed a considerable amount of money and labour,' added Aaron.

'Which will be repaid to the treasury ten-fold, if not more, my old friend,' Rsan assured him.

'As Lord Aaron says, it is not cheap ensuring water of the right quality is delivered at the right time and in the correct quantity to the fields,' said Almas.

Chrestus wore a bemused expression. 'Water is water, surely?'

'Alas no, general,' said Almas. 'Because Dura is a very dry kingdom, water used to irrigate crops can evaporate quickly, leaving a layer of salt behind. The very nature of irrigating crops, which means water is spread out in a thin sheet, encourages evaporation. Over time, salt builds up on the surface and makes the soil infertile.'

Aaron raised a hand. 'If irrigation is so damaging to the soil, why have we lavished a great deal of money establishing a new system?'

'A fair question, lord treasurer,' replied Almas, 'but rest assured the kingdom's money has not been wasted.'

'I'm relieved to hear it,' I said.

'The only way to deal with the problem is to apply enough water so that salt is flushed off or through the soil,' Almas informed us. 'Doing so means salt will not build up in the soil, though for it to work requires a large volume of good-quality water, together with rapid and efficient drainage systems.'

The cart trundled to a halt and we alighted from it to walk to a diversion dam built around two hundred yards from the Euphrates. Lined with stone, it was fed by a canal connecting it to the river. In turn, a system of irrigation ditches took water from the dam to the crops in the fields. There were gates on all the ditches to control the amount of water from them to the fields.

Sluice gates at the river were wooden and faced with copper to prolong their life, and the height of the bank had been raised to prevent any flooding when the spring melt waters came, though when they did, dams that had been built along the length of the Euphrates would be filled with water. The one we stood on was of modest size and located near the river, but others were larger and had been sited inland up to a distance of two or three miles from the Euphrates. The reservoirs were fed by wide canals, which had taken many months to dig, Chrestus loaning Almas cohorts of legionaries to speed up the work. In truth, it was still on-going, especially in the south of the kingdom where settlements were less well established. But there were now villages along the river for a distance of over two hundred miles from the city, and the new irrigation system would allow new settlements to be established further inland.

Hundreds had gathered at the spot, a century of Durans keeping the crowd at bay as we made our way to where a coterie of white-robed priests was burning incense to purify the air to welcome Shamash to the proceedings. The high priest was the same serious individual with a booming voice who had married Eszter and Dalir, his long arms rising when he spotted Gallia and me heading the official party. His voice seemed to fill the air as he began his invocation to Shamash, his eyes staring up at the heavens as he did so.

'Shamash, judge of heaven and earth, lord of justice and equity, director of upper and lower regions, Shamash, it is in your power to bring the dead to life, to release the captive. Shamash, I have approached you. Shamash, I have sought you out! Shamash, I have turned to you!'

On and on it went, hundreds standing with heads bowed as the high priest begged for Shamash's blessing, his voice never faltering as he paid homage to the Sun God. I searched the crowd around the reservoir, looking for a tall figure in a cowl but saw nothing. I glanced left and right to see Rsan, leaning on his walking stick, head bowed, eyes closed. Aaron, who was a Jew, wore a dignified expression, while Chrestus, who was from Pontus and had never visited the city's Temple of Shamash, looked bored to distraction. But he was a loyal servant of Dura and its king was a loyal servant of Shamash, so I hoped the Sun God would forgive my general.

The service ended with the high priest making a libation to Shamash by pouring water taken from the Euphrates from a terracotta pot into the reservoir. After emptying the vessel, he turned to me and bowed.

'It is done, majesty.'

I thanked him and nodded to Almas, who gave the signal to one of the army engineers who had been assigned to the project, the man picking up a red flag and waving it from left to right. Soldiers operating the sluice gates at the river end of the canal opened them. Moments later water began entering the reservoir, to cheers from the farmers and their families among the crowd and polite applause from the merchants and nobles present.

'My leg has locked,' I whispered to Gallia, who took my arm and helped me away.

'Come on, old man, back to the palace for you.'

A rider appeared among the now dispersing crowd, manoeuvring his horse through the throng, jumping down from the saddle and halting before me, bowing his head and holding out a note. I took the papyrus and broke the seal showing a horse, the mark of Aria. I read the words and smiled, Rsan, Aaron and Chrestus looking at me quizzically.

'Kewab is coming home,' I told them.

Chapter 3

All is as the gods will it. Man is but a puny, insignificant wretch who holds no sway over the way the world is ordered and the events that take place within it. A farmer may plant his fields and water his crops in the hope they will grow and provide him and his family with food after they are harvested. But a flood, drought or a plague of locusts may destroy his crops and condemn his family to starvation. A merchant may buy goods and ship them on a camel caravan to a distant land where they will be sold for a great profit. But the caravan may be attacked and his goods stolen, thus reducing him to poverty. A king may rule a kingdom and invest much of its wealth in a vast irrigation system to greatly increase the crop yield to not only ensure his growing population has enough food, but also to sell the projected enormous surplus to fill his treasury. But the gods had other plans.

It was now spring, and the Euphrates was rising, filled with the melt waters bringing torrents of water from the mountains in Pontus, in addition to a thousand smaller water courses bloated with melted snow and ice that fed into the great waterway. For over two hundred and fifty miles the border of Dura that abutted the Euphrates held back the swelling waters, city officials and engineers being able to control the flow from the river to water crops and fill canals and waterways. I was bursting with pride when I convened a special meeting of the city council to personally thank Almas in front of all of his peers, and to confirm him as deputy governor of not only the city but also the whole kingdom.

'Dura owes you a huge debt of gratitude, Almas,' I told him, 'you have made the desert bloom.'

'Hardly that, majesty,' he replied, 'the western bank of the Euphrates was already inhabited, thanks to your own peace treaty with the Agraci.'

I was having none of it.

'Thanks to you, Almas, Dura no longer has to rely on the Silk Road solely for its wealth. Increased crop production means an increasing population, which means a great surplus of crops that can be exported.'

'I was only following where you have already trod, majesty,' smiled Almas.

'Loathe as I am to break up this meeting of Dura's self-appreciation society,' said Gallia, 'but the king has some important news.'

'I do? Ah, of course, I had clean forgot.'

I briefly examined the letters in front of me. Aaron, Ira, Chrestus, Rsan and Almas looked at me expectantly.

'As you all know, Kewab was dismissed from his position as Satrap of Aria.'

'Bloody ridiculous,' muttered Chrestus.

'Akin to a crime,' I agreed, 'and a decision that is short-sighted at the very least. Be that as it may, Kewab is returning to Dura, along with his soldiers.'

Aaron and Ira exchanged concerned looks.

'Soldiers, majesty?' said Aaron.

I perused the second letter Kewab had sent me after the initial missive declaring his intention to return to Dura.

'Three thousand horsemen and another thousand dependents. Having fought and bled for Kewab, they have no desire to settle in

Aria ruled by the duplicitous Altan, who by all accounts has indicated no land will be made available to them in any case.'

I noticed Ira scribbling on a sheet of papyrus, a grave-looking Aaron shaking his head when he had finished.

'The new King of Aria must be mad to get rid of battle-hardened soldiers,' opined Chrestus.

'That is probably why he wants rid of them,' I told him, 'by all accounts Aria has few soldiers to call on.'

'That's because most of them were killed at Ctesiphon fighting for the traitor Tiridates,' said Gallia harshly.

I picked up another letter.

'Some of you may remember General Karys, my friend Nergal's loyal commander, who since the death of the King and Queen of Mesene had ruled that kingdom as satrap, and made a good job of it, by all accounts.

'However, in what appears to be the spirit of the age, High King Phraates has seen fit to dismiss him from his position and has made the Satrap of Susiana, one Sanabares, the new King of Mesene. Karys has requested, and both the queen and I have agreed, that he and his followers may have sanctuary in Dura, which means four thousand horse archers and their dependents, an additional two thousand people.'

Ira dropped his reed pen. 'That is ten thousand additional mouths to feed, majesty.'

Almas appeared thoughtful. 'Plus their horses and camels.'

'It will place a great burden on the kingdom's resources, majesty,' said Aaron, 'a great burden.'

Ira began scribbling again.

Rsan raised a finger. 'Is it wise to bring so many foreign soldiers into the kingdom, majesty?'

'I'm a foreign soldier,' said Chrestus, 'having been born in Pontus.'

Rsan nodded his head. 'But you are a member of Dura's army, general, who rose to command that army. But the soldiers of Kewab and Karys may cause much disorder within the kingdom.'

'We should bar them from entering Dura,' urged Aaron.

'And where will they go?' asked Gallia. 'I have fought beside Karys and his soldiers, soldiers that were trained by Nergal and Praxima. They are among the finest troops in Parthia, not a roving rabble of bandits.'

'And remember Kewab is a son of Dura, a man who graduated top of the Sons of the Citadel,' added Chrestus. 'Before the "Great Muster" and King Ali's campaign against the Kushans, Kewab and his men were the only things standing between Kujula and Parthia.'

'Both Kewab and Karys and their men will be welcome in Dura,' I stressed.

Ira sighed. 'But that will not only deplete the kingdom's food stocks, majesty, but will also mean the projected agricultural surplus that we intended to sell will effectively evaporate.'

'But the army will be reinforced by seven thousand veteran soldiers,' said Chrestus with relish.

Rsan raised a finger again. 'We are all comforted by the army's great strength, general, but with the king's retirement from the military affairs of the empire, what will the army be doing?'

'Perhaps the soldiers of Kewab and Karys will follow Deputy Governor Almas in pursuing civilian careers,' suggested Aaron.

'Perhaps,' I said without conviction.

But the plans of the gods are seldom revealed to mortals and Aaron, Rsan and Ira need not have wasted their energy fretting about the kingdom's finances. For Dura would soon be denuded of soldiers, both its own and foreign ones.

The first of those seeking sanctuary in Dura were those who travelled with Karys. Gallia and I rode south with the Amazons, a thousand horse archers and all of Azad's cataphracts, heading for the ford we had used many times to cross the Euphrates at the beginning of a campaign to save Parthia. And now we took the same route once more, to greet a man who had served Nergal and Praxima loyally and had decided, for whatever reason, to leave his homeland and live in another kingdom.

The ford was still navigable for a man on a horse, the level of the river yet to rise substantially due to the spring melt waters; indeed, it was brown, slow moving and very shallow in parts, allowing four thousand soldiers and their families to wade across. Professional to the last, companies provided flank and van guards for their woman and children, Karys and the bulk of his men remaining on the eastern side of the river until every civilian, cart and camel had crossed over to enter Duran territory.

I nudged Horns ahead so he entered the water, the riverbank either side lined with Duran horse archers, a phalanx of cataphracts behind me. Gallia accompanied me, together with Zenobia holding my griffin standard, and the Amazons. We waded through the water, avoiding the great column of civilians, camels, carts, donkeys and horse archers going the other way. Woman and children waved at us and I waved back, much to the amusement of Gallia and Zenobia. Klietas, now almost an accomplished horseman, stared in wonder at the ordered throng leaving Mesene, continually glancing behind at Haya in the column of Amazons.

'Is something wrong with your head, Klietas?' asked Gallia.

'No, highborn.'

'Then why does it turn backwards all the time?'

'Sorry, highborn.'

'She isn't going anywhere,' I said to him. 'Haya, I mean. That is what you were doing, checking to ensure she had not fallen off her horse?'

He blushed with embarrassment.

'Where will all these people live, highborn?' he asked, eager to change the subject.

'In the Kingdom of Dura.'

'Why are they leaving their homeland, highborn?'

'Because they are no longer welcome,' answered Gallia, 'and because loyalty is no longer valued in Parthia.'

She was bitter that Karys had been dismissed, seeing it as a slight against Nergal and Praxima, though I wondered if it was more a case of seeing what she and I had fought for over the years changing and slipping away. Once we had been the youngest king and queen in the empire, full of fire and determination to crush our enemies. The kings we had first fought alongside – my father, Farhad, Balas, Aschek and Gotarzes – were all dead, and Nergal and Praxima had joined them in the afterlife, along with Silaces. Now new kings ruled Parthia, appointed by a high king determined to stamp his own mark on Parthia and who owed their loyalty to him. From Phraates' point of view it made sense; to Gallia it was tantamount to a deliberate insult.

We emerged from the muddy water to meet Karys surrounded by a knot of his senior officers, men I recognised from our recent campaign against Tiridates.

Karys bowed his head to us. It was the first time I had seen him since the great victory over Tiridates at Ctesiphon and he had visibly aged in the interim. He still had a ruddy complexion but his thick hair and beard were flecked with grey and his grey eyes were filled with sorrow. When he spoke he did so with a voice laced with bitterness and anguish.

'On behalf of myself and those with me, majesty, we thank you for your generosity and benevolence.'

'Nonsense,' I replied, 'Dura does not forget its allies or its friends. Get your people over the river and we will speak more fully tonight in camp.'

'Thank you, majesty.'

He was nearly a king and had been a satrap, though he looked nothing like royalty or indeed a person of power and influence. Like his officers and horse archers, he wore a simple woollen kaftan, a *kurta*, dyed red that opened at the front and was wrapped across the chest from right to left. It was loose fitting, comfortable and entirely functional, like the leggings all Mesene's soldiers wore, called *saravanas*. Like his lowliest soldier, Karys wore simple leather ankle boots called *xshumaka* that were tied in place by leather bands that passed around the ankle and under the sole. Mesene had no cataphracts or mounted spearmen, being an impoverished kingdom well away from the riches of the Silk Road, and so could only field horse archers, but Nergal had managed to equip them all with scale-armour cuirasses – short-sleeved garments that reached down to the mid-thigh and were slit at each side to facilitate riding. Each cuirass, even Karys', consisted of horizontal rows of rectangular iron scales stitched onto the hide beneath, each row partly covering the one below. The only thing that differentiated officers from common soldiers was a red helmet crest. The helmets were solid affairs made from curved iron plates attached to a skeleton of vertical iron bands, complete with large cheek guards and a long leather neck flap.

'What's that?' said Gallia, pointing to a staff held by a soldier behind the group of officers, attached to which was a wax sleeve covering what I assumed was a furled banner.

'The old standard of Mesene, majesty,' said Karys softly, 'I thought I should bring it with us before it was consigned to history.'

'Unfurl it,' Gallia told him, 'the standard of Nergal and Praxima should never be hidden from view.'

'Yes, majesty.'

He ordered the wax sleeve to be removed and the yellow banner embossed with a double-headed lion sceptre crossed with a sword began to flutter in the easterly breeze.

'Much better,' smiled Gallia.

'What is Mesene's new banner?' I enquired.

'A viper,' spat Karys.

'History repeats itself,' remarked Gallia. 'Kings of Mesene who fly a snake flag are invariably reptiles and meet bad ends.'

Because the extreme south of my kingdom was still sparsely populated, it lacked the resources to feed, clothe and house six thousand people and their beasts. The plan, therefore, was to move Karys and his followers north to be nearer the city of Dura so supplies could be ferried to them on a regular basis, which would give the council time to decide the best course of action to ensure their welfare. That night I entertained Karys in my tent, Klietas serving us food and wine, as he briefed us on recent events in Mesene. He ate sparingly and I sensed he was weighed down by a great burden, which I hoped he would unburden himself of in our company.

'Sanabares, who has yet to take up residency in Uruk, has declared his intention to restore the old boundaries of Mesene.'

My heart sank. 'You mean try to conquer the Ma'adan.'

He nodded. Years before, when Nergal and Praxima had become rulers of Mesene, they had taken the bold step of granting the marsh people, the Ma'adan, who occupied the swamplands adjacent to the Persian Gulf, their freedom. At a stroke they gave away a third of their kingdom, but in return won peace and the lasting gratitude of the Ma'adan, many of whom went on to serve in his army.

'The Ma'adan will not tolerate being subjected to rule from Uruk after tasting freedom,' said Gallia.

'Sanabares is an outsider, majesty,' said Karys, 'he will only see a large slice of territory to the south that needs to be re-conquered.'

'What does High Priest Rahim say about the matter?' I asked.

He picked at his bread and olives. 'Alas, Rahim died last week, majesty. His successor is not a friend of the Ma'adan, or Jews.'

'Alas for Rahim,' I said.

The High Priest of the Temple of Anu in Uruk had been a formidable figure who had held great sway in the kingdom. It was he who had announced that Nergal and Praxima were gods made flesh, and in doing so ensured their reign would not be challenged. What he thought of Nergal's accommodation with the Ma'adan he never revealed, but now he was gone and so was his influence.

'The new high priest informed me he will declare a holy war against the Ma'adan once Sanabares is made king,' reported Karys. He pointed to the entrance to the tent.

'Half of those who came with me across the river today are Ma'adan, though their children were born in Uruk or outlying villages. The rest are from Mesene but have no stomach for butchering men they have fought beside for years. A small number are Jews, who are no longer welcome in Mesene.'

He sank into silence and I sensed the thing that burdened him was foremost in his mind.

'Continue, please,' I beseeched him.

'I have no wish to offend you, majesty.'

'Nonsense,' said Gallia, 'we have always valued the truth in Dura, however unpalatable.'

'Speak freely, Karys, one soldier to another.'

'The new high priest received instructions to eject all Jews from the kingdom, starting with me,' he said.

'Who made such a request?' I demanded to know. 'Was it Phraates?'

He shook his head. 'No, majesty, his chief adviser.'

'Claudia?' Gallia did not believe it.

'Yes, majesty,' confirmed Karys.

I looked at Gallia and we both knew he spoke the truth. I heard the same views regarding Jews from Dobbai years before: that they were disloyal, unreliable and followed a false god. I had dismissed her more eccentric beliefs as being the ramblings of an old woman. But I now realised she had infected Claudia with her opinions, which meant they formed part of the creed of the Scythian Sisters.

'I am sorry, Karys,' said Gallia.

'Sanabares will fail as a king if he replaces peace with war,' I said. 'The people of Mesene have got used to living in harmony with the Ma'adan. When I became King of Dura the then ruler of Mesene, Chosroes, had been waging unending war against the Ma'adan. History seems set to repeat itself.'

Karys looked at me. 'I did not incite insurrection, majesty, and nor did I force the people who crossed the Euphrates today to do so. They came willingly, though Sanabares may not see it that way and might want his subjects back.'

'Sanabares can think what he likes,' hissed Gallia, 'his words carry no power in Dura.'

'It is as my wife says, Karys,' I added.

We rode with Karys back to the city, leaving the horse archers to escort the refugees from Mesene north. Fortunately, Karys had made provision for his people and had ensured they had a month's worth of food and fodder for their journey, which would mean Dura's treasury would not have to subsidise them, at least not straight away. For their part, Chrestus, Azad, Sporaces and the army's other senior commanders were delighted by the addition of four thousand veteran, highly trained horse archers to the army, Aaron and Ira less so.

The treasury officials were even glummer when Kewab and his men entered Duran territory two weeks later, having been granted permission to journey through Elymais after leaving Sakastan, but being delayed in Susiana when the satrap of that kingdom, the soon-to-be-king Sanabares, insisted they be escorted all the way through Susianan and Babylonian territory. It was a deliberate slight designed to make Kewab feel disloyal and untrustworthy, but at least my brother gave the refugees from the east free rein to travel unaccompanied through Hatran territory before reaching Dura.

The whole army was paraded in front of the city to welcome back one of its favourite sons. The plumes that had been purchased to decorate the helmets of legionaries – red and white – were brought out of storage to once again adorn thousands of helmets. Azad's cataphracts literally shone in the sun, their burnished scale and tubular armour sparkling and the griffin pennants on the ends of every *kontus* adding a splash of colour to the brilliance. Sporaces and his horse archers had no plumes or burnished armour, but the coats of their horses shone in the sun and their tunics were a pristine white. Gallia and I wore our special scale-armour cuirasses, which still felt as light as a feather, the Amazons being attired in mail armour and helmets as they waited in the Citadel for Kewab and his senior officers.

The people of Dura were curious rather than ecstatic, Kewab having been away from the kingdom for some time and, crucially, only a small number of Duran soldiers having travelled with him to the east. But the fact the army was on display to welcome him back pointed to his importance, though many must have had trepidations about those that accompanied him. They looked like a bunch of refugees, all the soldiers wearing a variety of sun-bleached tunics that were kaftan-like coats with one breast crossed over the other and tied to one side. Both men and women wore loose-fitting leggings and ankle-length boots, though only the men wore armour, which comprised bands of hardened leather laced together to form a cuirass. Their helmets were also leather, with padded insides and neck and ear flaps.

They might not have cut a very prepossessing sight but each soldier was heavily armed. All, even Kewab when he rode into the Citadel, carried a recurve bow and three full quivers, in addition to a spear with a long blade designed for piercing armour. Every man also carried a sword, a straight, two-bladed weapon with a heart-shaped guard and knob-like pommel, plus a straight-bladed dagger.

The fanfare of trumpets from musicians flanking the colour guard did not spook the newcomers' horses, which were far removed from the magnificent beasts that carried Dura's horsemen. They had short necks and legs and solid bodies, but I could tell they were extremely sturdy animals. Kewab and his senior officers, all shorter than him with hard, flat faces and black eyes, dismounted and took a few steps to the bottom of the palace steps, before bowing their heads. I descended the steps and embraced the Egyptian.

'Welcome back, Kewab, it is good to see you.'

He gave me a wan smile. 'Thank you, majesty, it is good to be back.'

It was nearly ten years since the star pupil of the Sons of Citadel had dazzled us all with his knowledge of strategy and tactics when he had directed the Phraaspa campaign. The son of General Achillas had earned the gratitude of Phraates, who had agreed to my suggestion he should be sent to the east to contain the Kushans. He had performed that task admirably but I could see it had taken a physical toll on him. His hazel eyes looked tired and his circular face had a careworn look. Previously he had been clean-shaven but now he had a thick, slightly unkempt beard and his curly black hair was unruly. I rested a hand on his shoulder.

'At least now you do not have to worry about the Kushans.'

He gave a grateful nod. 'Perhaps I will be able to get some sleep now, majesty.'

The next day I invited him to the palace for an informal debrief on the terrace, only Gallia and Chrestus joining us. Provision had been made for Kewab's followers to camp ten miles north of the city until more permanent arrangements could be made, though he himself would be staying in the city. He looked slightly less tired when he arrived for breakfast, a change of clothes and a comb through his hair hinting at the younger, bright-eyed Kewab we had said goodbye to.

'I have purchased a house, a fine house by all accounts, for you and your family as befitting your status,' I told him. 'Deputy-Governor Almas will arrange for your effects to be moved in straight away.'

Kewab's brow furrowed. 'Who is Almas, majesty?'

Chrestus laughed. 'He used to be a dragon commander of horse archers but lost a hand during the Phraaspa campaign. You remember that, I trust?'

Kewab nodded. 'Yes, lord, though it seems a different lifetime now.'

Gallia cut straight to the point. 'What happened to the other seven thousand of your men, Kewab, for I seem to remember your force originally totalled ten thousand?'

The Egyptian picked up a small, freshly cooked loaf and broke off a chunk, using a knife to smear it with butter.

'A third had been killed fighting the Kushans before I was dismissed by the high king, majesty, so I gathered my officers together and informed them I was no longer their commander.

'I wrote to King Pacorus requesting leave to return to Dura, asking if any of those who wanted to travel with me would also be welcome, which the king kindly gave his assent to.'

Gallia did a quick tally in her head. 'And the other three thousand, have they dispersed to their homes?'

Kewab took a bite of bread and a mouthful of fruit juice.

'They did not wish to travel the breadth of the empire to live in a land they had never seen, majesty, so I sent them to King Salar, your son-in-law, to bolster Sakastan's army.'

'So the ones who journeyed with you are the more adventurous sort?' asked Chrestus.

'That is one way of putting it, lord, but truth to tell the ones who came with me wanted to fight beside King Pacorus of Dura, whose army has never lost a battle. They are warriors and want to fight beside Dura's ruler before they die.'

Gallia looked at me and then at Kewab, giving him a rueful smile.

'Allow me to bring you up to date, Kewab, the king has drawn his sword in anger for the last time. No longer will Dura's army march to war for its king has retired from the affairs of the empire.'

Kewab, about to put a chunk of buttered bread in his mouth, stared at me in amazement, melting butter dripping on to his hand.

'It is true,' I told him, 'I am done with war, save if the kingdom or the empire is invaded by foreign forces.'

'Such as the Kushans?' enquired Kewab.

I picked up a slice of melon. 'My daughter Claudia, now close adviser to Phraates himself, was here recently broaching the subject of another campaign against the Kushans. I told her Dura would not be sending any more soldiers east.'

A look of surprise again, so I told him about Phraates' duplicity regarding who ruled Media, our adventure at Irbil and the subsequent Battle of Diyana where Rasha was killed.

'We received reports of the attack on Irbil and the Armenian invasion, of course,' said Kewab, 'but not that these things were encouraged by the high king. Alas for Queen Rasha.'

'Hatra, Gordyene and Dura have forged an alliance with Media to guarantee the latter's safety,' Gallia told him, 'as well as preserve the lives of its king and queen.'

'I'm afraid I must inform you,' I said, 'that if you and your men are looking for war and glory, you might have to travel back to the east. But I hope not for many months because you and they deserve rest and peace. I'm sorry about Aria.'

I had thought not to mention the no-longer-vacant throne of Aria, recently filled by the skilled ambassador Altan, whose life I had saved after his master Tiridates had failed in his bid to seize the high crown. But seeing Kewab in the flesh and realising the toll fighting the Kushans had taken on him these past few years, I was intrigued as to whether he carried any resentment that his efforts had not been rewarded; indeed, had been cast aside.

'Aria, majesty?'

'We had hoped that you would be offered the crown of Aria instead of Ambassador Altan.'

'You did hold the east of the empire together, after all,' added Chrestus.

Kewab gave me a wry smile.

'Altan will need all his diplomatic skills to prevent his kingdom falling apart, along with Yueh-Chih, Anauon and Drangiana.'

'It is that bad?' asked Chrestus.

I bit into my melon as he relayed the tale of woe on the eastern frontier, making me fear for the safety of Isabella and Salar.

'How ironic it was that the high king despatched his lord high general with an army to the east *after* your majesty had destroyed the army of Tiridates outside Ctesiphon. That army contained the best soldiers drawn from Yueh-Chih, Anauon, Drangiana and Aria, leaving only two armies of note left to face the Kushans, my own modest mobile column and the larger army of Sakastan.'

'You are forgetting King Phanes and his Carmanians,' said Gallia.

Kewab nodded sagely.

'If the army of Carmania still exists, majesty, then I hazard its time is spent crushing internal dissent. King Phanes is, by all account, insane.'

'We heard he was a drunkard,' I said.

Kewab shook his head. 'That as well, majesty, and in any case he is currently engaged in a war.'

I grew alarmed. 'War against whom?'

'The Goddess Nanshe.'

'How does one fight a goddess?' asked Chrestus mockingly.

'And why?' asked a bemused Gallia.

Nanshe, the daughter of Enki, the God of Wisdom and Fresh Water, and Ninhursag, the Mother Goddess, was responsible for the waters of the Persian Gulf and all the creatures that dwelt therein. She was represented by the symbol of the pelican and the fish.

'A great storm from the Persian Gulf lashed the western coastline of Carmania,' Kewab informed us, 'resulting in many coastal villages being wrecked, with substantial loss of life. Enraged, Phanes sent his soldiers to the coast to kill all the pelicans and the fish, both symbols of Nanshe, or so I am told.'

Chrestus roared with laughter. 'He sent his soldiers to kill all the fish in the ocean?'

Kewab, straight-faced, nodded. 'His war is on-going, lord.'

'Let us hope the Kushans and Satavahanis are locked in combat for years to come,' said Gallia.

'It was a stroke of luck war broke out between the two,' agreed Kewab, 'which will give the eastern kingdoms, aside from Carmania, time to rebuild their armies and prepare. And King Salar has an excellent army under the command of General Shapur.'

'Elephants and all?' I quipped.

'Less elephants these days, majesty,' he told me, 'but more horsemen. And Sakastan is in close communications with King Silani of Persis, who has a broad knowledge of the art of war.'

I felt rather smug, having been the one who had proposed to Phraates that the former commander of his bodyguard should sit on the vacant throne of Persis, a kingdom that had long been a thorn in the side of the high kings of Parthia. My mind wandered to the haughty figure of Narses and the reptilian Prince Alexander, both of whom had ruled Persis.

'A bright spot amid the gloom,' I said. 'And let us not forget Prince Pacorus who rules Elymais until the son of Silaces comes of age. He too will be able to assist Sakastan if the worst happens.'

'Phraates desires a war of conquest against the Kushans,' I told Kewab.

'I'm afraid that is beyond the resources of Parthia, majesty,' he replied bluntly.

We continued our breakfast in silence and I pondered his words, which were not uttered in haste or without thought, but represented a sober assessment by one of the keenest military minds produced by the Sons of the Citadel. For so long Parthia had concentrated on defeating the Roman threat, which *had* been contained. But a new, perhaps even more dangerous menace now existed on the empire's eastern frontier. Like Gallia, I hoped the Kushan war against the Satavahana Empire would be long and bloody.

He may have been dismissed from his position but I detected no resentment in Kewab, only relief that the arduous task that had been wearing him down was over. His men were a rough-looking lot and some officers in the army raised eyebrows at their appearance and gaunt, small horses. But Chrestus was unconcerned, informing me that they had no uniforms as such but their armour and weapons were clean and their horses were well maintained and fed. But the fact remained Dura's population had been swelled by ten thousand people and a greater number of horses. The thousands of camels that accompanied the armies of Karys and Kewab could be accommodated easily enough, but an additional ten thousand mouths to feed would tax the food reserves of the kingdom, at least until the new arrivals could be re-settled in existing or newly established villages. It was ironic that the anticipated food surplus for export would be swallowed up feeding Dura's new guests. Such is fate.

But the immediate problems would not interrupt the increasing prosperity of the kingdom, in addition to a population that was also expanding. It was good to see villages filled with hearty, hale people and well-fed children. For the past forty years I had seen the face of war, rode through countless settlements laid waste by soldiers, wept at the sight of civilians butchered and their bodies left to rot in the sun, and witnessed the great waste and devastation conflict visited on kingdoms, cities and towns. I was not guiltless when it came to inflicting horrors on an enemy, though I had never sanctioned the wanton destruction of a region or given permission for a city to be sacked out of spite. Or perhaps it was only my vanity that prevented me from thinking I was not a murderer.

I was leaning against the stone plinth on which the griffin stood above the Palmyrene Gate, below me a press of people, camels, carts and donkeys seeking entry into the city and traffic going the other way. The air was filled with raised voices, the scent of spices and the more noxious aromas of animals and their dung. To the west was the legionary camp, a huge, sprawling collection of tents, field kitchens, stables and stores, all surrounded by a mud-brick wall to deter unwelcome guests and accessed by gates at the four points of the compass. Originally, it had contained nothing but tents, but over the years mud-brick armouries and storerooms had been constructed, along with stables. To the north, beyond the deep wadi that fronted the city's northern wall, was the great caravan park filled with tents and hundreds of camels carrying silk and other commodities for sale in Egypt and Syria. The park was full, the legionary camp was filled with Durans and Exiles, aside from those legionaries garrisoning the mud-brick forts north and south of the city, and all was well in the Kingdom of Dura.

'I thought I would find you here.'

A figure in black robes appeared next to me, her haggard features gazing at the legionary camp shimmering in the haze as the heat of the day began to take hold.

'It has been a while.'

'I've been busy, son of Hatra.'

'Waging war against the Jews?' I retorted.

'Sarcasm does not suit you.'

'Dismissing Karys was a poor reward for a man who has served Parthia well, to say nothing of Kewab.'

'You are responsible for their dismissals.'

I laughed out loud, the bustle below masking my mirth.

'By what tortuous logic do you arrive at that ludicrous conclusion?'

'I heard a rumour you were offered the high crown, which if you had accepted would have meant Karys and Kewab would still be in their posts.'

How did she know this? She spoke the truth but I was loath to admit it.

'Your silence speaks volumes,' she teased me. 'You are angry with Phraates?'

'Yes.'

'Even after all these years you are still endearingly naïve and idealistic, son of Hatra. Phraates is not like some old dog that will do your bidding for a treat and a pat on the head. As you have been told a thousand times, he has a malicious spirit and a cunning mind.'

'He is ungrateful.'

She emitted a cackle that was a cross between a laugh and groan.

'You believe he should be more appreciative of the efforts you have made to keep him on Ctesiphon's throne?'

'It would not hurt.'

'So by your logic, every king should spend his time thanking each and every one of those he rules, for their labours in the fields, for their bravery in the army, their devotion to the gods, and for bearing children to ensure future generations of his subjects.'

'Now you are being ridiculous.'

'Am I? A king expects loyalty from his subjects; a high king demands the same from the kings of the empire, especially after they have sworn oaths of loyalty to him. You did swear an oath of loyalty to him, son of Hatra?'

'You know full well I did.'

A wave of the arm. 'My memory is not what it was.'

'It is good to see you.'

A dismissive grunt. 'You see, incurably sentimental. And on that topic, I see you have managed to collect another waif.'

'Who?'

'Your new squire.'

I chuckled. 'Klietas?'

'History repeats itself, son of Hatra. I seem to remember another orphan you collected once, a marsh boy from the Ma'adan.'

So much for her memory failing. An image of Surena filled my mind, followed by a wave of guilt over his fate. She must have read my thoughts because she laid a bony hand on my arm.

'You could not save Surena, just as you cannot save Spartacus.'

'Spartacus is in danger?'

'Spartacus is beyond help,' she told me, 'Rasha acted as a restraint on him but now she has gone, there is no one to control him. The rage he has always carried within him has triumphed, and the roar of the lion of Gordyene will once again be heard throughout the north. He thinks he is a hunter, but he might be the prey.'

'What does that mean?'

'It means he will get his wish.'

'Another riddle.'

'Life is a riddle, son of Hatra. You asked why Karys and Kewab had been dismissed. I will tell you. They are needed here, to aid you.'

'Have not you heard? I have retired. Irbil was my last action and I shall spend my remaining days attending to my kingdom. That is what a king should do, after all.'

She began to clap and nod her head.

'What are you doing?'

'Oh, I'm sorry, I thought you came here to recite the lines of the play you are appearing in.'

'Play?'

'It must be a comedy, judging by the speech you just made. No man can escape his fate. Remember that, son of Hatra.'

There was a crashing sound below and I peered over the battlements to see that a wheel had come off a cart, spilling the contents – terracotta pots – all over the road, smashing many. The owner of the cart was holding his head in despair, others were remonstrating with him about the disruption and a flustered centurion and his men were shouting at individuals further back to remain where they were, prompting said individuals to begin gesticulating with their arms and demanding entry to the city. It was pure pandemonium. I smiled and turned to speak to my old friend, to discover I was alone once again.

Chapter 4

Papyrus. How the pith of the papyrus plant had shaped our world. Words scribbled on papyrus sheets had altered the course of history on many occasions, causing alliances to be forged, kings to be betrayed and the destinies of empires to be changed forever. The courier must have set off before dawn to reach Dura to deliver the roll of papyrus bearing a horse head wax seal. I had been on the training fields with Klietas to judge how his archery skills had been progressing, and in truth they were improving markedly. Each day, just after dawn when the sun had turned the eastern horizon blue and purple, he had ridden from the Citadel in the company of the Amazons to train. Gallia had initially been hostile to him joining her all-female group, but as he lived in the palace, in the servants' quarters, it made sense for him to join her and the Amazons before he began his duties. The squires of the cataphracts lived in various barracks in the city but Klietas was my manservant and his presence was required in the Citadel, so she relented.

They treated him appallingly, barely speaking to him save to ridicule him for his poor archery skills. But he endured their scorn and indifference like a Greek stoic, and of course to be with the Amazons meant being near Haya. But today he was with me. I had neglected my archery training, the new irrigation system and the arrival of Karys' and Kewab's followers having absorbed all of my time. But spring had arrived, the floodwaters of the Euphrates had been contained, controlled and channelled to serve the interests of the kingdom, and the thousands of new arrivals were being listed and organised for the same purpose. I could finally relax, just at the moment the papyrus scroll arrived from Hatra.

The courier arrived in the company of two horse archers, just to ensure he was not an assassin. But the note he carried was like a dagger to the heart of my plans to live a quiet life. The Amazons had left the training fields, the straw-filled targets that dotted the area shredded by their arrows. Later, the Daughters of Dura would travel from the city to repair the targets, so they would be ready for the following morning. Sporaces' horse archers had also been using the targets, hundreds of men performing battlefield drills to hone their response times and quicken their reactions to commands relayed by signallers. They too would return later to repair and replace the targets they had destroyed.

Train hard, fight easy.

'Bad news, highborn?'

I had been reading Gafarn's letter, going over the words again and again, my mood darkening with every reading.

I looked up at him, sitting on his horse beside Horns, still holding his bow though we had finished our shooting practice.

'How are your reading and writing lessons coming along?'

He looked downcast. 'Not good, highborn, my tutor is quick to anger and shouts at me.'

'How I envy you, Klietas,' I said, staring at the letter, 'to be unable to read would keep me in blissful ignorance, at least for a while longer.'

'Highborn?'

'Nothing. As you train with them, what do the Amazons divulge about the goings-on in The Sanctuary.'

'What does "divulge" mean, highborn?'

'It doesn't matter.'

'It is a great honour for me to ride with the Amazons, highborn.'

'Even though they treat you coolly.'

'They are warriors, highborn, whereas I am a poor farmer. I have to earn their respect. But the gods willing, I will prove myself to them on the battlefield.'

'I thought you already had proved yourself, with your expedition to Zeugma.'

He shook his head. 'Haya told me it is easy to kill a defenceless person when they feel safe, but only on the battlefield is a person's true worth tested.'

'That did not stop her, though, did it?'

'No, highborn,' he responded proudly.

'Well, you will be pleased to know you will have the chance to prove yourself on the battlefield, Klietas, though you might like to remind Haya and any of her she-devil friends, that you have proved yourself, at Irbil. But I must tell you there is no honour in being an assassin. You understand?'

'Yes, highborn. We are going to war?'

I examined his youthful features and saw the glint of excitement in his eyes. To him war was all about glory and the prospect of slaying enemies. He did not consider death, defeat or injury, only victory and a chance for personal advancement. I had been the same at his age. Only over the years did the illusion of glory fade, to be replaced by a marked reluctance to unsheathe a sword in anger. But peace meant no amusement for the gods, and so the immortals ensured the minds of young men and women were filled with a lust for bloodshed.

'It seems we are, Klietas.'

At the Citadel I showed Gallia the letter and convened a special meeting of the council, inviting both Kewab and Karys to attend. Chrestus was about to leave the city that afternoon, together with the cataphracts, horse archers and the soldiers of Kewab and Karys, for a large-scale desert exercise. This was to both take advantage of the presence of an additional seven thousand professional horsemen in the kingdom, and give said soldiers something to do rather than sit around in camp brooding.

I tossed the letter on the table, the eyes of all the attendees on the sheet of papyrus.

'This arrived earlier from King Gafarn of Hatra. It reports that Armenian troops are massing on the northern border of Media, prior to launching a second invasion of that kingdom. It would appear King Artaxias of Armenia, having failed in his first attempt to kill King Akmon of Media, is determined to try again.

'My brother informs me that King Spartacus of Gordyene is currently mustering his army, which he will march to the Araxes River to deter the Armenians. He also reports that Hatra's army is being mobilised to support Gordyene and Media.

'Having been in Irbil when the rebel army, financed by Rome and granted passage through Armenia, attacked the city, and having survived that close-call, subsequently being nearly killed on the Diyana Plain where Artaxias himself fought us, the queen and I are resolved to support Hatra and Gordyene in their efforts to protect Media. This is not only to honour the alliance we made with Akmon, but to put Artaxias firmly in his place, seeing as no one else has a mind to do it.'

Chrestus, Karys and Kewab rapped their knuckles on the table top to show their enthusiasm. Rsan's brow creased with concern and

Almas appeared thoughtful, no doubt regretting he would not be able to ride north with the army. I stood and turned to the hide map of the empire on the wall, pointing at Hatra.

'King Gafarn will march directly to Irbil to reassure Akmon and Lusin of Hatra's commitment to Media. I intend to do the same, where Lucius Varsas will re-join the army prior to marching north.'

Rsan cleared his throat to indicate he wished to speak. I retook my seat and nodded to him.

'Forgive me, majesty, but in the rush to war might it not be prudent to try to seek a diplomatic solution to the problem?'

'I am all ears,' I said.

He brought his hands together. 'As Armenia is in the Parthian sphere of influence, surely the intercession of High King Phraates will be enough to bring King Artaxias to heel without recourse to war.'

'The high king has no interest in defending Media,' said Gallia. 'It was Phraates himself who began this sorry episode, for he encouraged Atrax to attack Media.'

Rsan was shocked. 'I cannot believe…'

'Believe it,' I interrupted. 'I saw the letter from Phraates to Atrax myself. There is no use appealing to the high king to intervene, and in truth I have little appetite to involve Ctesiphon in this matter.'

'Phraates is more interested in a new crusade against the Kushans,' said Gallia, 'notwithstanding his dismissal of the man who offers the only hope of achieving victory against Kujula.'

She tipped her head at Kewab who bowed his head in appreciation. Gallia's blue eyes focused on Karys.

'The high king has displayed poor judgement of late, and it is highly unlikely his acumen will improve any time soon.'

Rsan was squirming at our disrespect towards the high king but both Gallia and I were disappointed to say the least at Phraates' attitude and actions towards those who had showed him nothing but loyalty.

'Dura is pledged to defend Media and it will honour its commitments. Chrestus, assemble the army.'

'It is already assembled, majesty,' he told me, 'though replacing the garrisons of the forts along the Euphrates with veterans will take a few days.'

'See to it,' I instructed him.

Thus far Aaron and Ira had been conspicuous by their silence, the two clerks always attending my chief treasurer as usual frantically recording every utterance on papyrus. I would have expected Aaron to side with Rsan regarding his appeal to the high king to avoid conflict, but instead he stared at the table top, only diverting his gaze to look at the map when I had been standing.

'What is your opinion, Aaron?' I asked.

'I concur with your majesty that Armenian aggression cannot be allowed to go unanswered.'

I was shocked. 'You do?'

'Yes, majesty.'

'Even with all the attendant costs involved in a military campaign?' said Chrestus.

'Wars are expensive, general, I agree,' replied Aaron, 'but Dura must be seen to uphold its obligations.'

This was all very disconcerting. I doubted Aaron cared a fig for alliances or pledges of support. He worried only about safeguarding the flow of trade caravans through the kingdom and citizens paying their taxes. During his long career at the treasury he had always been critical of the army regarding its size, excessive equipment use in peacetime and overall drain on the kingdom's resources. But his next question revealed he had not suddenly changed his mind regarding the army's worth.

'Will satraps Kewab and Karys be accompanying the army, majesty?'

'That is their decision,' I answered, 'though I am mindful they and their followers came here not to fight Dura's wars but to find a home.'

'Dura's wars are our wars, lord,' said Karys, 'when you march, the soldiers of King Nergal and Queen Praxima will be marching with you.'

Kewab, who now looked less tired after a period of rest, leaned back in his chair.

'As I told you, majesty, those who came with me from the east did so in the hope and expectation of fighting beside Dura's army. They will be delighted to learn their hopes are about to be realised.'

Out of the corner of my eye I saw Ira give Aaron a congratulatory smile and it suddenly all made sense. If the newcomers marched north with the army they would be leaving Dura, at least for a few weeks and perhaps permanently if they fell in battle or found a new home. Either way, they would not be making demands on Aaron's treasury in the near future.

'Ever considered working for the treasury at Ctesiphon, Aaron?'

'Majesty?'

'It doesn't matter. I will write to Gafarn and Akmon to inform them Dura's army will be marching in four days.'

Gallia was delighted, Chrestus was delighted and Kewab and Karys were looking forward to marching with the army again. The next day Malik arrived at the Citadel. I thought his visit was a coincidence but I was wrong.

He stood like a black stone statue in the throne room, staring at the griffin banner hanging on the wall behind the empty thrones. I had been talking with Farid about the camel train, the chief cameleer being his usual complaining self, but I would not have anyone else in charge of the army's fifteen hundred camels and their drivers. He and they were veterans of many campaigns and were an essential part of Dura's war machine. As soon as word reached me that the King of the Agraci was at the palace I hurried to the Citadel.

'My friend.'

He turned to face me when I walked into the throne room, giving me a half-smile before we embraced. His hair and beard were now heavily streaked with grey, offset by his black facial tattoos favoured by the menfolk of his people.

'Have you been offered no refreshments?' I said, looking around for Ashk.

'Your steward was most attentive, but I told him I wished to stay here, where it is quiet. How are you?'

'Old. Come, let us take the weight off our feet. You might be able to stand for long periods, but my leg won't take it.'

We walked to the door at the rear of the chamber giving access to the palace's private quarters. As we did so, Malik came straight to the point.

'You march against Armenia?'

'Yes.'

'I wish to accompany you, to avenge Rasha.'

I could have argued that we were going on campaign to curb Armenian hostility towards Media, according to the pact between Dura, Hatra and Akmon's kingdom. But so irritated was I with Phraates, King Artaxias and indeed Octavian for funding Atrax's rebels, that I saw no point in trying to dissuade him.

'You would be most welcome, my friend.'

'My son will stay at Palmyra to ensure there is a successor should I fall,' he said matter-of-factly.

'Hopefully it won't come to that.'

He shrugged. 'Death comes to us all. Far better to meet it when cutting down enemies.'

We reached the terrace and within minutes Ashk and a small group of servants were around us, ensuring we were settled into chairs stuffed with cushions and under the awning, so we were in the shade. Refreshments appeared, followed by Gallia, hot and flustered but glad to see Malik. He stood to embrace her, my wife holding him long and whispering into his ear. His hard features showed sadness and gratitude and then the warrior Agraci returned when she released him and they both sat. Ashk proffered a cup of water, which she quickly drained, a servant refilling it immediately after.

'Malik is joining us on our campaign,' I told her.

She beamed with delight. 'How did you discover we were marching north? Talib?'

Malik shook his head. 'Spartacus wrote inviting me to join him in punishing the Armenians for the murder of my sister. I agreed and rode here to request passage through Dura and Hatra for myself and the two thousand warriors accompanying me. But I saw the preparations in your legionary camp and knew Spartacus had also appealed to you.'

'Not to us,' I said, 'but to my brother at Hatra. But the result is the same. It will be good to have you by our side again, old friend.'

I heard Ashk's voice behind me.

'The king and queen are in a private meeting.'

'They will see me, I'm family. Get out of the way before I throw you off this terrace. It's me, princess.'

I raised my eyes to the heavens when I recognised Kalet's voice, but Gallia waved him past the protesting chief steward.

'Bring wine,' commanded my chief lord, whose eyes lit up when he saw Malik.

The Agraci king rose and they clasped forearms before Kalet waited until a chair had been stuffed with cushions for him before sitting himself down. He looked at me.

'So, off to war without telling me. A campaign to punish the Armenians, I hear.'

He rubbed his hands. 'Plenty of plunder to be had in Armenia.'

'Have you ever been to Armenia, Kalet?' I asked.

'No.'

'Then how do you know there is much to plunder?'

He tapped his nose. 'It's common knowledge the Armenians paid a high price in gold for the return of the girl who married Spartacus' son. Bad business.'

'I'm glad you do not approve of the abduction of young girls,' said Gallia.

Kalet was studying an attractive servant girl pouring wine into his cup, encouraging her to fill it to the brim. When she had done so he gave her a lascivious wink. He raised the cup to Gallia.

'Very bad business. Paying gold to get her back only to lose her again to the son of the man who had taken her in the first place. Not very clever.'

He looked at Malik. 'What brings you here?'

'I am accompanying the king and queen to Armenia.'

Kalet took a large gulp of wine. 'Me too.'

'That is a decision for me to make,' I said sternly.

He looked genuinely hurt.

'I was fond of Rasha, too.'

Malik nodded his head and I knew I had been outmanoeuvred. It was true Kalet and his lords had liked Rasha. She had known many of them, having spent much time in her youth in Dura, and I daresay the old rogue did have a soft spot for the Agraci princess turned Parthian queen. But he was like a hunting dog when it came to the possibility of killing and plunder: he was unrelenting. I looked at Gallia, who gave an indifferent shrug.

'King Malik is bringing two thousand warriors with him,' I said to Kalet, 'so you may select a similar number to ride north with you.'

'That few?' he complained.

'And no Dalir or Eszter,' said Gallia. 'This is the first time Dura's army will be leaving Parthian territory and we do not know if it will be coming back.'

Her words silenced the conversation and I realised that, save for the raid into Kushan territory after we had attended Salar and Isabella's wedding, no Duran troops had ever left the empire.

'What's the objective?' asked Kalet, smiling at the servant girl with the jug of wine and beckoning her over.

It was an excellent question. For Malik, there was no doubt.

'Revenge.'

Kalet sipped at his wine.

'Fair enough, lord, but what does that entail? Burning the Armenian capital, killing the Armenian king or taking hostages for ransom. If I may be so bold, I would recommend the latter option.'

'You would,' I said.

But he had raised an important point. What would we do once we had invaded Armenian territory?

'There is someone who will be able to provide an answer,' I announced.

Malik was unconcerned about campaign objectives. As an Agraci he had no concern for treaties, territorial acquisitions or Parthian honour. All he wanted was to spill blood to avenge the death of his sister and Spartacus had given him an opportunity to do so. Gallia also wanted revenge, along with the head of Prince Atrax, an objective I was also a supporter of after his dreadful behaviour at Irbil. As for Kalet, now Dura had become a kingdom where the law ruled, and it had peace with the Agraci, his only chance to reprise his raiding days was when he joined the army on campaign.

We sat eating and drinking for too long, Malik's stern disposition being replaced by the more easy-going man I had known for forty years, helped by Kalet whose infectious humour and carefree attitude helped to lighten the mood. Afterwards, Kalet being assisted to a guest bedroom to sleep off his drink-induced stupor and Malik accepting our offer of hospitality to stay in the palace, I went to search out Kewab. It was night, the air humming with the sound of crickets and filled with mosquitoes. To keep the insects at bay we smeared our limbs and necks with eucalyptus oil, though others used cinnamon oil or basil. The Citadel was unusually busy for the late hour, Rsan's clerks working late in the Headquarters Building organising the issuing of supplies and weapons for the forthcoming campaign.

I saw Almas talking to Kewab outside the armoury, both ceasing their conversation when they saw me approach.

'I would have a word with the satrap, Almas,' I smiled.

The deputy governor bowed his head, nodded to Kewab and took his leave.

'Logistical matters?' I enquired.

'No, majesty, we were reminiscing about the Phraaspa campaign. Seems like only yesterday.'

I felt a pang of guilt. 'I did not invite you and your followers to Dura just to reinforce the army, Kewab, but it seems events have dictated otherwise.'

'When I briefed my officers on the coming campaign, they were absolutely delighted and relieved.'

'Relieved?'

'Many who came with me from the east have known nothing but war for the past few years. They have developed a taste for it, and to be fair they are very good at it. They are eager to test themselves against the Armenians.'

'As you know, the Armenian army is massing just north of the Araxes River, prior to launching a fresh invasion of Media. Ideally, if they do we can intercept and destroy them before they reach Irbil.'

'As soon as they discover three of Parthia's finest armies are converging on them, majesty, more likely they will retire north.'

'That is what I fear. The least desirable outcome is a summer spent chasing Armenians around their own homeland.'

'Fortunately, there is a way to shorten the campaign to our advantage, majesty.'

I looked at him in anticipation, above us the sounds of guards reporting to the duty centurion as he made his rounds of the battlements.

'Take the siege engines and march directly to Artaxata.'

'The Armenian capital?'

He nodded. 'We do not need to take the city, but it is the royal seat of power and sooner rather than later the Armenians will have to mount a relief attempt; either that or try to intercept us before we reach their capital.'

'If we take the siege engines, our rate of march will average fifteen miles a day at best, which would take us a month to reach the Armenian capital. Without the siege engines, that time is reduced to around twenty days, less with a forced march.'

'There is little point in arriving before the walls of Artaxata without the means to batter down those walls, majesty. The best course of action would be to march directly to Vanadzor and then north into Armenia.'

In the pale light cast by oil lamps illuminating the interior of the armoury I caught sight of the dagger with the solid silver griffin pommel hanging in a sheath from his belt, the same weapon that had been presented to him when he had graduated from the Sons of the Citadel. I laid a hand on his upper arm.

'It's good to have you back at Dura.'

As the army mustered I wrote a series of letters: to Phraates, stating my reasons for taking Dura's army north to battle the Armenians; to King Ali of Atropaiene, Lord High General of Parthia, expressing my thanks to him for his services to the empire and to assure him I would do my utmost to ensure the northern border of his kingdom would not be violated by the Armenians; to Akmon at

Irbil, stating we were marching against Armenia to put an end once and for all to Armenian designs on his kingdom; to Gafarn at Hatra, suggesting he should wait for our arrival, in addition to writing to Spartacus to beg his son to show restraint (I feared he would launch an immediate attack against Armenia); and to Lucius Varsas to get himself back to Dura to take command of the army's siege engines.

Once put in motion, the gathering of the army was a wonder to behold. The majority of the Durans and Exiles were in the legionary camp, though some were garrisoning the mud-brick forts positioned at five-mile intervals north and south of the city along the Euphrates. Originally there had been fifty forts but the number had been increased by a further five south of the city to reflect the expansion of the kingdom's population and the number of villages to accommodate the increase. The garrisons of those forts – forty men per stronghold – were replaced by army veterans, who were put back on the army's payroll for the duration of the campaign. To safeguard the city itself, the replacement cohort would remain in the kingdom and Rsan could call on the lords should he feel imperilled. Additionally, Queen Jamal at Palmyra could always be relied upon to provide warriors to bolster Dura's defence.

Her husband's warriors arrived at Dura a day before we marched north, along with camels loaded with tents and supplies. Just prior to their arrival I was accosted by an angry Eszter and Dalir, both attempting to enter the throne room during an assembly of the army's senior legionary commanders, Zenobia, Azad and Sporaces and their company commanders, plus Farid and his chief cameleers, the chief veterinary and his staff, and Sophus and his senior doctors. They were prevented from doing so until I had finished addressing the assembled officers, briefing them on why the army was marching, the objectives of the campaign and expressing every faith in their professionalism and talents. Some kings viewed their armies as nothing more than instruments to do their bidding and paid no heed to the welfare of their soldiers. But I did not believe in blind loyalty or ruling through fear. If I expected a man to lay down his life for Dura, the least I could do was explain to him why he was marching to war. He already knew he had had the best training and was armed with the best weapons and armour money could buy. He had a right to know his king was not treating him as a worthless chattel. Morale was high, but the spirit of an army was like a delicate flower that required constant nourishment and care. It was not an understatement to say that I loved the army, but like all commanders I faced the unpalatable prospect of destroying something I loved when I marched it to war.

Gallia sat beside me as the officers filed out of the throne room, Eszter pacing up and down impatiently and Dalir fidgeting with his hands as he waited for the chamber to empty and guards to shut the doors. Our daughter looked like she was about to erupt when they were quietly closed.

'Why are we not allowed to go on campaign with the army?'

'And good morning to you, Eszter,' I smiled, 'and to you, Dalir. I hope you are both well.'

'Well, lord, thank you,' replied Dalir.

'Never mind that,' snapped Eszter, 'I demand an answer.'

'Demand!' I shouted. 'You will remember your place in this palace.'

'The king does not have to answer to you,' said Gallia harshly.

Eszter, usually enjoying the full backing of her mother, was taken aback and for once in her life was lost for words.

I stretched out my aching leg.

'It is time you assumed your responsibilities, Eszter. For too long you have behaved like a desert urchin, indulging your whims and bringing your position into disrepute.'

'What position?' she shot back.

'The heir to Dura's throne,' said Gallia.

'Should your mother and me fall in Armenia,' I continued, 'then you two will become Dura's rulers.'

Dalir swallowed. 'Us?'

'Yes, Dalir, son of Kalet. You. Of my three daughters, Isabella is Queen of Sakastan and Claudia is adviser to the high king at Ctesiphon. That leaves Eszter and you. You will vacate your half-built desert home and move into the palace until we return.'

'Or you receive news that we are not returning,' said Gallia.

When he had visited Dura, Phraates had gifted the couple gold so they could build a home of their own. Eszter had taken charge of the project and had invited Greek architects to the kingdom to indulge her every whim. The home was being built by the side of a small oasis located southwest of the city, away from the main highway from Dura to Palmyra and inland from the villages and agricultural strip adjacent to the Euphrates. It was one of many such oases dotted around the desert that had in the time before Gallia and I came to Dura been the preserve of the Agraci. The gardener Adel had been brought from Hatra to arrange the vegetation around the walled villa, the extant date palms to be joined by other fruit trees: citrus, olives, peach and plum.

'As your desert home is not yet completed,' I said, 'living in the palace will be more comfortable than sleeping in a tent.'

'You will both attend council meetings, hear petitioners and ensure the day-to-day affairs of the kingdom run smoothly,' added Gallia.

Eszter warmed to the idea of playing queen, her anger evaporating when the prospect of power was dangled before her.

'Though all your decisions will be ratified by Rsan before they are implemented,' I told them.

'But, father,' protested Eszter, 'surely if we are king and queen, we are not answerable to anyone.'

'You are *not* king and queen,' I told them firmly, 'rather, temporary administrators answerable to a man who has more experience of running the kingdom in his little finger than you two put together. A good king follows wise counsel, a useful lesson for you both to learn while we are away.'

A sense of dread enveloped me as the army prepared to march north. I said nothing to Gallia about it and I had no reason to doubt we would not triumph over the Armenians, in what would be a limited campaign of intimidation waged by three of the most formidable armies in the Parthian Empire, none of which had ever tasted defeat. And yet I felt something was wrong, like the taste of milk that was about to turn sour or biting into an apple that had a rotten core. But Gallia was invigorated by the prospect of visiting misery on the Armenians and exacting revenge for the death of Rasha, which became the Amazon motto for the campaign.

Before I left I visited Rsan and Almas in the Headquarters Building, both looking glum, though for different reasons. Rsan always viewed the prospect of war with dread, an attitude I had laughed at when I had been younger. But with age had come wisdom and I had come to realise that conflict was a waste – of lives, property, resources and the most precious assets of a kingdom – and was not to be entered into lightly. Almas was dejected because he wished to ride north at the head of his dragon of horse archers.

'While I am away, I am entrusting the care of the kingdom to my daughter Eszter and her husband.'

Rsan raised an eyebrow but said nothing, thanking one of his clerks for filling the cups before us with water. His office was like him: austere and basic, with not a trace of opulence. Indeed, it was a microcosm of Dura itself.

I took a sip of water. 'However, being fully aware of my daughter's volatile nature, you two are hereby authorised to keep a restraint on her, and Dalir is not to be encouraged to play an active role in the government of the kingdom.'

Rsan looked contented. 'It shall be as you request, majesty, though to be fair the princess did prove most able when news of you and the queen trapped in Irbil reached the city.'

'That is because the emergency harnessed her talents perfectly,' I replied. 'But the day-to-day affairs of a kingdom are very different. I expect her to become bored, which may prompt her to do something rash.'

'Rash, majesty?' said Almas.

'Such as mustering the kingdom's other lords and riding north to join what they believe will be a glorious affair,' I replied.

'You fear a hard campaign, majesty?' asked Almas.

'It is an unnecessary campaign,' I said bitterly, 'and if I had my way Dura's army would not be marching anywhere. But Armenia cannot be allowed to treat Media as its plaything and seeing as the high king has no interest in chastising it, it is left to others to do it.'

'I will pray for you and the queen,' said Rsan earnestly.

I stared at my cup. 'Everyone dies, Rsan, and Gallia and I are no different. But our wish is to see the kingdom safe and prosperous. At the end of the day, that is the only thing that matters.'

'You can rely on us, majesty,' Rsan told me.

I stood, prompting them to do likewise.

'This building sits on the top of a rock escarpment,' I said, 'but you have been the rock upon which the whole kingdom has relied on for many years, my old friend. I pray Shamash will give you many more years of life, so you may continue to be our rock, Rsan, the first minister and true son of Dura.'

I walked forward and embraced him, seeing tears in his eyes when I released him. He was lost for words, so I clasped forearms with Almas and took my leave, walking down the steps from his office to the building's ground floor and out into the courtyard. The guards flanking the doors snapped to attention as I paced towards the palace. To my left carts were being loaded with spare weapons and armour from the armoury. I glanced right and stopped when I saw what appeared to be Claudia standing in front of the duty centurion outside the guardroom. I diverted my journey to find out more, the centurion coming to attention when he spotted me.

The woman was not Claudia, though she was dressed exactly like my daughter in her black robes and *shemagh* that she had removed to reveal her face. It was a great pity to wear such dour apparel because she was a beautiful young woman, her skin flawless, her eyes an emerald green and her hair thick and golden. If I tried to place her I would say she was nobility of ancient Persian stock, though her hair colour made it difficult to place her ancestry anywhere in the Parthian Empire. My musings were interrupted by the gruff voice of the centurion.

'This woman says she is here to see the queen, majesty.'

' *This woman* has a name, centurion,' she said, 'if the king desires to know it.'

She had fixed me with her emerald eyes, which I found alluring but at the same time slightly disturbing. There was something behind the beauty that was unnerving.

'I do not think I have had the pleasure,' I said.

'I am Saruke, majesty, sent by your daughter Claudia to advise Queen Gallia.'

My instincts had not let me down.

'You are a Scythian Sister?'

She was delighted. 'Yes, majesty, your daughter said you were very perceptive. Long have I desired to meet the famous King Pacorus of Dura.'

I doubted that, but her smile, beauty and charm were difficult to resist. She reached inside her robe, prompting the centurion to stand between her and me and lay a hand on the hilt of his *gladius*. She giggled and slowly removed a papyrus scroll from her tunic.

'I would never harm such a legendary defender of the Parthian Empire.'

'It is fine, centurion,' I said, 'you may return to your duties. I will escort the Lady Saruke to the palace.'

He saluted, gave Saruke a cold stare and marched back to the guardroom. I took the scroll, unrolled it and read my daughter's words.

Father

This is Saruke, a Scythian Sister who will be an asset to mother in the months to come. Please do not pester her with questions. She has important work to do and has better things to do than answer your incessant queries.

Take care in Armenia and remember what I told you. The hunter thinks he is stalking his quarry but can unwittingly become the prey.

Claudia

Saruke was absolutely charming, listening to my questions and replying with grace and intelligence, but when we met Gallia and I had introduced the Scythian Sister to my wife and showed her Claudia's note, I realised she had told me absolutely nothing regarding why she had ridden to Dura and what use my wife might have for a sorceress. My curiosity was aroused further when Gallia despatched her immediately to The Sanctuary with an Amazon escort, brushing away my questions as to Saruke's presence at Dura.

'We have a war to win,' she reminded me as I watched the Scythian Sister ride from the Citadel flanked by a pair of Amazons.

The golden-haired beauty had been a minor distraction from the campaign that would begin the next day. The legionary camp was bursting with soldiers, wagons and mules, the siege engines having been broken down into their constituent parts and loaded on to carts prior to leaving. Farid had mustered his camel corps, the beasts corralled just south of the legionary camp, the odour of hundreds of camels drifting on the evening breeze towards the Citadel, along with the deposits of thousands of horses and mules. Azad's cataphracts and Sporaces horse archers were camped across the Euphrates, in Hatran territory, which was sparsely populated in the southern part of my brother's kingdom.

That night the army's commanders, Malik's warlords, Karys' senior officers, Kewab's easterners and Kalet's lords were feasted in the banqueting hall. But the mood was sombre and subdued. Malik sat in silence, staring into space and picking at his food. There was no drunken revelry, no bravado or boasting. Even Kalet and his lords were morose, though their muted conversations were probably complaints concerning how their numbers had been limited. Ideally, they would all have stayed at Dura, but honour dictated some of the kingdom's lords shared in the glory of their king when he marched off to war.

The feast ended early – men had to prepare for an early start when the army struck camp just after dawn. Afterwards, Gallia and I sat on the edge of our bed staring at the open chest before us. It contained the scale-armour cuirasses gifted to us by the immortals, and which had saved both our lives during the siege of Irbil.

'I thought I would gift them to the Temple of Shamash in the city,' I said.

'We have need of them before you do.'

'I vowed never to unsheathe my sword in anger again. And yet here we are, once again on the eve of a campaign.'

I turned to face her. She was still a handsome woman but now there were a few lines around her eyes and those eyes were weary, not the vibrant blue pools of yesteryear. But her skin was still smooth and free from blemishes, a result of shielding her fair complexion from the merciless Mesopotamian sun. And she still had all her teeth!

'Do you think we will ever be able to enjoy peace?'

She cupped my face with her hands.

'We are what we are, Pacorus. We have spent our entire lives fighting enemies, either Parthia's or foes within the empire. It is what we do, we are good at it and it is our destiny.'

'Like Sisyphus,' I lamented.

'Who?'

'Scelias told me the story of the King of Corinth, a part of Greece, who cheated death to return to the land of the living to live to a ripe old age. To punish him, he was sent to Hades, the Greek word for the underworld, where he had to roll a huge rock up a hill, only for it to roll down again once he had reached the summit. So, he had to walk down the hill and start the whole procedure again, and so on and so on. Dura's army is like Sisyphus – beating one foe only for another to appear, and after that another and another.'

She frowned. 'Don't be so morose. This is not the start of a long war; it is just a short campaign to punish the Armenians. We will be back here in no time at all, and then you can gift the two pieces of armour to the temple.'

I slept fitfully that night, trying to fathom why the Armenians, having been badly mauled on the Diyana Plain, would even consider a fresh invasion of Media. Perhaps they did not know of that kingdom's alliance with Hatra, Gordyene and Dura. But even if they did not, they were well aware that Spartacus needed only the slightest pretext to launch a war against them. As the old saying went: if one wanted peace, prepare for war.

The morning came soon enough and with it the movement of thousands of men, horses, mules and camels, all filing across the pontoon bridges spanning the Euphrates, to begin the march north. I stood on the terrace, burnished scale-armour cuirass shimmering in the early morning sunlight, my hands resting on the stone balustrade watching the legionaries marching to war. Like the Romans they were modelled on they marched six abreast, though unlike Rome's soldiers they wore white tunics and carried shields faced with hide painted white and embossed with a red griffin motif. Talib and his scouts had already left Dura, riding ahead, dividing into small groups and fanning out to provide advance reconnaissance. There were no hostile forces in my brother's kingdom, but procedures were never curtailed because we were marching in friendly territory. It was same regarding marching camps: irrespective of where the army was, its soldiers, equipment and animals slept behind a ditch and earth rampart topped with stakes every night when on campaign.

I became aware of another presence of the terrace and turned to see Klietas. He smiled, bowed his head and held out my *spatha* sheathed in its scabbard and attached to a leather belt.

'All clean and sharp, highborn,' he beamed, his eyes shifting to stare in wonder at the long line of legionaries across the river. I took the sword and buckled the belt around my waist. I pointed at the soldiers.

'That, Klietas, is Dura, the thing that keeps it safe and strong. Do you know why Dura's army is so strong?'

'Because you command it, highborn.'

I shook my head. 'No, Klietas, it is because every legionary, every cataphract and every horse archer knows his place on the battlefield and what is expected of him. He knows he has the best equipment money can buy, he knows he has had the best training in the world, and he knows his commanders have been promoted due to their talents. This gives him faith: faith in the man standing beside him in the battle line and faith in the ability of his officers to make the right decisions, which will give the army victory.'

'What of you, highborn?'

'What about me?'

'It is said the King of Dura has never lost a battle, that he is invincible and any enemy he faces in battle will always lose.'

'Only a fool thinks he is invincible, Klietas.'

'And when another silver disc is cast to decorate the Staff of Victory, highborn, I can say I was a part of the army that won it.'

He had not been listening to what I had been saying. His mind was filled with dreams of glory and conquest. When I had first encountered him, he had been a half-starved, scrawny urchin. But now he was lean, fit and his thick mop of hair tumbled to his shoulders. He had copied his king in being clean-shaven and he seemed to have grown taller since his arrival at Dura. I noticed the sling tucked in his belt.

'Old habits die hard, I see, Klietas.'

He went to remove the sling. 'I will discard it, highborn.'

'Nonsense, you should carry it with you at all times to remind you of where you came from. I once told another squire of mine a similar thing. He was like you, an orphan from a poor background. Know what happened to him?'

'No, highborn.'

'He became a king.'

The answer delighted him, and he gave me a broad grin.

'If I become a king then Haya will definitely marry me.'

I laughed. 'I think you can win her over without the aid of a crown.'

'You do?'

'Of course, just don't be too fawning. The Amazons respect strength and perseverance. And no slapping her on the backside.'

He was horrified. 'It is death to molest an Amazon, highborn.'

I thought of the time when Surena had slapped Viper's rump.

'Course it is. Come, then, let us write another chapter in the history of glory.'

Chapter 5

Though I had been reluctant to choose the path of war once again, the army I led across the Euphrates that spring morning was the finest I had commanded. The ten thousand foot soldiers – the Durans and Exiles – were far and above anything the rest of the Parthian Empire could field, and I counted Gordyene in that estimation. Spartacus' Immortals were good soldiers, but they did not have the superlative heritage and long list of battle honours accredited to Dura's legionaries. And to add to their potency on the battlefield they were trained to operate closely with Azad's dragon of cataphracts and Sporaces' five dragons of horse archers – six thousand professional horsemen. Kalet's two thousand horsemen had poor discipline and training in comparison, but they were hardy fighters and had proved at Ctesiphon they did not want for courage. Malik's warriors were also brave and rugged, though lightly armed and having no armour protection aside from their small round shields.

A different proposition altogether was the four thousand horse archers commanded by Karys. Trained to fight in exactly the same way as Dura's horse archers – Nergal had commanded Dura's horsemen before he became King of Mesene – they would be able to attach themselves seamlessly to Sporaces' men. It was true that because Mesene had no professional foot soldiers, aside from Uruk's palace guard, they had not been trained to work with legionaries, but their discipline was superb. As was that of the horsemen led by Kewab, who were fully conversant with combined battlefield tactics. Being armoured and equipped with spears, they could also be used to augment Azad's cataphracts if required. In all, I led just over twenty-seven thousand veterans east towards Hatra, and that figure did not include the two thousand squires attached to the cataphracts.

We arrived at Hatra after five days of a leisurely march. The desert was hot and dusty and most of the time the horsemen dismounted and led their mounts on foot, save for parties of horse archers serving as screens for the army. A permanent cloud of dust hung over the entire column, which covered a distance of fifteen miles each day.

'It's not going to jump up and bite you,' said Gafarn, noticing I had been staring at his leg.

It was good to be back at Hatra again, to relax in the quiet opulence of its grand palace, see peacocks strutting around the ornate royal gardens and watch white doves fly among the trees. The gentle sound of bubbling fountains and small waterfalls was both pleasing and comforting. Slaves in pristine white tunics and soft leather shoes served us delicious sweet pastries that melted on the tongue and filled our gold rhytons with fine wine. It was as if the troubles of the world ended at the doors of Hatra's gilded palace.

'The leg has fully healed,' smiled Diana, alluding to the ulcer that had prevented Gafarn from riding to Irbil the year before.

'The kingdom's prayers have been answered, majesty,' said the man who had ridden at the head of Hatra's horsemen to save mine and Gallia's hides.

Lord Orobaz, tall, slender, intelligent and one of the wealthiest men in the Kingdom of Hatra, took a bite of lemon cake. He was the governor of Nisibus, the kingdom's second city located in a huge fertile plain of the same name that in the spring is covered with white roses. He was used to sitting in the company of kings, as was Kewab who shared our company, though unlike Karys who said little as he stared into his rhyton. Gafarn had insisted they both be invited to the intimate gathering because as satraps they had been like kings, and he believed, as did I, that Karys should have been made King of Mesene. It was one of many grievances I harboured against Phraates. Malik, dressed in his black robes, looked like a cobra about to strike as he shared our company.

'How is the level of the Tigris, lord?' Kewab asked Gafarn.

Gafarn pointed at me. 'Pacorus' man at Irbil has built a pontoon bridge to span the river at Assur, so crossing it won't be a problem.'

'Good man, Lucius,' I stated, 'he will soon be joining us to take command of the siege engines.'

'As we are all here,' said Gafarn casually, 'what is the objective of the campaign we are about to embark on?'

'To punish the Armenians,' replied Gallia instantly.

'And how is that punishment to manifest itself?' Gafarn shot back. He had clearly returned to full health, which meant his tongue was as mischievous as ever.

'I assume the presence of Dura's siege engines means Artaxata is going to be besieged,' opined Orobaz.

'Correct,' I said savouring the taste of wine in my mouth. 'We cross the Araxes, crush the Armenian army and lay siege to the Armenian capital.'

'And then?' probed Gafarn.

'And then we force the submission of the city and take Artaxias, his family and senior officials into custody,' I announced, to the surprise of all those present.

'You have said nothing about this to me,' said Gallia.

I sipped at my wine.

'That is because I have just thought of it. Either that or occupy the Armenian capital and exact reparations from the Armenians to compensate Media for the damage done to it by Atrax and his Armenian allies last year.'

'Phraates might object to us interfering in the grand strategy of the Parthian Empire,' cautioned Gafarn.

I finished my wine and indicated to a waiting slave my rhyton should be refilled.

'Ah, yes, Phraates. I had forgotten about him, just as he forgot about Akmon and Lusin when he encouraged Atrax to invade Media.'

'She's pregnant, by the way,' interrupted Diana.

We all looked at her.

'Lusin,' she continued, 'such a lovely girl. They were here a few weeks ago, along with your Roman, Pacorus.'

'Indeed, well,' I said. Diana held up a hand.

'Lusin is an Armenian, Pacorus, as you know, so I do not think it is advisable to humiliate the Armenian people if you are desirous of peace with our northern neighbours.'

Malik now spoke. 'What Queen Diana says has merit. But there is no point in going to war unless you intend to win that war. We are not here to punish Armenia but to exact revenge for the death of Rasha.'

He fixed each of us in turn with his cold stare.

'Retribution is a bloody business and should be so if it is to deliver the proper message.'

'Would you care to elucidate further, Malik,' said Gafarn.

Malik tipped his head at me. 'Dura has brought its siege engines, so I assume they will be used to batter down the walls of the

Armenian city and put its inhabitants to the sword. As for the Armenian king, he should be the first to die.'

There were sharp intakes of breath from Orobaz and Kewab, to say nothing of the look of horror that spread across Diana's face.

'Hatra will not sanction the wanton murder of innocent women and children,' she stated firmly. 'We have known each other a long time, Malik, and Rasha was our daughter so you do not have a monopoly on grieving for her. But while I am queen of this kingdom, I say to you all that its soldiers will not become butchers and enslavers of people. We are not Romans, after all.'

They were fine words and rather than erupt in anger at her naïve view of warfare, Malik merely smiled and nodded in submission. And Orobaz was delighted.

'I know the Agraci way is not the Parthian way,' admitted Malik, 'but if you are not going to raze the Armenian city to the ground, I see little point in dragging siege engines a further how many miles for nothing.'

'Around four hundred, majesty,' said Kewab.

'There is another way,' teased Malik.

'We are all ears, my friend,' said Gafarn.

Malik emptied his rhyton. 'Leave the foot soldiers and siege engines here. Take the light horsemen and let us spend a summer enjoying the hospitality of the Armenians. That should persuade them to refrain from invading Parthia.'

Diana was not amused. 'They say the Agraci are an uncouth people, unfit to share the company of civilised races, but that is entirely wrong. King Malik has given us a perfect demonstration of saying one thing and meaning another, which would not be out of place in the court of Ctesiphon itself.'

The Agraci king watched a slave refill his rhyton.

'I am a simple desert lord, Diana, I know not what you mean.'

Diana fixed him with her brown eyes.

'Oh, I think you do. You submit to my objection to butchering the entire population of Artaxata, yet at the same time propose turning the whole of Armenia into a charnel house, reasoning it is the better option.'

Malik took a slow sip of wine.

'I am just a brother seeking justice for my murdered sister.'

Gafarn clapped his hands. 'My friend, we will make a diplomat of you yet. So, by way of compromise, may I suggest that when we have Artaxias and his family in our hands, they stay here until such time as we deem fit to let them return to their homeland.'

'Here?' queried Gallia.

'They would find Dura dreary and I dread to think what would happen to them if they fell into Spartacus' hands, so Hatra makes perfect sense.'

'Talking of Spartacus, where is he?' I enquired.

'He said he would link up with us at Lake Urmia,' replied Gafarn.

'I hope he will wait for us,' I said in hope.

Kewab reassured me. 'It will take us another month to reach the Araxes, majesty, by which time the current and level will have ebbed. To try to cross the river when it is bloated with spring melt water would be to invite disaster.'

'Geography comes to our rescue,' quipped Gafarn.

Malik glanced at Orobaz. 'You are concerned about Malik the Agraci barbarian, but you should be more worried about Spartacus, whose rage will be difficult to control once unleashed against those who killed his wife.'

It was what everyone was thinking, though no one said as much. And in truth one of the reasons for joining the war against Armenia was to try to restrain Spartacus, who had the capability to launch a war against his northern neighbour without the assistance of Dura or Hatra, or Media for that matter.

'He is very distant since the death of Rasha,' lamented Diana.

'Well, we'll make sure he stays close to all of us in this war,' said Gallia.

I glanced at Karys who had remained silent throughout.

'This war is not only to punish Armenia, but also to remind Phraates that the empire is not a box of toys that he may pick at and discard some according to his will.'

'If only Pacorus of Dura had taken the high crown when he had the chance,' lamented Gafarn.

'That's ancient history,' I told him.

'And history has a habit of repeating itself,' he grinned. Diana was right: he was back to his old, irritating self.

The mass of tents, camels, wagons and soldiers that ringed Hatra, like a huge besieging army, was on the move the next day, striking east for the city of Assur. General Herneus, the commander of Hatra's army, arranged a parade through the city of the kingdom's soldiers to display its military might. In the vanguard was the Royal Bodyguard: five hundred cataphracts riding white horses fully encased in scale-armour suits, the torsos of their riders protected by the same armour, on their arms and legs tubular steel armour. They wore open-faced helmets adorned with white plumes and a red pennant decorated with a white horse head motif fluttered from every *kontus*. They were the cream of Hatra, nobles and the sons of nobles who had sworn to defend to the death their king and queen. Behind them came their squires: a thousand teenage boys between the ages of fourteen and eighteen in half armour – scale-armour cuirasses and helmets – riding horses also protected by scale armour, though not covering their heads or necks.

Next came a thousand cataphracts, armed and equipped exactly the same as the Royal Bodyguard, each man carrying a *kontus* and being armed with sword, mace and axe, the latter two highly effective in a mêlée with enemy horsemen. Behind them rode two thousand squires, without armour but equipped with bows and swords and capable of fighting both as cataphracts and horse archers as circumstance dictated. The last contingent was a long column of horse archers led by Orobaz, who had been appointed their commander for the duration of the campaign. Five thousand were professional soldiers based at Hatra itself, the other ten thousand being raised in Nisibus and the surrounding villages.

Hatra had a population of one hundred thousand and every one of its citizens appeared to be on the streets to bid their soldiers farewell and to wish them good luck. At the same time as the military parade was taking place, Dura's army was marching east across the desert. Gafarn and Diana and over sixteen thousand soldiers would join it later. Forty-three and a half thousand troops were heading for Assur to link up with the army of Gordyene, which I hoped was still south of the Araxes River.

We reached the city of Assur in three days, the weather curiously overcast and a northerly breeze making marching less arduous than tramping across the desert under a blazing sun. When we reached the stronghold and thriving commercial centre on the western bank of the Tigris, now swelled by the melt waters from the mountains in the north, I smiled when I saw a pontoon bridge spanning the waterway. I recognised it from the one Lucius had constructed during the campaign against Tiridates – a row of boats, or pontoons, secured by anchors to the riverbed arranged side-by-side, over the top of which was a roadbed comprising wooden beams lashed together and topped by a road of wooden planks nailed to the framework. It made perfect sense to replicate Dura's pontoon bridges across the Euphrates and I wondered why no one had thought of it before.

The governor of Assur, a nephew of General Herneus, was like his relative, albeit with a full head of hair. When we were shown into his mansion after arriving at the city, he came straight to the point.

'I have received a demand for half the costs incurred building the pontoon bridge, majesty,' he said to Gafarn after accosting him as soon as the formalities of welcoming royalty were over. 'It was not our idea, so why should we pay for it?'

Gafarn laughed. 'I don't think we should highlight our lack of foresight. Who makes this demand, the King of Media?'

We had left the mansion's courtyard to enter the cool of the building, its floors covered with white marble tiles, its rooms and corridors spacious and airy.

The governor shot me a glance. 'General Varsas, majesty, a Roman.'

'A Roman who is Dura's quartermaster general,' I told him, 'and a man of many talents.'

The governor, his ire obviously aroused, was going to respond but Herneus beside his king glared at him to remain silent.

'Surely,' I continued, 'as both Media and Hatra will benefit from the bridge, both should share the costs, which I assumed were considerable. It looks a very sturdy bridge. And it will expedite the crossing of the army over the Tigris greatly.'

Gafarn rolled his eyes. 'We will pay half, as our illustrious Roman friend desires, if only to shut his king up.'

Gafarn suddenly stopped to face me.

'That reminds me, my treasurer informed me before you arrived, Pacorus, that he had an official approach from Lord Aaron at Dura, your own treasurer, concerning the purchase of Duran grain.'

I knew what was coming but feigned innocence.

'Really?'

'The price quoted was a third higher than the grain normally purchased from Media,' continued Gafarn, 'which is interesting as Media's recent troubles mean its exports will be markedly reduced this year. One might think Dura is taking advantage of Media's misfortune.'

'It is a seller's market, or so Aaron told me,' I replied.

'I always wondered why Dura's palace was sited atop a rock escarpment,' mused Gafarn, 'and now I know.'

'Please enlighten us,' said Diana.

'It is quite simple, my dear,' he told his wife, 'it is so the treasury vaults can be dug deep to accommodate all the gold that Dura exhorts from other kingdoms.'

'I preferred it when you were laid up at Hatra with a bad leg,' I told him.

Assur was a somewhat bleak mud-brick stronghold, which had been substantially strengthened when Hatra and Media had not been allies. Its layout took advantage of the Tigris that protected two sides of the city and there was a moat that covered the other two sides. Behind this water obstacle on the landward side was a double wall, the space in between filled with buildings to house troops of the garrison. On top of the outer wall was a parapet protected by battlements, the latter containing narrow slits from where archers could shoot down on attackers below. But the only people who occupied the spaces beyond the city wall were the drivers and guards of the camel caravans on their way to Hatra and on to Syria.

At least it was spring, which meant the current of the Tigris was rapid, because in the autumn and winter when its brown waters meandered slowly south, the stench from the river could be overpowering, a result of the city authorities using it as a giant sewer. But the builders of the governor's mansion had also taken advantage of the Tigris to tap into it upstream to bring fresh water to the building via grooves in the paved floor. Thus, the kitchens, latrines and private chambers had fresh water, and other tiled channels beneath the floors carried wastewater to the city's sewer and thence to the nearby Tigris.

My whole body was aching as I removed my dust-covered clothes to ease myself into the large round bath sunk in the floor. It had been filled by slaves and had a plug to take away the water after we had bathed in it. Gallia joined me, and we closed our eyes as female slaves massaged our heads, necks and shoulders with oils. Slowly the hours in the saddle were eased away and my mind and body became relaxed and free of worry.

'So, we have a Roman bridge across the Tigris.'

I opened my eyes and looked at Gallia, the slave using the ends of her fingers to gently massage her blonde locks.

'Mmm?'

'The pontoon bridge over the Tigris built by Lucius. I was just thinking of Dobbai.'

'Really?'

'Do you remember her letter that accompanied the griffin banner she sent to you, when we were at Hatra?'

I did not. 'Vaguely.'

'She was so perceptive and wise,' she said wistfully.

I thought of Dobbai's barb tongue. 'I suppose so.'

'She said your fate would be bound up with the Romans and so it has proved. Your foot soldiers mimic those of Rome, they and your horsemen sleep in a Roman camp when on campaign and a Roman trained your army. I was just thinking about him, Domitus I mean. Remember when we were trapped in this city and he saved us?'

'Like it was yesterday.'

'I miss them, Pacorus, all our old friends that have died. It seems like we are being kept alive so we may witness the passing of those we are closest to. We should have died at Irbil but instead Rasha fell, and at Ctesiphon when Phraates lost his crown and had to flee, Nergal and Praxima died. And at Irbil we were given armour that could defeat all weapons.'

'If you try to fathom the minds of the gods you will go insane,' I said. 'The only thing we can do is remain steadfast in our aims.'

'Which are what?'

'To keep Parthia free and strong so it may determine its own destiny.'

After we had bathed, been massaged and had slept, we were woken by an apologetic steward who informed us Lucius Varsas had arrived at the palace and was desirous of an audience. Refreshed and wearing clean clothes, we made our way to the audience chamber where we found him pacing up and down, helmet in the crook of his arm. From a distance he looked like Domitus with his cropped hair and shaven face, though my quartermaster general was taller and not as solid.

'You look like a sentry,' I told him.

He turned, snapped to attention and bowed his head.

'It is good to see you, Lucius,' I said, 'and my compliments on the pontoon bridge. I look forward to seeing Irbil's new perimeter wall.'

He wore a most severe countenance and when he spoke I understood why.

'The wall is not the only thing you will see at Irbil, majesty. King of Kings Phraates is in the city.'

Chapter 6

I harboured hopes Phraates would mature to become like his father: a good, just high king who dedicated his life to the service of the empire. In retrospect, I was naïve to believe that anyone could live up to the example that Orodes had set. In the aftermath of the defeat of Tiridates, when Phraates had been grateful to Dura, Hatra and Gordyene for saving not only his rule but also his skin, he had shown magnanimity and gratitude, and had taken my advice regarding making King Ali Lord High General of the Empire and appointing Silani to the vacant throne of Persis. But I had forgotten Claudia's warning that Phraates had a malicious and scheming nature, or perhaps I had hoped that with age and experience the baser aspects of his nature would disappear. How wrong I was.

The news that Phraates was in Irbil was greeted with pained expressions and heavy sighs. Gafarn and I had liaised closely with Akmon regarding the march of the army through his kingdom to the Araxes River, assuring him there would be no destruction of crops or property, and urging him to remain in his capital. There was little point in fighting for the security of his reign if he himself fell in battle in Armenia. He had agreed to the transit of the army through his realm but had remained silent regarding staying in his kingdom.

When we crossed over the Tigris we struck northeast, which would take us past Irbil, so there was no possibility of avoiding Phraates, not unless he left the city before we arrived. But, as Gafarn pointed out, why would he leave before we arrived as his visit was intended purely to intercept us before we reached the Armenian border? And it would be impossible to meet with Akmon and Lusin without greeting Phraates.

'He will be like a viper in a tent,' said Malik, 'an unwelcome visitor but impossible to ignore.'

One of the things, among many, that annoyed me about Phraates was his ability to bring out the petulant and childish side of individuals, and I was not immune to this. Four days after crossing the Tigris we approached Irbil and I ordered every Duran cataphract to wear his scale armour and full-face armour, shoulder a *kontus* and ensure his horse was fully covered with armour. Similarly, the legionaries were ordered to march in full equipment rather than carrying their shields and *furcas* on their backs and helmets hanging from their belts. Not to be outdone, Gafarn ordered all his cataphracts and squires to march as on a parade, complete with white plumes and companies of horse archers carrying a profusion of horse head banners. And to add to the display I heard a sound that made my blood boil, an irritating thumping sound making me swing in the saddle. Gafarn beside me grinned like an impish child.

'Please tell me that is not what I think it is.'

Another impish smirk. 'Hatra's first kettledrummers, and I have to say they sound magnificent.'

The dirge was like a woodpecker tapping at my skull. I caught sight of Irbil's citadel in the distance and my heart sank further. Boom, boom, boom. Shamash give me strength, I knew this day would be long and arduous.

'Dura should get itself a corps of kettledrummers,' said Gafarn, strumming his fingers on one of the front horns of his saddle to the rhythm of his mounted musicians, 'they are rather invigorating.'

'That is one word for it,' I groaned.

Fortunately, we left the column before my headache got worse to head towards the city; the same city Gallia and I had been trapped in the year before. Then a simple ditch, earth bank and wooden wall surrounded Irbil, but now the defences looked much more impressive. Lucius, who accompanied us on our visit, explained that the mud-brick wall that would eventually surround the city was as yet unfinished, but by the end of the year would be completed. The western gates into the city, the same portal Gallia and I had defended when Atrax had attacked the city, had been considerably strengthened. The ditch in front of the gates had been widened and made deeper, sharpened stakes decorating its base, while the drawbridge over it could be raised and lowered by chains operated by soldiers in the impressive gatehouse. Soldiers in blue tunics eyed us through narrow slits in the walls above, archers I assumed. On the other side of the drawbridge an imposing figure wearing shining armour sat on his horse at the head of a party of cataphracts, a huge blue plume atop his open-faced helmet. He nudged his horse forward, which trotted over the bridge before halting in front of us. General Joro, scion of an ancient Median family and head of the kingdom's army, such as it was, bowed his head.

'Welcome to Irbil, majesties, King Akmon is eager to see you all. If you would follow me.'

He showed no trace of emotion when he spotted the black-robed figure of Malik among us and I wondered what a very traditional Parthian made of an Agraci king entering the capital of one of the oldest kingdoms in the empire. But Joro was a professional and he would never debase his position with unseemly behaviour. I urged Horns ahead to draw level with the general as we rode through the city. There were no longer any tents housing refugees behind the walls on the city side.

'The villagers have returned to their homes, I see.'

'Yes, majesty, the north of the kingdom is returning to some sort of normality at last. That was why the king was so aggrieved to learn the Armenians are planning a fresh invasion.'

'There will be no fresh invasion, or any future invasion, be assured.'

His worry-lined face cracked a smile. 'That is good to hear, majesty.'

Irbil also looked to be on the road to recovery, its streets packed with people and its shops doing a brisk trade, those I saw anyway. At the citadel, the walled stronghold atop the stone mound in the centre of the city, it was more peaceful, a guard of honour lining the ramp that led to the huge gatehouse on the mound's southern side. I recognised the palace guard I had fought beside to defend the city the year before: soldiers in helmets with large cheek guards and neck protectors wearing short-sleeved scale-armour tunics and carrying large oval shields faced with hide painted black and sporting a white dragon motif. A huge dragon banner fluttered from the gatehouse, alongside the flags of the kingdoms Phraates ruled: one showing the horned bull of Babylon, the other an eagle clutching a snake in its talons – the emblem of Susiana.

Gafarn pointed at the latter. 'If Susiana's banner was redesigned to show Phraates being held in an eagle's talons, do you think everyone would understand what it meant?'

Gallia laughed but I was not in a humorous mood.

'Try not to make this more uncomfortable than it already is, Gafarn.'

The citadel stood in stark contrast to the bustle and energy of the city that surrounded it; its narrow streets and alleyways largely empty save for white-robed priests and servants going about their business. It was the home of the king, his wealthiest and most powerful nobles, and the Temple of Shamash, the home of the Sun God. The royal palace a short walk from the temple was enclosed by a wall and contained stables, barracks and storerooms, as well as the king and queen's living quarters. When we rode into the courtyard I saw an honour guard of Median cataphracts commanded by Joro's son and a line of Babylonian Guards – big, powerful men sitting on large horses wearing purple leggings and tunics and dragon-skin armour comprising a leather vest covered with overlapping silver plates protecting their torsos. Their burnished steel helmets sported purple plumes and their purple saddlecloths were edged with gold with golden bulls stitched in each corner. No expense had been spared to equip the high king's bodyguard, which numbered five hundred men, each one armed with a lance, bow, sword and long knife. The trumpeters played a fanfare and slaves walked forward to take our reins after we had halted and dismounted, my gaze being drawn to the figure of the high king at the top of the palace steps. Now broad shouldered and tall like his father, he wore a purple silk robe fastened at the waist by a wide leather belt with gold stitching, on his feet a pair of purple leather boots. Behind him was the strapping figure of Adapa, the commander of his bodyguard, previously Adapa the leper and social outcast, condemned to wander the earth shunned by all, until Claudia had intervened in his life. And now he stood at the right hand of the king of kings of the Parthia Empire. Such is the will of the gods.

Beside Phraates stood Akmon and Lusin, the queen looking radiant in a blue silk dress that had obviously been specially made to accommodate her bulging stomach. I wondered when she was due to give birth. Akmon, no longer the pale, lean teenager who had fled to Palmyra with his love to escape her forced marriage to the repulsive Nabu Egibi, now long dead, was a young man in his prime who had shown his kingly virtues in battle. He grinned at his grandparents – Gafarn and Diana – as we halted at the foot of the steps and bowed to Phraates, Malik doing likewise, though he was not a king of the empire.

Phraates, all smiles, brought his hands together and walked down the steps, Akmon and Lusin following, his eyes immediately focusing on the armour cuirasses worn by me and Gallia.

'So, this is the famed armour I have heard so much about. It puts that worn by my bodyguard to shame. I hear it was a gift from the gods themselves, King Pacorus.'

'Exaggerated gossip, highness,' I lied. 'It is good to see you looking so well, and you as well, Lusin. Pregnancy suits you.'

She was blooming, her chestnut curls more lustrous than I remembered and her cheeks rosy and healthy.

'I have prayed in the Temple of Marduk at Ctesiphon that the child will be a boy,' Phraates told us with not a trace of irony, 'so it will grow up to be a future ruler of Media.'

'We all pray for that, highness,' said Gallia, 'and for Akmon's reign to be prosperous and free of usurpers.'

Gafarn supressed a smirk but Phraates merely smiled at her, took Lusin's hand and walked back up the steps.

'Come, you all must be tired after your journey. We watched your army approach from the south from the citadel's battlements, a most impressive sight.'

He was all charm and disarming smiles that evening, engaging all of us in convivial conversation about nothing in particular. There was no mention of Rasha's death, the reason why we were at Irbil, or the defeat of Prince Atrax and King Artaxias. In truth, no one had the stomach to bring these subjects up, especially as Akmon was clearly blissfully happy with his wife's pregnancy and she in turn obviously felt at home in Media. So we talked, smiled, toasted the rulers of Media with excellent wine and feasted on a wide range of meats, cheeses, vegetables and fruits. When the evening had finished we retired to the same bedroom we had occupied during the siege of the city.

The next morning Gallia and I took breakfast on the balcony, before us magnificent views of the city below and the Zagros Mountains in the distance. We ate only slices of melon, as our stomachs were still full from the meal the evening before, but as Gallia picked at her fare I knew something was troubling her.

'He's here for a reason,' she said at last, 'Phraates, I mean.'

'Not here to convey his felicitations to Akmon and Lusin, then?'

She chuckled. 'Only if there's something in it for him. It is a pity Claudia is not here.'

We had been surprised our daughter, supposedly chief adviser to the high king, was not with Phraates, but he had explained that she had travelled north to the Alborz Mountains to attend a meeting of the Scythian Sisters. When I asked when she would be returning he had merely shrugged and told me Claudia had not informed him as to the date of her return.

'Talking of the Scythian Sisters,' I said casually, 'what is Saruke doing at Dura?'

It was easy to discern when Gallia was annoyed. Her eyebrows squeezed together and her mouth twisted slightly sideways to create a crease in her cheek, which was the facial expression she now adopted.

'I hope we are not going to argue once more concerning the Amazons.'

'I did not mention the Amazons.'

'Don't be clever, Pacorus, it does not suit you. As for Saruke, she is at Dura to serve Dura's interests.'

'Which are what?'

Her eyes narrowed. 'As king, I would have thought you knew them well enough.'

A knock at the door interrupted the first rumblings of an argument.

'Come,' I shouted.

Klietas came from the corridor, bowing his head to me and then Gallia.

'Should I have your horse saddled, highborn?'

I looked up into the sky to discern the position of the sun. It was mid-morning.

'Yes, we will be leaving Irbil immediately.'

Gallia regarded my squire for a few moments.

'Are you glad to be back home, Klietas?'

'Dura is my home, highborn,' he told her.

'Quite right,' I said.

'Why do you like Dura?' she probed.

'Because its king and queen saved my life and offered me a roof over my head and food in my belly, highborn, and for that I will be forever grateful.'

'Nothing to do with wanting to be near Haya?' she teased.

Klietas blushed and avoided her eyes.

'I, I, well…'

'Leave the boy alone,' I said, 'there's nothing wrong in falling in love with a beautiful young woman, even if she is a killer.'

Gallia was far from amused. 'Killer?'

I shook my head. 'Apologies, wrong word. Assassin.'

Gallia was about to rise to the bait when there was another knock at the door, the palace's chief steward entering when told to do so. He glided over and bowed his head to me.

'Apologies for interrupting your meal, majesty, but High King Phraates has requested your presence in the royal garden. I am to escort you there at your earliest convenience.'

Which meant straight away. I dabbed my mouth with a napkin and stood, rolling my eyes at Gallia who wore a triumphant smile.

'Looks like we won't be leaving Irbil just yet.'

I pointed at Klietas. 'Come on, meeting the king of kings will be good for your education.'

He was dumbstruck. 'The king of kings, highborn? What will I say to him?'

The steward was horrified by the idea.

'Keep your mouth shut at all times,' I told him, 'and don't smile at him, and avoid his eyes. But keep your ears open.'

'Yes, highborn.'

Phraates was standing beside the pool in the garden, as at Hatra positioned in the front space of the garden to reflect the image of the palace and the sky, thus binding the realm of the earthly to the heavenly. Royal gardens were images of paradise on earth, and water, with its scarcity in the more arid parts of the empire, was a sacred and precious element. Irbil's citadel was blessed in having its own springs that brought cool water from deep in the earth all-year round, which meant the royal gardeners were able to create waterfalls and fountains in the garden to produce pleasing, calming sounds.

The steward left us and I walked up to Phraates and bowed.

'They say they can live for up to forty years.'

'Highness?'

He pointed at the goldfish in the pond.

'Goldfish, King Pacorus. Just think, King Farhad probably stood on this very spot feeding these very fish all those years ago. Sinatruces was high king then.'

He looked at me. 'And now I am high king.'

'Indeed.'

He walked towards the white gazebo in the centre of the garden, positioned so Media's royal family could enjoy the beauty of the surroundings and breathe in the fragrant air.

'Let us take the weight off our feet, King Pacorus.'

Adapa standing a few feet behind Phraates shadowed his master, giving a cursory glance at Klietas who walked behind me to the gazebo. The commander of the high king's bodyguard bowed his head to me and I smiled back. It was hard to believe this was the same man who had been the rotting corpse at Seleucia all those months ago. The steward reappeared with slaves carrying refreshments and drinks, waiting for us to sit on couches with gold feet in the shape of dragons. Phraates waited until the slaves serving fruit, pastries and wine had retreated before speaking, reclining on his couch with a silver rhyton in the shape of a crouching dragon in his hand. He said nothing for a few minutes, staring at the different varieties of trees that had been planted in the garden – cypress, flowering almond, apricot, and peach. He took a sip of wine and noticed I had not picked my rhyton.

'Wine not to your liking, King Pacorus?'

'I have a long ride ahead, highness, and prefer to keep a clear head.'

He placed his drinking vessel on the low table between us and leaned back, Adapa standing behind his couch and Klietas behind mine.

'You intend to invade Armenia, then?'

'Yes, highness. King Artaxias led his army into Media last year in support of the renegade Atrax, and now Armenian troops are once again mustering on Media's northern border. Such provocation cannot go unanswered.'

I stared at him intensely.

I dare you to order me to stand down my army.

'If you and King Gafarn had not taken it into your own hands, I would have commanded King Ali to lead an expedition against the Armenians.'

His answer put me on the back foot and he saw the confusion in my eyes.

'You have always been a loyal servant of Parthia, King Pacorus.'

Flattery will get you nowhere, Phraates.

'It would have been better if Atrax had not been encouraged to seize Media's crown, highness.'

'I made a mistake, I admit it. I thought a close ally in Irbil would, with the cooperation of the Armenians, be a counterweight to the seemingly insatiable appetite of King Spartacus to wage war against his neighbours. I was wrong.'

'You have a close ally in Irbil, highness,' I told him. 'If given the opportunity, Akmon will prove loyal to Ctesiphon.'

He smiled. 'He and Lusin are a pleasant enough couple and they have the support of Media's lords, which is imperative for outsiders.'

'Outsiders, highness? Akmon is the son of King Spartacus.'

'And Lusin is an Armenian, who are hardly popular in Media. And if we want to be pedantic, Akmon is half-Agraci and half-Thracian.'

Not all this again. We fought against Atrax to defeat not only him but also his ludicrous ideas about Parthian purity.

He leaned forward. 'But I am hopeful their child will be a boy, born in the empire's oldest capital city, a true Parthian who will grow up to rule unchallenged the first kingdom of the empire.'

He looked around at the green, lush garden.

'Your sister never understood that a child born in a particular kingdom becomes an offspring of that realm, irrespective of his or her parents. Take your namesake, for example.'

'Prince Pacorus?'

He began to wag a finger at me. 'The epitome of what a Parthian prince should be: handsome, brave, with impeccable manners and morals and heir to the throne of Hatra, a most prestigious kingdom. Perhaps *the* most prestigious. There is talk that one day he many become high king himself.'

If only.

'Not for many years I hope, highness.'

He stopped wagging his finger and looked most serious.

'I do not wish Armenia to be humiliated, thus forcing it into the arms of Rome.'

'Neither do I, highness, but at the same time foreign aggressors must learn that to invade Parthia carries consequences.'

'Try to restrain your nephew, that is all I ask. King Spartacus has shown some worrying tendencies when it comes to ignoring the power balance that currently exists between Parthia and Rome. Negotiations are at a delicate stage.'

He was referring to the diplomacy surrounding the return of the captured Roman eagles currently in the Hall of Victory at Ctesiphon, in exchange for his young son being held in Rome. By all accounts Octavian had grown very fond of the boy and had taken him under his wing, which made me wonder if Phraates' son would want to return to Parthia. He had been abducted when a baby by Tiridates and the only knowledge he would have about Parthia would be from the Romans – hardly an unbiased source.

'I pray that your son will be returned to you soon, highness,' I said truthfully.

'I am surprised Akmon and his army is not accompanying you.'

'In truth, highness, Media's army needs rebuilding, much like the north of the kingdom that was so recently ravaged by war.'

'Including King Spartacus, who now attacks Armenia in defence of Media,' quipped Phraates.

'Akmon better serves his kingdom by remaining here, continuing with the strengthening of Irbil's defences and rebuilding his army,' I continued. 'Besides, it would be cruel indeed if he fell in a campaign launched to guarantee his future.'

'Of course, if the campaign was cancelled no one would die,' he remarked casually.

'Parthia cannot appear to look weak, highness.'

'No, of course.'

He remained silent for a few seconds before speaking.

'I worry that King Spartacus will invade Pontus, thus provoking a confrontation with Rome. If he does, I will state publicly that Gordyene will get no support from Parthia should Rome retaliate.'

I was confused. 'Why would he invade Pontus, highness?'

'Did I not tell you? Forgive me. The chief troublemakers who caused Media such injury recently are currently in Sinope, guests of King Polemon, I believe.'

'May I ask how you know this, highness?'

'A by-product of the seemingly unending correspondence and diplomacy between Ctesiphon and Rome. Like flies drawn to dung, Atrax, Tiridates, Laodice and that rogue Titus Tullus are all in the Pontic capital. Let us hope the gods send an earthquake to level the city. But I do not wish your siege engines to do it, as I am reliably informed they are with your army.'

'They always accompany the army when it marches, highness,' I lied. 'And I can assure your highness they will not be battering down the walls of Sinope, or indeed any other Pontic city.'

He looked relieved, if not entirely happy. An all-powerful king of kings would have simply ordered me to take my army back to Dura, and would have issued the same command to Gafarn. But Phraates was only just beginning to re-establish his power following the revolt of Tiridates. He had appointed loyalists to the thrones of Persis and Mesene, and had made an astute choice with regard to the throne of Aria, though whether Altan would prove a dutiful king remained to be seen. But Dura, Hatra and Gordyene represented a powerful alliance; one that potentially could remove him from power had it a mind to. Not that I for one had any intention of doing so – Dura had shed too much blood keeping him as high king – but he could not as yet order around the kings of those realms.

'I also do not desire for Artaxias and his family to be killed. It was the murder of his father in Alexandria that alienated Artaxias from Rome. It would be the height of folly for Parthia to force Armenia back into Rome's embrace.'

'I agree, highness, but Artaxias must realise he cannot invade Parthia without consequences. As for him and his family, I pledge they will not be harmed.'

He seemed satisfied by my answer, stood, wished me a safe journey and return and left the garden, Adapa trailing in his wake.

'You can look up now,' I told Klietas.

He did so and grinned in his endearing way.

'What did you think of the high king, the demi-god who rules all Parthia, or so his priests would have it?'

He clamped his lips together before speaking.

'He is not as tall as I thought he would be, highborn.'

'Ha, I assume you expected him to be seven feet tall and surrounded by a glowing light, with the face of a god. This is a useful lesson for you, Klietas. As you go through life you will discover that people, both high and low, are a constant source of disappointment.'

'He is not happy with you, highborn.'

'Oh, why do you say that?'

'I was not looking at him, as you ordered, but I could hear the tone of his voice. I heard anger in his kind words.'

'Mm. What did you make of his bodyguard?'

'A mighty warrior, highborn,' he beamed.

'He used to be a leper.'

Klietas looked askance at me. 'That is impossible, highborn, he was strong and healthy. Lepers do not get better.'

I slapped him on the arm. 'That one did. Come on, time to ride north.'

The army was already on the march, having struck camp just after dawn. It would take it five days to reach the southern shore of Lake Urmia and a further five to reach the Araxes, the boundary between Parthia and Armenia. By then I hoped the current would have abated enough to allow us to cross the river to strike for the Armenian capital. When staring at a map it all seemed very straightforward, but I had no doubt the reality would be very different.

In the palace courtyard we said our farewells to the high king, Akmon and Lusin. Gafarn and Diana hugged their grandchildren and there were tears in the Queen of Hatra's eyes when she walked to her waiting horse. Despite her age she was still slim and agile, vaulting into the saddle without any assistance. Malik waited on his black stallion and Gallia sat on her mare chatting to Zenobia, who held Dura's griffin banner. Before I gained my saddle, I had a quiet word with the brooding Joro, who was far from happy.

'I and my king would prefer to be leaving with you, majesty.'

'I know that, Joro, but this campaign is about Media's security and the stark truth is that Media's army, which is still being rebuilt, is needed here to defend the kingdom and its king.'

'It sits uneasy with me, majesty, remaining here while you fight on my behalf.'

'I can appreciate that, general, but I will leave you with this thought. If I were Artaxias and saw Media's dragon banner among the army opposing me, I would command a raiding column to strike south to devastate this kingdom. With you and Akmon here, that option is not available.'

He nodded half-heartedly.

'There is another reason for keeping Media's army here, general,' I said.

'Which is what, majesty?'

'If we face disaster across the Araxes, only you and Akmon will be able to save us.'

It had been heartening to see Irbil thriving and its defences being strengthened, and we were all pleased to see Lusin looking so healthy and happy with her husband. But what really filled me with hope as we trotted north to catch up with the army, was seeing villages, previously abandoned and in a state of disrepair, once again filled with inhabitants and working in the fields and orchards around them. It was a visible sign that the kingdom was reviving following years of conflict and invasions. Unfortunately for Media, its geography was ideal for campaigning, comprising in large parts of rolling to flat grassland blessed with fertile soil. The landscape was a beautiful green, fed all year round by underground water and thousands of natural springs, the location of which was indicated by the plethora of villages build beside them.

Commanders were under strict orders not to let their men graze their horses on crops but there was such an abundance of grassland between settlements that the army was able to move north without troubling the civilian population or their fields and orchards.

I told Gallia, Gafarn and Diana about my conversation with Phraates in the royal garden, and his revelation about the location of Atrax and Tiridates.

'I thought Tiridates was in Syria,' said a surprised Gafarn.

'It makes sense for rebels and traitors to gravitate towards each other,' remarked Gallia.

'As long as they stay in Pontus, then they do not concern Parthia,' I said.

Gallia howled with derision. 'They are in Pontus because they are planning a new invasion of Parthia, supported once more by Octavian, and Artaxias, probably.'

'It does seem more than a coincidence, Pacorus,' agreed Gafarn.

'Will you tell Spartacus?' queried Diana.

Gallia was adamant. 'He deserves to know where the people responsible for murdering his wife are skulking.'

'He probably already knows,' I said without conviction, 'after all, his Sarmatian allies have raided deep into Armenia and I'm sure a merchant divulged the whereabouts of Atrax before he had his throat slit.'

'Not a big devotee of the Aorsi, then, Pacorus?' said Gafarn.

'Thieves and bandits the lot of them,' I told him, 'and their presence in northern Gordyene serves only to provoke trouble between Parthia and Armenia.'

'Spartacus believes them to be his only true and loyal allies,' said Diana, 'and that includes his own parents. Sometimes I wonder if

Orodes made the right decision in making him King of Gordyene. I worry for him.'

I worried for him, though my concern was not so much for Spartacus' sense of isolation but his mood when we arrived at the Araxes, for the last time I had seen him was when he had departed Irbil to visit Hatra to report Rasha's death to his parents. Since then neither I nor Gafarn or Diana had set eyes on him and correspondence between Hatra and Vanadzor had been sporadic. Only when he received news that the Armenians were massing for a fresh invasion of Media did he become a writer, invoking the treaty made with Media and asking for our aid. I fully expected to meet a man eaten away with grief who wanted to unleash his pent-up fury against the Armenians.

Chapter 7

By dint of an ancient treaty that no one remembered, Media owned a small strip of territory adjacent to the eastern shore of Lake Urmia right up to the Araxes River. This was the route Atrax and his rebel army had used to advance against Irbil the year before, and happily for him and the Armenians that followed him, using this land meant they did not wander into Atropaiene territory, thus ensuring the neutrality of King Ali. I had sent Talib and his scouts ahead to make contact with the forces of Gordyene, but he returned to the army with news that Spartacus and his army had not left Gordyene territory but were camped directly north of Lake Urmia a few miles south of the Araxes. I found it strange that he had not placed his soldiers in the path the Armenians would take if they launched an invasion of Media, but when we arrived at the great encampment that housed Gordyene's army, I understood why.

We arrived on a beautiful late spring day, the sun high in a sky dotted with small puffy white clouds, a gentle breeze blowing to ruffle the dozens of banners among my nephew's army. This region of northern Gordyene abutting Armenia was one of contrasts. Around us were high mountains with snowy peaks, with red rock faces below, from where cool, fresh air invigorated lungs and bodies. But the valleys and mountain steppes were lush and green, fed by ample supplies of rainwater, streams and rivers. Bitterly cold during the winter months, in spring they were pleasant and fertile. There were no settlements in this part of Gordyene, which had been raided and criss-crossed by warring bands for decades, although now the only raids were launched north by the Aorsi across the Araxes.

The valley Gordyene's army occupied was lush and verdant, being watered by numerous streams running into the Araxes some five miles further north. In the middle sat the large marching camp the Immortals had created to house the thousands of men, mules, camels, horses and dozens of carts that accompanied the army. The carts were the only thing missing from the grand parade organised by my nephew to welcome the rulers of Dura and Hatra to his kingdom, though I suspected it was more for Gafarn and Diana's benefit than Gallia's and mine. Nevertheless, it was a fine spectacle and showed the army of Gordyene in all its glory.

Long gone were the days when that army had been nothing more than a ragtag band of men and women armed with a variety of weapons riding anything that could bear their weight. That had been in the days when the Romans had occupied Gordyene and the spirit of freedom had been kept alive by groups of hardy raiders living in the forests and mountains. They had been replaced by professional soldiers, men equipped by the armourers and workshops of Vanadzor, which worked day and night to produce the weapons and armour that kept the kingdom safe. Though like the freedom fighters of yesteryear, it had been a long time since Gordyene had had to defend itself. Now it exported war and its troops were among the finest in the Parthian Empire.

We rode down the corridor separating the two parts of my nephew's army, either side of us battalions of Immortals deployed in open order. In front of each company was a scorpion bolt thrower such as used by my own soldiers. The Immortals, like their famed Persian namesakes, were maintained at a strength of ten thousand men, the replacement battalion at Vanadzor ensuring there was a constant supply of new recruits to make up losses. They were to all intents and purposes legionaries, being equipped in a similar fashion – mail armour, helmets and large oval shields faced with hide painted red bearing a white lion's head motif – and armed exactly the same as Dura's legions and indeed Rome's: two javelins, short sword and dagger. Their tunics were even red like their Roman counterparts, though they wore black leggings.

Either side of the Immortals were companies of medium horsemen, men in helmets, scale armour cuirasses, with pteruges hanging from the waist. They carried round wooden shields faced with red-painted hide and embossed with a white lion's head motif. Their main weapon was a spear, though each man was also armed with a sword, axe and dagger.

Outnumbering the medium horsemen were Gordyene's horse archers: men riding hardy, swift horses, wearing no armour except soft pointed hats. Attired in red tunics and black leggings, their hats also red, each horseman carried two full quivers, a recurve bow and a short sword.

As we trotted past the horse archers, medium horsemen and Immortals, the élite of Gordyene's army came into view: the King's Guard and Vipers. The latter had existed when Surena had ruled Gordyene with his queen Viper, the former Amazon who had died in childbirth. Then they had been called Lionesses, but their name had been changed in honour of the woman who had formed and led them. They now numbered five hundred women and were commanded by Narin, whose name meant 'delicate' but who was anything but, and who was as effective on the battlefield as Zenobia. The Vipers were striking for the sex of their ranks, but the King's Guard would not have looked out of place on the parade square at Ctesiphon. Like the other members of the army they wore red tunics and black leggings, but whereas the medium horsemen wore iron scale-armour, the King's Guard sported cuirasses of alternating steel and bronze scales that shimmered in the sun like fish scales. Each horseman also wore pteruges at the shoulders and thighs, a burnished helmet and carried a round shield bearing a lion emblem. Originally armed with spears, the King's Guard were armed with ukku swords, recurve bow, two quivers and a dagger. To finish off his appearance each horseman wore a red cloak and his horse was fitted with a large red saddlecloth.

Red was the colour of the day and hinted at the blood that would be spilt in the coming days, my eyes being drawn to a huge red banner showing a silver lion fluttering behind the king and his two sons mounted on their horses in front of the camp's entrance. The Durans and Exiles were already building our own camp a couple of miles away, Lucius and his engineers laying out the dimensions of the ditch and rampart to provide shelter and security for forty-three thousand soldiers, thousands of squires, hundreds of non-combatants and tens of thousands of animals.

It was a happy reunion between Spartacus and his parents, Diana walking her horse forward to kiss her son on the cheek and share a few private words with him. Spartacus was all smiles as he greeted Gallia and me.

'Welcome, aunt, uncle, this is a great day for Parthia; for now the empire's three greatest powers are united in the defence of Media. I trust my son and daughter are well?'

'Akmon and Lusin are thriving,' I assured him.

'And you will soon be a grandfather,' beamed Gallia, 'and you two uncles.'

Castus and Haytham were now fine young men, the former with blue eyes and dark blonde hair tumbling from beneath his helmet, the latter's hair black as night like his dead mother's.

General Hovik, dependable, austere and slightly weathered looking, was behind his king, next to the cutthroat Shamshir, commander of the King's Guard.

'It is good to see you, general,' I called. 'How did you find the east?'

'Hot, dusty and humid in equal measure, majesty,' he replied. 'I am glad to be back home.'

I ignored Shamshir who showed disdain in his cold eyes. And the man next to him, the swarthy Spadines, the leader of the Aorsi tribe and the man who had devoted his life to inflicting misery on the Armenian people and anyone else who crossed his path. Rated a valuable ally by Spartacus, I had nothing but contempt for him and his Sarmatian bandits. I turned in the saddle to peer at the immaculately dressed ranks of Gordyene's army.

'Something troubles you, uncle?' said Spartacus.

I turned back to face him.

'Are all your soldiers present?'

'They are,' he told me, 'though Prince Spadines' troops are deployed along the Araxes to keep the Armenians amused until we determine our plan of campaign.'

I caught a glance of Spadines smirking and nodding knowingly at Shamshir. I wondered if the ugly commander of the King's Guard was related to the uncivilised Spadines, long-lost brothers, perhaps. I laughed. Quizzical stares were directed at me.

'I must compliment you on your army, Spartacus, it is a credit to both you and all Parthia.'

It was no lie. Every man and woman who wore a red tunic was a professional and trained to operate with the other constituent parts of the army. Thus the horsemen could operate closely with the

Immortals, and vice-versa. This meant the Immortals could form a square with the horsemen inside it, to fight a defensive battle, which could change in an instant if the ranks of the foot soldiers opened to allow the horse archers and medium horsemen to attack. They were the same tactics used by Dura's army, the only significant difference being that Gordyene possessed no cataphracts, the steel fist of my own army and that of Hatra's. But that had not prevented Gordyene's soldiers from tasting victory after victory on the battlefield.

We rode into camp, passing neat blocks of ten-man tents, each one the campaign home of a company of Immortals, or ten horsemen. In the Roman and Duran armies, troops slept in eight-man tents called a *papilio*, which was made of oiled goatskin, though the Romans also used calfskin. But to differentiate Gordyene's soldiers from the Romans' whose training, organisation and weapons they had copied, ten-man tents were the norm. I thought it churlish but to Spartacus such gestures spoke volumes, as did enforcing a prohibition on calling the short sword, javelin and shield *gladius*, *pilum* and *scutum*, respectively, on pain of a flogging, even though they were exact copies.

In the centre of camp stood the headquarters tent, a rather dour, functional structure far removed from the exotic pavilions served by armies of slaves used by most Parthian kings, except me, when on campaign. The eating and general reception area of the tent was small, made more diminutive by the stout oak table placed in the centre, around which we all sat on wooden stools, soldiers serving us wine and water. Laid on the table was a hide map of northern Gordyene and southern Armenia, the Araxes the dividing line between the two. Spartacus remained standing to dominate the proceedings, his two sons standing behind him and Hovik and Spadines loitering nearby. After we had been served drinks Spartacus came straight to the point.

'Due to our presence, the Armenians are camped beyond the Araxes, five or six miles from here.'

He pointed at the map. 'We are here, and the enemy is here.'

He moved his finger a few inches to indicate a spot north of the river.

'Now the spring melt waters are abating,' he continued, 'the current has slowed, and the level has dropped to four feet.'

'How wide is the river?' asked Gafarn.

'Around fifty yards, perhaps more. It is an ideal crossing point where the river flows south and then east to create a bend just over a mile in length. The bend in the river slows the current, making it safer for an army to cross.'

I studied the map. 'The Armenians will also be aware of this, and to undertake a river crossing in the face of enemy resistance is no small thing, Spartacus. Foot soldiers and horsemen wading through water are very vulnerable to enemy slingshots, arrows and spears. And they can be struck when they are just exiting the water, when they will be disorganised and at their most vulnerable. It could quickly turn into a disaster.'

'Pacorus has a point, son,' said Diana.

Spartacus gave her a reassuring smile.

'Which is why, mother, we will not be crossing at that point. Rather,' he indicated a spot to the east, 'the horsemen will cross five miles downstream. The current is stronger and the water deeper, but it is possible to get horsemen across without too much difficulty. Is that not true, Prince Spadines?'

The wild man of the north gave a leer and nodded.

'True, lord.'

I groaned when Spadines walked forward to speak.

'We have used this crossing place many times to raid Armenia.'

'Small parties of horsemen, I assume?' I said.

He smiled and nodded. 'Yes, lord.'

'Ever seen a camel swim, *prince*?'

His smile disappeared as he looked at me warily.

'I do not understand, lord.'

I drank a mouthful of wine. 'Horses can swim if they get into difficulties, but I have never seen a camel swim, which is unfortunate as we will need camels to supply the horse archers with spare arrows.'

'We can leave the camel train behind, uncle,' said Spartacus. 'The horse archers can carry additional quivers. The most important thing is that our horsemen get across the river while the rest of the army holds the attention of the Armenians in the bend of the river. Then our horsemen will strike the enemy from behind and push them into the river.'

I took another mouthful of what was a most excellent wine.

'It is a good plan, my congratulations,' I told Spartacus, which elicited smug smiles from Spadines and the two princes. 'Fixing the enemy's attention by a secondary operation while the most important element marches to envelop the foe's rear, thereby severing his lines of communication and making his position untenable. *If* it is successful.'

'The army of Gordyene has never tasted defeat,' boasted Spadines, making Hovik wince with embarrassment.

'The risks are high,' agreed Gafarn. He looked at his son and the Aorsi chief. 'I assume the Armenians also have scouts who are monitoring our own movements?'

'It is a good plan,' insisted Spartacus.

'It is a *risky* plan,' I corrected him, 'but one that we should adopt in the absence of an alternative. Having marched all the way here, we cannot now dither. I will get my scouts to undertake a thorough reconnaissance of the two crossing points to satisfy myself the river is at least fordable.'

'There is no need for that,' insisted Spadines, 'my men know the river like the backs of their hands.'

'Crossing a desert at night under a full moon requires much concentration,' stated Malik, who thus far had remained silent, 'but fording a river is fraught with risks. What about rocks and boulders on the riverbed?'

'The riverbed is just mud and sand at that point,' Spadines told him.

I ignored him, as I did not want to waste my time arguing with a bandit. I looked at Hovik, the careworn commander of Gordyene's army who looked like an over-worked shop owner but who had forged that army into a war-winning instrument.

'General, I would hear your opinion on this operation.'

Hovik's red tunic had seen better days and his boots could have done with a clean, but he was one of those individuals who garnered instant respect, not only for his keen mind but because he had been a common foot soldier when Balas had ruled Gordyene, a mere teenager armed with a spear. In a career spanning four decades he had fought the Romans, Armenians and indeed other Parthians when Orodes had defeated Surena before the walls of Vanadzor. He cleared his throat.

'One way or another, we have to cross the Araxes, defeat the Armenian army and encircle the city of Artaxata to bring this campaign to a successful conclusion, or at least exact reparations from the Armenians for what they did in Media last year. We are all agreed on that.'

He looked at Gafarn and me in turn. 'I understand your misgivings, majesties, but we must strike now, while the iron is hot, so to speak. Therefore, and to reduce the risks involved, I propose the horsemen should cross the river in two days' time. At night.'

Absolute silence met his words and I wondered if he was attempting some sort of levity.

'It will be a full moon,' continued Hovik, 'and visibility will be adequate. More to the point, even if they are watching the river, the Armenians will not be expecting us to attack at night.'

'Crossing a river at night is risky at the best of times, general' said Gafarn.

'That it is, majesty.'

'And yet you still propose it?' I asked him. 'Why?'

'Because Dura, Hatra and Gordyene have the best trained troops in the world, majesty,' he told me, 'and it makes sense to make the most of their talents. Speed and surprise will get us across the river.'

'And then?' I asked.

'The road leads directly north to the Armenian capital,' said Spartacus.

'We do not desire the deaths of Artaxias or his family,' stated Gafarn bluntly, 'or the annexation of Armenia by Gordyene. We are here to enforce the territorial integrity of Media.'

'And to avenge Rasha,' said Gallia, to the satisfaction of Spartacus and his sons.

'I do not covet any Armenian territory,' declared Spartacus, 'but rather desire to see the Armenians respect others' borders.'

'I think General Hovik's plan is a good one,' said Gallia. 'We have all fought at night before.'

'But I still insist my scouts carry out a reconnaissance of the area beforehand,' I added, 'so they may familiarise my commanders with the terrain.'

Spadines was going to say something but Spartacus shook his head.

'As you wish, uncle.'

'There is one more thing,' I said, 'I wish to be overall commander during the campaign. I say this not out of a desire to order anyone about but rather because I have had experience of being the leader of armies composed of disparate elements.'

I expected Spartacus to argue that he should lead the expedition, but he merely shrugged.

'As you desire, uncle.'

Malik nodded.

'I always knew you would make lord high general again, Pacorus,' joked Gafarn.

Spadines, his nose put out of joint, insisted his men accompany Talib and his scouts during their reconnaissance. So, for the remainder of that day and the next, small parties of scouts rode up and down the river, on the opposite bank parties of Armenian horsemen shadowing their movements. It was clear the enemy was very aware of our presence, though unless they had troops across the Araxes they would have no idea of our numbers.

There were now sixty thousand Parthian soldiers massed five miles south of the Araxes, three thousand more if one counted the Aorsi, which I did not. With their shabby appearance, wild assortment of weapons and armour, most of it either stolen or gifted, they presented a sorry spectacle. The fact their ranks included many women did not concern me, but their lack of tactics, discipline and training did. They were born raiders, thieves, cutthroats and brawlers good only for mopping up after victory had been secured. If that.

'That Sarmatian was right, majesty, the river is shallow enough for a man on a horse to wade across, though at night the risks are magnified many times.'

I gestured to Talib he should sit on one of the stools arranged by Klietas around the table in my command tent. The light was beginning to fade outside and Talib looked tired. He and his men had spent the afternoon carrying out a detailed reconnaissance of the southern shore of the river. Klietas filled a cup with water and handed it to him.

Karys, Chrestus, Kewab and Lucius were also in attendance, along with Gallia and Malik. Klietas hovered over us like a hornet, water jug in hand ready to refill empty cups. Everyone ignored him as he did so.

'Did you see any Armenians?' asked Chrestus.

'Yes, lord. A few horsemen, scouts, I assume.'

The general looked at me. 'I don't like it, majesty, any general worth his salt would know the river is fordable in many places and would plan accordingly.'

'We must make a lot of noise and a great display at the main crossing point,' said Kewab, 'to focus the enemy's attention on that spot rather than further downstream.'

'How many horsemen will be crossing at night?' asked Malik.

'Ten thousand,' I answered, 'divided equally between the Agraci, Kewab's soldiers, the horsemen of Mesene, Duran horse archers and Gordyene's medium horsemen.'

Chrestus exhaled disapprovingly.

'We don't need the horsemen of Gordyene, majesty, we should stick with the soldiers we know and trust.'

'You don't trust Spartacus' men, general?' queried Gallia.

He ran a hand over his cropped crown.

'They are good soldiers, majesty, no doubt about that. But operations at night are risky and if I was taking part in one I would prefer to have soldiers around me who I knew and trusted implicitly.'

'I agree,' I told him, 'but for diplomatic reasons we must include a contingent from Gordyene.'

'The key to success will be to distract the Armenians,' said Kewab, thinking out loud.

'That is where you come in, Chrestus. The Durans and Exiles will leave camp before dawn, link up with the Immortals and march to the main crossing point, making as much noise as possible. When the sun comes up the rest of the horsemen of the army will join them. Use every whistle, drum, horn and trumpet to make as much a racket as you can. Gafarn and Spartacus will instruct their soldiers to do likewise. As soon as you see us on the opposite bank, attack.

'If we do not appear, you will know we were surprised at the river and butchered.'

Klietas, who had been taking a keen interest in what was being said, laughed.

Every pair of eyes turned on him, making him blush.

'You think the death of your king is funny, boy?' growled Chrestus.

'No, highborn, my apologies.'

'If the king falls, I will take you to the river myself and drown you,' threatened Chrestus.

'Let's concentrate on killing Armenians, shall we?' I advised. 'Besides, I do not intend to fall, unless it's into the water if Horns panics in the dark and throws me.'

'Perhaps you should stay on this side of the river,' advised Gallia, 'and let younger men carry out the river crossing.'

'A commander leads from the front,' I replied, 'besides, I've never forded a river at night.'

Hovik was right about the full moon, which appeared overly large in the night sky above us: a huge grey disc casting the land in an eerie silver light. The brightness certainly aided our journey from camp to the crossing point five miles downstream of where the main force would ford the river, but such was the brightness that we became very visible. I scanned the mountains and craggy hills on the opposite side of the river and imagined them filled with Armenian soldiers ready to report our presence as soon as we came into view. It was also very quiet, unnervingly so, and I worried that the jangle of bridles, the snorts of horses and the dull crump of thousands of hooves on the ground would carry long distances, to the ears of our enemies.

'It looks wider at night,' I said to those with me.

We had halted at the riverbank, around us officers organising the horsemen into five columns to ford the river, using hand signals instead of shouting orders, the use of horns and trumpets prohibited.

'Darkness acts as a strong stimulus to the imagination, majesty,' Kewab told me, 'and exaggerates a feeling of insecurity. Objects seem bigger and distances greater.'

'It looks a mile wide,' said Karys, pointing at the river, which resembled a massive black snake slithering through the mountains and lowlands. Black and dangerous.

'The other riverbank is empty, that is something,' said Malik, his tattooed face like a black mask in the moonlight.

I turned to the commander of Spartacus' medium horsemen, a man in his early thirties with a thick black beard.

'Your men are ready?'

'Yes, majesty.'

I looked at Sporaces beside him.

'Ready, majesty.'

'Then let us get wet. May whatever gods you follow be with you this night.'

After Malik had clasped my forearm I closed my eyes and said a silent prayer to Shamash, requesting the Sun God smile on our efforts and watch over Gallia. I opened my eyes and saw Klietas.

'Keep close to me. Can you swim?'

'No, highborn.'

'Then don't fall off your horse.'

I turned Horns and nudged him forward to join Sporaces' horse archers, which were divided into four long columns, each five hundred strong. Beyond them were Malik's Agraci, then Karys' horse archers and Kewab's eastern recruits. Finally, some half a mile away but still visible in the luminous silver light, were Gordyene's medium horsemen, each rider carrying a spear, the points of which looked like pale torches in the ethereal landscape.

I stroked Horns' neck and whispered into his ear to walk forward. He grunted and entered the cold, black waters of the Araxes. In Armenian tradition, the river was named after Arast, a great-grandson of the legendary hero Hayk, the *nahapet*, and the original patriarch of the Armenians. According to legend, two-and-a-half thousand years ago Hayk led his household of three hundred from servitude in Babylon to Armenia, being pursued by his lord called Bel. A great battle ensued in which an arrow shot by Hayk killed Bel, thus ushering in the beginning of Armenian history, or so legend would have it.

Horns slowly entered the water and began to move forward, the cold water lapping around my legs and covering his limbs and lower half of his belly. As we left the riverbank I prayed it would not rise any further. Our bows and quivers were slung on our backs, which meant if we were attacked before we reached the opposite bank we would be helpless. Now spring was over the river was no longer raging, though in its many gorge-like sections along its nearly seven-hundred-mile length the torrent was always strong. But here the river was wide – over one hundred yards – though even here in early spring the river would be raging. For this reason, there were no bridges along the entire length of the Araxes.

Mid-point and my legs were chilled, which meant Horns would also be feeling the cold. His breathing was short and hurried but I reached forward to stroke his neck and speak soothing words into his ears. I glanced at the approaching riverbank to try to discern any movement. Praise Shamash there was none. I looked right to see the other columns, now slightly ragged but still intact, Malik and his Agraci ahead of mine. The depth of the water remained unchanged and I grudgingly recognised that Spadines had been right – this was an excellent crossing place. And there were no hidden obstacles on the bottom to impede our movement.

I felt the water around my legs drop and heaved a sigh of relief when Horns exited the water, urging him forward. In front of us, around a mile distant, reared up a large rocky hill. I turned to Sporaces.

'Get a couple of companies ahead to scout that rock, and two more east and west to guard the track.'

It was around three hours before dawn and when all the contingents had left the water, a council of war was held on the riverbank. Filling our minds had been whether we would be able to cross the river safely and would the crossing be contested. Now we were on the north bank of the Araxes and had suffered no casualties save for a score of men who had drowned during the passage. We shivered in the cold night air, our legs soaked and a slight breeze chilling us further. I rubbed my hands and tried to ignore the throbbing pain in my leg.

'We wait until dawn and then ride west to attack the enemy in the rear.'

'We should attack now, Pacorus,' suggested Malik, 'while we have the element of surprise. Ten thousand horsemen can kill a lot of Armenians.'

'You are right, my friend,' I agreed, 'but we are the sting in the scorpion's tail and our success depends on the rest of the army drawing the Armenians into the bend in the river, so they can be surrounded and annihilated. A little patience now, my friend, will save many Parthian and Agraci lives later.'

'And with the dawn the sun will be behind our backs,' said Kewab, 'increasing our chances of success.'

Malik was not happy but accepted my point, and so we established patrols and a defensive perimeter, stuffed ourselves with strips of cured meat, re-fastened our quivers and bows to our saddles, paced up and down to keep warm and waited for the sun to appear in the east. Klietas was beside himself with excitement.

'If I do well in the battle and kill an Armenian, will you tell Haya, highborn?'

'You can tell her yourself.'

'It would sound better coming from you, highborn.'

'Ah, so you want me to embellish your exploits.'

'Embellish?'

'It means to exaggerate, Klietas. In any case, you are the king's squire, a position of some importance. I'm sure if you switched your affections to someone else, Haya would be more amenable to your advances.'

The idea dismayed him. 'Why would I want to do that, highborn?'

'To make her take more notice of you.'

'By loving someone else?'

'Well, by showing some interest in someone else.'

'I do not want anyone else, highborn.'

'I know that.'

'Then why do you suggest I love someone else?'

'I didn't.'

He looked totally bemused and lost.

'I will mention to Haya that you are a brave and loyal squire. In return, I command you to take great care during the battle and stay by my side.'

'Yes, highborn,' he replied.

He stared down at the ground.

'I thought…'

'You thought that after your little trip to Zeugma Haya would fall into your arms like a grateful girl.'

'Yes, highborn.'

'When men see the Amazons, they are drawn to their alluring looks, shapely bodies and lustrous hair. They think the bows, swords and daggers they carry are just for show, and they smirk when they see them wearing helmets and armour. But the weapons and armour are not for show, Klietas, they are the tools of the Amazons' trade, and that trade is killing. An Amazon is like a wild horse, which needs a lot of taming. Some can never be tamed.'

'Can Haya, highborn?'

'That is something you will need to discover for yourself.'

It was now very cold, and my leg was throbbing like fury, causing me to wince with pain and hobble when I walked. But the eastern horizon, previously black, hinted at salvation as white light peaked over the crags. Within minutes the light had increased and the sky, previously black and twinkling with a thousand stars, began to turn purple and blue. Dawn had arrived. The atmosphere, previously calm and subdued, suddenly became frenetic as officers spoke in hushed tones to their men and horses became agitated as they sensed their masters' heightened tension. Within minutes the warlords were around me, waiting for me to gain Horns' saddle, which I did with some difficulty after my leg's immersion in cold water and then being chilled by a cool night breeze.

'You are getting too old for all this, Pacorus,' grinned Malik, himself no teenager.

'That is why I retired, my friend,' I groaned, settling myself into the saddle, 'and look how that turned out.'

The sun was rapidly rising behind our backs to herald a beautiful early summer's day, for some among us their last on earth, and hopefully the same for many more Armenians.

'Any questions? I asked.

We had spent most of the previous day working out our plan of attack once across the river, the latter causing more concern than the former. Our tactics were simple enough: ride west along the riverbank in two columns. In the vanguard of one, Gordyene's mounted spearmen. Leading the other Malik and his Agraci. Behind both would be the horse archers – six thousand mounted bowmen ready to lend missile support should we encounter trouble. Once we had arrived at the bend in the river where the main force would cross, we would attack the rear of the Armenian army, hopefully lured into the bend by the racket made by the legions, Immortals and Gafarn's kettledrummers. Then we would strike the rear of the enemy, with any luck inflicting many casualties and spreading panic. At the same time, our own foot soldiers would be wading across the river, though not until we had arrived.

'Shamash be with you all,' I said. 'Time to go.'

The crisp morning air was filled with the rumble of ten thousand horses cantering over the ground, men controlling the urge of their horses to break into a gallop. The ground was moist because of the rain that had been falling during the previous days, which meant there was no choking dust cloud enveloping us. It also meant visibility was excellent, though the same was also true for the enemy.

The Armenians would have heard us before they saw us, but it made no difference. When we arrived at the giant bend in the river we achieved almost total surprise. Shamash was smiling on us this day for my expectations of victory were not only met but exceeded. Malik led his warriors straight into the attack with no regard for tactics or discipline, his men hollering war cries as they rode straight at the mass of enemy soldiers facing south to meet the attack of our foot soldiers.

The width of our army's crossing point in the bend was around a mile and a half, the Armenians filling this extent with their foot soldiers. As our columns galloped west, swung south and fanned out into line – apart from the Agraci who attacked in a mob – the enemy foot archers deployed behind the spearmen, turned around and loosed a few volleys into our ranks. Riders fell from saddles and horses collapsed on the ground when arrows hit them. But archers on foot are very vulnerable and after two volleys at most they scattered, running back to the spearmen for protection.

They were not quick enough.

The Agraci and Gordyene's mounted spearmen were among them in minutes, skewering them with their spears and cutting them down with their swords. With Horns' reins wrapped around my left wrist, I pulled out my bow from its case, plucked an arrow from my quiver and nocked the missile. Around me Sporaces' men, according to Duran doctrine, formed into several columns, ready to shoot at the enemy shield wall that would inevitably be formed to meet enemy horsemen.

But there was no shield wall.

Klietas beside me whooped with delight when he saw his arrow hit a spearman around fifty yards ahead, the missile striking his torso, causing him to crumble to the ground.

'Did you see, highborn, did you see?'

'I saw.'

I also saw no enemy shield wall; indeed, no enemy army to speak off, just desperate men trying to escape the carnage unfolding around them. Kewab threw his armed spearmen straight into the mêlée, dozens of Armenians dying on the ends of those lances as his horsemen cut their way through to the river to link up with Dura's legions and Gordyene's Immortals exiting the water, thereafter forming a screen around them. There was no need. The Armenians, the majority levy spearmen carrying rectangular wicker shields as their only protection, were already trying to flee. But they were trapped between the horsemen that had crossed the river the night before and the foot soldiers emerging from the river.

Sporaces and Karys, keeping a tight control over their men, abandoned company columns deploying their soldiers into lines to shoot at the Armenians running hither and thither in their desperate efforts to escape. For men trained to hit targets riding at the gallop and twisting left and right in the saddle as they did so, sitting stationary in the saddle picking off men wearing no armour was not war; it was sport. A series of trumpet calls announced the cessation of shooting and suddenly there were no Armenians still standing, only hundreds of corpses strewn over the ground, some twitching and others crawling pitifully and moaning in pain, their bodies pierced by one or more arrows. The 'battle' was over in around fifteen minutes. The arrow I had first nocked in my bowstring was still there.

I sat on Horns in the centre of what had been the Armenian battle line, if such a term could be used to describe the rabble we had easily brushed aside. At the river, around half a mile to the south, the Durans, Exiles and Immortals were slowly emerging from the water, along with horsemen, which included Spartacus, Gallia, Gafarn and Diana. The banners of Gordyene, Dura and Hatra fluttered in the morning breeze to announce our invasion of Armenia. Malik arrived next to me, his face flushed with triumph, his sword covered in blood.

'If that is what we can expect from the enemy, then Armenia will fall to us with ease.'

Kewab and Karys arrived to report, the former scanning the ground around us with professional eyes.

'These were civilians pressed into service, majesty, and suffered accordingly,' said Kewab. 'It is very strange.'

'Strange?' Malik's voice was mocking. 'There is nothing strange about slaughtering one's enemies.'

'Losses?' I asked.

Malik smiled contentedly. 'Too small to worry about.'

'Insignificant,' said Karys.

'The same,' added Kewab.

'Unfurl your banner,' I told Karys, 'the standard of Mesene should be flying beside the others.'

Karys beamed with delight. 'Yes, lord.'

I reached over to kiss Gallia when she and the Amazons arrived, Gafarn and Diana offering me congratulations and Spartacus viewing the dead Armenians with satisfaction.

'How far to the Armenian capital?' I asked.

'About twenty miles,' Spartacus told me. 'Through these hills and we will be on the Ararat Plain, good campaigning land.'

'It will take the rest of the day to get the troops, camels and wagons across the river, and another to reach the Armenian capital,' I said.

'The Armenians were foolish to build their capital so close to Parthian territory,' commented Diana.

'Artaxata was built one hundred and fifty years ago, mother,' Spartacus informed her, 'when Armenia fancied itself as a great power.'

'Now it is your plaything, lord,' gloated Spadines, who had appeared with half a dozen of his motley followers.

'We should get scouts out,' suggested a concerned-looking Kewab, who suddenly held up a hand.

Spadines observed the Egyptian with barely concealed mirth but Kewab had a keen ear and I too became aware of something on the wind, a faint humming noise.

'What is it?' asked Malik.

'The army of King Artaxias,' replied Kewab without hesitation, shouting in frustration. 'That is the reason we encountered only light resistance, to delay the army's crossing so we could be trapped against the river with only half or less of our soldiers on this side of the Araxes.'

The humming had given way to the familiar sound of drumming and in the distance, heading from the north between the two mountain ridges that flanked the valley, was a black line – Armenians.

'We must retreat back across the river,' said Kewab.

Spartacus glared at him. 'Impossible, to do so would give the enemy an easy victory and I did not come here to withdraw.'

He pointed ahead, to the space at the neck of the bend, a span of around half a mile.

'We defend the gap there with our foot soldiers, and once the Armenians have wasted their strength on trying to break through, we unleash the horse.'

Gafarn looked at the gap, turned to stare at the Immortals and Dura's legionaries still wading through the water and shook his head at me. His son saw the gesture.

'Perhaps those who are too old and cautious should seek shelter back across the river.'

'Have more respect for your father,' I reprimanded him.

He threw back his head and laughed, then spoke with a very loud voice so all nearby could hear.

'Is this the same King Pacorus who won the Battle of Carrhae against a Roman army five times larger than his own, who defeated the Armenians but last year on the Diyana Plain?'

'Are you insane?' I shouted in a most unseemly manner. 'We know nothing of the strength of the enemy bearing down us, but we do know less than half of our own army is yet to cross the river.'

Hovik had ridden over to his lord. His face betrayed his anxiety and I hoped he would voice his concern. But the veteran general knew not to cross his master when his Thracian blood was up. Before he could open his mouth, Spartacus was issuing orders.

'The Immortals will form a line across the neck of this bend.'

'It will be a thin line, majesty.'

'Unless we have assistance,' replied my nephew, turning to stare at me.

What could I do? Abandon him and his army to their fate, along with Gafarn, Diana and the thousands of other troops exiting the river to march into what could easily become a death trap?

'I will need your medium horsemen,' I told him, turning to Gallia.

'Ride to Chrestus and order him to deploy as many Durans and Exiles as possible next to the Immortals.'

I pointed across the river as I spoke to my wife. 'Next, you and Gafarn must lead all the cataphracts along the riverbank, cross the river in the same place we used last night and attack the Armenians in the rear.'

I looked at Gafarn. 'You agree?'

He was already turning his horse. 'Consider it done.'

I reached over to grab Gallia's hand 'Shamash be with you, and in the name of the Sun God hurry.'

'And you?'

'I am going to buy us some time.'

I ordered Kewab and Karys to deploy their men either side of Sporaces' men, in company columns.

'What of us?' demanded Malik.

'Alas, my friend,' I said, 'this is a task for horse archers alone. But comfort yourself that you have no need to sheath your sword. We are about to be deluged by the Armenians.'

Though the earlier action had been an easy affair, the horses were tired from the exertions of a night march and their riders had had no sleep the night before and should have been looking forward to a day's rest. Instead, six thousand horse archers cantered across the grass towards the thickening mass to the north, while around them Immortals and Duran legionaries frantically tried to create a battle line. I glanced at my bow, which was still nocked with the original arrow I strung earlier.

'Looks like you will see some use today after all, old friend.'

'We go to kill more Armenians, highborn?' beamed Klietas.

Unless we get killed first.

'That's right, Klietas. Remember your training and don't waste your arrows. Keep close.'

'Yes, highborn. If I do well, you will tell Haya?'

'I will.'

He grinned with delight, unaware we were riding into the jaws of a monster. If we survived that, then we would have to fight for our lives to stop the Armenians from pushing us into the river.

The Battle of the Araxes was about to begin in earnest.

Chapter 8

Six thousand horse archers, arrayed in company-sized columns, trotted forward to try to halt the huge mass of horse and foot that was bearing down on the makeshift battle line thrown across the neck of the river bend. Chrestus and General Motofi, the grim but no-nonsense commander of the Immortals, were desperately marshalling their respective foot soldiers to prevent the Armenians from advancing into our perilous bridgehead. The easy victory earlier had lulled us into a false sense of security, reducing any sense of urgency and giving the quartermasters more time to organise the river crossing. But their plans had turned to ashes.

'Keep close,' I said to Klietas beside me, behind us a company of Duran horse archers. Our tactics were tried and tested and every one of my men and those of Karys and Kewab were professionals who knew their task. I glanced at Klietas – he alone was inexperienced. But I hoped all those hours on the training fields with the Amazons would stand him in good stead.

'Remember your training. Focus. And blot out the noise from your mind.'

'Yes, highborn.'

Easier said than done. The Armenian army was a vivid splash of colours and the trumpets, drums and horns among its ranks were making a racket fit to raise the dead. Artaxias' army had deployed into line prior to attacking our forces in the bridgehead, in the centre an unbroken length of foot soldiers carrying spears and shields, with the sun glinting off thousands of helmets and whetted spear points. Fluttering among their ranks were dozens of red banners, the colour being the symbol of bravery in Armenia. As we cantered forward I could see that the banners were actually crimson, with golden stars in the centre flanked by two reverse-looking eagles also in gold – the standard of the Artaxiad dynasty.

Company signallers blew their horns to order their men to break into a gallop, the enemy line becoming more formidable and intimidating as we rode directly at it.

'Focus.' I shouted to Klietas.

A hundred paces from the unbroken lines of shields and spears I shot my arrow, releasing the bowstring to send the missile high into the sky. To drop vertically among the dense ranks of the enemy. Then I turned Horns to the right to ride along the Armenian battle line, plucking another arrow from my quiver and again shooting it high into the sky, before turning Horns right again to retrace my steps back to our own army, twisting in the saddle to shoot a third arrow at the enemy before the rider behind me – Klietas – blocked my aim.

The companies of horse archers raked the Armenian army with a hurricane of missiles, each company shooting one arrow every five seconds once the attack commenced – sixty companies discharging three thousand, six hundred arrows a minute in total. The air was thick with black missiles arching into the sky before falling among the enemy's foot soldiers. Many would hit shields and the ground, but others would strike helmets, torsos and legs, inflicting casualties but, more importantly, stopping the Armenians in their tracks.

The companies withdrew and prepared to gallop forward again to unleash fresh volleys against the enemy, buying our own foot soldiers valuable time to form a battle line. But from the flanks of the Armenian foot soldiers came horsemen, thousands of them. They carried lances and round shields, wore scale-armour cuirasses and helmets and I knew they would slaughter us easily if they caught us.

'Sound withdrawal,' I shouted at the signaller behind me.

Seconds later, the sound reverberated through the air and was copied by the signallers in other companies. Kewab, seasoned general that he was, was already leading his men back to the relative safety of the bridgehead – some five hundred paces away. The horse archers of Karys were also falling back, swiftly followed by those of Sporaces. The Armenians were moving slowly, knowing that horse archers armed only with bows and perhaps swords were no match for heavily armed and armoured lancers, and that our men would withdraw out of their way, as indeed they were now doing. Like the foot soldiers, the standard bearers of the enemy lancers were carrying red banners sporting golden eagles. These men were the lesser nobles of Armenia and their retainers, not as rich and powerful as the men around their king who formed his corps of cataphracts, but landowners able to raise sizeable numbers of armed horsemen nevertheless.

'Highborn, we should go.'

Klietas interrupted my musings. I tugged on Horns' reins to turn him and dug my knees into his sides to get him to gallop, my squire following, glancing back at the mounted horde pursuing us.

'They will not harm you,' I told him, 'unless you fall off your horse and they catch up with you.'

'There are many of them, highborn. They will sweep aside our foot soldiers.'

'No, Klietas, they will not.'

Horsemen cannot break through unbroken ranks of disciplined foot soldiers. But the Armenians would not use their horsemen against the Immortals and Exiles that were now parting ranks to allow our horse archers to pass through them. They would instead use their foot soldiers to batter their way through our defensive line. That line reformed as the horse archers, riding tired horses that had had no rest or fodder since the day before, withdrew to water their mounts in the river. I slid off Horns' back and handed his reins to Klietas.

'Take him to the river and water him, your horse, too.'

An impromptu council of war took place behind the Exiles, Chrestus with a face like thunder marching over to me, Kewab and Karys joining my general, the King of Gordyene speaking to a clearly concerned Motofi nearby. When they arrived, Chrestus vented his spleen.

'We have been well and truly duped. Only the Exiles are across the river and how many Immortals?'

His eyes bored into Motofi.

'Four divisions,' replied the general.

'Four thousand men, in case you are unaware of the organisation of Gordyene's army,' smiled Spartacus.

Chrestus ignored him.

'Any scorpions?' he asked Motofi.

The general shook his head. Chrestus sighed.

'So, we have half our foot soldiers on the wrong side of the river, together with all the scorpions and spare javelins.'

'We still have thousands of horsemen on this side of the river,' I said.

'Six thousand blown horse archers and two thousand mounted spearmen of Gordyene, also fatigued,' Chrestus shot back, 'plus Malik's men, who are also riding tired horses. That leaves the Vipers and King's Guard of Gordyene. A thousand fresh riders.'

'You are forgetting Prince Spadines and his three thousand Aorsi,' remarked Spartacus.

Chrestus said nothing but merely tapped the vine cane he was carrying against his leg. Always a bad sign.

I looked back across the river, to where the wagons, mules, squires, camels and rest of our foot soldiers were massed. Lucius, quite rightly, had halted any further crossings of the river and had withdrawn the army away from the river, just in case we had need to ferry soldiers back across the Araxes.

'We hold until the cataphracts and Hatra's horse archers arrive,' I said. 'We still may prevail.'

A loud cacophony of drums and trumpets signalled the start of the Armenian attack and Chrestus and Motofi departed in haste, Spartacus indicating to the lingering Shamshir he needed his horse.

'Shamash be with you,' I said to him.

My nephew looked around, smirking.

'Shamash? Is an ally, one who has brought more men to reinforce our position?'

'You know he is not.'

'Then I have no use for him.'

His blasphemy was something to behold and I prayed the Sun God would not punish him for his insolence. He vaulted into the saddle, Shamshir handing him his reins.

'You spend too much time praying to man-made idols, uncle. Battles are won and lost by men, not gods, and I do not intend to lose this one.'

With that he was gone, riding over to where his Immortals were arrayed in two lines to the left of the Exiles, also deployed in two lines. Behind the Immortals stood the Vipers and King's Guard, and to the rear of them Spadines and his raiders, many lolling around on the grass with seemingly not a care in the world. As if reading my thoughts, Kewab voiced his opinion, and mine.

'A great pity we cannot swap the Sarmatians for the Durans, majesty.'

'Indeed. Do you think we can hold them?'

He scanned the half-mile gap protected by the Immortals and Exiles, glancing at the horsemen behind our foot soldiers.

'It will be close. We are deprived of the luxury of manoeuvre, so will have to withstand their assaults until the queen and King Gafarn and Queen Diana arrive. But with Montu's help we will overcome.'

'Montu?'

'The Egyptian God of War, majesty, whose name originally derived from the term for a nomad, which I became until Dura offered me a home.'

'Egypt's loss is Dura's gain,' I told him. 'May your god go with you.'

'They will soften us up first,' he said, gaining the saddle of his horse held by one of his officers, 'and you have no shield to take cover under, majesty.'

I raised a hand in acknowledgement as he trotted back to his own men now withdrawing back to the river, some half a mile distant and well out of range of enemy slingshots and arrows. I began to follow them when I heard the cracks of slingshots hitting shields and the dull thuds of arrows doing likewise. I increased my pace, pain shooting through my leg, forcing me to hobble.

'Get on this horse, old man.'

I turned left to see a grinning Malik holding a spare mount.

'Do you want me to assist you into the saddle?'

'I'm quite capable, thank you.'

I hoisted myself up with difficulty and he tossed me the reins. An arrow thudded into the ground a few yards away. Malik urged his horse forward; I did the same.

'These Armenians cannot shoot straight,' he grinned, enjoying the possibility of our imminent slaughter immensely.

But he was wrong. The Armenians could shoot well enough and they were bringing the full weight of their slingers and archers to bear on our battle line. That line comprised five thousand Exiles in two lines, the first made of six cohorts, the second four cohorts, and to their left four thousand Immortals in two lines, both lines comprising two divisions. All the divisions and cohorts – covering a space half a mile in width – were now in *testudo* formation: all soldiers were kneeling, the first rank forming a shield wall, the second and third ranks lifting their shields to form a forward-sloping roof, and the subsequent ranks holding their shields horizontally above their heads. In this way, the Armenian arrows and slingshots struck leather and wood instead of flesh and bone. But while the cohorts and divisions were battered by the missile storm, the Armenians tasked with breaking through our battle line deployed into formation.

A giant wedge took shape in the centre of the Armenian battle line, composed of the élite soldiers of Artaxias' army: heavy spearmen and heavy swordsmen. The latter, all professionals, wore mail armour, helmets and carried oval shields faced with bronze. Armed with two spears, their primary weapon was a long sword that they used to attack the enemy after they had thrown their spears. A mixture of mail and scale armour protected the heavy spearmen, and all wore helmets. They carried round shields and long spears and were trained to fight in close order. If their spears broke or got stuck in an enemy, they used their short swords in the mêlée.

Either side of the wedge were blocks of light spearmen: soldiers wearing no armour or helmets and carrying only a wicker shield. Nevertheless, every man was equipped with a heavy war axe and three javelins that they hurled before attacking. The flanks of the Armenian line comprised levy spearmen: civilians impressed into service and armed only with a spear and a knife, though a few may have had swords. Their wicker shields offered poor protection against the *gladius* carried by the foot soldiers of Dura and Gordyene, but their purpose was to keep the soldiers they faced fixed in the same place, thereby preventing either Motofi or Chrestus from reinforcing the spot the Armenian wedge would strike.

Having retrieved Horns from Klietas, I sat in the saddle alongside Malik and Spartacus, behind us his King's Guard and Vipers, and waited for the tell-tale sounds that signalled men were locked in mortal combat.

'They will never break our line,' said Spartacus.

He was right; they did not. But when the war cries of thousands of men and a horrible rasping sound reverberated through the air, my stomach turned over. The grinding noise was focused in the middle of our battle line, meaning the Armenians had thrown all the momentum of their attack against that one spot. The subsequent incessant clicking sound filling our ears was the cut-and-thrust of close-quarter combat: spears being thrust forward, javelins impacting on shields and bodies, and the hacking and stabbing of swords.

Normally, once the enemy's slingers and archers had finished their work there would be a lull, akin to a pause for breath, before the foe attacked. This gave the foot soldiers of Dura and Gordyene time to break free of their *testudo* formations and organise their ranks before unleashing a javelin storm against the onrushing enemy. As they were trained to do, the legionaries and Immortals would not wait to be assaulted while stationary, but would rather advance to meet the enemy, the rear ranks hurling their javelins to slow down or stop the foe. And if given the opportunity, the scorpion crews would shoot one or two volleys for added effect. But today there were no scorpions and the Armenians threw thousands of men against just one spot in our battle line: where the Immortals ended, and the Exiles began. Their light and levy spearmen also launched a frontal assault, but the weight of Armenian arrows and slingshots was brought to bear in support of the huge wedge that now fractured our battle line.

'This does not augur well.'

Kewab put into words what we were all thinking as we saw red enemy banners appear as the Immortals on the left and Exiles on the right give way. They did not break or run away, but the Armenian wedge forced battalions and centuries to face right and left respectively, to prevent the enemy infiltrating between the first and second lines of our battle formation. This meant the tip of the wedge forced its way through the Immortals and Durans, who were still battling to their front against a numerically superior foe. But the deluge of missiles – arrows, spears and slingshots – combined with the number of enemy soldiers thrown against one point in the line, had prised the two sections of our battle line apart.

Spartacus curled his lip.

'Shamshir, the King's Guard and Vipers will advance to plug that gap.'

The sinister commander of his bodyguard saluted and turned his horse to canter to the thousand riders waiting patiently in the sun.

Spartacus turned his attention to Malik.

'I would welcome your assistance, brother.'

'And you shall have it,' grinned the Agraci king.

'Karys, Kewab,' I said, 'bring your horse archers forward. We will support the King of Gordyene.'

The breach in our battle line was widening and time was of the essence. Spartacus was already at the head of his King's Guard, and ahead of him the Vipers were ready to unleash volleys of arrows against the Armenian wedge that was now slowly turning into a column as more and more soldiers were fed into the gap. Gordyene's medium horseman were cantering behind the King's Guard, ready to skewer the enemy foot soldiers with their lances, but only if the enemy broke.

I heard a loud, continuous hissing noise as the Vipers began to shoot at the enemy, columns of female riders unleashing arrows against the enemy column. Then the King's Guard slammed into the Armenians, Spartacus' men armed with ukku blades slashing down at spearmen in close order forming an impenetrable wall of shields and spear points. They achieved very little. The Agraci were similarly frustrated as they tried and also failed to hack their way into the Armenian mass. But at least they had halted the enemy column, which appeared to be a minimum of two hundred paces wide. And then saddles were emptied as foot archers within the Armenian column began shooting at the horsemen lapping around the edges of their formation.

Spartacus and Malik immediately pulled back their troops, which became literally sitting targets for the enemy as they hacked with their swords and jabbed with their lances against the heavy spearmen, to little avail.

When the medium horsemen, Agraci, King's Guard and Vipers withdrew, I led six thousand horse archers forward to form a semi-circle around the Armenian column. Both horses and men were tired but if the Armenians were allowed to extend and widen their column they would reach the river to condemn us to defeat. So once more companies formed into columns and attacked the enemy. But the limited space within the bridgehead meant only around ten companies at a time could attack the Armenians, who continued to shoot back with arrows and now slingshots.

I aimed my arrow at one of the shields bearing a tree of life symbol, released the bowstring and turned Horns sharply right, plucking an arrow from my quiver, nocking it in the bowstring, twisting left in the saddle and shooting the missile. Behind me Klietas also shot his arrow before following me right and then right again to gallop back to the rear of the company. On the way back, I saw a horse archer shout and clutch his face, an arrow lodged in his eye socket, before tumbling from the saddle. The air was thick with missiles. More and more enemy arrows were now being shot at us; an indication the enemy commander was feeding more and more missile troops into the column. I glanced back to see our own arrows had made no discernible impact on the enemy.

At least the Armenians had halted, which was something, but when I took up my position at the rear of the column to begin the attack process again, I noticed an increasing number of our own horse archers dead on the ground and horses without riders milling around, some with arrows stuck in them.

'You are with me,' I said to Klietas, turning Horns to direct him towards a small red griffin banner denoting the presence of Sporaces.

When I reached him, he was issuing orders to his officers to pull the horse archers back out of range of the Armenian column. He saw me and for a split-second appeared hesitant.

'I was going to suggest the same thing,' I reassured him.

'The Armenian commander knows what he is doing, majesty.'

'With no ground to manoeuvre on we are hamstrung.'

He pointed to the flanks where both the Immortals and Exiles were slowly giving ground, maintaining their formation and discipline while being assaulted on their front and flanks.

'We may have to withdraw back across the river, majesty.'

'There is still time, Sporaces. In the meantime, deploy your men for long-range shooting. We don't want that enemy column splitting into two with each part wheeling left and right to surround the Immortals and Exiles.'

Sporaces nodded his head towards the loitering Sarmatians lining the riverbank, seemingly without a care in the world.

'What about them, majesty?'

'Hopefully, if we are forced to withdraw, many of them will drown in the river. Every cloud has a silver lining, as the saying goes.'

Kewab and Karys, veterans that they were, had also recognised the futility of getting too close to foot soldiers that had been reinforced with missile troops, and they also ordered their men to fall back and shoot at long range, though as our backs were almost against the river, 'medium range' would have been a more appropriate term. From a range of over three hundred paces we shot at the enemy column, aiming our arrows high into the sky so they would drop vertically on the Armenians, hopefully striking slingers and archers who carried no shields, wore no armour and were mostly devoid of helmets.

An irate Spartacus and his equally angry sons galloped over, behind them a huge red banner emblazoned with a silver lion. The King of Gordyene pulled up his horse.

'Why did you order your horse archers to withdraw?'

'The same reason you pulled back your own horsemen, nephew,' I said slowly, slipping my bow back into its leather case fixed to my saddle.

I pointed at the now stationary Armenian column that jutted forward in the centre of what had been our line, around it a semi-circle of horse archers taking leisurely shots at it. Their rate of shooting was deliberately slow to conserve their limited ammunition.

'The Armenians have placed slingers and archers within their column, therefore it makes sense to withdraw and shoot arrows on a high trajectory into the column.'

'In the hope they withdraw?' scoffed Castus.

'That is correct, young prince,' I shot back, 'for our efforts are merely secondary.'

'To what?' demanded Haytham beside him.

The ground beneath us suddenly began to tremble and an ominous rumble filled our ears. I smiled at Prince Haytham.

'To that.'

Spartacus cracked a wry smile. 'Luck is with you, uncle.'

'The gods are with us,' I corrected him.

He turned his horse to ride away.

'They are mere fantasies, uncle, whereas cataphracts are real.'

Two and a half thousand cataphracts – big men wearing scale and tubular armour riding big horses with iron-shod hooves, smashed into the left wing of the Armenian army, supported by fifteen thousand Hatran horse archers. The still-battling Exiles on our right flank and beyond them Armenian foot soldiers in front of Artaxias' horsemen blocked our view of what must have been a magnificent spectacle. But the results soon became evident.

The Armenian column of foot soldiers began to withdraw, spearmen in the front ranks shuffling back and maintaining their unbroken shield wall. But no arrows came from behind the red-uniformed wall tipped with glinting spear points.

'Help them on their way,' I said to Sporaces, my spirits lifted by the sounds of battle erupting on the right where Gallia, Gafarn and Diana were hopefully mauling the Armenians.

Moments later, Dura's horse archers were once again riding forward in company-sized columns to shoot at the retreating foe. Karys and Kewab also sent their men forward, though unfortunately their low ammunition stocks resulted in their volleys being sporadic at best. Spartacus led his King's Guard forward once more, but the discipline of the Armenians was impeccable and for a second time the ukku blades of Gordyene's finest enjoyed only meagre pickings.

One by one the companies of horse archers ceased shooting as their quivers emptied, wheeling away to fall back to the river where Spadines and his Aorsi bandits finally gained their saddles.

'A great victory, highborn,' smiled Klietas, who still had most of his arrows left.

'A great escape, more like.'

I nudged Horns forward and he broke into a canter, heading for the rear cohorts of the Exiles. The colour party guarding their silver lion still held their javelins. The signaller sounded his trumpet to indicate the approach of a senior officer, all two hundred men snapping to attention. I raised my hand in salute as I passed and halted Horns a few paces from where a medical orderly was bandaging the arm of a wounded legionary. In front of him tired men had rested their shields on the ground, all of them without javelins but still holding *gladius* blades in their hands. The nearest centurion spotted me sliding from my horse.

'Stay here, I will return shortly,' I told Klietas.

'Stand to attention, the king approaches.'

'As you were, rest easy,' I commanded.

The centurion, his face beaded with sweat, saluted smartly.

'Hard fight?'

'I've known harder, majesty,' he said without emotion.

The damaged white crest atop his helmet told a different story but I smiled and walked on, passing the second-line cohorts that had obviously been in the frontline before being relieved, and on to those standing directly opposite the enemy, though the lack of screams and battle cries indicated all fighting had now ceased. I caught sight of Chrestus standing behind a cohort circled by a group of officers and walked over, a sharp pain shooting through my leg causing me to stumble and fall.

'The king is injured.'

An eagle-eyed legionary had spotted my fall and within seconds had rushed over to assist me, followed by what appeared to be a small army that closed in on me, each member shouting 'the king is wounded'.

'Make way,' I was relieved to hear Chrestus' voice, the general grabbing my arm as I hoisted myself up with difficulty. He looked me up and down and saw no wound or blood.

'The old leg wound, majesty?'

'The old leg wound,' I confirmed.

'Back to your positions,' he bellowed, 'the king is fine.'

'Want to see our handiwork?' he grinned.

'Of course.'

'Want a walking stick?'

'I think I can walk a few yards.'

He escorted me to where the battle had been fiercest, where the Armenians had launched a frontal assault against the Exiles, all around me tired men raising their swords and cheering when they spotted me. I drew my *spatha* and saluted them in turn, stopping when I saw the ground carpeted with dead men, hundreds of them. Men who had been stabbed with *gladius* blades, their tunics heavily stained with blood, their faces moulded into grotesque shapes by multiple sword cuts.

'Not a good idea to throw men wearing no armour or helmets with wicker shields and armed only with a spear against the Exiles.'

'Farmers and townsmen,' I told him, 'who always suffer the most in war.'

A loud cheer went up and I turned to accept the accolade. But they were not cheering me but a group of riders approaching from the right, their horses carefully threading their way through the carpet of dead. I heaved a sigh of relief when I saw Gallia and Zenobia, the latter holding my griffin banner, alongside Gafarn and Diana, a red banner showing a white horse behind them. Also with them were the Amazons and at least two companies of Hatra's Royal Bodyguard.

I walked forward to greet Gallia, my wife removing her helmet and bending down so we could kiss, prompting whoops and whistles from the legionaries behind us. I also kissed Diana and shook Gafarn's hand.

'You are a sight for sore eyes,' I told them.

'The river crossing took longer than anticipated,' said Gallia, 'but once across the Armenians had no answer to our strength.'

'Azad, Herneus and Orobaz are currently dancing with the enemy,' Gafarn told me.

'How is Spartacus?' asked a concerned Diana.

'Like a wolf deprived of his prey,' I answered. 'He was hoping to slaughter the entire Armenian army in this river bend, but his hopes have been dashed.'

'The Armenians are retreating in good order,' said Gafarn, looking around at the horror, 'what is left of them.'

'We will be before the walls of Artaxata within two days,' I said, 'and once King Artaxias has agreed to pay reparations, we will be back home within a month.'

There was a rumble of thunder overhead and we all looked up to see the sky was suddenly full of grey clouds. But had I realised what the immediate future held, I would have known it was not thunder but the mocking laughter of the gods.

Chapter 9

Spadines and his bandits finally roused themselves to pursue the Armenians once they began to fall back north towards their capital. Azad used Dura's cataphracts to shield our own army, over half of which had yet to cross over the Araxes. Herneus assigned Hatra's cataphracts to Azad to fulfil the same function, leaving Orobaz to lead Hatra's horse archers against the Armenians, though with orders not to pursue too far lest they were ambushed by fresh enemy forces. We had given the foe a bloody nose but Artaxias' army was far from finished, though whether he would offer another battle before we reached his capital remained to be seen.

It was just past midday when the Armenians commenced their withdrawal, which meant the army had eight hours of daylight in which to cross over the river, evacuate the battlefield and find a place to camp. Lucius, who had prevented any forces from crossing over to the northern side of the river while the battle was going on, including an incensed Kalet and his lords, selected a place two miles upstream of the river bend, which would ensure a supply of fresh water untainted by dead bodies, while also being close to the river should we be forced to withdraw over the Araxes if the Armenians returned in strength. Spartacus derided the notion.

'There is no Armenian strength,' he boasted. 'We beat them today with half our army.'

We sat on blown horses while behind us thousands of Immortals and legionaries, thousands of camels and mules, thousands of horsemen, and dozens of wagons navigated their way across the Araxes and then headed west to the camp being established by our engineers.

'We mauled the Armenians, son,' said Gafarn, 'I will grant you that. But they are far from beaten.'

The King of Gordyene looked around at the enemy dead.

'I estimate there are perhaps ten thousand enemy dead on this ground. What are our own losses?'

'What I have garnered thus far, majesty,' said Lucius, 'is that our own losses number around two thousand, including wounded.'

'Tomorrow, we must conduct a forced march to reach Artaxata,' demanded Spartacus, 'there to lay siege to a city that will be filled with enemy soldiers as well as the population.'

'There will be no storm,' I emphasised. 'We are here solely to exact reparations from the Armenians and deter them from launching any more wars against Gordyene and Media.'

'Levelling Artaxata will do that,' smirked Spartacus.

'We are not butchering innocent civilians,' Diana reprimanded him.

Lucius' concern was of a more immediate nature.

'If I were King Artaxias, I would send my army away from the city while I defended it. In this way, he would know there is a relief force being organised, which would force us to dilute our own forces to guard against such a relief.'

'Artaxias is a weak figure, Roman,' said Spartacus, 'with little talent for war.'

'The enemy's battle plan today would suggest otherwise,' I opined.

Spartacus sighed with annoyance.

'The commander of the Armenian army is a man called Geghard, who has more backbone than his king, I'll grant you.'

He looked at Gallia. 'You might be interested to know, aunt, that Geghard is the father of Lusin, now Queen of Media, who arranged for his daughter to marry Nabu Egibi before my son stole her away.'

His words elicited the response he desired.

'This Geghard deserves to be punished,' growled Gallia.

'Regrettable though the arranged marriage between Lusin and Nabu Egibi was,' I said, 'which never took place anyway, it is irrelevant to the current situation.'

But Gallia's blood was up. 'Irrelevant? How would you feel if one of your daughters was sold into slavery? This Geghard needs to be taught a lesson.'

'He will, aunt, that I promise,' said a smug Spartacus.

'I'm sure we would all feel better able to make rational decisions after a good night's sleep,' interrupted Gafarn. 'I know I would.'

'Me, too.'

Everyone turned to look at Klietas who had uttered the words. He blushed with embarrassment as Spartacus and Gallia glowered at him and Gafarn gave him a bemused look.

'My squire echoes my own thoughts,' I said.

I sent Talib north with his men to scout the terrain and shadow the retreating Armenian army, ignoring Spartacus' dubious claim that Spadines would provide timely and accurate intelligence regarding the enemy.

Parties of Immortals and Durans were tasked with the grisly duty of collecting our own dead for cremation, the fuel to do so being provided by the thousands of wicker shields left on the battlefield by the Armenians. Enemy dead would be left to rot, their corpses picked clean by the flocks of ravens that would descend on the area once human activity had ceased. At least a couple of miles away we would be spared their grating croaks as they feasted on dead flesh.

Only when the army and its civilian servants were safely in camp could I finally relax. After a change of clothes and a meal my limbs and eyelids felt like lead and I had to lie down to sleep. Younger men can do without sleep for a night and a day but I was no longer a young buck. Neither did Gallia have unlimited reserves of energy, though she was loath to admit it. She joined me in our cot, though she insisted she did so only to provide me with body warmth after my immersion in the Araxes the previous night. When I reminded her that she too had carried out a river crossing, she put a finger to my lips and told me to get some sleep. I needed no second prompting but after what seemed to be less than a minute of blissful slumber, I was woken by the sound of Azad's voice.

'The king and queen are resting,' I heard Klietas say.

Azad muttered something under his breath I could not hear.

'Can I offer you some wine, general?' asked Klietas.

I raised myself up, swung my legs off the cot and stood, shaking my head to clear the drowsiness. I walked into the reception area of the tent and Azad bowed his head.

'How long have I been asleep?' I asked Klietas.

'Two hours, highborn.'

'That long?'

I walked over to a bronze bowl on a stand, filled it with water and washed my face, Klietas handing me a towel.

'How can I help you, general?'

Klietas filled two cups with wine, handed me one and the other to Azad. We toasted each other.

'I thank the gods we are alive and still have all our body parts.'

Azad beamed. 'As one gets older, that becomes more and more important. I have someone who might be of interest to you?'

I gestured for him to take a seat and sat myself down.

'When we hit their left flank, the Armenians sent in their cataphracts to support their foot soldiers. But their foot soldiers, just farmers, really, panicked, turned tail and ran straight into their own horsemen. We took advantage of the ensuing chaos to inflict many casualties. We also took some prisoners.'

My interest was pricked. 'Oh?'

'One of them was a lord called Vahan.'

The name meant nothing to me.

'He is the son of General Geghard, commander of the Armenian army, majesty, and he is very free with his tongue. He has some interesting information you should hear.'

How strange is fate and the lives of men, which are entwined like the strands of a rope, one woven by the hands of the gods. Some would dismiss the capture of the son of Geghard as a mere coincidence, with nothing to do with the gods or destiny. But I believed the immortals to be at work when the young man with a heavy brow and black hair and beard was brought before us later, Gallia having roused from her slumbers, washed and changed her clothes. He was tall and handsome in a sort of intimidating manner, with broad shoulders and a slightly haughty manner, even in captivity. I offered him a seat and commanded Klietas to serve him wine in an attempt to put him at ease. Azad stood behind him and Chrestus, whom I had invited to attend, stood next to my commander of cataphracts.

'I assume you will be handing me over to King Spartacus,' he said in Greek, his eyes studying Gallia's face and hair.

'Why would you assume that?' I asked.

Vahan sipped at his wine, his eyes registering surprise when he discovered it was not vinegar.

'We have fine wines in Parthia,' Gallia told him, 'and we are not barbarians. We certainly do not prostitute our own daughters in Parthia.'

'Not now,' I said softly to her.

She ignored me. 'Tell me, Vahan, how much was your father paid to marry his daughter to Nabu Egibi?'

He was shamefaced, staring into his wine.

'I did not hold with that decision,' he muttered.

'And yet last year you and your father invaded Media in an attempt to kill its king and queen, after first allowing the traitor Atrax to march through Armenia.'

He looked up. 'I know nothing of the agreement made between our king and Lord Atrax.'

'How convenient,' she sneered.

'But we did not purposely invade Media.'

'You just happened to find yourself there?' I said. 'Perhaps you took a wrong turn on a track and went south instead of north.'

Chrestus and Azad smiled and even Gallia smirked.

'We were pursuing the army of Gordyene,' Vahan told me, 'which had been plundering my homeland but then suddenly turned back south and crossed the Araxes into Media. We followed.'

'You will have to do better than that, Vahan,' I told him. 'I remember the battle on the Diyana Plain where your king's army and that of the rebel Atrax combined to give battle to your brother-in-law.'

'It is the truth,' he insisted in a raised voice.

'Watch yourself, boy,' growled Chrestus, placing a hand on the Armenian's shoulder.

'She is well, by the way,' said Gallia, 'your sister, I mean. She is a fine queen and her people love her.'

'And is soon to be a mother,' I added.

Vahan's eyes lit up. 'Lusin is pregnant?'

'Her son will make a fine future King of Media,' I said. 'But enough small talk. What information do you have that I might be interested in?'

He took a long sip of wine.

'Parthia has invaded Armenia because of a lie,' he told me.

'We invaded your land because your army was mustering to launch a fresh invasion of Media,' I corrected him. 'Do you deny your army was being assembled?'

'No, majesty,' he said. 'But the reason was not to invade Media but to launch a campaign against the Aorsi, to finally rid Armenia of their murdering and plundering.'

'What has that to do with Media?' said Gallia.

'Nothing, majesty,' answered Vahan. 'That is why my king did not take the bait.'

I looked at Gallia in confusion and then at Azad, who spoke to Vahan.

'Tell King Pacorus. He will not think ill of you for speaking the truth.'

'What truth?' I asked.

Vahan emptied his cup. 'The King of Gordyene thought he could deceive us by sending his Sarmatian allies into Armenia wearing the uniforms of the soldiers of Media, thus provoking my king into launching an invasion of that kingdom.'

'What nonsense is this?' snapped Gallia.

'Not nonsense, majesty,' he insisted. 'For years the Aorsi have tormented my people, burning villages, killing civilians and carrying off the young and women to sell as slaves. You think horsemen wearing blue tunics, grey leggings and carrying dragon banners would be mistaken for Media's soldiers? Men who used the same tactics, carried out the same atrocities and spoke the same language as the Aorsi?'

'We have only your word for that,' said Gallia.

But I knew he was speaking the truth. I knew the Aorsi had, with the blessing of Spartacus, used Armenia as their plaything for years, and their bandit leader had even been given the Armenian city of Van to abuse, before he and his bandits had been evicted by the Armenians.

'I will speak with the King of Gordyene on this matter,' I said.

'I ask for a noble's death, majesty,' he pleaded, 'rather than a lowly end at the hands of the Sarmatians, for that will surely be my fate if you hand me over to King Spartacus.'

I nodded to Klietas to refill Vahan's cup.

'You will not be staying with us, it is true,' I said, 'but nor will you be handed over to King Spartacus. In the morning, you will be riding south with an escort to Irbil, to be entertained by your sister and brother-in-law until such time as a ransom for your return to Armenia can be arranged and paid.'

'You will find much to interest you in the city,' Gallia told him, 'not least its strengthened defences, which you can report to King Artaxias when you see him again.'

A mixture of surprise and relief spread across Vahan's face and he enjoyed his second cup of wine more than the first. In the now more relaxed atmosphere, I probed him concerning the fortifications of Artaxata and the remaining strength of the Armenian army. He was cagey about the latter but effusive regarding the former, being clearly in awe of a city that was relatively new, having been founded only one hundred and fifty years ago. After more than an hour of conversation, I indicated to Azad that Vahan should be returned to his quarters.

'In the morning, send him south with a party of mounted wounded,' I told Azad. 'Impress upon the commander that he should be watched closely at all times. If he proves difficult, have him bound. Get him to Irbil. I will pen a note for the party's commander to present to King Akmon.'

'Or you could just hand him over to King Spartacus, majesty.'

'I have never sanctioned the killing of prisoners, Azad, and I do not intend to start now.'

The 'walking wounded' were soldiers who had suffered sprained wrists or ankles, or incurred cuts that were not life-threatening but which would exclude them from military duties in the short term. Any head wounds tended to exclude men from the ranks for long periods, so those suffering them left the army if circumstances permitted. Fortunately, we were next to the Araxes, on the other side of which was Gordyene, so those wounded in the battle could be speedily evacuated to Vanadzor. The party of injured horse archers escorting Vahan, however, would ride south to skirt the eastern shore of Lake Urmia and then head for Irbil.

Afterwards, sitting alone with Gallia as the oil lamps flickered in our tent, I wondered if I should take Dura's army home.

'Vahan spoke the truth,' I stated bluntly.

She did not disagree.

'I do not blame him, Spartacus, I mean. The Armenians supported Atrax and were complicit in the death of Rasha.'

'That does not excuse him from luring us here on false pretences, to say nothing of the dead we have incurred after his deception.'

Gallia's face was a pale yellow in the half-light, her hair appearing white.

'What are your intentions?'

'My initial thought was to leave for Dura tomorrow,' I replied. 'However, to do so would mean abandoning both Spartacus and Gafarn and Diana in enemy territory, which I am not prepared to do. And we only have friend Vahan's word that Spartacus has deceived us.'

'Though you are convinced he spoke the truth.'

'Yes, I am.'

She looked at me expectantly. 'So?'

'So, I intend to pull the rug out from beneath my nephew's feet.'

'What does that mean?'

I stood, cupped her face and kissed her on the cheek.

'You will see, my love.'

The next day Spartacus was deliriously happy, smiling to all and sundry, whistling to himself, handing out compliments and generally being far removed from the snarling, menacing figure that had cast a black shadow over Armenia for many years. The cause of his happiness was the return of Spadines, who reported he, his men and women had raided far and wide, up to the walls of Artaxata itself. The Armenian army had withdrawn into the city after a forced march covered by its horsemen, but not before hundreds of its more poorly trained soldiers had drifted away from the colours, to be butchered by the Sarmatians. Like the wolves they were, the Aorsi had hovered around the retreating Armenians, ready to pounce on the lost, wounded and vulnerable.

'We killed many, lord,' he boasted as we conducted a leisurely march from the Araxes towards the Armenian capital. 'The enemy has withdrawn into the city where they wait for the siege engines of Dura.'

As much as I loathed Spadines, he had carried out a near-perfect harassing exercise, picking off enemy stragglers to weaken and demoralise the enemy.

'The Armenians have been debilitated by two defeats,' said a contented Spartacus. 'They lost thousands of men last year on the Diyana Plain and now they have suffered fresh losses. Artaxias will not offer another battle; he will ask for terms.'

'This campaign will be over before the month is out,' said Gafarn. He looked at his son. 'What are your terms, by the way?'

'I have three demands,' he answered instantly. 'First, a pledge from Artaxias that he will no longer wage war against Gordyene or Media. Second, an indemnity of five thousand talents of gold shall be paid to the treasury in Vanadzor for the costs incurred during this year's campaign and last year's. Third, Artaxias will immediately surrender Atrax and Titus Tullus so that summary justice can be served on them.'

Castus behind his father smiled at Haytham, the former tapping the hilt of his sword. I assumed this meant their father had promised them they could cut off the heads of those responsible for their mother's death, indirectly at least.

'Atrax and Titus Tullus are not in Armenia,' I told Spartacus.

'And you know this how?' he demanded.

'Phraates informed me in a conversation we had at Irbil. They have fled to Pontus where I assume they currently reside, along with Tiridates.'

'They will pay, you have my word,' said Gallia. 'Nothing is ever forgotten.'

Spartacus smiled at her. 'There is plenty of time, aunt. In the meantime, I will raise the indemnity the Armenians will have to pay to ten thousand talents of gold.'

It was a staggering sum, the equivalent of three hundred tons of gold.

'Do the Armenians possess such a sum?' asked Diana.

'Their temples are full of gold,' answered her son.

Gafarn looked at Haytham. 'Remember what happened last time you plundered an Armenian temple, son. I would not wish any more harm to be visited on your family.'

'I will not be plundering any temples, father,' he assured Gafarn. 'It will be up to the Armenians to source the gold.'

'And if they do not?' I asked.

'Then my horsemen will support my Aorsi allies in their on-going dispute with the Armenians.'

I was going to enquire what 'on-going dispute' he was alluding to but realised it would be futile. The Aorsi raided Armenia and the King of Gordyene was more than happy to sanction their depredations. But I was far from happy.

'You will need to offer the Armenians something in return,' I said.

'Why?' came the retort.

'Because, Spartacus, you will create a festering resentment that will condemn you and your kingdom to unending war with the Armenians if you do not.'

'Pacorus has a point, son,' said Gafarn.

Spartacus sighed loudly. 'What offer would you suggest, uncle?'

'Peace,' I answered. 'In return for a pledge of non-aggression and ten thousand talents of gold, you promise that neither you nor the Aorsi will raid Armenia or seize Armenian territory or those living in it.'

Spadines was indignant and went to object, but Spartacus raised a hand to still him.

'I will think on it, uncle.'

We left the river to enter the beautiful Ararat Plain, dominated by the volcano Mount Ararat, the top third of which was always covered with snow and ice. But the plain itself was a place of abundance, filled with forests of oak and pine and dotted with many villages. Because this part of Armenia was far from the sea and of a high altitude, spring and summer temperatures were mild, though winters, as in nearby northern Gordyene that shared the same elevation, were long and harsh. But the absence of blisteringly hot summer temperatures and an abundance of rain, meant the ground was fertile, villagers cultivating almonds, figs, apricots, wheat, cherries and hazelnuts, as well as keeping goats and sheep as livestock. Not that we saw any as we headed for the Armenian capital, villages being deserted of both people and animals.

Lucius sent his engineers with parties of Talib's men to scout the area for supplies of wood that would be needed to establish siege lines around Artaxata, now visible in the distance, especially the promontory of Khor Virap, upon which the city's palace, temples and homes of the nobles had been constructed. Lucius' enquiring mind found Mount Ararat fascinating, though we just regarded it as another snow-capped mountain.

'You may be interested to know, majesty,' he said, 'that Mount Ararat is the place the Jews believe the huge ark landed during the great flood. That is what Aaron told me. He would love to see the mountain, I'm sure.'

'What great flood?' asked Spartacus.

'The Jews believe that their god made it rain for forty days and forty nights to flood the entire world, majesty.'

Castus was curious. 'Why would he do that?'

'Because the people were acting wickedly, prince,' answered Lucius. 'Only a man called Noah was listening to the Jewish god, who instructed him to build a huge ark, a boat which he would fill with a pair of all the creatures of the earth, one male, one female, as well as his own family.'

'Childish stories,' scoffed Spartacus.

Castus ignored his father. 'And did this Noah collect all the animals, general?'

'He did, prince, with the assistance of the Jewish god who instructed the animals to make their way to the ark. When it began raining, the ark began to float and did so for seven months before it came to rest on Mount Ararat, though Noah and the animals had to remain on board for several more months until the earth dried out.'

Castus was clearly impressed by the story, gazing in wonder at the mountain, which to be fair was an impressive feature dominating the landscape. The low chuckle of Spartacus diverted his eyes away from Mount Ararat.

'These Jews, how foolish they are. The story of this great ark makes no sense.'

'In what way?' I asked.

'Simple,' replied Spartacus smugly. 'Let us take as an example just one animal. A horse. It requires ten pounds of fodder and ten pounds of grain daily, plus around eight gallons of water. Multiply these requirements by thousands, and the notion that this ark could house and feed two of every type of animal in the world is nonsensical.'

'He has a point, Pacorus,' agreed Gafarn.

'And who would shovel all the shit?' asked Spartacus, prompting raucous laughter from his sons.

'Language, Spartacus,' a stern Diana rebuked him.

'How many people aboard this ark?' he asked Lucius.

'Er, well, I believe there was Noah, his wife, three sons and their wives, majesty,' replied Lucius.

'Eight people? To muck out thousands of animals? The Jews are even more deluded than I thought.'

'But you forget one thing, Spartacus,' I said.

'Oh?'

'This Noah had the aid of a god, who presumably provided the food, water and other things needed to stay alive aboard a boat for months.'

Spartacus rolled his eyes. 'The universal answer to all the nonsensical myths and fables in the world, which all happened thousands of years ago. Interesting that. We never see the handiwork of the gods on an everyday basis.'

I glanced at Gallia who gave me a mere hint of a smile.

Spartacus pointed at the mountain. 'Is it still there, general, the ark, I mean?'

'I do not know, majesty, the tale of Noah is thousands of years old.'

Spartacus laughed mockingly. 'So, it would have rotted away thousands of years ago. How convenient.'

He seemed to have forgotten about the legend of Gordis and how it had nearly cost the life of one of his sons. But Spartacus had always been more concerned with the here and now, though I often wondered if being raised in Hatra, a city and kingdom where the gods were treated with great respect and honoured daily, had cultivated his resentment against all things religious. That and the fact Gordyene, always been a wild, godless place devoid of grand temples and armies of male and female priests, had encouraged his disdain for religion.

'Tell me, general,' said Spartacus, 'how do you intend to deal with the formidable defences of Artaxata?'

'That is for my king to decide, majesty,' replied Lucius.

'It is your plan, Lucius,' I said, 'so there is no point in me taking the credit. Tell my nephew your intentions.'

'The intelligence I have collected on Artaxata reveals a city with stout stone walls and a moat surrounding it. It has paved streets, public buildings, baths, shops and many workshops. It is also filled with many fine bronze statues of Greek gods.'

'It will be a hard nut to crack,' agreed Spartacus.

'I do not intend to crack the nut, majesty,' said Lucius, 'more roast it.'

'Explain,' snapped Spartacus, not appreciating the Roman's witty retort.

'We must assume the Armenian king has sent his horsemen to the north to rally fresh forces,' opined Lucius, 'or at the very least saved the city granaries from having to feed thousands of horsemen and their horses with a siege imminent. But we have forty thousand horsemen to both reconnoitre far and wide to warn of the approach of any relief force. Not that it will make any difference.'

'How so?' asked Gafarn.

'Because King Artaxias will have asked for terms long before a relief army can be organised, majesty,' said Lucius. 'Our siege engines will see to that.'

'It takes time to batter down a city's walls, Roman,' said Spartacus, 'and these walls are thick and high.'

'I do not intend to batter down the walls, majesty, more shoot over them. King Artaxias has by all accounts a beautiful city. He will not wish to see it burn. Our siege engines will shoot over the walls to bring Artaxias to the negotiating table.'

'Shoot what?' asked Castus.

'You would call it "dragon fire", prince,' smiled Lucius.

It had been many years since Dura's siege engines had been used in anger, but the army's engineers had not been idle when it came to developing more effective ammunition for when they were employed. The most potent machines were six giant ballista, each one weighing several tons, three times the height of a man and around thirty feet in length. They worked like a bow, with a strong wooden frame holding two skeins of animal sinew in place vertically. Two horizontal wooden arms pass through each skein and are linked by a strong bowstring. As the arms are pulled back the sinews become twisted to create great tension for propelling a missile forward, the latter resting in a groove in the horizontal stock of the ballista. The bowstring is pulled back using winches and held in place by a rotating trigger. There was also a score of smaller ballistae, which could throw a metal-headed bolt, solid metal balls and stones over great distances. Worked by two-man teams, they were essentially scorpions but were employed exclusively by Lucius' men.

His corps of engineers did not drag large stones from Dura. There was no need – the same quarries that had been used to build Artaxata would provide ammunition should it be needed. But they did bring along metal balls that were shot by the smaller ballistae to decapitate enemy soldiers standing on the walls – small victories that had a devastating mental effect on those of the garrison who witnessed them. But the ammunition wagons also contained clay pots filled with a dangerous material; so dangerous that these wagons and their drivers travelled away from the rest of the engineers and the disassembled siege engines. It was stored in a cool storeroom beneath the armoury in Dura's Citadel, where oil lamps were forbidden and candles were carried in containers with metal grilles to prevent flames spilling on the floor if dropped.

The substance in question was highly flammable and was a concoction of a number of ingredients, chief among them being the sticky, black, highly viscous liquid that was found in the southern regions of Agraci lands. In the desert could be found pools of the black liquid, which was poison to drink and which caught fire for no reason at all. The Agraci viewed it as useless and in truth no one could think why the gods had created such a substance. But Marcus Sutonius, may the gods treasure his soul, realised its flammable properties could be harnessed for siege warfare.

He employed a team of experts in noxious substances that devised Dura's equivalent of 'Dragon Fire'. They combined the black sticky substance termed bitumen with quicklime, which raised the temperature when the liquid was ignited. Sulphur was added to increase flammability and pitch sourced from trees to bind all the materials together comprised the final ingredient. Poured into clay pots, which were sealed with a pitch-soaked wick, they shattered after being shot from a ballista, spewing burning liquid in all directions. Difficult to extinguish once it stuck to surfaces, it burnt at high temperatures for long periods. It was truly a dreadful substance but it made Dura's siege engines extremely powerful weapons.

Artaxata was surrounded by green pasturelands and vineyards and the city itself looked pristine in the sunlight, its walls and towers constructed from well-dressed stone. Those walls were lined with soldiers, the sun reflecting off their burnished helmets and whetted spear points, red eagle banners flying from every tower. The drawbridges spanning the moat had all been raised and archers stood ready to repulse any assaults we mounted, the ground beyond the moat having been cleared of anything that would impede the field of view of an archer or slinger.

It took a whole morning to assemble and site the ballistae, the soldiers on the walls shooting a few arrows and slingshots in their direction but giving up once they realised the engines were beyond their range. Lucius had positioned them some three hundred and fifty yards back from the moat, which meant their crews would not be disturbed by enemy missiles.

Malik, Spadines and Kalet had grown bored by the slow proceedings, wishing to see the machines in action straight away. So they decided to explore the Ararata Plain, hoping to run into the Armenian lords and their retainers they had encountered in the battle at the river. Spartacus had his own scouts out, and Talib and his men had left camp, a mile south of the city, at dawn to search for the enemy.

'They are wasting their time,' said Spartacus, leaning on his saddle, clearly bored. 'The Armenian horsemen will have fled to the north and east, to their clan homelands, there to raise fresh forces. But it will take time to organise a new army, though at the rate your Roman is going, uncle, it will be autumn before your siege engines are in operation.'

'Patience is a virtue,' I told him.

He had arrayed his Immortals in front of the city and I had ordered Chrestus to deploy the Durans and Exiles on the other side of Artaxata. But as the day wore on there seemed little point in having thousands of men standing idle and so most had returned to camp. A thousand Durans and the same number of Immortals stood either side of the siege engines, reinforced with scorpions, just in case the Armenians tried a sally to destroy Lucius' machines. Companies of horse archers enforced a Parthian perimeter around the city to ensure no one left or got in.

'It is a beautiful city,' remarked Diana. 'I hope King Artaxias sees sense and agrees to terms.'

'He will,' I said.

'Either that or dies of old age,' quipped Spartacus.

Finally, Lucius reported that the machines were ready and did Gallia or Diana want the honour of shooting the first projectile? They both turned down the offer but Spartacus, eager to amuse himself, said he would pull the trigger. So we rode over to the first ballista, its crew bowing their heads as we dismounted to gather in a semi-circle around the end of the machine, where a team of engineers used winches to pull back the wooden throwing arms. On a nearby cart were clay pots carefully packed in crates stuffed with straw to secure them in place when the vehicle was on the move. Lucius gave the order for one to be brought over, the two men assigned to the duty having the utmost care not to drop the container. The pitch-soaked wick was only lit when the pot had been placed in the machine's slider, ready to be launched. They stepped back and Lucius turned to Spartacus.

'At your convenience, majesty.'

Spartacus looked at the pot resting against the strap fitted to the thick cord and then glanced at the city walls beyond the moat.

'You sure you've got the range right?'

'Range and elevation have been established, majesty,' said Lucius.

Spartacus released the trigger, there was a loud crack and the clay pot was propelled forwards and upwards, arching through the air over the walls to disappear behind them. Lucius raised his right arm to signal to the crew of the second machine positioned twenty-five paces away. Seconds later, its thick bowstring shot forward and the whole machine shook, another clay pot arching into the sky to land in the city. The third, fourth, fifth and sixth ballista shot their pots in turn, their crews then commencing the reloading process.

'Continue shooting for an hour,' I told Lucius, 'then we shall see if the Armenian king is willing to talk.'

As soon as the ballistae began shooting, Chrestus and Motofi moved the rest of Dura's legionaries and Gordyene's Immortals out of camp and deployed them facing the city's southern entrance; the route any force sent out to destroy the machines would take. Gafarn deployed Hatra's cataphracts and horse archers to support them – nearly forty thousand soldiers arrayed before the city walls to deter a sally.

After an hour, each ballista shooting one pot every fifteen minutes – twenty-four in total – thick black smoke began to appear from inside the city, legionaries and Immortals cheering and banging the shafts of javelins on the insides of their shields to signal their delight at the destruction being visited on the Armenian capital.

We reassembled near Lucius' engines, the banners of Dura, Hatra, Gordyene and Mesene fluttering in the refreshing northerly breeze that had picked up, the sky now filling with light grey clouds to banish the sun. The flapping of the banners was the only sound now the ballistae had ceased shooting. I turned to Chrestus.

'Send forward a herald to the walls with a message for King Artaxias that the rulers of Dura, Hatra and Gordyene wish to speak to him.

'I will go, highborn,' said Klietas.

Chrestus froze him with a stare. 'Silence, boy, no one was asking you.'

'Do you speak Greek, Klietas?' I asked.

'No, highborn.'

I pointed at the city.

'They do not speak Parthian, so we have to use a language that both sides understand. I therefore need a Greek speaker.'

'Besides,' said Gafarn, 'we don't want the king's squire being killed after so recently being appointed to such an august position.'

'Forgive me, highborn, but why would they kill a herald?'

Gafarn pointed a finger at the black smoke.

'The enemy might take exception to their city being set alight.'

'If the herald is killed, the king will burn the city to the ground,' stated Klietas with conviction.

'We might burn it to the ground anyway,' threatened Spartacus.

Chrestus sent one of his senior officers to the city walls, the officer in mail armour and white-plumed helmet carrying a bow aloft with the bowstring removed, a traditional sign he came in peace. It was considered the height of ill manners to kill a herald making such a gesture, but manners are singularly lacking in war and there was an even chance he would be felled by one or more arrows when he rode within range of the walls. We all held our breath as his horse plodded forward, reaching the edge of the moat, many bows trained on him. We could not hear what he shouted up at the walls but the fact he remained in his saddle as he apparently conversed with someone on the battlements was a good sign. After what seemed like an age, he turned his horse and cantered back to us.

'The Armenian officer will report your offer to King Artaxias, majesty, as long as no more flame pots are launched into the city,' he reported.

'Describe the officer,' ordered Spartacus.

'Tall, majesty with broad shoulders, black hair and a heavy brow.'

'Geghard,' said Spartacus. 'At least he will talk directly to his king.'

'I am to return in an hour to learn the Armenian king's answer, majesty,' stated the herald.

The tension was unbearable as the clouds thickened overhead, ballista crews waited for the order to either stand down or re-commence shooting, and thousands of soldiers focused their attention on the drawbridge to see whether it would drop to herald an enemy assault. Low rumblings in the sky to the north signalled a storm and the breeze turned into a brisk wind that carried spits of rain. Servants brought cloaks and warm wine to fortify our bodies as each of us mulled over in our minds whether we would be forced to storm what was a formidable stronghold. When the hour was up the herald returned to the walls, to be told Artaxias was willing to speak to us.

The news was met with disappointment by Spartacus, who I sensed wanted the Armenians to defy us, thereby leaving us no choice but to storm the city. The reality, however, was that neither Gafarn nor I wished to see Artaxata reduced to rubble, and neither did Diana or Gallia for that matter. Only my wife and myself knew what the son of Geghard had told us regarding the Aorsi dressing up as Medians to provoke the Armenians. He could have been lying, of course, but what did he have to gain from such deceit? If anything, he had risked his life to divulge such information, for as family we could have been outraged by his words and had him killed on the spot. But we knew Spartacus better than he did and our nephew was more than capable of such a ruse. When it began to rain, the dreariness suited my mood, for I was angry and morose that a family member had deceived us.

Gallia was more sanguine about the matter back in our tent, bringing her hands together and resting her elbows on her shins as Klietas rubbed balm into my leg suffering the effects of the old arrow wound.

'He is grieving over Rasha and his judgement is impaired.'

I winced when Klietas' strong hands provoked a spasm of pain in my leg.

'Apologies, highborn.'

'You have nothing to apologise for. The wet always brings on a constant pain. I thank Shamash Dura is at least hot and dry.'

'Will you tell Gafarn and Diana?' asked Gallia.

'What, that their son is as conniving as Phraates? No, with a bit of luck the negotiations tomorrow will be concluded to the satisfaction of all parties and then we can go home.'

'What if the Armenians refuse Spartacus' terms,' she said.

'They won't. And he won't renege on his promise not to torment the Armenians any further.'

'Ten thousand talents is a lot of gold.'

'The Armenians must learn that the actions they take have consequences, and they must take responsibility for those consequences.'

'Even if Spartacus agrees to stop his aggression towards the Armenians, I doubt Spadines and his warlords will stop their raiding.'

I looked at Klietas massaging my leg.

'Perhaps I should send Klietas and Haya to cut off his head, like they did the former governor of Mepsila.'

He stopped kneading my leg and looked up.

'It would be an honour, highborn.'

I looked at Gallia. 'There is no honour in assassination, Klietas.'

She leaned back in her chair.

'But you do believe in justice, don't you?'

'Justice, yes. Murder, no.'

I could see her anger rise but I shook my head.

'I have no desire to fight old battles. What's done is done. Hopefully, Artaxias will agree to Spartacus' terms, peace will be restored on the northern border of the empire and we can all go home.'

I could tell by her expression she was sceptical but she said nothing. I thanked Klietas and asked him to request the cooks send us some hot porridge. The rain had chilled the air and I suddenly felt cold.

It got colder as day gave way to night and it continued to rain, a light pattering on the roof of the tent that increased in intensity and volume as the night wore on. The new day dawned bright but cool, the rain having stopped to leave the air fresh and invigorating and the land soaked. Soldiers wrapped in cloaks huddled round campfires while cooks prepared breakfast and horsemen groomed and fed their mounts. I walked into the morning air, my breath misting when I breathed, much to my surprise.

'Late spring can be cool in the Armenian highlands, uncle.'

I turned to see a beaming Spartacus, his boots and bottom of his red cloak splashed with mud. The tents of the kings were in close proximity so I assumed he had been out before dawn, fortifying his men's spirits.

'Good morning, Spartacus, I trust you slept well.'

He slapped me hard on the back.

'Like a newborn. So, today we relieve the Armenians of a large amount of gold.'

'Remember, you must offer them something in return. Do not humiliate Artaxias, for if you do you will be sowing the seeds of resentment and future conflict.'

He held up his hand and smiled. 'I will be both conciliatory and humble.'

I doubted that but it augured well he was in a good mood. Both Gafarn and Diana were also in high spirits, though their cheery mood was due to the prospect of their imminent return to Hatra. The only person unhappy was Lucius, who reported to me as Gallia and I were eating our breakfast. I ordered him to sit and told Klietas to fetch more porridge and warm wine.

'The ground is waterlogged, majesty, which means it will take longer to transport and re-assemble the ballistae in front of the city walls.'

The machines had been dismantled, their constituent parts loaded onto carts and transported back into camp, just in case the Armenians were tempted to launch a night-time raid to destroy them.

'As the Armenians have agreed to negotiate, do we need to re-assemble them at all?'

Klietas placed a bowl of porridge in front of Lucius.

'The presence of the ballistae will encourage the enemy to be more amenable, majesty,' said my quartermaster-general, who proceeded to devour the porridge. I ordered my squire to refill his bowl.

'Take Klietas with you,' I told Lucius, 'it will be good for his education to see how Dura's siege engines are assembled.'

'And used?' said Lucius.

'Only if negotiations go badly.'

The process to begin said negotiations was long and tortuous. Heralds went to and from the city to transmit messages between us and Artaxias, or rather his chief advisers. Where were the talks to be held? Inside our camp? Artaxias refused point-blank. Inside the city? *We* refused point-blank. At a spot halfway between the camp and the city? Artaxias refused, fearing our forces that now formed a cordon around the city would seize him. What about a short distance from the northern entrance to the city, which would be within range of archers on the walls?

Midday came and went.

Artaxias agreed to the location of the meeting place near the northern entrance. What about respective delegations? The Parthian party would naturally include the kings and queens of Hatra and Dura and the King of Gordyene. To prevent him from feeling 'threatened', Artaxias insisted the commander of his army, the commander of his bodyguard and the high priest of the Temple of Aramazd be present to equal out the numbers. We agreed. His other demands were: no weapons to be worn in the tent, slaves to test wine before it was served as a defence against poisoning, all parties to remain seated throughout the negotiations, all hands to be visible at all times, and no raised voices.

Gafarn could not contain his laughter.

'No raised voices? Are we meeting a king or a novice of a silent religious order?'

'Artaxias is a weak vessel,' shrugged Spartacus, 'like most Armenians.'

'As you are the only one who has met him,' I reminded my nephew, 'I think most of the terms of the meeting are directed at you.'

'Try to remember your manners,' Diana told him sternly.

Spartacus bowed his head. 'Of course, mother.'

It was four hours after midday, the sun showing its face only intermittently as thick white clouds began to gather in the sky, when we rode from camp in the company of the Amazons, a company of Hatra's Royal Bodyguard and a hundred King's Guard. On our right before we swung left to skirt the western side of the city, Lucius' re-assembled machines stood in a line, around them centuries of Exiles standing at ease, though ready to form a square around them should the garrison launch an attack. But the drawbridge was in a vertical position and there were few soldiers visible on the battlements. The drawbridge spanning the moat in front of the northern entrance into the city had been lowered, however, and when we reached the large circular tent that had been pitched not more than fifty paces from the bridge, the ramparts were lined with soldiers. There was also a small army of slaves, frightened individuals who avoided eye contact as they stood around the interior of the tent, the floor of which had been covered by wooden planking, in top of which had been laid a thick purple carpet. Spartacus pointed at it.

'To the Armenians, purple is the colour associated with wisdom. It would be a travesty if it was red.'

'Why, what does red symbolise?' asked Gafarn.

Spartacus laughed. 'Bravery.'

'Remember what I told you,' I snapped. 'You might like holidaying in Armenia; I do not.'

We stood waiting for the King of Armenia, slaves brushing the luxurious couches that had been positioned in a large circle, a man with a huge belly who informed us he was the marshal of the court asking if we carried any weapons.

'None,' Spartacus told him, Gafarn and I doing likewise.

Interestingly, he did not pose the same question to either Gallia or Diana, not that they were carrying any weapons. Neither was Artaxias when he appeared shortly after our arrival, striding across the drawbridge in a striking purple and white striped robe, a black leather belt at his waist and a tall conical, jewel-encrusted hat that accentuated his height. The king was in his late twenties, tall with low eyebrows and brown, narrow eyes. He was also pale and that plus his rich attire reminded me of a younger Phraates.

When he and his entourage had entered the tent, Spartacus stepped forward and tipped his head to Artaxias.

'It is good to see you again, lord.'

Artaxias, obviously surprised by my nephew's apparent conviviality, was initially lost for words, his mouth opening but no words coming out. Spartacus extended an arm to his parents.

'May I introduce King Gafarn and Queen Diana of Hatra, my parents, and my uncle and aunt, King Pacorus and Queen Gallia of Dura?'

I bowed my head to Artaxias. 'It is an honour to meet you, lord.'

'Hatra salutes a noble son of the Artaxiad dynasty,' said Gafarn.

Whatever Artaxias had expected of us, it obviously did not include politeness and respect, which resulted in him being uncertain how to proceed. But the tall, thin, black bearded man I assumed to be his high priest, wearing a simple white robe, took command of proceedings.

'The king thanks you for your courtesy and asks you to share wine with him before we sit.'

He clapped his hands and slaves carrying trays hurried forward, each one holding beautiful gold chalices. We watched as wine from silver jugs was poured into wooden cups so slaves could taste it before we were served. There was an awkward couple of minutes as we studied the slaves who had tasted the wine, waiting for any signs of poisoning. I smiled when I realised Artaxias had missed an opportunity to rid himself and his homeland of the man who had plagued it for years, along with his family members. So not much like Phraates, after all.

The slaves served the wine, we took our seats and Artaxias spoke at last, introducing the tall, heavily built commander of his army, the severe Geghard with sharp cheekbones and a heavy brow. The commander of his bodyguard, Toros, was younger and less stern looking, though just as broad. The high priest was called Voski, which Spartacus whispered in my ear meant 'gold' in Armenian, though we conversed in Greek, the language of diplomacy.

'An entirely apt name for these proceedings,' he said.

He flopped back on his couch, chalice in his left hand.

'I will come straight to the point, lord. Artaxata is surrounded by a great Parthian army, an army that reluctantly ventured north to settle long-held grievances.'

'Grievances, King Spartacus?' said Artaxias.

Spartacus ignored him.

'Our terms for withdrawing from Armenia are as follows. First, you will pledge to no longer wage war against Gordyene or

Media. Second, an indemnity of ten thousand talents of Armenian gold shall be paid to the treasury in Vanadzor for the costs incurred during this year's campaign and last year's.'

Geghard shook with anger. 'You insult King Artaxias.'

Spartacus took a long sip of wine.

'Or we could resume the burning of Artaxata. Tell me, general, how long will it take for your lords to organise another army to march to the relief of Artaxata? Unless they can be here within two days, the city will burn for certain.'

'Aramazd is watching you, King Spartacus,' growled the high priest.

'Who is Aramazd?' asked Diana.

Voski was all smiles when it came to the Queen of Hatra.

'The father of the gods, majesty, all-powerful and all-seeing.'

'Then he must have seen Armenian soldiers in Media last year,' smirked Spartacus, 'and wondered, as did we all, why they were there. But let us not talk of the gods. Let us instead talk of what I can do for you, lord.'

Artaxias was again surprised. 'Me?'

'In return for your pledging to never again attack Gordyene, I in turn promise not to wage war against Armenia, and that includes the Aorsi.'

Geghard laughed. 'The Aorsi obey only their own insatiable desire to plunder and kill.'

'The Aorsi are under *my* control,' said Spartacus forcefully.

Geghard leaned forward to fix Spartacus with his black eyes.

'So, you admit the Aorsi are under your command.'

'Naturally, they are loyal servants of the crown.'

Geghard looked fit to burst.

'And the years of raiding and atrocities, they were all at your command?'

Spartacus held his stare. 'Every one of them.'

'We are not here to rake over the past,' snapped Artaxias. 'I would hear what Hatra and Dura have to say on Gordyene's proposals.'

'Hatra stands firmly with Gordyene,' said Gafarn.

'As does Dura,' I added.

'And do Hatra and Dura also pledge not to attack Armenia in the future?' queried Artaxias.

'As long as Armenia does not attack Parthia,' I answered, 'then Dura will not wage war against your kingdom.'

'And neither will Hatra,' confirmed Gafarn.

'Ten thousand talents of gold is a significant sum,' said Artaxias. 'We will need time to assemble such an amount.'

Spartacus smiled. 'As long as it is paid by the end of the year, lord, by which time you will see that it is I who controls the Aorsi, then Gordyene will count Armenia as a friend. And the border between our two realms will no longer be soaked in blood.'

Artaxias' eyes shifted from him to Gafarn and then to me, briefly alighting on Gallia, who thus far had been like a stone statue.

'What of Spadines?' he said to Spartacus.

'What of him? He does what I tell him and his warriors do what he tells them.'

'I agree to your terms,' said Artaxias, 'subject to the peace you propose between our two kingdoms becoming a reality. If the peace holds, then I promise to pay ten thousand talents of gold to Gordyene at the end of the year.'

'Plus the immediate reimbursement of campaign costs incurred by Gordyene, Hatra and Dura.'

Spartacus did a quick calculation in his mind.

'Another three thousand talents of gold, payable within the month.

Geghard jumped up. 'Your terms are unacceptable.'

'You treat Armenia with disrespect,' roared Voski.

'I offer Armenia a lasting peace, priest,' Spartacus retorted. 'You would trade that for a few pieces of gold?'

'You call thirteen thousand talents a few pieces of gold?' said an exasperated Artaxias.

Spartacus held out his chalice to be topped up, pointing it at the city walls visible through the open tent flaps.

'I'll warrant the fine ladies of Artaxata wear more than that around their necks. Time for your nobles to pay up, lord, so their gilded lives can continue uninterrupted.'

'I agree it is a large sum,' I said, 'but if I have learnt anything over the years, it is that peace brings trade and trade brings wealth. A little inconvenience now will reap rich rewards, of that I am certain.'

Artaxias sighed. 'I inherited a kingdom occupied by the Romans, King Pacorus, who murdered my parents and sought to make Armenia a part of their empire. After the defeat of Mark Antony, Armenia was tormented by the soldiers of Gordyene and Aorsi raids. I gave Prince Atrax permission to march his army through my kingdom in the hope it would lead to peace with Parthia. I was wrong and my mistake has brought Parthia to the door of my palace. I cannot undo what has happened but I have no wish to embroil Armenia in any more wars. My people have suffered enough. I will pay the gold and you all will depart my kingdom forthwith.'

'We will be marching south tomorrow, lord,' I promised without consulting Spartacus.

Artaxias stood, gave each Parthian king a curt nod and turned on his heels.

'We have your son, Lord Geghard.'

I shook my head at Gallia but she ignored me. Artaxias stopped and Geghard's jaw dropped.

'That's right,' gloated Gallia. 'Our soldiers captured him at the battle at the river. He is on his way to Irbil to visit his sister. You remember her, general? The girl you tried to sell into slavery?'

'Not now, Gallia,' I pleaded.

'Perhaps you wish to buy him back?' Gallia goaded him. 'I know you like to barter your children to the highest bidder.'

'We give thanks to the gods he is alive, general,' said Diana, seeking to calm a seething Geghard.

'And assure you he is perfectly safe and indeed unharmed,' I added hastily.

'The price for his return is ten talents of gold, general,' said Gallia, 'payable immediately.'

Geghard's fists clenched but he held his rage.

'How do I know he is safe, or indeed if you even have him?' he said to Gallia.

'You will just have to take my word for it, general.'

'I had no idea Dura was so impoverished that its queen had to resort to extortion,' remarked Artaxias.

Her blue eyes bored into the Armenian king.

'Dura is rich, lord, but in this particular matter money is immaterial. There is a point to be made.'

'What point?' demanded Geghard.

'That daughters are not chattels. If you wish to see your son again, you will ride to Irbil.'

Geghard was confused. 'Irbil?'

'There to hand over the gold to your daughter in exchange for your son,' she told him, 'and at the same time apologise to Lusin for your despicable treatment towards her.'

The general's cheeks were red with rage but she cleverly disarmed him.

'She is pregnant, by the way.'

'Pregnant?'

'You are going to be a grandfather,' I said, 'my congratulations.'

'Lord Geghard will pay the gold,' said Artaxias, eager to be out of our company. 'Our business is concluded here. General.'

He glared at Geghard who withdrew in fury, followed by a glowering Voski and a bemused Toros.

'Was that necessary?' I said to Gallia.

'Entirely necessary,' she replied.

'I think the phrase rubbing salt into the wound is appropriate to what just happened,' remarked Gafarn.

Spartacus rubbed his hands together. 'Went better than I expected. Never thought they would agree to pay the gold. Still, kicking a kingdom when it's down is always worthwhile.'

Diana shook her head with disapproval but I was relieved Artaxias had agreed to peace. The war was over and we were going home.

I was wrong on both assumptions.

Chapter 10

The ballistae were disassembled later that day under the watchful eyes of archers on the walls. Once loaded on carts, they were carried back to camp as the sun descended in the west. The next morning, the air crisp and cool following more rain during the previous evening, the march south began. The horsemen provided a large rearguard and flank protection, while Talib and his men rode ahead to ensure there would be no nasty surprises at the Araxes. There were no Armenian soldiers waiting to ambush us, but there were plenty of black, bloated corpses of their former colleagues providing a rich feast for hordes of ravens, vultures and crows that created a screeching racket fit to raise the dead. The nauseating stench of rotting flesh filled our nostrils and tickled the back of our throats as we were forced to wait at the river until the lengthy process of getting the siege engines, supply wagons and mules, camel trains and foot soldiers back across the river was completed. Finally, after eight hours in the river bend where the battle had taken place only a few days before, the last of the horsemen waded across the Araxes to return to Gordyene and Parthian territory. That night Spartacus feasted his parents, Malik, Gallia and me in his tent.

Castus and Haytham were beside themselves with joy, having defeated and forced a peace on the Armenians, their mother avenged and the treasury at Vanadzor about to be filled by a huge amount of gold. They gorged themselves on freshly killed venison and drank copious amounts of wine, the scruffy Spadines sitting next to them also taking advantage of his lord's generous hospitality. I wondered when Spartacus would inform him that his days of rape and plunder were over. That would certainly wipe the smirk off his thin face.

Spartacus seemed remote from the proceedings, eating sparingly and barely touching his wine. But he did speak a great deal to Spadines, the Aorsi chief nodding his head and laughing loudly at regular intervals. Spartacus clearly was not ordering him to curtail his raiding habits. Spartacus caught my eye and raised his cup to me.

'To you and Aunt Gallia, uncle, whose siege engines made the first part of this campaign quick and painless.'

My blood ran cold. 'The *first* part of the campaign?'

'Tomorrow I march west to serve justice on my wife's murderers.'

Spadines belched. 'Pontus will burn for its crimes.'

'You are going to invade Pontus?' I could not believe what I was hearing.

Spartacus curled his lip into a thin smile.

'Atrax, Titus Tullus and Tiridates think they are safe behind Sinope's walls, uncle. But they will discover that Gordyene's reach is long, as will that hill chief Laodice.'

'Pontus is a Roman client kingdom, son,' warned Gafarn. 'If you wage war against it, you wage war against Rome.'

A broad grin replaced the thin smile.

'That would be the same Rome that financed Prince Atrax's attempt to seize the crown of Media, the same Rome that has tormented and invaded Parthia for decades?'

'The same Rome we now have peace with,' I said.

Spadines wore a smug expression as his lord raged.

'Peace! There can be no peace with the Romans. You delude yourself, uncle. The Romans are just using Phraates for their own ends. The high king was foolish to allow his son to be taken by Tiridates, who handed him over to Octavian, who dangles him like a piece of bait in front of Phraates. The high king debases himself by entering into negotiations with his son's jailers. The boy is dead, uncle, and the world laughs at Phraates' weakness.'

'The boy is not dead,' I insisted.

'But my wife is,' he shot back.

Out of the corner of my eye I saw Gallia and Diana nodding, the knot in my stomach twisted some more.

'I ask you to reconsider,' I pleaded. 'Laying waste to Pontus will not bring back Rasha.'

Spartacus drank some wine. 'My mind is made up, uncle. I know you embarked upon this campaign reluctantly, but you have fulfilled your part in it. You can leave Gordyene with a clear conscience.'

I glanced at a grim-faced Malik.

'And you, my friend?'

'My sword is pledged to Spartacus, Pacorus. I will have vengeance on my sister's killers.'

' *We* will have justice on Rasha's killers,' hissed Gallia.

I once thought Spartacus was the exact opposite of Phraates. Whereas the latter was manipulative and cunning, the former was forthright and straightforward. But the times the King of Gordyene had spent in the company of the high king had corrupted his soul, or perhaps it was always debased, and I chose not to see it. But now I realised he had engineered this evening with one aim in mind only: to reinforce his army with the soldiers of Hatra and Dura. He knew neither Gafarn nor I would agree to march with him into Pontus, but we both had weak spots that he now fully exploited.

'I wish you both safe journeys back to Dura,' he said earnestly.

I saw Gallia holding the lock of Rasha's hair hanging from the chain around her neck and knew we would not be going back to Dura.

'I will be coming with you,' said Gallia.

'Me too,' added Diana.

My mind went back to the first time we had met Rasha, when a frightened girl had been brought into the Citadel's throne room when we had first arrived at Dura. From that moment on a special bond had formed between her and Gallia, a bond that had only strengthened as the years passed. A bond that endured still. I turned to Gallia and saw the steely determination in her eyes I had seen so many times before. But I was not defeated just yet. Perhaps I might take the wind out of my nephew's sails.

'My siege engines will be going south tomorrow regardless, Spartacus.'

He shrugged. 'I do not need them. They brought the Armenians to heel but I do not need to capture King Polemon's capital to get him to surrender the renegades.'

'How then?'

'As my friend Spadines says, we lay waste to his kingdom, or threaten to as a start. He will give them up rather than see his kingdom burn.'

I looked at the swarthy Sarmatian.

'Did your king tell you he promised the Armenians there would be no more Aorsi raids against them? What will you do now, *prince*?'

Spartacus gave me a wry smile.

'My lord informed me he would deceive the Armenians,' Spadines told me.

'I do not control the Aorsi, uncle,' said Spartacus. 'They are my allies, not my subjects.'

'You gave your word,' I countered forlornly.

'My word? To those who were complicit in the murder of my wife? I would tell a thousand lies to trick the Armenians. There will never be peace between Gordyene and Armenia.'

'Never,' echoed Castus.

'Our vengeance has just begun,' boasted Haytham.

They were so consumed by hatred and a thirst for revenge that everything else became secondary and irrelevant. That was the legacy of the arrow that had killed Rasha on the Diyana Plain. There was no point in pleading for restraint and reason, but I tried anyway.

'I ask you to be a father to your sons, Spartacus. They have already lost one parent. Would you risk your life, theirs, and the welfare of your subjects, for the sake of revenge?'

'We march at dawn, uncle,' he replied, 'regardless of whether Dura marches with us or not.'

In the morning, a long line of Immortals tramping west out of camp, I sat on Horns with my commanding officers, watching Lucius' siege engines on carts trundling out of the southern entrance to the camp, heading for Vanadzor. From there they would continue to Irbil and then Assur, before striking west for Hatra and then Dura. Normally Lucius would have gone with them, but I wanted him with us for the journey to Pontus. I had a feeling we would need his knowledge when it came to the return journey.

'You will be going home, Chrestus,' said a smiling Lucius.

'You can look up old family members,' urged Azad.

'I have no family in Pontus,' replied a grim-faced Chrestus, 'they were killed by the Romans. My family and home are in Dura.'

'I have looked at the maps we possess on this area,' said Kewab, 'and it is at least four hundred miles to Sinope, though how we find a way through the many mountains I have no idea.'

I sighed. 'Spartacus informs me his Aorsi are intimately acquainted with the many tracks through the mountains leading to both Cappadocia and Pontus.'

'So, we are in the hands of Spadines and his Sarmatians?' grumbled Chrestus.

'A man who would sell his own mother if given the opportunity,' said Sporaces.

'If any woman did give birth to such a creature,' remarked Lucius.

'Just remember to urge your men to sleep with one eye open,' Chrestus advised them.

They fell into mirth, but it was no laughing matter. They were professionals, the best that Parthia could muster, though Hatra and Gordyene might disagree, and with some justification. But I had not created and maintained Dura's army to risk it on some insane foreign venture. And yet here we were, about to invade a Roman province on the flimsiest pretext and risk wrecking the peace that now existed between two mighty empires. In the distance I discerned a rumble in the mountains, which sounded like thunder but must have been the laughter of the gods.

The first part of our new campaign was a delight.

We marched parallel to the Araxes, moving south of the river in Gordyene territory, which was inhabited by the Aorsi. The Sarmatians had now lived in this part of my nephew's kingdom for nearly two generations and they were firmly established. Their villages were located in narrow valleys next to streams or beside one of the dozens of lakes in the region, their huts having stone walls with thatched roofs. But the settlements were invariably small as the area's steep slopes, eroded soil and severe winters made farming difficult. In the summer the small fields grew wheat and barley, but barely enough to subsist on. As sixty thousand soldiers and thousands more civilians threaded their way through northwest Gordyene, I realised why the Aorsi resorted to banditry to supplement their meagre existence, and why there would never be peace between them and the Armenians.

But the region was rich in game. The vast forests of oak, ash and juniper that blanketed the hillsides as far as the eye could see were teeming with deer, brown bear, wolves, lynx, hyena, leopards and Caspian tigers. Hunting parties of horse archers were despatched into the woods to kill anything edible, so at night the camp filled with the pleasing aroma of cooking venison, goose, pheasant and grouse. A competition broke out between the horse archers of Dura and Hatra concerning who could kill the most eagles, though the birds mostly flew at high altitudes and perched on lofty mountain crags. But at least there was no need to use up our rations as we lived off the land and cut a swathe of destruction of wildlife as we marched west.

Loath as I was to admit it, the Aorsi provided an invaluable service, scouting ahead and acting as guides to steer the army through the many passes and, crucially, leading us to open spaces at the end of each day to allow us to construct a marching camp. The spirits of the soldiers were high after our easy and relatively bloodless victory in Armenia and the march took on the feel of a training exercise, with pleasant temperatures, an abundance of water sources, grazing and hunting, and an absence of hostile forces.

'This terrain reminds me of Cisalpine Gaul,' remarked Gallia, looking around at the tree-covered hillside in front of us. 'That was filled with game as well. In addition to Romans.'

I plucked an arrow from my quiver and nocked it in the bowstring.

'And Gauls,' I smiled.

We were standing by the side of a stream running with clear, cool water, lancing through a valley with steep, tree-covered sides. Half a dozen empty carts stood in a line on the track near the stream. In front of them, some thirty paces from the treeline, stood a much longer line of archers, comprising most of the Amazons and a company of Sporaces' horse archers. On the other side of the track stood groups of horses tended by every tenth man, or woman, of the companies. Klietas stood on my right next to the commander of Dura's horse archers, Gallia on my left. Above us, in the dense forest, came the muffled sounds of voices and whistles.

'Now remember,' I said to Klietas, 'the animals will appear quickly and will veer left and right when they emerge from the trees and are startled by our presence.'

'Yes, highborn,' he grinned, gripping his bow with his left hand, the fingers of his right ready to pull back the bowstring.

'And don't snatch at your target.'

Three companies of dismounted horse archers had been sent into the forest earlier to act as beaters, equipped with whistles, flags and sticks to crack on tree trunks. They also used their voices to drive the game in the desired direction, forming a long line that began at the top of the hill and slowly made its way down – three hundred men hopefully driving dozens of animals towards us.

A bird suddenly flew from the trees, a fleeting shape of frantically flapping black wings, followed by a crack and the animal falling to the ground. I looked left and saw Haya with an empty bowstring and a look of satisfaction on her face.

'You are getting old and slow, Pacorus,' said Gallia softly. 'Did you even see it?'

'Did you?' I retorted.

'Did you see that, highborn?'

I pointed at the trees. 'Concentrate.'

Beating is hard work: men pushing through dense undergrowth or stepping over fallen branches, all the while trying to stay level with those on their left and right. A line extending some eight hundred paces through the forest, making a lot of noise to drive any animals in front of them down the hill, being careful not to allow any gaps to form through which animals might escape.

All chatter ceased as the whistles and shouts got louder and every archer concentrated on the trees, straining to catch sight of game breaking cover. A deer jumped out of the trees and was immediately hit by two arrows. Gallia struck another deer that ran straight at her, hitting the animal square in the chest, causing it to spin head-over-heels before crumbling in a heap a few paces from her. Sharp cracks filled the air as arrows were shot at the increasing number of animals bolting from the trees: deer, squealing boar and lynx. All felled by multiple arrow strikes.

'We will eat well tonight,' I grinned.

Animals were going down to my left and right, arrows hissing through the air to demonstrate the shooting skills of the Amazons and Sporaces' horse archers – professionals showing their deadly skill with a recurve bow. I caught sight of movement in the trees directly ahead and raised my own bow. To see a brown bear break cover and run straight at me. He must have weighed over a thousand pounds, a great hulking mountain of muscle and claws with rage-filled eyes.

'Defend the king,' shouted Sporaces, archers on my left and right directing their arrows at the beast hurtling towards me. I released my own bowstring, the arrow shooting forward to strike the bear in the shoulder, the arrowhead failing to penetrate its thick fur. Two arrows stuck fast but they made no difference to its momentum or direction, the bear giving a mighty roar as it suddenly reared up on its back legs, ready to lock me in a deadly embrace.

The brown bear is a killing machine, each of its paws having claws up to six inches long that are capable of ripping bark off a tree. Their jaws contain teeth that are akin to a saw and can chew through a six-inch-thick branch with ease. Arrows were slamming into it, bouncing off its fur, making it more enraged. I strung a second arrow and shot it into its belly, the metal head penetrating the fur and piercing its flesh. It did not even feel it. I tossed my bow aside and drew my sword, bracing myself for the monster's deadly embrace, when I witnessed one of the bravest acts I have ever seen.

Klietas, knife in hand, screamed and sprang forward, his voice distracting the bear for a split-second as my squire threw himself at the head of the animal, stabbing the point of his knife into the bear's left eye socket. The beast roared in pain and anger and swatted Klietas away with his right front leg, my squire shrieking as he was clawed across the chest, knocking him to the ground. The few seconds of distraction allowed Gallia to put an arrow through the bear's right eye, Sporaces crouching low to shoot another missile into the animal's throat. The bear groaned, swayed on his hind legs and flopped down onto all fours. I dashed forward and dragged Klietas out of harm's way, Amazons surrounding the animal to unleash arrow after arrow into the bear, which collapsed on the ground, gave a loud sigh and expired.

'Cease shooting,' ordered Zenobia, walking forward to kick the bear with her boot to ensure it was dead.

Animals were still coming from the trees, the archers that had not seen the drama continuing to shoot them down. I knelt beside a bleeding Klietas, the right side of his chest lacerated by the bear's claws.

'Is he dead, highborn?'

I glanced at the bear with the knife embedded in his eye socket.

'He's dead. Don't talk.'

Haya, her eyes moist with tears, threw herself on the ground beside him, causing him to smile.

'You are an ignorant fool,' she said through sobs, kissing him on the lips just before he passed out.

We staunched the loss of blood with a bandage, used a belt to secure it in place and I held him as Horns took us both back to camp at the gallop, Gallia and the Amazons in tow. We rode straight to the hospital tent, Sophus commanding orderlies to take Klietas to a bed, all but two being mercifully empty. The Greek unbuckled the belt, removed the now bloody bandage and examined the wound, Haya and Gallia crowding round.

'I must have space,' snapped Sophus. He looked at Haya. 'Get out of my hospital, now.'

Gallia ushered a pale Haya from the tent, Sophus shaking his head as he examined the wound.

'What caused this?'

'A bear. He saved my life.'

'How brave. Fortunately, though there are several lacerations, they are not deep. He will have several scars, however.'

'You will cauterise the wound?'

He frowned at me. 'Clean bandages, pressure and a regular application of vinegar will suffice. Cauterisation is only used in extreme circumstances, as it can lead to deadly infection. Now if you will excuse me, King Pacorus.'

He waved me away like I was an irritant. Clearly Alcaeus had trained him well when it came to disrespecting royalty.

Outside the hospital tent an anxious Haya was pacing up and down, Gallia standing with arms folded and nostrils flared.

'Sophus should have more respect,' were her first words when I exited the tent.

'Alcaeus waxes lyrical about his medical talents, so we will forgive him his republican tendencies.'

Haya stopped and looked at me with distraught eyes.

'Klietas will be fine, though Sophus told me he will have scars on his chest.'

A look of utter relief spread across her face.

'Thank you, majesty.'

'Report to the Amazons,' Gallia told her.

Haya saluted and sauntered away, a spring in her step. We followed at a slower pace, around us Durans and Exiles cleaning their equipment and sharpening their swords. The camp was huge, far bigger than the city of Dura, and was infused with the aroma of horses and camels.

'I would be dead were it not for Klietas,' I reflected, shivering. 'A close shave with mortality.'

'You will reward him?'

'Of course.'

'How?'

I gave a sly smile. 'I will marry him to Haya.'

She was not amused. 'Amazons are not gifts to give away, not even for kings.'

'But you saw her distress when he was wounded. They clearly love each other.'

'Then he must ask her for her hand in marriage, and she must give it willingly. But all talk of marriage must wait until we get back to Dura. Minu is pregnant. She told me last night.'

I stopped in my tracks. 'Does Talib know?'

'Not yet, and you are forbidden to tell him. She wants to keep it from him until the campaign is over.'

' *If* the campaign ends.'

'What do you mean?'

'After we have finished meting out justice on Atrax, Laodice, Titus Tullus and Tiridates, Spartacus will probably suggest marching on Rome itself to exact reparations from Octavian.'

'You are being ridiculous.'

'History always repeats itself,' I said. 'Forty years ago, we were obeying the orders of another Spartacus in Italy, and now we are doing the bidding of a second Spartacus in a foreign land. All we need is a descendant of Marcus Licinius Crassus to appear and the picture will be complete.'

When we reached the border with Pontus after sixteen days of marching, all hunting parties were withdrawn and the army was put on high alert. The terrain remained much the same, with densely wooded narrow valleys cutting through the Pontic Mountains. We expected the passes to be contested, but each day our scouts returned to report encountering only deserted mountain villages and an absence of humanity. Spadines told us the Pontic hill men, which we had encountered at Irbil, were cowards who preferred to run rather than face the might of Parthia, but I was not so sure. The hill men presumably knew every pass and track through the mountains intimately and could have launched dozens of small attacks on our stretched-out column, inflicting casualties and slowing down our rate of march to a crawl. But instead the only thing that delayed our progress was logistics: the process of getting thousands of foot soldiers, thousands of horsemen, thousands of mules and camels and dozens of carts through narrow valleys and along rocky tracks. The need to safeguard against ambush combined with severe congestion reduced our rate of advance to a maximum of five miles a day, resulting in an extra ten days of marching before we reached the interior of Pontus.

It was a land of mountains, valleys, spectacular waterfalls, lakes and basins that the gods had sprinkled with small villages. It was summer now, but the temperatures were pleasant, with frequent rainfall and fog that rolled through the valleys at regular intervals like white celestial beings, alternately revealing and covering mountain peaks. It was a beautiful, enchanting land and the more I saw of it the more a sense of impending doom enveloped me, not least because not one Pontic soldier had showed himself since our arrival.

'King Polemon will muster his army, such as it is, at Sinope, here on the coast.'

Spartacus pointed a finger at a map on the table before us, at the city-port on the Black Sea coast. 'He lost many men on the

Diyana Plain last year, even though he himself was not present. Pontus does not have an inexhaustible reserve of men, uncle.'

Spadines next to him was nodding like the obedient dog he was.

'Prince,' I asked him, 'have your men reported any signs of enemy troop movements in this area?'

He shook his head. 'The terror of your name sends them fleeing, lord.'

I caught Gafarn's eye and he sighed.

Spartacus was unconcerned. 'We avoid the coastal strip and head straight for Sinope, there to force Polemon to give up those we wish to serve justice on.'

'Just like that,' I said.

'Yes, uncle, just like that.'

'What troubles you, Pacorus?' asked Malik.

'Thus far we have encountered no resistance, despite being in the enemy's homeland. No ambushes, raids, no night-time attacks, nothing, despite traversing terrain ideally suited to ambush. That is what troubles me, my friend.'

'Even if Polemon wanted to contest our advance,' said Spartacus, 'he would have scant forces to do so. He lost his best foot soldiers on the Diyana Plain, and Laodice's hill men are all but worthless.'

'He has a point, Pacorus,' nodded Gafarn. 'How long will it take to reach Sinope?'

'Another ten days,' answered his son.

'We will be back in Gordyene in another twenty,' said Spartacus. 'We have sixty thousand soldiers, that is why Polemon has not dared to face us. He thinks he is safe behind the walls of his capital, but he is wrong. There are many villages around his capital, which we will destroy if he does not surrender the rebels.'

Diana shuddered at the prospect but unless we backed up our threats with actions we would be a like a tiger whose fangs had been removed. I looked at Malik and Spadines, both of whom led warriors very adept at spreading death and destruction. We had the numbers, it was true, and it was also true that Pontus had lost thousands of men supporting Atrax's abortive attempt to capture Media. But still…

Spartacus beamed at Gallia.

'And the omens for victory are excellent. After all, Sinope was established by the Amazons and named after their first queen, Sinope. It is surely no coincidence that your Amazons and my Vipers are about to march on the city named after the first queen of the Amazons.'

I thought the connection was tenuous at best, for though Gallia was well acquainted with the mythical history of the Amazons, even she would find it hard to justify a campaign on the grounds she and her female warriors wanted to pay homage to the city of their first queen.

'What a pity the city is not currently ruled by women,' was her only comment.

The Aorsi and Agraci provided a plundering vanguard as the army left the mountains and descended into gentle hills filled with evergreen trees and finally the area of great beauty and fertility that surrounded the city-port of Sinope itself. Polemon had obviously evacuated the entire population of the many villages that dotted the lush landscape, either to the city itself or to another stronghold,

Trabzon, further east on the coastal strip. It was a rich land, more than capable of feeding our army and all its animals.

As a massive camp was erected less than a mile from the gates of Sinope itself, our horsemen were sent out to pick clean the fruit trees and vineyards that littered the area. They returned with saddlebags bulging with apples, pears, figs, peaches, plums, apricots and cherries. The horsemen were under strict orders not to molest civilians or destroy their property, though the Sarmatians were under no such constraints and when Sporaces reported to me at the end of the first day of our siege of Sinope, he relayed stories of farms and villages burnt and many dead civilians. The lucky ones had either fled into the hills or sought sanctuary inside Polemon's city.

That night I slept fitfully. Dura's army had always fought in defence of the Parthian Empire, but now it was part of an army of aggression waging war in a foreign land, a realm that was moreover a client kingdom of Rome. I feared our presence would lead to a cooling of relations between Octavian and Rome, which might even lead to an outbreak of hostilities between Parthia and Rome. This had always been at the back of my mind the moment we had crossed the border between Gordyene and Pontus. But in the morning my nagging doubts were pushed to the back of my mind due to fresh woes revealing themselves.

Chapter 11

Klietas was beaming from ear to ear, holding up the necklace so I and Gallia could see it. His chest was still bandaged, and his right arm was in a sling, but he still insisted on cleaning my weapons and armour and serving meals. It was a precarious exercise, both for him and us, wooden platters of food sometimes being spilt over the floor, and us! Still, his enthusiasm was infectious and whereas Gallia would normally have given him short shrift for such clumsiness, the fact he had saved my life meant he was something of a hero, making her more forgiving.

'Haya gave it to me, highborn,' he cooed.

Forged by an armourer, it was a simple necklace holding one of the bear's claws that had lacerated his chest. The chain was made from rings from mail armour and was rather blunt and unattractive. But that it had been gifted by his love made it the most beautiful thing he had ever seen. With one hand he tried the impossible task of putting it on. I stood.

'Let me, don't reopen your wounds.'

He stood still as I fastened the necklace, Klietas smiling like an imbecile at Gallia.

'Very fetching,' she admitted.

'Haya gave it to me, highborn,' he said a second time.

She indulged him. 'I'm sure she is very fond of you.

'Go and report to Sophus,' I told him, 'so he can put a fresh dressing on your wounds.'

He bowed, 'Yes, highborn.'

He passed Kewab and Lucius on the way out of the tent, both wearing scowls of concern.

'Have we become the besieged?' I joked, failing to elicit a smile from either.

'We wish to show you something, majesty,' said Kewab.

'It will affect our conduct of the siege,' added Lucius, 'and ultimately the outcome of the whole campaign.'

Half an hour later I and Gallia were sitting on our horses some half a mile east of Sinope, the sun glinting off a blue Black Sea, a pleasing breeze blowing into our faces. That was the only pleasing thing that morning.

'We captured a merchant yesterday,' Kewab informed us, 'a man who does much trading inside Sinope. He owns a large vineyard further up the coast and sells wine to nobles inside the city, or at least he did.'

I shuddered. 'You have executed him?'

Kewab was shocked. 'No, majesty, but his vineyard was wrecked by a large party of Aorsi. A patrol of my horsemen saved him from being nailed to one of his vine trees.'

'Animals,' spat Gallia.

'After interrogation, he was allowed to leave by sail boat,' Kewab continued, 'but what he divulged was very interesting.'

He pointed at the peninsula jutting into the sea, on which Sinope had been built.

'The peninsula is two miles in length and a mile wide at its broadest point. It has its own water supply, as well as being endowed with two ports. There is one on the eastern side and one on the western side. You can see the sails of the boats in the harbour, majesties. This means the city can be supplied with ease by merchant ships.'

Lucius continued the tale of woe. 'The landward wall of the city, the one we would have to breach if we launched an attack, is strongly fortified and bristles with arrow ports. In addition, because we are unable to enforce a sea blockade of the city, King Polemon is free to land soldiers both up and down the coast.

'This means we will have to establish both outer and inner siege works if we are to prevent any force being landed on the coast interfering with our own forces.'

I shook my head at Gallia, who raised her eyebrows in acknowledgement.

'So we cannot starve the city into submission, we have no engines with which to batter down or scale the walls, and the garrison can be supplied with food and fresh troops without interruption.'

They both nodded.

'Suggestions?' I asked.

Kewab turned away from the sea to gaze at the tree-covered hills behind us.

'We could construct boats to raid the harbours and burn all the shipping therein, as there is an abundance of wood in the area.'

'And level every settlement in the area within a radius of fifty miles,' added Lucius.

'A very Roman tactic,' said Gallia, clearly unimpressed.

'With no siege engines, majesty, it will almost impossible to take the city,' he told her.

'Not without heavy losses,' admitted Kewab. 'If I may be frank, majesty.'

'Be my guest,' I told him.

'The first half of this campaign has been masterful, resulting as it has in the defeat and humiliation of the Armenians at very little cost, at least in the short term. But to march into this kingdom without the means of capturing the objective and having no desire to conquer Pontus, is frankly folly.'

'Perhaps you should tell King Spartacus that,' said Gallia.

Kewab gazed back at the city surrounded by a shimmering sea.

'There is no guarantee the renegades we seek to capture are even in Sinope. They could have left at any time, or if they are still in the city, they could still be evacuated with ease. We do not even know if King Polemon is in the city.'

'I would suggest that a policy of destruction will make Polemon more amenable to enter into discussions to bring about the resolution we desire,' said Lucius.

'No,' I replied firmly, 'I will not wreak destruction on a kingdom and condemn innocent civilians to starvation, which is what will happen if we destroy their homes, farms, fields, orchards and vineyards.'

'Then we will fail,' stated Lucius flatly.

Our horsemen ranged far and wide, collecting supplies and keeping watch for any enemy forces. But though they sometimes came upon small groups of hill men, who were easily dealt with, they encountered mostly a deserted land. The heralds sent to the city walls to request a parley with King Polemon met with no answer and on the third day of our 'siege', I called a meeting to discuss our strategy.

We feasted on venison and boar shot that morning, apricots and apples plundered from a nearby orchard and wine taken from villas whose owners had fled. Spartacus brought Castus and Haytham, both having led raiding parties of King's Guard earlier. They were in high spirits, the enemy having seemingly melted away to leave them free to ride far and wide and indulge their every whim.

Before they got too drunk, I informed their father, Gafarn, Diana and Malik of the opinions of Kewab and Lucius regarding our visit to Pontus.

Spartacus finished picking clean a boar rib and tossed the bone on his platter.

'When Polemon sees his kingdom burning from his palace, he will be willing to enter into negotiations.'

'He has shown little inclination to do so thus far,' remarked Gafarn, smiling at the excellent wine he was drinking.

'Have we become murderers and bandits?' asked a shocked Diana.

'Hostages,' said Castus.

We all looked at him in expectation. He drank his wine greedily.

'Send horsemen far into the west and east, round up anyone they come across, bring them back here and line them up before the walls of Sinope.'

'Line them up?' asked a confused Haytham.

'On crosses, like the Romans do,' said his brother, bursting into laughter.

Diana's jaw dropped in horror.

'Hatra will have no part in such barbarity.'

'Neither will Dura,' I confirmed.

Castus looked at the austere Malik.

'Uncle, surely it is the Agraci way to exact vengeance on your enemies.'

Malik nodded slowly. 'Vengeance, yes, but what you desire is to spill blood for its own sake, Castus, to drench your sword in the blood of innocents. In doing so, you become like the ones you seek to serve justice on.'

Castus was deflated by Malik's sage words and Haytham sank into silence. Their father was not to be deterred, though.

'Before we begin weeping over the wrongs committed against King Polemon, let us remember he was part of the army led by Mark Antony that invaded Parthia ten years ago, and his soldiers formed the backbone of the rebel army of Prince Atrax. Pontus has a lot to answer for.'

His sons murmured their agreement.

'You are right, Spartacus,' I admitted, 'but that does not assist us in the slightest. I have no desire to spend weeks or months in this land, nor do I have any appetite for wanton destruction or wholesale murder.'

'Pacorus speaks for Hatra in this,' said Gafarn. 'Before we condemn Polemon outright, remember he is in the unenviable position of being a Roman client king.'

'Roman puppet, you mean,' sneered Gallia.

Gafarn nodded. 'And Phraates' puppet also, for let us not forget it was our esteemed high king who encouraged Atrax to try to seize the crown of Media, thus creating a sequence of events leading to King Polemon offering his soldiers to Atrax, paid for by Octavian.'

Spartacus bit into an apricot. 'Tomorrow, we change the tone of our requests for a meeting with Polemon, informing him we will turn his kingdom into a desert if he does not speak with us.'

He took another bite of apricot.

'He does not know that Hatra and Dura do no not have the stomach for it.'

'I will give you a month, Spartacus,' I told him, 'after which Dura's army will be marching back to Parthia. But I expect Polemon to meet us before then, if only to save his honour, his kingdom from destruction and his people from starvation.'

Castus and Haytham spent the rest of the meal sulking and making derogatory comments about Klietas and his arm in a sling, until I told them to desist. Spartacus chastised his sons for their boorish behaviour, which darkened their mood further. Their father was in an altogether more agreeable mood, having acquired a taste for being a conqueror. He was more like the Romans than he thought in that respect. Malik kept his counsel but was happy to engage Gafarn and Diana in conversation, about Rasha, his father and how all three had been outsiders in Parthia and probably always would be, notwithstanding their many labours in defence of the empire.

'Of all of us,' he reflected, 'only Pacorus is accorded respect, because he comes from a great and noble family resident in a famous city.'

I gestured at all of them seated at the table.

'All of us are accorded respect in the empire, not least for what we have done for that empire.'

Malik stared into his cup of wine.

'In your kingdom, where men are judged purely on merit, that is the case, Pacorus. But since you and my father made peace I have travelled to many parts of Parthia, rubbed shoulders with many nobles and kings, and seen the looks of horror on the faces of their fine ladies when they see the tattoos on my face. Old fears and prejudices take generations to die, my friend, if they die at all.

'I look around this table and see the faces of friends, blood brothers and sisters whose origins are irrelevant. But we and what we have created is an aberration, an exception.'

'Times change, and people change, my friend,' I argued. 'As a young boy, if someone had told me an Agraci woman would be Parthian queen, I would have laughed in his face. And yet did not Rasha become Queen of Gordyene? Did not her son, half-Agraci, half-Thracian, become King of Media?'

Malik shrugged his shoulders. 'Perhaps you are right.'

'But Akmon and Lusin can never rest easy while Atrax still walks the earth,' warned Gallia. 'Whatever happens in Pontus, Atrax must die, and sooner rather than later.'

Spartacus raised his cup. 'Well said, aunt.'

Not long after our guests had departed, Klietas busying himself clearing up the cups and platters one-handed, Chrestus appeared, removing his helmet and saluting. I offered him wine, but he refused.

'There's a man outside, majesty, turned up at the northern entrance to the camp saying he has a massage for you, from King Polemon.'

I looked at Gallia.

'What proof does he hold of his authenticity?' I asked.

'Words he says you will remember, majesty.'

'He must be mad,' said Gallia, 'either that or an assassin sent to kill the king.'

'He carries no weapons, majesty,' Chrestus informed her, 'and his hands have been tied behind his back.'

'I will hear what he has to say,' I said.

The prisoner, a young man in his twenties with a handsome face and kind eyes, was bundled into my presence. He bowed his head and Chrestus was about to force him down onto his knees, but I stopped him.

'That will not be necessary, Chrestus. You are from King Polemon?'

The man smiled. 'Yes, majesty, he sends his greetings and asks you to remember the last time you and he met.'

I did remember. It was near the shore of Lake Urmia after we had him and what was left of his men cornered like rats in a trap – a small band of dismounted horsemen determined to sell their lives dearly. Gallia had wanted to shoot them to pieces but I wanted their surrender to save time, and had demanded to meet with their commander, who turned out to be Polemon himself.

'Go on,' I told him.

'When you saved my lord's life, you asked him if it was worth dying on a wind-swept plain for Rome? Let the Romans fight their own wars, you said, saying further that a tactical withdrawal was no shame.'

'Release him,' I ordered Chrestus.

My general was at first hesitant but cut the man's bonds with his dagger when he realised I was not joking. They were the exact words I had spoken to Polemon during our brief discussion at Lake Urmia. I poured wine into a cup and offered it to the man.

'I can taste it first if you suspect poison,' I said.

He smiled and took the cup. 'That will not be necessary, majesty, it is well known King Pacorus is a man of honour.'

'How do you serve King Polemon?' I asked.

'As a dutiful son,' he replied.

Gallia was surprised. 'You are Polemon's son?'

He bowed his head to her. 'Prince Zenon at your service, majesty.'

'When does your father wish to meet with me, Zenon?' I asked.

'Tonight, majesty.'

'Tonight?'

'Yourself and one other can meet my father at the gates of Sinope. I will stay here as surety for his promise that no harm will come to you.'

'Why the urgency?' asked Gallia.

'King Pacorus once saved my father's life, majesty, and he now wants to return the favour.'

It was late, but I was intrigued, and so after acquiring a cloak with a hood I set out with Chrestus for the gates of Sinope. We journeyed on foot as there was no moon and I did not want to risk Horns twisting or breaking an ankle for the sake of a short walk. To see we carried torches, which could be seen for a great distance, much to the consternation of the army's commander. Chrestus was like an old grump beside me, muttering and cursing under his breath, which I ignored for the first ten minutes after we had left camp, but then stopped to confront him.

'I take it from your barely disguised utterings that you disapprove of our midnight walk.'

'I do.'

'Why?'

He looked around at the darkness.

'There could be a dozen assassins lying in wait. The King of Dura risks his life because a man recounts some words spoken in a meeting ten years ago? Madness, utter madness.'

'I respect your candour, but there are times, Chrestus, when one must have faith that what seems simple and true are in fact so.'

I started to pace towards the flicking torches on the ramparts of Sinope's gatehouse, Chrestus resuming his muted ramblings, hand firmly on the hilt of his *gladius*. We slowed when the drawbridge over the moat in front of the gates descended and two figures carrying torches strode across the wooden boards. We instinctively slowed as the figures got nearer, stopping around ten paces from them.

'King Pacorus, I presume.'

He had not changed much in ten years. His beard was still thick, and his scale-armour cuirass was still very kingly in appearance, though it paled beside my own magnificent example. It was my armour that first caught his eye.

'I see Dura has prospered in the years since our last meeting, which makes your presence in Pontus even more baffling.'

'We are here, lord king, to apprehend those responsible for crimes against Parthia, namely Prince Atrax, Titus Tullus, Tiridates and Laodice.'

'Crimes against Parthia or against Gordyene?'

'They are one and the same thing,' I answered. 'May I ask if those individuals are in Sinope?'

He smiled. 'They are. And may I ask if my son is unharmed?'

'He is quite safe. Dura does not harm envoys.'

'I know that you are a man of honour, King Pacorus, which is why I sent Zenon to you. Ten years ago, you saved my life and allowed me to watch my children grow up. Now, by dint of current circumstances, I am in a position to save your life, and that of your wife. I will even allow King Gafarn and Queen Diana to leave with you, though Pontus owes Hatra nothing, especially considering the outrages its army has committed on my soil.'

'If we want to speak of outrages, lord king,' I replied, 'I could mention innocent people crucified on the streets of Irbil by Pontic soldiers under the command of Titus Tullus, as well as depredations committed by the savages led by Laodice. Shall we compile a tally of who has slaughtered the most innocents?'

'I will come straight to the point, King Pacorus, as I wish you and your army to be gone from my kingdom. The individuals you desire to apprehend have been used as bait to lure you here, or rather King Spartacus and his army. The character of the King of Gordyene is well known not only in Parthia but also in Rome. Surely a great military commander such as yourself must have wondered why the mountain passes into Pontus were not contested.'

I felt a knot tighten in my stomach. I tried to maintain my dignity.

'How easy has been your progress,' continued Polemon, the man holding the torch beside him wearing a helmet that sported a magnificent crest, the commander of his bodyguard, I assumed.

'Pontus lost many soldiers on the Plain of Diyana,' I said, trying to convince myself that was the reason our advance had not been contested.

'It is true Pontus suffered losses in Media last year,' he conceded, 'but my army is not the only one you will soon be facing.'

The knot in my stomach tightened some more.

'The hour is late, and I have no appetite for word games, King Pacorus. The combined might of King Archelaus of Cappadocia and

King Amyntas of Galatia are converging on Sinope, where my own soldiers will reinforce them. In addition, Herod of Judea has also sent soldiers north to take part in ridding the world of King Spartacus.'

'He stands not alone,' I said. 'You fight Gordyene, you fight all Parthia.'

'*All* Parthia? High King Phraates wants rid of Spartacus, King Pacorus, for it was he, with the support of Octavian, who is behind this grand scheme. It was Octavian who expressed concerns that a plot to destroy Spartacus would result in a war involving Dura and Hatra. But Phraates assured him it would not lead to a wider conflagration.'

I wanted to be sick. I felt my knees weaken and for a moment was unsteady on my feet.

'Are you all right, majesty?' asked Chrestus.

I took a deep breath and composed myself, avoiding Polemon's eyes. It all made sense now. I remembered the conversation in the royal garden at Irbil with Phraates when he had casually mentioned the presence of the renegades at Sinope. He knew I would pass on the information to Spartacus. And my nephew needed no second prompting when it came to vengeance. He thought he had been most clever in engineering conflict with Armenia, but it had been he who had been manipulated, like a puppet. And Ctesiphon rather than Rome had been pulling the strings.

'My offer is this,' said Polemon. 'You and your wife, together with King Gafarn and Queen Gallia, may avail yourselves of a ship that will take you east to Trabzon. From there guides will take you south through the mountains to the border of Gordyene and safety.'

He glanced at Chrestus. 'You may also take those closest to you if you wish. But your army will stay here, its soldiers to be disbanded and sold into slavery.'

'If you knew me, King Polemon, you would know that I would never abandon my soldiers.'

He sighed. 'I knew that, but I had to make the offer. A matter of conscience, you understand.'

'I appreciate your courtesy, lord king, and regret that Parthian soldiers have invaded your land. I assume you had little choice when it came to aiding Prince Atrax.'

'There was a time when Pontus was a great power in these parts, King Pacorus, but that time has passed. But I comfort myself with the thought that a native king is better for my people than a Roman governor, though Pontus is still paying for the mistakes of its former rulers.'

'I thank you for your honesty, lord king, but if what you say is true, our army will have left this area before your allies arrive.'

He looked at me with sympathetic eyes. 'It is too late, King Pacorus. A carrier pigeon arrived at my palace earlier with news that Archelaus and Amyntas are but two days' march from Sinope.'

'I will see to it your son is escorted back to your city,' I told him, eager to be away. 'I thank you for your generosity, lord king, but in the morning you will be my enemy again.'

'You are still my enemy tonight, King Pacorus.'

I was glad Polemon did not see me limping back to camp, my old wound rousing itself from its slumbers to torment me afresh. Chrestus tossed the torch away when we left the King of Pontus, just in case an eagle-eyed archer on the walls decided to make his lord's work easier. For a while my general said nothing but again began to mutter to himself. After a while I found it unbearable.

'In the name of the gods, Chrestus, spit it out.'

'That king spoke the truth. Our eyes have been focused on the city and the land to the east and west of it. But we gave scant regard to the south and the tracks through the mountains.'

'We have patrols out in all directions.'

'Up to a day's march from camp, yes. What worries me is that if we quit camp in the morning and retrace our steps back to Gordyene, we will find the mountain tracks and passes full of hill men.'

'And with a hostile army snapping at our heels,' I said.

When we reached camp, we sent Zenon back to his father with an armed guard. Gallia had been entertaining him with stories about Spartacus the slave leader, our time in Italy and the Amazons. When he had gone, I entertained her by recounting my meeting with his father.

'Send men to rouse Spartacus and the king and queen of Hatra,' I told Chrestus, 'and Malik, too.'

Bleary eyed and irritable, they listened to what king Polemon had told me in silence, though not about the plot of Phraates to rid the world of the King of Gordyene. As I did so Spartacus yawned frequently, and Malik demanded wine to keep him awake. It was perhaps two hours after midnight and the night was cool and still. Diana wrapped a thick cloak around her and Gafarn rubbed his eyes in an effort to stay in the land of the living. When I had finished speaking, Spartacus spoke first and predictably.

'Polemon bleats like a lost lamb. So what if the armies of Galatia and Cappadocia are on the march? We stay here and defeat them before the walls of Sinope, after which we burn everything in Pontus. Polemon will surrender those we want after he has seen his enemies destroyed.'

His arrogance was breath-taking, but he had the support of Malik.

'We have no choice but to stand and fight. To run would be dishonourable.'

With that Spartacus stood, kissed his mother on the cheek and walked from the tent, turning at the entrance.

'You made a mistake not bringing your siege engines, uncle. The old Pacorus would not have made such an error.'

Malik slapped me on the arm before taking his leave, Gafarn stretching out his legs as he did so. When they had left I told Diana and Gafarn about Phraates' twisted plot.

'How could he?' was Diana's lament.

'Because he has no morals, no loyalty and a very short memory,' Gafarn told her.

Diana looked at me with tired eyes. 'I apologise, Pacorus.'

I was surprised. 'For what?'

'For supporting my son instead of listening to you. And for what may befall us all in the coming days.'

Gafarn took her hand. 'At least we will face it together.'

'Just like old times,' said Gallia with a wan smile.

Even she sounded deflated and I wondered what we would be facing when the new allies of Pontus arrived.

Chapter 12

'The enemy king was right, majesty.'

I nodded. In my heart I knew Polemon had been telling the truth, but I sent Talib and his scouts out anyway, just to put my mind at rest. I pointed at the stool to indicate my chief scout should sit, Klietas handing him a cup of water. It had been another beautiful summer's day, the wind blowing off the sea fresh and invigorating, the temperature warm but not unpleasant. In camp morale was high. Why wouldn't it be? The land was fertile and teeming with fruit and game, the enemy was cooped up inside Sinope and the ease of our march here had lulled everyone into a false sense of security. It was the most pleasant trap I had been lured into.

Gallia was all ears as Talib reported what he and his men had seen earlier.

'The foothills that we used just days ago are swarming with soldiers,' he told us. 'Tens of thousands of them, mostly men on foot, lightly armed with spears and shields, hill men from Pontus, like the ones we encountered on the Diyana Plain last year. But there are also others, lord.'

He glanced at Gallia. He was reluctant to speak for some reason.

'Spit it out,' I told him.

'Gauls, majesty, thousands of them.'

'Gauls?'

'Galatia derives from a Latin word meaning "land of the Gauls",' Gallia told us. 'It is the stuff of legends. Over two hundred and fifty years ago, three tribes of Gauls, the Trocmi, Tolistobogil and Tectosages, were invited into this region to aid a king called Nicomedes. They stayed.'

'The leader of the Gauls, King Amyntas, has a reputation as a great warlord,' reported Talib. 'He has boasted he will tie the severed head of King Pacorus to the saddle of his horse.'

'How do you know this?' I asked.

'My men mixed freely with the Gauls, majesty, who have made camp at the base of the hills. They told them they are waiting for the Parthians to come to them.'

'Sensible,' agreed Gallia. 'On the plain they would be vulnerable to our horsemen. But in the hills…'

'In the hills, conversely, *we* would be vulnerable to constant ambushes launched by lightly armed warriors,' I said.

'The soldiers of King Archelaus of Cappadocia are also approaching, majesty,' said Talib.

'A pity Byrd is not with us,' mused Gallia, 'he could have paid a bribe to Archelaus to let us pass through his land.'

'A pity we are here, more like,' I said bitterly.

The sun was dipping in the west when I called together the other kings and queen and their senior commanders, plus Kewab and Karys, who deserved to hear first-hand about the grave situation they were now in. I admit I was in a testy mood, not least because Spartacus seemed oblivious to the great danger we all faced. He was flanked by his sons and Spadines, the agreeable Hovik standing behind his king. Kewab and Lucius were deep in conversation with a concerned Karys, while a grim-faced Chrestus was shaking his head as he conversed with Malik. Gafarn and Diana stood with Herneus and Orobaz, the general examining the scruffy Spadines with barely concealed contempt. We all stood, as I did not intend the meeting to last long. The atmosphere in my tent was stuffy and was about to get heavier.

'As you all know, last night I met with King Polemon outside Sinope,' I announced. 'He told me a large army composed of Cappadocians, Galatians and Israelites was marching north to trap us between the mountains and the sea. Following scouting parties conducted by Talib and his men, I can confirm that army is now in the foothills of the mountains, using the same tracks we traversed to reach this accursed place.'

'What is your inclination, Pacorus?' asked Gafarn.

'Retreat,' I answered, 'though I am open to suggestions regarding the route we should take back to Parthia.'

'What?' roared Spartacus. 'Why speak of retreat when we can slaughter our enemies with ease? Once this army of Rome's puppets reaches the plain we can unleash our soldiers against it. Polemon can watch the slaughter from the walls of his city.'

Castus and Haytham laughed. I did not.

'Except Rome's puppets will not be entering the plain. They will stay where they are and wait for us to try to force our way through them.'

'And you know this how, uncle?' queried Spartacus.

'Talib's scouts spoke to the soldiers of Archelaus and Amyntas this very morning. They may be Rome's puppets, but they are not fools. They know our strength lies in our cataphracts and horse archers.'

'And Immortals,' said Castus.

'Have you ever conducted a campaign in the mountains, Prince Castus?' I said heatedly. 'Fighting on every narrow pass, in every valley and defile? In such terrain, a man armed with only a spear is at least equal to a cataphract.'

'We must leave, that much is certain,' said Diana. 'Even I, a mere woman, can see that to stay is to endure a lingering death. We have to get through the mountains to get back to Parthia, so instead of bickering among ourselves I suggest you turn your minds to how we are going to achieve it.'

'There is one way,' said Chrestus.

All eyes turned on him in expectation, including my own.

'When I left Pontus thirty years ago, and those of the Exiles who made the journey more recently, the route we took was west of here, via Galatia and going through Cappadocia before reaching the Kingdom of Hatra. If you want to hear my opinion…'

'We are depending on it, general,' said Diana.

'We leave tomorrow and strike south to the Gokirmak Valley,' continued Chrestus, 'passing the ancient track that was once used by the Hittites and Persians to continue on south. We keep west of a river called the Halys, which marks the boundary between Pontus and Cappadocia. From there we continue south.'

'How long will the journey take?' enquired Kewab.

'It took me a month walking on foot to reach Hatran territory,' replied Chrestus, 'but I was young then.'

There was a ripple of laughter.

'At least a month, probably longer,' said Chrestus, 'and that is hoping we will have a head start on the enemy.'

'Who will soon be snapping at our heels,' remarked Malik.

'We leave in the morning,' I told them.

'What about the criminals we came here to apprehend?' asked an angry Spartacus, pointing at the tent's entrance. 'They are in Sinope, laughing at us. If we leave Pontus they will escape justice.'

It was true. We had come to Pontus to capture Atrax, Titus Tullus, Laodice and Tiridates. We had failed to do so. But at least if we managed to extradite ourselves from the situation we currently found ourselves in, we might serve justice on them at a later date.

'We cannot have vengeance on anyone if we are dead, Spartacus,' I told him. 'Dura's army will be leaving in the morning. You can do as you see fit.'

He probably hated me at that moment, but I did not care. If I included Malik's warriors, the horsemen of Kewab and Karys, and Dura's squires, I had brought nearly thirty thousand fighting men and boys to Pontus, in addition to hundreds of cameleers, muleteers, servants and wagon drivers. I would not allow them to perish in this foreign land. I looked at Gafarn who gave me a slight nod. Hatra would be marching with me, which meant Spartacus would have no choice but to follow.

The legions and Immortals left camp before dawn, preceded by Talib's scouts, half of Sporaces' horse archers, all of Kalet's horsemen plus Malik's warriors. As we were only a mile from the walls of Sinope, it would not have taken a genius to work out we were marching west instead of east. All we could hope for was Polemon would be uncertain as to our intentions, and I prayed that he might even believe it was a ruse to lure the large relief force on to the coastal plain where we could engage it. Guessing the intentions and thoughts of the enemy was a risky business, and so the cataphracts of Hatra and Dura, reinforced by Kewab's mounted archers-cum-spearmen, were deployed near the gates of the city, to deter any attempt by the garrison to launch a raid. I led the rest of Hatra's horse archers and the horsemen of Mesene east to keep the enemy relief army in the foothills. Behind us, Orobaz with Hatra's horse archers provided a sizeable reserve to assist either Kewab or myself. Spartacus, still sulking regarding our intention to quit Pontus, had declared his forces would stay with the wagons, camels, mules and foot soldiers to provide flank and rear protection for the army.

Klietas' arm was no longer in a sling, which meant he could ride in the saddle, though his wound was still bandaged and dressed every day. As such, it made shooting a bow difficult for him. But he was in a happy mood, whistling to himself as we trotted across the verdant terrain, much to Gallia's chagrin.

'Silent! Keep watch,' she hissed.

Over the centuries the trees had been cleared from the plain, to be replaced with neat vineyards, fields and orchards. White-washed stone farmhouses dotted the land, along with villages composed of stone huts with thatched roofs. The hillsides were different, being blanketed with trees: oak, beech and maple. Higher up were great stretches of birch and pine, the track we had used to descend on to the plain weaving its way up the hills like a long yellow snake.

I held up a hand when a strange noise reached my ears, like a thousand woodpeckers tapping at tree trunks. Then we saw them, just a few at first, small groups slowly exiting the treeline, increasing to a multitude as more and more came into sight. Karys ordered his men to deploy into company columns and Sporaces did likewise. Ahead, around four or five hundred paces, more and more warriors exited the trees.

'Gauls,' spat Gallia bitterly.

As they got closer they began to taunt us in a language I barely recognised. It was Gaulish, but it had been so long since I had heard it that it was like listening to a foreign language. Even though Gallia was a Gaul, she rarely spoke it, saving for when she was cursing or hurling insults.

'They are calling us women, sons of whores and frightened children who dare not fight them on foot but prefer to sit on our horses, so we can run away quicker,' she reported, as the horde made a fearful racket.

And then horsemen appeared, just a minority compared to the huge throng that had vomited forth from the trees, but well attired in what appeared to be bronze armour, helmets and mounted on horses with shiny coats. They rode to within around a hundred paces of our position, one jumping down from the saddle and striding forward, before spreading his arms and venting his spleen. He was around fifty paces from where I sat on Horns, my horse flicking his ears in annoyance in response to the king's booming voice. He was a great slab of a man, his cone-like helmet decorated with what looked like a pair of eagle wings. His over-sized chest was covered with a burnished scale-armour cuirass, beneath which he wore a long-sleeved blue tunic. His baggy grey leggings were striped, and his hair and thick beard were ginger. In his right hand he held a mighty war hammer. Gallia translated for me as his voice thundered across the grass.

'I am Amyntas, King of Galatia, and I demand to speak to Pacorus, ruler of a land called Dura. I see his griffin banner but where is this Pacorus? Is he hiding behind his warrior women?'

The insult was for the benefit of his tribesmen, who began to whistle and whoop derisively, some sticking out their tongues or turning around and bending over to show us their buttocks. It was very boorish and infantile, but I was more than pleased to indulge it. I nudged Horns forward,

'You are wasting your time, Pacorus,' said Gallia, 'all he wants is to ridicule and belittle you.'

'Exactly,' I smiled, 'the more time the Gauls spend insulting me, the longer the army has to get into the hills. I would appreciate a translator.'

Gallia urged her horse forward.

'If he tries anything with that hammer, drop him,' she told Zenobia.

'With pleasure,' replied the commander of the Amazons, though as she carried my standard it would be others who would shoot the Gaul dead if it came to it.

When we left the line of Amazons the Gauls gave a mighty cheer and began banging their spear shafts on the insides of their shields. Those shields were a variety of shapes – square, oval and hexagonal – being wood covered in hide with metal ribbing, spines and edges and decorated with spirals, circles and animal motifs.

Gallia rolled her eyes as the noise reached a crescendo, our own soldiers in contrast sitting in silence on their horses. The hubbub died down when we halted our horses less than ten paces from the man mountain that was King Amyntas. His large brown eyes flitted between Gallia and me. Then he grinned.

'King Pacorus and Queen Gallia, we meet at last,' he said in perfect Greek.

He saw the surprise in my eyes. 'You thought I was a brainless barbarian? Never underestimate an opponent. Surely a commander as long in the tooth as yourself must know that?'

He was brimming with confidence and energy, his eyes always moving as they examined me, Gallia and the companies of horse archers behind us.

'Are you going to sit on your horses and speak down to me?' he asked, feigning hurt.

'Our weapons are sheathed, lord king,' I answered; tipping my head at the huge two-handed hammer he gripped in his hand.

He tossed it aside. 'My apologies.'

I slowly dismounted, as did Gallia.

'I assume you will now demand our surrender.'

He shook his giant head. 'I know too much about you and your Gaul queen to waste my words. To be honest, I just wanted to meet the pair whose fame has spread far and wide. You are older and smaller than I expected, but that is the nature of meeting legendary figures. They invariably disappoint.'

He beamed at Gallia. 'It is an honour to meet you, lady. I promise that when this campaign is over, and the soldiers of Parthia are either dead or enslaved, you will have free passage to travel back to Dura.'

He looked past us. 'You and your women.'

'There is no need, lord,' she smiled, 'because if, by some quirk of fate, you and your allies are victorious, I shall be dead. A great man once told me it is better to die on your feet than live on your knees.'

He roared with laughter. 'The stories do not do you justice, lady. Is the man you speak of standing beside you?'

'No, his name was Spartacus,' she told him.

'The slave leader, I have heard of him. Even now, he provokes rage and disgust among the Romans. But we stand here because of another who shares the same name. Octavian wants him dead,' he stated bluntly.

'Wanting and having are two different things,' I replied casually.

He jerked a thumb behind him.

'King Archelaus and his soldiers are but a few hours' march away. When they arrive and join with my warriors and the soldiers of King Polemon, our combined forces will overwhelm your own troops. Not that I need the help of Pontus and Cappadocia, you understand. There is no escape.'

'We do not seek to escape, lord king,' I said, 'rather conduct a leisurely withdrawal in pleasant weather and in scenic terrain, after our summer holiday in Pontus.'

His warriors and mounted warlords were silent now, many Gauls leaning on their fearsome two-handed war axes as they watched their king converse with the enemy. Amyntas looked at Horns.

'I heard you rode a white stallion.'

'He died.'

'After *you* are dead, King Pacorus, I will take your horse and provide him with many mares to service. He will be happy, I promise you.'

'I assume we are done here,' said Gallia.

Amyntas bowed his head to her. 'I am a man of my word, Queen Gallia. Your life shall be spared.'

She gained her saddle. 'If we meet in combat, I will show you no mercy.'

He beamed at her again. 'I would not expect any less of a fellow Gaul.'

I hauled myself into my saddle. 'Farewell, King Amyntas.'

'Until the next time we meet, King Pacorus.'

He retrieved his hammer, whistled to his warlords who turned and galloped to their subordinates. When we had walked our horses back to the waiting Amazons and turned them around, the Gauls had disappeared back into the trees, Amyntas halting at the treeline to raise his hammer in salute before he too vanished. We stood on the grass for another hour to ensure it was not a ruse to entice us into the hills. But the Gauls did not reappear and so we too departed, cantering through the fields and vineyards to re-join Lord Orobaz and his waiting horse archers. We had bought the army some time, but whether it would make any difference remained to be seen.

Chapter 13

The first two days were nerve shredding, scouts reporting seeing the enemy in every direction. Talib aged overnight as he and his men, plus the scouts of Gordyene and Hatra, rode for hours reconnoitring every track, ravine, hill, forest and lake. The main road leading south was wide enough for the legions to march six abreast, but the pace was slow for fear of ambush. We thus made only ten miles on the first day and the same distance the day after. On the third day we reached the great plateau that extended into Galatia, Pontus, Cappadocia and western Gordyene, a place of stunning mountains, lakes, deep valleys and remote passes.

The hills and mountainsides were blanketed with trees: pine on the upper slopes and oak, maple and beech lower down. But the plains were wide and largely open save for small villages, around which were fields and orchards. The soil was fertile, and our horses and camels could feast on the short grass that gave the valleys and plains their lush appearance. But it was hot.

Gafarn took off his floppy hat and wafted it in his face.

'I thought the mountains were supposed to be cool. This heat reminds me of the deserts of Hatra.'

'It is always like this in the highlands in summer, majesty,' Chrestus told him.

'Do you miss your homeland, general?' asked a glowing Diana, her cheeks flushed by the heat.

'I left when I was sixteen, majesty, so it is no longer my homeland, not since it became a Roman province.'

'Client kingdom,' I corrected him.

'Same thing,' he shot back.

Spartacus, still offish with me, had decided to take command of the rearguard with his sons, which meant he was some twenty miles north of our group. The army was marching in a column some twenty-five miles long, and so the horse archers were providing flank and rear protection, as well as forming a sizeable vanguard. And I was glad Spartacus was with the rearguard, because north was where our enemies would attack from when they showed their faces.

'Perhaps Polemon will not pursue us,' said Diana.

'His pride will not allow him to sit on his backside in Sinope,' I told her, 'especially with Amyntas and Archelaus having marched to his relief. They will join forces and pursue us, of that I am certain.'

Gafarn looked around at the low-lying hills and expansive grassland.

'At least we will be able to deploy our horsemen to full effect.'

'Let us assume the enemy makes an appearance sooner rather than later,' I said. 'And let us also assume we defeat the combined forces of our foes. I hope you will emphasise to your son that any victory is to facilitate our withdrawal and not an excuse to return to Sinope.'

Gafarn laughed. 'I cannot guarantee that, my friend. For all I know, Spartacus might be thinking of annexing eastern Pontus.'

'Why would he do that?' queried Gallia.

'To give his friend and ally Spadines a new kingdom to rule,' replied Gafarn. 'It saddens me to say it, but I believe Spartacus only truly trusts his Aorsi allies, plus his sons, of course.'

'Even the King of Media?' asked Gallia.

'He is proud of Akmon,' said Diana, 'he told me so. And he has forgiven Lusin for stealing his son away.'

I was going to say that if Spartacus had not stolen Lusin in the first place, she would not have met Akmon and they would not have fallen in love. But there was no point in raking over the past.

'He should think of his first grandchild instead of fanciful schemes in Pontus,' I said.

The temperature continued to rise as we headed south, watering our beasts in the cool waters of the Halys River and the various lakes and waterfalls that littered the area. The pace was slow, Lucius' engineers mapping out the site of the next evening's camp as the last troops were leaving the previous night's encampment. But after ten days and after covering around one hundred miles, the sense of apprehension hanging over the army had vanished, and everyone was congratulating themselves on escaping the trap we had walked into at Sinope.

Until we reached Corum.

This ancient Galatian town was reportedly nearly two thousand years old and had been ruled in turn by the Hittites, Persians, Macedonians and Armenians, before falling under the influence of Rome. And it was our old adversaries who now barred our way.

'How many?' growled Spartacus, chewing a piece of cured meat.

'Difficult to say, majesty,' answered a dust-covered Talib, 'but they have built a wooden wall across the valley we need to march through to continue our journey.'

I had called a council of war the moment Talib had returned to the army with the news that the route to Corum, a walled town that we intended to skirt as we headed south, was blocked a couple of miles north of the town. It was late afternoon, but the temperature was still high, causing us all to sweat, though not as much as the legionaries hacking at the bone-dry ground around us as they constructed the ditch and palisade for our new camp.

'What else have they built?' asked Lucius, removing his helmet to wipe his sweat-beaded brow with a cloth.

'The wall sits on top of an earth embankment, in front of which is a ditch. Beyond the ditch are pits lined with stakes to break up the advance of an assault force,' reported Talib. 'There are no gates in the wall.'

'Can we go around the valley?' asked Gafarn.

'Either side of the valley, which is wide and flat, the hills get steeper, rockier and higher, majesty,' said Talib. 'We would have to retrace our steps before finding a new, more circuitous route.'

'Unacceptable,' snapped Spartacus. 'We must go through this wall. There are enough trees in the area that we can fell to make bridges to cross the ditch and ladders to scale the wall.'

'Attacking such obstacles is a costly and time-consuming business,' warned Lucius, whose own defences at Irbil the year before had impeded Atrax's rebel army.

'It is obviously a trap,' mused Spartacus, spitting out the strip of meat he had been chewing on. 'I doubt there are many Roman soldiers manning that wall. But they have created an obstacle that will slow us down, which is what they want.'

'Who, son?' enquired Diana.

He pointed at the mountains in the background.

'Somewhere out there is the combined army of the kings of Pontus, Galatia and Cappadocia. They obviously anticipated our movements, knowing the King of Dura would not allow himself to be trapped against the sea. You have been out-foxed, uncle.'

What a pity he did not stay with the rearguard, was my thought as he leered triumphantly at me.

'I yield to your superior military knowledge, nephew. What would you do?'

He answered without hesitation.

'What we should have done at Sinope. Stand and fight. Destroy the Gauls and their Cappadocian allies and then continue our retreat back to… Remind me, uncle, where are we fleeing to?'

'We are heading for Hatra, and have more respect for your uncle,' Gafarn chastised him.

'Sixty thousand of the world's best soldiers and all we can do with them is run away from the foe. History will not look kindly on our campaign,' lamented Spartacus.

'Very well, Spartacus,' I shouted, causing Gallia and Diana to jump. 'You can have your battle. We will wait here until the enemy appears and then you can cover yourself in glory. But, as ever, it will be the common soldiery who will pay the price.'

The next day I rode with Talib, Chrestus, Kewab, Karys, Lucius and Gallia to see for myself the obstacle that blocked our way. It was another hot day and the army welcomed the opportunity to have a day's rest, to say nothing of the civilian muleteers, cameleers and wagon drivers who lacked the stamina and resolution of the soldiers they served. As my chief scout had reported, the wooden wall and rampart blocked a wide, largely flat and featureless valley, the hills on either side of which had steep, grassy slopes. But beyond them in the distance were more steeply sided, higher inclines showing limestone outcrops.

The road ran straight through the middle of the valley, the wall, rampart and ditch bisecting it at right angles around a mile distant. I estimated the length of the wall itself to be around half a mile. We trotted towards it in silence, the sun glinting off the helmets of soldiers patrolling its ramparts. As we neared the wall, Talib pointed out what he and his men had discovered.

'In front of the ditch are rectangular pits filled with sharpened stakes. Further out are small, round pits containing a single stake with a fire-hardened point.'

'The enemy made no attempt to interrupt your scouting?' asked Kewab.

'They did not bother shooting at a few riders at a range of over two hundred paces, lord,' Talib told him. 'They seemed content to allow us to examine their defences.'

When we trotted closer to the wall, which comprised horizontal tree trunks arranged in a curious zigzag fashion, the enemy slingers and archers took shots at us, lead pellets thudding into the ground before we reached the first row of circular holes cut in the earth. Arrows arched into the sky to land harmlessly well ahead of where we had halted.

'They were content to allow our scouts to see the extent of their works,' commented Kewab, 'but now they deny us any further examination of their defences.'

'The question is,' I said, 'how many soldiers defend that wall? A legion, more?'

Kewab discounted the idea. 'I doubt if King Amyntas can call on a full legion, majesty. Rome would not trust a client king with the use of its best soldiers, not in a war against the finest that Parthia can offer, anyway.'

'Perhaps the governor of Syria has joined our enemies,' said Karys.

I discounted the notion. 'Byrd would have alerted me if his friend the governor was sending any soldiers north.'

'Most likely,' theorised Lucius, 'there are two or three cohorts of Romans, supported by slingers and archers from the garrison of Corum. Enough to man the barrier we see before us and delay our journey long enough.'

'For what?' asked Gallia.

'The main enemy army, majesty,' he replied.

But the enemy army did not appear and so thousands of Immortals, Durans and Exiles spent two days chopping down trees in the area, thereafter fashioning the branches and trunks into scaling ladders and platforms to span the ditch in front of the enemy wall and climb the wall itself. Other parties were sent forward to mark the exact location of the potholes and trenches in front of the ditch, a risky business as the groups attracted the attention of enemy archers and slingers. To provide them with cover, Chrestus deployed Dura's scorpions to rake the rampart with iron-tipped bolts. It became a desultory, albeit deadly, exchange of missiles that cost us over a hundred dead.

As our horse archers provided security for the tree-felling parties, I sent Talib and his men to search for a route around the wall that the army might use. They found numerous tracks that circumvented the valley, but they were narrow and winding and impossible for wagons to negotiate. Our only option was to overcome the wall. Normally, such an assault would be costly in the extreme, which must have crossed Gafarn's mind as we watched the cohorts of the Durans and Exiles, plus the battalions of the Immortals, deploying into position prior to their attack. Overhead the sky was devoid of any clouds and the sun roasted everything below.

The air was already warm, the earth dry and flies were irritating the horses and camels. The mules had been left in camp a couple of miles to the north of our position, the wall around five hundred paces to our front and hills on our flanks.

Gafarn pointed at the wall. 'I am mindful of Rhegium where we lost many good men.'

'What a terrible night that was,' said Diana.

'The night when Burebista fell, though he did not die. We left him to be enslaved by Rome once more,' I lamented.

Gallia reached over to grip my hand. 'It was not your fault, my love, and we did rescue him from slavery in the end.'

Spartacus, who had heard the story of the slave army's breakout from Rhegium a hundred times, rolled his eyes. He was clearly bored and made no attempt to disguise it. The prospect of a time-consuming assault on a defensive position did nothing to raise his spirits. He was still brooding over what he saw as a lost opportunity to engage the enemy at Sinope, and his avoidance of any polite conversation with me since indicated he held me responsible. His two sons flanking him also had morose expressions, and the unseemly Shamshir always looked glum.

At least the swarthy Spadines was absent, though no sooner had that happy thought crossed my mind than the Aorsi leader appeared at the head of a party of his scruffy Sarmatians, pulling up his horse in front of Spartacus.

'The enemy is here, lord,' he said loudly.

Spartacus frowned in annoyance. Any fool could see that hostile forces manned the wall. Spadines cast a glance at the rampart and shook his head.

'Not here, lord, to the north. Enemy horsemen are approaching.'

All our ears pricked up.

'What horsemen?' I demanded to know.

Spadines gave me a triumphant leer.

'The horsemen of Pontus, Cappadocia and Galatia, lord. My men were looking for supplies.'

'Looting, you mean,' said Gafarn.

'As you will, lord,' shrugged Spadines, 'but they saw a great mass of horsemen to the north.'

He looked at Spartacus. 'Atrax is with them. My men report seeing a black banner emblazoned with a white dragon.'

His words were enough for the King of Gordyene. Atrax was the last remaining male link to a time when Media had treated Gordyene as a land of inferiors, to be plundered and abused at will. Atrax, whose invasion of a Media now ruled by his eldest son had led directly to the death of his beloved Rasha. Spartacus turned in the saddle to address Hovik, his trusted general.

'Ride to Motofi and give him my compliments. Instruct him to march the Immortals north to support our horse soldiers who will be engaging the enemy.'

Hovik hesitated for a second before bowing his head and wheeling his horse away. The general was above all a professional and knew that to divide an army in the presence of the enemy could lead to a disaster. But he was also loyal, loyal to his king, the king's family, and to his homeland. And he would never diminish his lord's authority by questioning his decisions in front of foreign kings and queens.

'How many horsemen?' Spartacus questioned Spadines.

'A few thousand, lord,' came the vague reply.

'We should wait until we have ascertained the strength of the enemy force approaching from the north,' I advised.

'Pacorus is right, son,' said Gafarn.

'There are no foot soldiers with the enemy horsemen, lord,' reported Spadines.

Spartacus smiled.

'We have enough soldiers, father.'

As he commanded a third of the army, he was unworried about the numerical strength of the force approaching from the north. And he knew, as did I, that the army of Gordyene was a formidable force, easily capable of defeating a numerically superior opponent.

'Time to avenge your mother,' he said to his sons.

He looked at Malik, who thus far had remained silent, his black-robed warriors grouped in a compact mass a hundred paces to the rear. The Agraci king nodded, drew his sword and wheeled it around to join his brother-in-law.

Malik's Agraci, Gordyene's Vipers, lancers, horse archers and King's Guard followed their ruler as he cantered north back towards camp, while to our front Immortal signallers sounded their trumpets to turn ten thousand men around and march them away from the wall. They left hundreds of scaling ladders and wooden platforms dumped on the ground. Their departure prompted the arrival of Chrestus, my general sweating as he halted his horse before me.

'What the hell is going on? I've just lost half of my foot soldiers.'

He peered past me to see the rumps of thousands of Gordyene's horses.

'Enemy horsemen have appeared to the north. The King of Gordyene marches to meet them,' I told him.

Concern showed on his face. 'Bad idea to split the army, majesty. We should join him.'

'What of our assault on the wall?' queried Gafarn.

'It will be there tomorrow, majesty,' said Chrestus.

'Chrestus is right, Pacorus,' said Gallia, 'we cannot sit here while Spartacus fights the enemy.'

'We must help him,' agreed Diana.

'Very well,' I conceded, 'give the order to about-face and retire.'

Chrestus saluted and rode back to his waiting legionaries. As he departed Kewab and Karys arrived, having left their horsemen who were deployed behind the foot soldiers to provide missile support if needed. I briefed them on the new situation we found ourselves in.

'It will take time to withdraw in an orderly fashion,' stated Kewab.

The valley was half a mile wide, which for small bodies of soldiers was ample room for manoeuvre. But for sixty thousand troops, their horses and Farid's camel train to the rear of the army, plus the ammunition trains of Hatra and Gordyene, it was a small space that could become congested very easily. Like a mighty warship on the sea, it would take time for the army to turn around.

Which is precisely what the enemy had reckoned on.

Kewab stayed with the abandoned scorpions and camel trains, there being no room to accommodate thousands of the humped beasts as we cantered north with Dura's and Hatra's professional horse archers and the cataphracts of those kingdoms, riding through the Immortals as they tramped after their king and passing the western entrance to our camp. Spartacus was a mile or so ahead of them, a great red banner emblazoned with a silver lion showing his exact position.

Not only to us but also to the enemy.

Gordyene's horsemen and their Agraci allies barred my view of the enemy horsemen but I could make out a dozen or more banners, one of them black, marking the presence of Atrax. A blast of horns from among the Gordyene riders signalled the beginning of their charge, followed by a roar of hurrahs as Spartacus' horsemen screamed their war cries and their horses broke into a gallop. The gap between them and us was around a mile, increasing by the second as Gordyene's soldiers hurtled towards the enemy horsemen. When suddenly the hills on either side of the valley were filled with figures running down the slopes to enter the valley floor. Behind Spartacus' horsemen! Tens of thousands of them. The majority were equipped with spears and shields only, though among them were also men wearing leather armour, bronze breastplates, mail and even scale armour. These individuals also wore cone-like helmets with a long, straight plate to protect the neck, and decorated with a variety of feathers, bird wings or horse tails.

'Gauls,' sneered Gallia, as she and all of us pulled up our horses as the great mass in front of us grew bigger and thicker.

And separated us from the horsemen of Gordyene.

'We must break through them,' shouted an alarmed Diana, who instantly realised her son and grandsons were in great danger.

Already foot archers beyond the mass of warriors were shooting arrows at the mounted troops of Gordyene, who now faced a battle to their front and rear. My apprehension grew as I continued to see arrows being shot at Gordyene's horsemen and the line in front of us solidify to present a dense phalanx of spears and shields across the breadth of the valley. There must have been over fifty thousand warriors facing us, though I could see no missile troops among them. The Gauls were in the front ranks, their long shields resting on the ground, the ends of their spears thrust into the earth and the points pointed directly at us. The rear ranks had hoisted their shields above their heads to present a makeshift roof of wood and hide that extended to the rear of the phalanx. Clearly Amyntas and Archelaus had been taking lessons from their Roman overlords.

'Shoot them to pieces,' shouted Gallia, Sporaces saluting and wheeling away to order his companies to attack. The commander of Hatra's horse archers was already marshalling his men, who now rode forward in lines to shoot at the inviting target.

A tightly packed *testudo* could withstand volleys of arrows, as long as its members kept their shields locked and maintained their discipline. Even so, being under volleys of arrows for sustained periods is not only an assault on the body; it is also an attack on the nerves. And these men were not professional soldiers but farmers, villagers and townsfolk. To compound their difficulties, their shields were a mixture of oval, square and hexagonal shapes. A Roman legionary and his Duran and Gordyene equivalents carries a shield that is identical to those equipping his comrades, which means when locked together they present an unbroken wall. Not so the shields of the Galatians.

Ten thousand horse archers, plus the Amazons, began shooting at the dense phalanx, individuals finding gaps in between shields to hit faces, flesh and bone. Each archer was shooting up to seven arrows a minute, though because of the restricted space we were fighting in, only three hundred and fifty horse archers could shoot their bows at the enemy at any one time. But it still equated to nearly two and half thousand arrows a minute being directed at the front ranks of the phalanx – nearly five thousand after two minutes. To add to the deluge of missiles being directed at them, the rear ranks of horse archers were shooting arrows at high angles over the front ranks, to drop vertically on the rear ranks of the phalanx – an additional thirty-five thousand arrows a minute.

It took less than five minutes to reduce the phalanx to a bloody, shattered pile of dead and dying, after which Azad and Herneus led forward the cataphracts of Dura and Hatra. The commanders of the horse archers commanded their signallers to sound 'company column' and instantly ten thousand horsemen deployed into files to allow the cataphracts to pass through them. It was a marvel to behold and testament to the professionalism of our soldiers.

The cataphracts attacked in a series of wedges, each one a company in strength – one hundred men – in two ranks, though as with the horse archers there was insufficient room for all twenty-five companies to attack at once. But the result was satisfying enough: *kontus* points driving through shields and torsos with ease, leaving dead Gauls standing upright, the long lances driven through their bodies sticking in the earth at an angle of forty-five degrees to pinion them in place.

The warriors were running now, fleeing from the armoured horsemen who were slashing left and right with their swords, the ukku blades of Dura's cataphracts splitting heads covered by helmets and cleaving torsos. I saw an unclothed Gaul – what my wife's people call 'naked swords' – charge at a cataphract, gripping a longsword with both hands and screaming at the top of his voice. He stumbled and tripped over the dead, arrow-pierced bodies between him and the horsemen, his face contorted in rage. He raised up his sword on his right side, ready to deliver a downward cut to the cataphract's armour-clad left leg, when another horseman closing on him from behind took his head clean off with a swing of his ukku blade.

Company after company of cataphracts surged forward, but now the piles of dead and dying Gauls presented more of an obstacle than living enemy warriors, horsemen having to steer their mounts through the fresh carrion.

Those warriors still living were fleeing to the hills to reach the tracks and trails they had presumably used to spring their surprise. Amyntas obviously knew his realm well and had used his geographic knowledge to move thousands of warriors unseen into positions that allowed them to appear seemingly out of thin air when they attacked. But the price in blood had been exorbitant. A carpet of dead measuring half a mile wide and around four hundred yards in depth lay before me – thousands of men shot down by our horse archers and cut down by cataphracts. In terms of numbers we had won a spectacular victory.

But the aftermath of the bloodletting would reveal we had suffered a crushing defeat.

Chapter 14

Diana was inconsolable when the dreadful news reached her that Spartacus was dead. In the furious battle he and his horsemen and women fought against first the enemy horsemen and then the slingers, archers and Laodice's Pontic hill men that swarmed in on their flanks and rear, during which a lance had penetrated beneath his cuirass to pierce his stomach. Like the lion he was, he carried on fighting; the King's Guard and Vipers becoming enraged when they heard their king had been wounded. Despite being under a hailstorm of slingshots and arrows, they cut down thousands of hill men, slingers and archers. Hovik told me later that Atrax was the first to turn tail and run, leaving the horsemen of Pontus, Galatia and Cappadocia heavily outnumbered. Spartacus, dismissing his belly wound as a mere scratch, sent Hovik, Spadines and his two sons to chase after the now-fleeing enemy horsemen with Gordyene's medium horseman and half the horse archers, while his King's Guard, Vipers, balance of horse archers and Malik's Agraci dealt with the enemy foot soldiers. The two princes, not knowing their father had been mortally wounded, relished the task and pursued the enemy for miles, the Aorsi excelling in cutting off and slaughtering isolated groups of enemy horsemen. They returned with boasts of decorating the landscape with enemy dead. But their father was no longer alive to hear their tale of glory. And neither were eighteen hundred men and women who had ridden with Spartacus to attack the enemy horsemen – nearly one in six of the riders from Gordyene and their Sarmatian allies.

That night the King of Gordyene was cremated on a huge pyre outside camp, tens of thousands gathered around the raging fire to pay their respects. Shamshir wept like a child as his lord's body was incinerated and his soul went to join Rasha in the afterlife. Castus and Haytham stood like stone statues, their faces showing no emotion but their spirits no doubt crying out for vengeance. Their father would have been proud of their defiance and stoicism. Their uncle, his mood matching the black tattoos that adorned his face, placed a comforting arm around Haytham's shoulders when the pyre began to roar like an angry lion. The gods were paying homage to the passing of a great warlord, of that I had no doubt.

But the hissing, spitting and roaring of the flames had a competitor in the sobbing of the Queen of Hatra, who would have collapsed had it not have been for the strong arms of her husband holding her up.

She had been the one who had carried the infant Spartacus during our flight from the Silarus Valley following the death first of Claudia and then of Spartacus. She had subsequently raised him in Hatra after we arrived back in Parthia, and had seen the shy, reticent boy turn into an angry young man and then a king in his own right. Spartacus had always been like a lion with a short temper, quick to lash out and slow to forgive. But he had always respected his mother and father, being at ease in their company, probably because they had been slaves and he was the son of a slave. He also carried a heavy burden when he had been named after his natural father, and that probably contributed to his rage against the world. All speculation now.

I saw Shamshir, who had finally managed to compose himself, hand a sword to Castus. It was his father's sword, one of the precious ukku blades forged by the swordsmiths of Vanadzor. The young man, barely twenty years of age, took it. Shamshir grabbed his right arm and hoisted it aloft.

'Castus, King of Gordyene.'

The King's Guard and Vipers behind began shouting 'Castus, King of Gordyene', and hundreds and then thousands of others proclaiming the new ruler of Gordyene soon joined them. I found myself participating, the chorus of thousands reassuring on this bleak night.

'I am going to Corum,' hissed Gallia beside me.

The next day she left camp in the company of Talib, Haya, a pair of Daughters of Dura, two of Talib's scouts and a sizeable group of soldiers. I begged her not to go but she was adamant she would have revenge for Spartacus. Before she left, she called Spadines to our tent, the Sarmatian as surprised as I regarding the invitation. His eyes were dark-rimmed, and his normally ebullient, irreverent attitude was mercifully absent when he settled himself into a chair and accepted a cup of wine offered him by Klietas. He had lost two hundred men in the clash with the enemy, which still weighed heavy on his mind.

'We do not have our siege engines,' said Gallia, 'so I intend to walk to Corum and seize one of the gates giving access to the town. After I do so, I want your warriors to sweep into the town and put everyone to the sword.'

Spadines' eyes lit up but then his brow furrowed.

'Why us, majesty? You have thousands of your own soldiers to call on.'

Gallia did not spare his blushes.

'It is well known the Aorsi are skilled raiders and not averse to butchering civilians when the opportunities arise. My husband will never sanction Dura's soldiers being used to slaughter a town's inhabitants.'

Klietas handed me a cup of wine.

'That is true,' I said.

Gallia took the jug being held by Klietas and poured more wine into Spadines' cup.

'You will do it to avenge King Spartacus?'

Spadines drained his cup. 'We are in. But how will you get into the town?'

She gave him an evil grin.

'Let me worry about that. You just make sure your men are ready.'

Spadines was many things but he was no fool. He looked at me with a sceptical expression.

'What does the King of Dura have to say about this?'

What could I say? Gallia was determined to exact revenge for Spartacus, though some might say the thousands of enemy dead that littered the ground north of the camp was payment enough for one death. But I had neither the energy nor, frankly, the inclination, to argue with her. I just shrugged and drank more wine.

'He is supportive of his queen,' I answered.

Gallia and her three female accomplices led the column of riders that threaded its way across a mountain track to the east of the town: a hundred Amazons, hundreds of Aorsi and a small detachment of Durans on horseback commanded by the redoubtable Centurion Bullus. Amid the gloom that hung over the army in the wake of Spartacus' death, it was good to talk to the bluff soldier who had been a hero in the defence of Irbil a year before.

'Bad business with King Spartacus, majesty,' he grunted.

'Bad business, yes.'

We were riding through a beautiful stretch of pine trees on the lower slopes of a mountain, the track an ancient one though only wide enough to accommodate two horsemen riding side-by-side.

'How is the leg now, majesty?'

'Still giving me grief. I heard you refused the promotion I recommended you for.'

'Yes, majesty. I'm too old to learn new skills.'

'How old are you?'

'Thirty-eight, majesty.'

I nearly fell off Horns. He looked ten years older. But then, tramping the length and breadth of the empire took its toll on even the hardiest constitution. I should know. I winced every time I saw my reflection in a mirror.

'How is morale?' I asked him.

'The boys are itching to avenge King Spartacus, majesty, and are pissed off, sorry, annoyed, they didn't get to slaughter a few of the enemy yesterday. They feel cheated. They would have liked to have been in on this mission, whatever it is.'

Gallia was riding in front of us with Spadines and Zenobia, her face emotionless and determined. She had said nothing since we left camp, which was why I took the opportunity to speak with the trusty centurion.

'I will tell you what it is,' I said loud enough for Gallia to hear. 'My wife and three of her female companions are going to infiltrate themselves into the town of Corum later today. Then, without aid, they are going to open one of the gates to give us entry. Do you have a wife, centurion?'

'Me, majesty? No. I have a son, like, a bastard who lives in Dura. I make sure he and his mother don't starve.'

'Very noble. But let us say for the sake of argument that you did have a wife. Would you allow her to go on a mission, knowing that it might lead to her capture and execution?'

Bullus inhaled deeply, pondering the question, but did not have the chance to answer before Gallia turned in the saddle.

'Your wife would be free to make her own decision, centurion,' she said sternly.

'Even if her judgement was clouded?' I said.

'The queen's judgement has never been clearer,' stated Gallia.

'We have not heard Centurion Bullus' opinion on the subject,' I said.

'I'm just a soldier who obeys orders, majesty,' answered Bullus.

'How I envy you,' I sighed.

It was mid-afternoon when we arrived at a forest of oak and beech three miles to the east of Corum. Gallia handed the reins of her horse to Zenobia, slipped from her saddle and called her accomplices to her. All four donned loose-fitting robes to cover their tunics and leggings, swapping their boots for poor-quality shoes and smearing dirt on their faces. They would leave their bows and swords behind but took knives with wicked thin blades, ideal for slitting throats or thrusting into eye sockets.

'I beg you to reconsider,' I pleaded with my wife.

'You waste your words, Pacorus. The enemy must pay for what they did to Spartacus.'

I tried to keep my voice down. 'The enemy did pay. There are thousands of dead Galatians, Cappadocians and Pontic hill men littering the valley to the north.'

She flicked a finger across the blade of the knife, smiling with satisfaction at its sharpness.

'A message needs to be sent to the arrogant Amyntas, that he tangles with us at his peril.'

Before I could answer she sheathed her knife, pulled me towards her and kissed me passionately on the lips.

'If it goes wrong, I will wait for you in the next life.'

She turned to Spadines loitering nearby with a knot of his warlords, like him wearing an assortment of mail, leather and scale armour.

'Wait two hours and then lead your men with all speed to the eastern gates into the town. They will be open.'

'Yes, majesty,' he smiled, his warlords wearing evils leers at the prospect of plunder and slaughter.

Talib had only reconnoitred the town from afar, which was of modest size and had four entrances in the stone wall that encompassed all its buildings and inhabitants. He had no information regarding the size of the garrison or its population.

I prayed to Shamash to keep Gallia safe as she and the others ambled from the trees along the track that led to Corum's eastern entrance. Klietas ran forward and kissed Haya on the cheek, the young Amazon pushing him away. I watched them walk along the track, deliberately maintaining a slow pace to give the impression they were weak from their ordeal. They would be spotted from the battlements soon enough and the deception had to begin the moment they exited the trees.

'Do not worry, lord,' said Spadines beside me, 'it is well known the Queen of Dura cannot be killed in battle.'

'Who told you that?'

'At Irbil last year, I heard she survived a blow unscathed that would normally have cut a man in half.'

My mind went back to an enemy weapon shattering on Gallia's cuirass inside the city of Irbil. The incident had obviously become common knowledge.

'Tales are often exaggerated,' I said.

'The Queen of Dura has never been injured in battle, despite having fought in many wars. That is no exaggeration.'

I realised he was right. During the dozens of battles she had fought in, Gallia had not suffered even a scratch. Strange to say his words cheered me. Perhaps the gods had always watched over her. A sharp pain shot up my leg.

Unlike me!

The gods must have been with Gallia that day because the torment I had endured while waiting two hours before we saddled up and cantered west, vanished completely when I first clapped eyes on Corum's eastern gates. They were wide open. It had been easy for a grandmother and her three grandchildren to request and be given sanctuary in Corum, especially after news reached the town of the great slaughter suffered in the battle against the Parthians to the north. Gallia, speaking Gaulish, told a heart-rending tale of how the soldiers of the accursed King Pacorus had killed her husband, son and his wife, leaving her homeless and responsible for her three grandchildren. My relief on seeing the open gates mixed with elation made me urge Horns on, behind me hundreds of Aorsi drew their swords, levelled their spears and gripped their axes in anticipation of loot and murder. To date they had existed on meagre pickings – Armenian villages and travellers on the road – but now a whole town seemingly lay at their mercy. And they took full advantage of the opportunity.

Corum had an ancient past but its layout corresponded to the Greek style of town planning. The main street – the *decumanus* – ran east to west and the shorter street ¬– the *cardo* – ran north to south, with other streets running parallel and at right angles to the two thoroughfares. In this way the town was divided into rectangular blocks, with public buildings in the centre.

Corum was a neat, tidy and prosperous town. Its streets were clean, its houses and other buildings well maintained and its temples ornate and impressive. When the Aorsi swarmed through the eastern gates, Gallia was waiting on the steps leading to the battlements, three dead bodies at the foot of the steps and Haya on the wall standing over another corpse. Gallia came down the steps when the Aorsi had passed, gaining the saddle of her horse that had been brought into the town by Zenobia. I reached over and embraced my wife and thanked Shamash for keeping her safe.

'Old men and boys,' she said triumphantly, nodding at the dead men. 'The town had only a scratch garrison, one of them told me so before he died.'

Out of the corner of my eye I saw a triumphant Haya vault into a saddle, Amazons around her congratulating her on gaining entry to the town. The two Daughters of Dura who had accompanied her and Gallia likewise gained their saddles. They looked a picture of childish innocence, but their knives were smeared with blood.

Gallia pulled her bow from its case and nocked an arrow.

'Ready,' she shouted, prompting a hundred Amazons to nock arrows.

Zenobia began to remove the wax sleeve protecting my griffin banner.

'No, Zenobia,' I said. 'There is no honour to be had in killing innocents. Leave the cover on.'

Gallia rolled her eyes and nudged her horse forward. I heard the first screams and shuddered. It had begun.

I had always considered the Aorsi to be an undisciplined rabble on the battlefield, but in Corum they displayed a thoroughness for looting that was a wonder to behold, if one had a taste for plunder. Homes and small buildings were pillage by groups of four or five warriors. One held the horses, one covered the rear and the rest forced an entry and ransacked the interior. Spadines knew the rulers of Dura and Hatra would not tolerate the taking of slaves, so he had instructed his warlords to order their men, and some women, to kill everyone they encountered before robbing the corpses. They proved ruthlessly efficient doing so.

I hung my head in shame as we journeyed to the centre of the town, ear-piercing screams coming from the buildings on our left and right. How I wanted to draw my bow and shoot down leering Sarmatians coming from buildings holding loot – metal ornaments, gold and silver jewellery, coins and silks – that they then shoved in their saddlebags. Soon enough, pillars of smoke appeared in the sky. The Sarmatians were burning the town.

Gallia smiled with satisfaction. 'A signal to King Amyntas that we have taken Corum.'

The Sarmatians were not only burning; they were killing everything. I saw a dog limp from a shop, its shutters smashed open, its owner and his family dead on the floor. An Aorsi warrior threw a spear at the animal, which gave a hideous yelp as it was skewered. The bearded brute wrenched his spear free and joined his comrades in looting the shop, smashing open amphorae filled with wine, which they guzzled greedily. Their raucous laughter disgusted me. I heard a crack behind me and saw a fleeing man, aged judging by his grey beard and hair, collapse on the street. I spun in the saddle and saw a gloating Minu with an empty bowstring.

'No shooting,' I raged. 'Your duty is to protect the queen, not murder innocent civilians.'

I turned Horns to address the two files of Amazons, bellowing at them.

'No shooting at unarmed civilians. Bullus!'

The centurion trotted forward, bowing his head to me. I spoke to him in a voice loud enough for many Amazons to hear.

'If you see any Amazon take aim at an unarmed civilian, confiscate her bow.'

'Yes, majesty.'

I pointed at Minu. 'And you can put your bow away.'

She glanced at Gallia.

'Now!' I shouted.

She did as she was told, grudgingly.

'The Amazons have become a law unto themselves,' I said loudly, turning Horns. 'It is time they realised they serve the Kingdom of Dura, not themselves.'

Gallia said nothing as we trotted to the centre of the town, the location of a splendid assembly hall with a red tile roof and fronted by white stone Corinthian columns decorated with intricate leaves and floral patterns. Spadines was already on the scene, directing his warlords and pointing at the half a dozen temples standing on stone plinths accessed via steps on all four sides of each plinth. Groups of beaming warriors were coming from the temples clutching gold and silver candle holders, coins, rich robes and jewellery.

'Amazons to me,' Gallia shouted, urging her horse towards the largest temple, an outstanding example of Greek architecture, six columns wide and fourteen columns in length. It had a large terracotta roof with wooden beams and rafters. She dismounted and bounded up the steps, shoving aside surprised Sarmatians with armfuls of loot. I followed.

'Surround the temple,' shouted Gallia, 'no one gets in or leaves.'

The Amazons took up positions around the columns, ninety archers keeping guard while the other ten held the horses.

'You are with me,' I said to Bullus, who ordered half his men to stay with their mounts, the others to follow him.

The interior of the temple comprised an inner room, a *cella*, containing a statue of whatever god the temple was dedicated to. It was filled with scruffy Sarmatians, all standing in awe before a gold statue of a bare-chested warrior with wild hair and long moustache, holding the hilt of a huge longsword with both hands before him, the point resting on the marble plinth. On his head was a helmet decorated with what appeared to be ram's horns. There was a room behind the statue, an *adytum* or treasure room, the door of which had been prised open.

'Everyone out,' commanded Gallia, her voice echoing around the *cella*.

The Aorsi turned and stared at her, unsure what to do but reluctant to leave the great treasure they had stumbled upon. They began to move when the gruff voice of Spadines told them to.

His brown eyes lit up when he beheld the statue.

'Camulus,' Gallia told him, 'the Gauls' God of War. He is not to be touched.'

Spadines walked past us, halted at the statue, which was twice the height of a man, and stroked the precious metal.

'There is great wealth here, Queen Gallia,' he purred.

'There is wealth enough in the town to satisfy the greed of your warriors,' she shot back. 'You have heard of how King Spartacus plundered the Temple of Anahit in Armenia?'

Spadines continued to caress the gold. 'It provided much gold, enough for him to purchase his magical swords. Perhaps I desire such swords.'

'The day he plundered the temple was the day his life was cursed,' she said harshly. 'And now he is dead.'

She pointed at the open door to the *adytum*. 'And those of your warriors who took the god's gold are also dead men walking.'

Spadines stroked the statue one last time, sighed and turned around, smiling through gritted teeth.

'As you say, Queen Gallia, there are rich pickings to be had in the town.'

He ambled from the *cella*, muttering under his breath.

'It comforts me to know you still revere the gods,' I said.

'I should have cut off Spadines' hand for touching the statue,' she uttered. 'There is no respect left in the world.'

As the smell of burning wood reached my nostrils in the sanctity and quiet of the temple, she failed to see the irony in her words. Nevertheless, she was obviously moved to be in the presence of a god she had last worshipped over forty years before.

'I would like some time to myself, Pacorus,' she whispered.

I bowed my head to the statue, turned and took Bullus with me to leave my wife to converse with a god from her youth.

The screaming had stopped now, to be replaced by dozens of smoke stacks rising into the sky as Corum burned. The stench of bloated, decomposing bodies would come later, along with the incessant buzzing of flies and cawing of crows as they feasted on human flesh. The area around the temples and assembly hall was now filling with Aorsi with bulging saddlebags and blood-smeared weapons.

Bullus looked at the thickening smoke hanging over the town.

'If there are any enemy soldiers in the area, they will have seen this, majesty. We should be away sooner rather later.'

'I agree, centurion.'

He nodded towards the groups of Aorsi, many of them now drunk and rowdy.

'Perhaps we could persuade them to stay and sleep off their drink. When the enemy comes and sees what they have done, they will slaughter them all.'

'Killing two birds with one stone, as the saying goes.'

He nodded.

'I am sorely tempted, believe me,' I told him.

But Spadines was too skilled in raiding to allow his warriors to be caught by a vengeful enemy. Already parties of horsemen were leaving the town, cantering to the eastern gates to retrace their steps back through the forest track we had used to reach Corum. They would ride hard and fast, pushing themselves and their horses to put as much space as possible between themselves and any pursuit force, arriving back at camp before the sun dipped below the mountain peaks in the west. I doubted there would be any force chasing us. To support Gallia's raid, the rest of the army had made a display of strength in front of the enemy's wooden wall a few miles north of Corum, to avert the eyes of the enemy.

'Mount up.'

I heard Gallia's voice and turned to see her leading the Amazons from the temple with an expression of serene calm on her face.

'Are we finished?' I asked.

'We are done,' she replied.

We rode from a burning, ransacked Corum with the sun on our backs, a cool breeze in our faces and a sense of exhilaration due to taking the enemy completely by surprise. Gallia was happy, Spadines and his Aorsi were ecstatic and we had avenged the death of Spartacus with the slaughter of thousands of unarmed civilians. But just as we had sought retribution, so surely would the enemy, and I was mindful that we were still in hostile territory many miles from home.

Chapter 15

When we returned to camp, when the sky in the west was a shade of dark red, thousands of soldiers cheered the returning heroes, Chrestus' foot soldiers chanting 'Dura, Dura' as their queen accepted their applause. We halted outside camp to talk with Gafarn, Diana and their grandsons, Castus pulling his sword from its sheath and holding it aloft in salute.

'The enemy have fled,' he shouted, to raucous cheers from the Immortals within earshot.

The scene was reminiscent of the aftermath of a victory, which it was, of sorts, as Gafarn explained as we rode into the camp together. Diana and Gallia chatted excitedly about the raid on Corum, the Queen of Hatra, much to my surprise, delighted the town had been put to the torch. Clearly the death of her son had affected her greatly.

'Your men Kewab and Lucius probed the enemy defences with small parties when we spotted the smoke to the south.'

'Corum burning,' I said.

He nodded. 'Soon after, the wall appeared strangely absent of soldiers, so Chrestus and Motofi ordered an assault, your engineers having marked the location of the pits and trenches the enemy had dug. The soldiers reached the ditch, crossed it and scaled the rampart without any resistance.'

'The enemy must have fled when they saw the smoke,' I said. 'Their commander probably believed we had outflanked them and were marching north to trap him.'

'Well, they've all gone, to where no one knows,' reported Gafarn. 'Our scouts are scouring the area. Your man Lucius has already assigned parties to create a passage through the wall. We will be able to leave this accursed place in the morning.'

'It would have been better if we had stayed in Parthia.'

He sighed, his eyes full of sorrow.

'Cappadocia has always been unlucky for us. Remember the last time we were here?'

'How could I forget? We lost Bozan on that campaign, and then our liberty.'

'Bozan,' he said. 'There's a name from the distant past. And Vata, his son. Both long dead. It seems we have been kept alive to see our friends and family die before our eyes, Pacorus.'

'That is why we must get back to Parthia with all haste,' I said, 'before we lose anyone else.'

But that evening, as the kings and queens gathered in my tent to decide on our route home, thoughts of home were not uppermost in the minds of some of those present.

'We must sack Kayseri,' announced Castus, his blue eyes darting left and right to seek approval of his plan.

I had to confess I had not heard of the place.

'Where is Kayseri?' I asked, taking a sip of wine.

'It is the capital of Cappadocia,' Haytham told me, 'and should be destroyed.'

He sat next to his brother, Haytham seventeen, he twenty and now head of Parthia's most fearsome army. Malik smiled at the two, admiring their bullishness, while Kewab and Karys, both of whom I had invited to attend as they commanded sizeable contingents of the army, looked concerned. I had to tread carefully for I had no desire to prolong this campaign any longer than was necessary. But neither did I want to provoke Castus in particular, who might march on

Kayseri anyway. The oil lamps hanging from the tent poles around the table flickered, giving Castus a malevolent appearance.

I took another sip of wine.

'I understand your desire to avenge your father,' I said, 'but we do not know anything about this city: its size, defences, the strength of its garrison or whether it has its own water supply. And I would remind you we no longer have any siege engines.'

Gafarn was nodding in agreement but Castus' eyes narrowed.

'You have just taken a town without the aid of siege engines,' he replied, 'and with only a few hundred horsemen. There is no reason why we cannot do the same to Kayseri. Besides, it is on our route back to Parthia. We know King Archelaus has lost many soldiers already, as have his allies.'

'The army thirsts for vengeance,' said Haytham.

I looked at Gallia for support but she merely stared at her cup, tracing a finger around the lip. Gafarn was also strangely quiet. I tipped my cup at Kewab.

'I would hear your opinion concerning capturing Kayseri, Kewab.'

The Egyptian ran a hand through his curly black hair, deliberating for a few seconds before speaking.

'It is true we have inflicted losses on the enemy, though at a great price to Gordyene. But I would advise against delaying at Kayseri, even though it lies on our route. Speed is our ally in our objective to get back to Parthia as quickly as possible. The more time we stay in Cappadocia, the more time we give to the enemy to reorganise and hinder our withdrawal.'

I watched Castus and Haytham as Kewab gave his opinion, which made great sense. But I saw them bristle when he uttered the word 'withdrawal'.

'An army that has just won a great victory does not withdraw, satrap,' snapped Castus.

'It marches with impunity through the enemy's heartland,' added Haytham, whose rosy cheeks indicated he had imbibed too much wine.

'If we are not here to conquer Cappadocia,' said Karys.

'Which we are not,' I emphasised.

'Then why bother capturing a city we will have to relinquish immediately afterwards?' asked the former ruler of Mesene.

'To teach King Archelaus a lesson,' said Castus, 'to show him that his part in the killing of my father carries a heavy price that his people will have to pay.'

'You speak well, Castus,' said Diana.

I closed my eyes and knew I had lost the argument.

'Your father would have been proud of you,' continued Diana, smiling at Haytham. 'Both of you.'

Castus leaned back in his chair with satisfaction, just as Klietas was pouring wine into his cup, wine that he spilt on the young king's tunic when the royal head knocked the wine jug he was holding. Castus immediately jumped up and struck Klietas on the cheek with the back of his hand, causing my squire to drop the wine jug. Without thinking, Klietas struck him back.

For a few seconds Castus stood, open mouthed, staring in disbelief at my squire, before calling for assistance.

'Guards!'

Two Durans rushed in with swords drawn.

'Halt!' I shouted.

'I demand he is taken away and executed,' roared Castus.

I waved the guards away. They saluted, sheathed their swords and left the tent.

'Very well, I will do it myself,' said Castus, drawing his father's sword.

I jumped up. 'Put that away. Now!'

'It is death to strike a king,' seethed Castus, ramming his sword back in its scabbard.

'He's right, Pacorus,' agreed Gafarn.

'You should let Castus kill him,' growled Malik.

Klietas, aware of the gravity of his offence, went pale and swayed on his feet. I walked over to him and laid a hand on his shoulder.

'Apologise,' I said softly.

'I, I am sorry, highborn,' he babbled to Castus, who was uninterested.

'Your life is forfeit, slave,' he hissed.

That was the final straw. I had been deceived into joining this campaign, which I considered a complete waste of time. Worse, I had been dragged hundreds of miles from Dura on a fool's errand, which might yet cost us all our lives. Much as I had respected Spartacus, he had duped me, as had Phraates and indeed Octavian. But what really riled me was that Dura's army, *my* army, would be in grave danger if we loitered in Cappadocia trying to capture a city that served no strategic value save for satisfying Castus' blood lust.

'Make yourself scarce,' I told Klietas, who bowed and ducked out of the tent.

I turned to face Castus. 'To draw a sword in another king's tent is also to incur punishment. You would do well to remember that, Castus. And for your information, Klietas is not a slave but my squire. In Dura, we do not kill servants just because they make a mistake.'

'This is not Dura,' he grunted.

'No, indeed. It is a foreign land that we have no business being in, and we have yet to make a journey of several hundred miles to get back to Parthian territory. But allow me to congratulate you.'

He gave me a quizzical look. 'For what?'

'For assembling such an impressive list of enemies. As well as being in an armed truce with Armenia, you are now at war with Pontus, Galatia and Cappadocia, to say nothing of their Roman masters, who might take a dim view of your rampaging through their client kingdoms. I would have thought you have more urgent things to consider than a few drops of wine on your tunic.'

'Leave the boy alone,' Diana scolded me as I walked back to my seat.

' *Boy* being the operative word,' I replied.

Diana had always been one to try to soothe tempers, who was invariably the voice of reason and the arbiter of disputes. But not tonight. In my naivety I had not realised how the death of Spartacus had wounded her, until she spat venom in my direction.

'I blame you for this, Pacorus.'

I was astounded. 'Me?'

'For years, you persuaded Hatra and other kingdoms that the ingrate Phraates was the rightful high king. That decision cost Silaces, Nergal and Praxima their lives, and for what? So that Phraates could stab us all in the back. And now my son has died because of a secret pact between your high king and Octavian. How many more must die before you realise that Phraates is a treacherous snake?'

I tried to reason with her. 'Phraates is the son of Orodes and therefore…'

'Orodes is dead, Pacorus, killed by his own son. In the name of all that's holy cannot you at least admit that?'

'Who else is there, then?' I demanded. 'Tiridates, who decided to seize the high crown by force and who plunged the empire into civil war?'

'You know very well who should have been high king,' said Gafarn sternly.

'You, Pacorus,' spat Diana. 'You should have been high king, and if you had taken the high crown then our friends and my son would still be alive.'

'You speak harshly, Diana,' said Malik. 'Pacorus did what he believed was honourable.'

The Queen of Hatra now turned her wrath on the Agraci king.

'Honour? The honourable thing would have been for him to take the high crown and save us all the bloodshed we have had to endure since Orodes died. Do you think Mark Antony would have invaded Parthia if Pacorus had been high king instead of that fool Phraates? And Tiridates would not have dared raise his sword against a Pacorus sitting on Ctesiphon's throne. Becoming king of kings would have been the honourable thing to do, Pacorus. We all had to suffer the consequences of your ridiculous sense of honour.'

Kewab and Karys, squirming in their seats, stared at their cups, Gallia said nothing and Malik was taken aback by the revelation of a side of Diana he had not seen before. Castus broke the awkward silence.

'I will accept your squire's apology if Dura commits its army to the capture of Kayseri.'

'A most kingly gesture,' said Diana.

'Dura accepts,' Gallia answered for me, which did nothing to improve my humour.

'Never was the life of a squire so dearly bought,' I remarked caustically.

The evening ended soon after, the guests hurriedly leaving the tent while I sat and fumed. Klietas reappeared after Castus and Haytham had departed, to be lectured by Gallia.

'You must be more careful when serving food and wine. The king and I are more forgiving than other rulers. You may be free, Klietas, but others see you as a slave. You understand?'

'Yes, highborn.'

He began to clear away the platters and cups on the table.

'I did not like the side of Diana on view this evening,' I complained.

Gallia poured herself some wine and flopped down in the chair beside mine. Klietas refilled my cup.

'She is a grieving mother,' she said, 'people who are hurting strike out at those they love.'

'Thank you for pledging Dura's support to the absurd idea to capture the Cappadocian capital, by the way.'

She rolled her eyes. 'I know you would not divide the army in the middle of enemy territory, and as the soldiers of Gordyene and Hatra will be laying siege to the city, we have no choice but to remain with them.'

'I have a bad feeling about this,' I warned.

Klietas' ears pricked up. 'It might be the meat, highborn, sometimes it is under-cooked.'

'What? No, I was not referring to the food. Tell me, Klietas, if you were a king, would you try to capture a place knowing that you would have to give it up immediately afterwards?'

'Yes, highborn,' he beamed.

'Why?'

'To show the whole world my power, highborn,' he answered without hesitation.

I sighed. 'You really are not helping.'

The next day we continued our march south, making use of the gap cut through the enemy's wooden wall and earth rampart by Lucius' engineers and the entrenching tools of Dura's foot soldiers. It felt good to be away from the valley where Spartacus had fallen and where thousands of corpses lay rotting in the sun. We had cremated our own dead but the enemy slain stayed where they were, which meant the area was full of ravens, crows and vultures, to say nothing of hyenas and wolves that came at night to gorge on and fight over human flesh.

Corum was an empty, burnt-out husk when we passed it, smoke hanging over the town and the smell of dead flesh and charred wood filling our nostrils and making our horses skittish. Gallia said nothing as we passed the town, and I wondered if the gold statue of Camulus was still extant. More likely it had been stolen by the Aorsi and broken up. Bits of the god were probably stuffed into the saddlebags of Spadines and his Sarmatians. Camulus meant nothing to me but what worried me more was when Amyntas discovered the wreckage of his town and the sacrilege committed in its temples, he would be more determined than ever to serve vengeance on us.

'Vengeance' was certainly the word of the moment. Spartacus had wanted retribution for the death of Rasha, which had led us to Sinope; Diana and Castus wanted revenge for the death of Spartacus; and Amyntas would want recompense for the atrocities committed in Corum, to say nothing of the thousands of his warriors butchered by our arrows and lances north of the town. With forced marches, we could have been out of Cappadocia before the enemy had time to re-organise and mount a pursuit. But now we would march to Kayseri to lay siege to the city, which would give the enemy the very thing I wished to deny him: time.

It did not augur well.

During our march to Kayseri the landscape changed from one of verdant valleys and forested hillsides to bare, rock-strewn steppes littered with tall rock cones, needles and outcrops in a rainbow of colours. But at least the somewhat barren landscape provided good visibility and reduced the chances of any enemy force creeping up on us unawares. But to ensure we enjoyed an uneventful march, Talib and his scouts were despatched to reconnoitre our route and provide an outer screen for our flanks. Nearer the army were patrols of horse archers organised by Sporaces, Herneus and Hovik. The latter shared my misgivings about besieging Kayseri but his sense of duty and honour forbade him from saying anything to his new king. He looked like an impoverished mercenary in his tatty red tunic, old scale-armour cuirass and battered helmet. The hair beneath his headgear was thinning and streaked with grey, but for all his shortcomings when it came to apparel, he had a keen military mind, the product of over forty years' service in the army of Gordyene. It comforted me to know he would be a steadying and guiding influence on the young Castus. He would need it, for like a hyena sniffing blood, when

Armenia and Pontus discovered Spartacus was dead, they would surely test his resolve when it came to maintaining Gordyene's borders. And I doubted Artaxias would now pay the exorbitant amount of gold extorted from him by Spartacus.

Of the Cappadocians we saw none. We came across abandoned villages with stone huts and straw roofs, and Talib reported cave dwellings among the rock formations. However, they too were deserted, their inhabitants having fled before us.

It took ten days to reach Kayseri, the enemy conspicuous by his absence. Another ten would see us safely back in Parthian territory and I argued again with Castus and Diana about the sense of laying siege to the city. But they, and also Gallia, were adamant that King Archelaus should pay for his support of Pontus and Galatia, and by inference the rebel Atrax. To their voices was added that of Malik, who was aggrieved he and his warriors had taken no part in the raid on Corum. And so we entered the fertile oasis surrounding the large city of Kayseri and prepared to seize Archelaus' capital.

Kayseri was huge: a sprawling city, surrounded by a stone wall, on the northern slopes of a mountain called Argaeus. The mountain itself was massive, a dormant volcano that towered over the city, its peak covered in snow, its lower slopes wreathed in forests. All around the city the land was green and fertile, watered by underground springs, mountain streams and the nearby River Halys. The abundance of water produced a bounty of crops. There were vast areas of vine and fruit orchards, fields growing barley, wheat and flax, and expansive meadows where cattle and sheep grazed. Or they would have done had they not been evacuated before our arrival, along with the inhabitants of the outlying villages and farms, presumably into the city.

Kayseri itself projected power and strength, its long circuit wall constructed of black stone with towers at regular intervals. Each tower comprised two storeys, with arrow slits on the second storey and an open fighting platform on the roof. The sun reflected off whetted spear points held by soldiers on sections of the walls and on the fighting platforms, though I did not see a mass of troops lining the walls. Either side of all the gates into the city were towers, which like the others allowed flanking shots to be taken at attackers trying to scale the walls. As the army established a camp a mile from Kayseri, I rode in the company of Kewab, Chrestus, Lucius and a score of horse archers to take a closer look at the city Castus wanted to storm, being careful not to stray too close and tempt an archer or slinger to try his luck.

'Well-trimmed and fitted stone,' observed Kewab, examining the wall. 'I would advise ramps.'

'My thoughts exactly,' agreed Lucius. 'Aristotle stated a circuit wall ought to be an ornament as well as a defence, and these walls certainly fulfil both functions.'

'I would estimate the wall to be around twenty-five feet in height,' said Kewab, 'and ten feet thick.'

Chrestus was far from happy.

'Ramps take time. How many do you propose, Lucius?'

'At least two,' replied my quartermaster general, 'each one capable of accommodating two centuries side-by-side, plus archers, with a wooden wall on both edges to give cover from enemy missile troops.'

Chrestus shook his head. 'Madness, utter madness.'

'The King of Gordyene wants this city,' I said.

'The King of Gordyene should be put in his place,' said Chrestus bluntly.

'Allow me to provide a summary of coalition warfare, Chrestus,' I replied. 'The King of Gordyene is supported by Hatra concerning attacking this city, and the Queen of Dura fully supports the Queen of Hatra in believing King Castus should have his day in the sun. So you see, far from the King of Gordyene being put in his place, it is the King of Dura who has been out-flanked.'

Chrestus looked at the city, at the tree-covered lower slopes of the volcano and then at the verdant terrain behind us.

'If I was King Archelaus, I would not have surrendered the area around the city so lightly. I would have at least tried to interrupt the construction of our camp. But the enemy merely sits behind his walls.'

'The Cappadocians lost many men at Corum,' said Lucius, 'perhaps the army of Archelaus is a mere shadow of what it was.'

'Perhaps,' mused Chrestus. 'But the longer we stay here the more vulnerable we become.'

'General Chrestus is right, majesty,' said Kewab. 'Each siege ramp will require around twenty-five thousand tons of stones and soil, the felling of hundreds of trees to provide horizontal and vertical beams to provide bulwarks, as well as the labour of a thousand men fully committed for up to four weeks.'

'Four weeks sitting on our arses over two hundred miles from friendly territory is madness, utter madness,' grumbled Chrestus.

'You are right,' I agreed, turning Horns, 'work begins on the siege ramps in the morning.'

The garrison did nothing as we established siege lines around the city – small, fortified, self-contained camps manned by horse and foot soldiers – and watched as thousands of men went to work felling trees to provide timber to make beams to strengthen the siege ramps. The ramps themselves, which would enable two assaults to be made against the northern wall of the city, were started well away from the wall. Lucius organised dozens of work parties to fill baskets of freshly dug earth to create them. Under the direction of his engineers, hundreds of men emptied these baskets every hour to build up the ramps, each of which would be over a hundred paces in length.

From the beginning those working on the ramps were protected from enemy missiles, at the front of the ramps by large convex wicker shields over the height of a man and covered with rawhide to act as a defence against fire. Behind them were light wooden structures with open ends and wicker sides and roofs, likewise covered by rawhide to make them fire resistant. Each structure had four vertical wooden posts in each corner for support, and when arranged in a line, they formed tunnels that allowed soldiers to haul their baskets of earth under cover.

Engineers arranged wooden beams to be laid horizontally at regular intervals in the ramps to act as a framework for each structure, along with vertical beams along the sides for additional support. But the ramps took shape slowly, work ceasing when the sun went down for fear of enemy night-time sallies. But no attacks came from the city, and indeed very few arrows or slingshots were directed at the multitude working on the siege ramps, leading me to believe there were few troops inside Kayseri. But the thought of assaulting a city filled largely with civilians filled me with dread, and so I gladly accepted the offer to talk with a representative of King Archelaus, a herald being lowered down the outside of the city wall on a rope ladder a week after we had arrived outside Kayseri.

Sieges are dull affairs, save for the bloodletting at the end of them. Endless days filled with digging trenches, building ramps, chopping wood, collecting supplies, patrolling and leading horses to water and grazing. Cleanliness and preventing the outbreak of pestilence become of paramount importance, so the siting and digging of latrine trenches, cleaning up animal dung and ensuring troops attend to their personal hygiene become the obsession of officers, medics and veterinaries. As we settled down to isolate Kayseri and prepare for its storm, men such as Sophus and Lucius Varsas became influential figures, for the fate of the army rested in their hands. On a day-to-day basis, there was very little to do aside from menial chores, and I began to envy the patrols of horse archers who at least had a change of scenery during their duties. I therefore jumped at the chance to speak to a representative of King Archelaus.

'Not the king, majesty, the queen mother.'

Klietas poured wine into a silver chalice for our guest, a bald, plump, slightly effeminate courtier I assumed, judging by his rich purple silk tunic, red shoes and yellow silk leggings. Klietas poured me some wine and also Gallia, who entered the tent in full war gear, having taken the Amazons on a patrol to alleviate her boredom. At first the messenger, thinking she was an ordinary soldier reporting to his king, did not acknowledge her appearance. But he rose in haste when she removed her helmet to reveal the blonde hair and blue eyes of the Queen of Dura.

'Forgive me, majesty,' he said in Greek, bowing his head, 'I bring greetings from Glaphyra, mother of King Archelaus.'

'This is Levon,' I told her, 'an emissary from the city.'

Gallia took the wine and eyed him wearily. She noted his rich attire, delicate hands and fawning demeanour, which he emphasised by the fixed smile on his plump, blemish-free face.

'It is an honour to meet the Queen of Dura, whose fame is known throughout the civilised world.'

Gallia rolled her eyes, tossed her helmet to Klietas and removed her mail shirt.

'Your mistress rules Kayseri?' she asked, flopping down in a chair, her cheeks flushed for it was another very hot day and the tent was dry and airless.

'In the place of her son, yes, majesty,' he replied.

'Sit, Levon,' I told him, 'it is too hot to stand on ceremony. I assume you have a message from your mistress?'

He bowed his head to me, still smiling.

'She is desirous to meet with you, majesty, to find a solution to the current predicament.'

'There are two other kings who need to be consulted first,' I told him.

His smile disappeared. 'My mistress believes that a face-to-face meeting between you and her, majesty, would be more productive than including King Gafarn and King Castus.'

I glanced at Gallia, who looked surprised. So this Glaphyra had learned of the death of Spartacus.

'The meeting would be informal,' emphasised Levon, 'more a discussion between like-minded individuals than an occasion of high diplomacy.'

'Where?' I asked, intrigued.

'There is an apricot orchard two miles from the city's western entrance, majesty. My mistress will be there tomorrow two hours after dawn, at a cottage with stone walls painted white with a red-tiled roof.'

'Her leaving the city will draw the attention of our soldiers,' I told him.

'My mistress will not be leaving the city via the gates, majesty,' he replied.

I was now more intrigued than ever. Was this a woman or a sorceress who could become invisible to pass through our lines unseen?

'Until tomorrow, then, Levon,' I said.

He rose, bowed to me and then Gallia and took his leave, halting at the tent entrance.

'My mistress has heard you are a man of honour, majesty.'

'Don't worry, Levon,' I assured him, 'I promise not to harm or try to seize your mistress.'

He was delighted. 'The rumours are indeed true, majesty. Until tomorrow.'

I had him escorted back to the wall, just in case a bored legionary or archer decided to brighten up their day by killing an enemy eunuch.

'Eunuch?' chuckled Gallia.

'Perhaps I am being unkind.'

'Probably not. He was wearing perfume, did you notice?'

'I did. Made a pleasant surprise from sweat, leather and horses.'

'It might be a trap,' she cautioned. 'If she can move in and out of the city by way of a concealed passageway, so can soldiers. You should take an escort.'

'Klietas,' I called.

He came running from the bedroom area.

'Highborn?'

'You like apricots?'

'Yes, highborn.'

'I'll take you with me. There, I have my escort.'

Gallia, however, insisted I was accompanied by a score of Amazons, who were waiting for Klietas and me when we walked from our tent the next morning. It was another warm, sunny day, a few white puffy clouds in the sky, which would disappear by midday. Parties of legionaries and Immortals were filing out of camp to continue work on the siege ramps, as well as replace the garrisons in the smaller fortified camps that ringed Kayseri. Gafarn kept Diana company in their tent. She had withdrawn into a state of melancholy and shunned all company, mine especially. Castus and his brother, bored by the logistics of siegecraft, rode off with a large escort of King's Guard and Vipers every morning on hunting expeditions. Malik and Kalet surprised us all when they announced they and their men would take part in the construction of the siege ramps, after Kalet had lectured the Agraci king on his men, and women, being stronger and fitter than the Agraci on account of them having to build their own mud-brick strongholds in the desert, whereas the Agraci lived in tents that required little manual effort to erect. And so a competition began to decide whose followers could dig and haul more earth, which delighted Lucius and speeded up the work on the ramps. A little.

Klietas was delighted to see Haya among the score of Amazons, the pregnant Minu their commander. He gave her a broad grin and clutched his claw necklace, and she in turn gave him a smile.

Perhaps he was breaking down her wall of resistance. Good, they would make a well-matched couple. Gallia kissed me on the cheek.

'Ensure the king comes to no harm,' she called to Minu.

'Yes, majesty,' replied the Amazon.

I hauled myself into Horns' saddle and nudged him forward. In front of us loomed the impressive feature of Mount Argaeus, on its lower slopes the sprawling city of Kayseri. We had not trotted a hundred yards when Sophus walked into the main avenue leading to the camp's southern entrance. He had a lean frame anyway but he seemed to have lost weight, giving him a gaunt appearance. He bowed his head to me.

'Are you fasting, Sophus?' I joked.

He raised a disapproving eyebrow.

'I have a query, majesty.'

'The king is on an important mission,' snapped Minu.

'Then I will not delay him any more than necessary,' the Greek shot back.

'What is your query, Sophus?' I asked.

He pointed at the city. 'Is Cappadocia going to be absorbed into the Parthian Empire?'

'No.'

'But you intend to capture the city.'

'Yes.'

'And presumably give it up afterwards?'

I nodded.

He stroked his thick beard.

'We, or should I say you, lay siege to a city, storm it, butcher its population, plunder the ruins, and afterwards march back to Parthia.'

'Is that your query, Sophus?' I asked wearily.

'Oh, no, majesty. My query relates to the care of the wounded civilians in Kayseri. If we assume that when the soldiery breaks into the city and they do not manage to slaughter everyone, do you wish me to administer medical aid to the wounded survivors? Or let them die a slow death?'

I leaned forward.

'You are impertinent, Sophus.'

'And you are an unhappy man, majesty.'

I was taken aback. 'How so?'

'You are not a butcher devoid of morals. The King of Dura does not sack cities for the mere pleasure of it. It would be a great pity if your reputation were to be irrevocably damaged at Kayseri, to say nothing of the self-reproach that would torture you afterwards. You are, above all, a moral man, majesty.'

He stepped aside. 'I have said my piece.'

'I respect your honesty, Sophus, and it may interest you to know that I now journey to prevent the slaughter you have predicted.'

He looked surprised. 'I will pray that you succeed, majesty.'

'Pray to whom?'

'Dike, the Greek Goddess of Justice, majesty.'

I tapped Horns' flanks with my knees to prompt him to move, raising my hand to Sophus.

'Let us hope she hears your prayers.'

The designated place for the meeting with the mother of King Archelaus was an old apricot orchard, the trees having been planted in a grid formation, in rows from north-to-south to maximise the number of hours daily each tree was exposed to the sun. The orchard was deserted, the ground showing signs of iron-shod hooves where our horsemen had ridden through the area. When we spotted the whitewashed cottage on the edge of the orchard, I ordered Minu to remain with her women while I rode on with Klietas. I could see no signs of life and wondered if Glaphyra had been forced to remain in the city. When we arrived at the cottage, however, I saw two horses tethered near a water trough, both with red saddlecloths and bridles decorated with silver discs. And then Levon came from the cottage, smiling and bowing his head.

'Welcome, King Pacorus. My mistress awaits you inside.'

Glaphyra was beautiful, a woman who despite her middle age had retained her slim figure and a fair skin free from blemishes. She smiled when I entered the hut, the interior filled with the pleasing aroma of her cedar perfume. She was standing behind a simple wooden chair, though Levon had placed a cushion on its seat. She spread her arms.

'Alas, King Pacorus, all I can offer is a chair and a cushion, a far cry from what a lord of war like you is used to.'

I removed my helmet, bowed my head to her and walked to the other chair, arranged opposite hers. She noticed my limp.

'You are wounded, King Pacorus?'

I eased myself into the chair; she did the same.

'An old wound, lady, that has never left me.'

She wore little makeup and her only jewellery comprised a simple silver necklace and a silver ring on her left hand. But she had no need to paint her skin because her oval face was framed by long, auburn hair. Her blue eyes went from me to the sparse interior of the hut, which nevertheless was free of dust and cobwebs.

'I like to come here from time to time. I own the orchard and it is nice to escape the bustle of the city.'

She looked at me. 'Though I will have to endure the oppressive heat of the city uninterrupted this summer, it would appear.'

I thought of her living a life of luxury in a palace filled with slaves and officials attending to her every need. Hardly a taxing existence, even during a siege.

'How may I help you, lady?'

'Straight to the point, I like that. You should know I have full authority to treat with you as the representative of my son, King Archelaus.'

'May I enquire as to the whereabouts of your son and his army?'

She ignored my request.

'It grieves me to see a Parthian army outside my city, King Pacorus, especially as Cappadocia has no quarrel with you or the other kings who currently sit outside its walls.'

'We are here due to an unhappy sequence of events, lady, and you are right, Parthia has no quarrel with Cappadocia. But may I remind you that your son was part of the army that attacked us at Corum.'

'Cappadocia has a treaty of friendship with Pontus, King Pacorus, under the terms of which my son is obliged to provide military aid if Pontus is attacked by a foreign power. You must appreciate that obligations must be honoured. After all, is not your presence here the result of your pact with Gordyene?'

I did not wish to engage in a conversation about treaty obligations, especially as I believed Dura had been deceived into joining what was turning into an ill-judged campaign.

'You are well informed, lady, but I am still at a loss as to why you requested this meeting.'

She smiled alluringly. 'I have a proposal for you.'

Surely she was not going to attempt to seduce me.

'What kind of proposal?'

'A monetary kind.'

I had to admit I was disappointed. 'Oh?'

'I know you are incorruptible, King Pacorus, so I humbly request you act as an intermediary between King Castus and myself. If the new King of Gordyene refrains from attacking Kayseri, I will pay him twenty thousand talents of gold.'

The sum caught me by surprise. It was the equivalent of six hundred tons of gold.

'That is a lot of gold. But I am reluctant to mention it to Castus, that is King Castus.'

She was surprised. 'May I ask why?'

'For the simple reason, lady, that he will conclude Kayseri is filled with gold, which will merely intensify his efforts to take the city by storm.'

'Kayseri does not hold such a treasure,' she told me.

Now I was confused. 'Making promises you cannot fulfil is guaranteed to incur King Castus' wrath, and believe me you do not want that.'

'He is cast in the same mould as his late father?'

'Very much so,' I informed her.

'We have gold, King Pacorus, but not all of it is in the city. However, if you promise to restrain your soldiers for a period of two weeks, the balance can be collected and brought to Kayseri. I am eager to save the city of my birth from destruction, King Pacorus.'

I believed her, but whether Castus would be convinced or indeed interested in her offer I doubted.

'Mark Antony believed you were a man of honour,' she said suddenly.

'Mark Antony?'

'We were lovers once, and he often talked of you, about how you had shown him mercy and friendship when he had been captured in Syria. He respected you as a great commander, king and moral man.'

'I liked him,' I admitted. 'I had no idea you were a close friend of his.'

She tossed back her auburn hair and laughed. 'How upright and proper you are, King Pacorus, which is why I desired to meet with you. Everything I have learned about you leads me to believe that you would not purposely butcher civilians, but that is what will happen if your army, and those of Hatra and Gordyene, storm Kayseri.'

She looked at me with pleading eyes. 'I beg you to show mercy, if not for me or my son, then for the tens of thousands of innocents within Kayseri's walls.'

She reached over to grab my hand. 'I beg you.'

I doubted not I was being manipulated. However, twenty thousand talents of gold was an enormous sum. Castus was young and impressionable; perhaps he too could be manipulated.

'I cannot speak for King Castus, or indeed King Gafarn,' I told her. 'But I believe I might be able to avert more bloodshed. But I will need a gesture from you, lady.'

When I ordered the work on the siege ramps to be halted, I received a visit from Castus and Haytham, their tunics drenched in sweat after a day spent hunting ibex in the hills to the north. They were joined by an equally rank Spadines, his clothes so tatty, his hair and beard so unkempt I thought a pack of ibex must have ambushed him in the hills.

'General Motofi has told me you halted the work on the siege ramps,' panted Castus, clicking his fingers at Klietas to indicate my squire should pour him and his two companions cups of water. Klietas obliged.

Gallia regarded the ruler of Gordyene coolly, clearly unimpressed by his lack of manners.

'And good afternoon to you, too, Castus,' I said sarcastically, 'I trust you had a successful hunt?'

He looked at me and then Gallia, snatching the cup from Klietas before nodding at Gallia.

'Great aunt.'

'Take the weight off your feet,' I said to all three, 'and allow me to explain myself.'

Spadines, showing his age, was sweating profusely and so I tossed him a towel to prevent him dripping all over the carpet that covered the tent's wooden boards. I then lifted a sheet that had been placed over eight gold bars that had been stacked on the floor. Castus' eyes lit up when he saw them.

'A talent of gold, Castus,' I said, 'a gift from the good people of Kayseri. Two days ago I met with the mother of King Archelaus, who informed me her son is willing to pay you twenty thousand talents of gold if you march your army back to Gordyene.'

I doubt Castus could even conceive of twenty thousand talents. But he would have seen the gold his father had extorted from Phraates, and that had been 'only' thirteen hundred talents. Then there was the gold plundered from the Armenians, but that was a mere trifle compared to the vast sum Glaphyra had promised. His blue eyes, filled with excitement, looked up at me.

'Twenty thousand talents?'

'That is what she said.'

'When we take the city, it will fall into our hands anyway,' said Spadines, whose breathing had almost returned to normal.

'Except it will not,' I told him. 'The gold will have to be collected from other parts of Cappadocia, which will take at least two weeks.'

Castus rose from his chair and squatted beside the gold, and then proceeded to run his hands over the illustrious metal. He stopped and peered at me with narrow eyes.

'How much do you want?'

'Nothing, Castus. Dura has its own gold. All I desire is to be out of this kingdom and back in my palace among my friends and family.'

The answer pleased him and he returned to his chair, though a scowl soured his handsome features when Gafarn and a pale Diana entered the tent. Klietas pulled up two more chairs for the rulers of Hatra, Gafarn's eyes alighting on the pile of gold.

'Been mining, Pacorus?'

'It's mine,' snapped Castus, who instantly regretted speaking to his grandfather in such a curt manner, blushing in embarrassment.

'A tidy sum,' said Gafarn, 'a gift?'

'More a bribe,' I said, accepting a cup of water from Klietas.

I provided details of my meeting with Glaphyra and her generous bribe in return for our withdrawal from Cappadocia.

'And you believed this woman you have never met before, Pacorus?' asked Diana, her eyes red from weeping over the death of her son.

'I believed she wanted to save her city from destruction, yes,' I answered.

'Twenty thousand talents of gold is a tidy sum,' admitted Gafarn.

'Very tidy,' agreed Spadines, rubbing his hands.

'This woman, this Glaphyra, will provide more gold as surety for the soldiers of Gordyene halting work on the siege ramps,' insisted Castus, 'as a sign of her good faith.'

'Excellent idea, brother,' agreed Haytham, 'a thousand talents should suffice.'

I frowned at the young pup but Castus thought it an excellent idea.

'A thousand talents, delivered to my tent,' insisted Castus. 'In two days. Your friend in the city can arrange that, lord?'

'She is not my friend, Castus,' I emphasised, 'but I will convey your demand.'

'One thing, Pacorus,' said Gafarn, 'how did this Glaphyra exit the city unseen past our patrols?'

I shrugged. 'I have no idea, though if I was to hazard a guess I would say a secret passage from the palace, constructed to allow members of the royal family to flee in times of peril.'

'Or perhaps it was a sewer,' suggested Gafarn.

I thought of Glaphyra's perfect skin, her alluring perfume and her long auburn hair.

'It was not a sewer.'

A message was shot into the city tied to an arrow, which prompted a similar reply from the besieged, a letter from Glaphyra tied to it stating she would deliver the amount demanded by Castus, but it would require one of the city gates to be opened and would I ensure there would be no storm of Kayseri when they were unlocked.

On the allotted day, the city's northern gates were opened and half a dozen large carts, each one with four thick wooden wheels and pulled by a pair of oxen, trundled from the city and drove between the quarter-finished but now abandoned siege ramps. Their nervous drivers kept glancing left and right when the party of King's Guard flanked them as they left the city and then halted the convoy four hundred paces from the gates, which had been hurriedly shut after the last cart had exited Kayseri. Castus, Haytham, Shamshir and Hovik then examined each of the carts, Castus instructing the drivers to walk back to the city on foot. After the gold had been meticulously counted and recounted, Shamshir allocated a King's Guard to drive each cart, which continued their journey to the tent of Castus. The young ruler was beaming from ear to ear when he passed me and Gallia, being barely able to contain his excitement. He had only been king for a few weeks and already a thousand talents of gold had fallen into his lap, with another nineteen thousand due in less than a fortnight. It made his father's prizes look paltry in comparison.

The days passed and the spirits of the army soared. Not only had the soldiery been spared a potentially bloody and costly storm of the city, they would be setting off for home in a matter of days, with the largest sum of booty ever won by a Parthian army.

And it was all illusion.

Chapter 16

It was Talib who brought news that a Roman army was approaching from the southeast, the route we would have to take to return to Parthia, and specifically the Kingdom of Hatra. It was with a heavy heart I called a council of war soon afterwards, the knowledge I had been duped by the enticing Glaphyra uppermost in my mind.

Gafarn was surprised 'A Roman army?

'I have identified seven Roman legions, majesty,' said Talib. 'They are accompanied by auxiliary foot soldiers and horsemen.'

'How many?' asked Castus.

'At least thirty thousand in total,' my chief scout informed him.

The young king shrugged. 'We still outnumber them. We have a strong position here. I say send horsemen to harry them and interrupted their march. How far away are they?'

'Two days' march, majesty,' said Talib.

'My warriors could slow them up,' proposed Malik.

'And mine,' added Kalet, winking at the Agraci king.

I discounted the idea. 'Even if you delay their march, it will give us two days instead of one. I would rather use our light horsemen to form a strong rearguard to allow us to leave this place.'

Castus was unimpressed. 'Why would we want to leave? We defeat this new army, take Kayseri, put all the inhabitants to the sword and then continue our march back to Parthia.'

How simple and straightforward the world seems to the young. He failed to realise that a Roman army meant we would be fighting Octavian himself indirectly, the first occasion in a long time when Parthian had faced Roman across the battlefield.

'We have no choice,' said Diana bluntly. 'The Romans want us dead, all of us, and that includes you, Pacorus. Phraates colluded with

Octavian to bring about the death of Spartacus, and now they both sniff an opportunity to deal with the other members of his family.'

'I say we fight,' growled Gallia. 'Let's send a message to Octavian and Phraates that their unholy alliance will fail.'

'I'm with you, princess,' smiled Kalet.

I looked at Kewab and Karys, who together commanded a total of seven thousand horsemen.

'You two are quiet.'

We were all sweating as we sat at the table, the tent warm and airless, despite Klietas' efforts to cool us down with copious amounts of water.

'In my deliberations, majesty,' replied Karys, 'I have always considered what my lord and his wife would have expected of me. To them, there would be no hesitation. So I and my men will fight beside their old allies.'

Gallia smiled triumphantly, and Diana gave a cool nod. The Queen of Hatra turned her brown eyes on Kewab. They were no longer red and blotchy but cold and determined. She wanted revenge for her dead son; nothing else mattered.

'My horsemen are at King Pacorus' disposal,' he stated matter-of-factly.

'I still do not understand how seven Roman legions have seemingly sprung from the earth,' I complained.

' *Evocati*, probably,' explained Kewab.

'What's that?' said Haytham.

'Romans who have fulfilled their terms of service and obtained their discharge,' explained Kewab. 'However, such veterans can voluntarily enlist again if asked to do so, enticed by the promise of reward.'

'Old men,' sneered Castus.

'Roman veterans,' I said firmly, 'men with vast military experience. Our four legions will be outnumbered by the Romans.'

'The Immortals are not legions,' hissed Castus.

I was tiring of his immaturity. 'Very well, Castus, my two legions, plus the Immortals who fight, dress and are equipped in an identical manner to Roman legionaries, will be outnumbered. Is that more pleasing to your ears?'

'We will see who triumphs between the Romans and our Immortals,' boasted Haytham.

Castus nodded, Malik frowned and Gallia roller her eyes. There was silence as everyone reflected on the coming battle. For Castus and Haytham it was an opportunity to win glory; for Diana, simple revenge against the enemy. Any enemy.

'Are there any other routes we might take to extricate ourselves from the predicament we find ourselves in?' I asked Talib.

He shook his head. 'The road south leads to Cilicia, a Roman province, while the road northeast would take us back to Pontus.'

'The only way is east,' insisted Castus.

'It is settled, then, we remain here and await the enemy,' I said with little enthusiasm.

After the council meeting I desired to get some fresh air and be away from the tiresome bravado of Castus and Haytham. Their young age and volatile natures bothered me, especially as Castus commanded a third of the army. Whatever his faults, Spartacus always had a calculating head on his shoulders when it came to battle. He had created the army of Gordyene, lavished it with high-quality weapons and equipment, and ensured good officers staffed it. And he was always careful to ensure it was never committed to battle unless the odds were stacked in its favour, though even he had been out-smarted at Corum. I worried Castus would show no such restraint.

'May I walk with you, majesty?'

I turned to see Kewab following me. I nodded to him.

'Something is bothering me, majesty,' he said after catching up with me.

'Apart from being deep in enemy territory, cornered like a rat in an alley, and about to ignite a war between Rome and Parthia, you mean?'

He flashed a half-smile. 'Kayseri is located at a crossroads, majesty, and as such it is an ideal place for separate armies to converge on. We know there is a Roman army approaching from the southeast, but what of the forces of Pontus, Galatia and Cappadocia?'

'You think they will join with the Romans before the battle?'

'No, majesty, I believe we will be assaulted on multiple fronts.'

We walked to the stable bloc to the rear of the royal tent and those of the Amazons, a sizeable area of sheeting and poles arranged to create stalls, with canvas roofs to provide shade for horses. Squires were shovelling dung into wheelbarrows and rubbing down horses, while others were leading mounts away to the workshop area of the camp to be re-shoed by farriers.

'That assumes a high level of coordination, Kewab, and a central directing hand.'

'Exactly what I was thinking, majesty.'

I walked over to the stall holding Horns, an old stable hand about to commence brushing his shining black coat. He bowed, I held out a hand and he passed me the brush. I began to brush my horse from the head to neck to begin with, the strokes being in the direction of the natural lie of his hair.

'Please elaborate,' I said.

'I believe Queen Glaphyra is coordinating the movement of enemy forces, majesty. My men have detected pigeons flying into and out of the city, leading me to believe they are carrying messages for the kings converging on Kayseri.'

I stopped brushing. 'Or they could be just birds doing what birds do.'

His hazel eyes narrowed. 'I do not believe so, majesty.'

Kewab was a genius, a man who could conceivably have risen to become pharaoh of Egypt had not Cleopatra killed his father, General Achillas. But Egypt's loss was Parthia's gain, and specifically Dura's. Over the years I had come across many generals, warlords and kings, all with various strengths and weaknesses. Crassus was rich, intelligent but vain, and it was vanity that had led to his defeat at Carrhae: the belief he could easily conquer Parthia after he had defeated Spartacus. Narses and Mithridates were ruthless and calculating and not without talents. But they both believed they were chosen by the gods to rule Parthia and because of that they grossly underestimated their adversaries. They also took little interest in the organisation, tactics and equipment of their armies. After all, why bother with such trivialities when the immortals are on your side?

Mark Antony was certainly a charismatic figure who inspired devotion among those he commanded. But he was also a gambler; indeed, when I had first encountered him he was in Syria after fleeing gambling debts. Bright, resourceful and likeable, he was at heart a romantic who believed he could enchant and seduce his way to glory. He almost succeeded, but his obsession with Cleopatra cost him the eastern half of the Roman Empire and eventually his life.

But Kewab was the complete commander, whose mind could focus on both details and grand strategy. In this way, he came to know the strengths and weaknesses of the troops he commanded, allowing him to plan campaigns and battles to maximise their advantages and minimise their deficiencies. And he never underestimated the enemy. He went out of his way to discover as much as possible about the adversaries he faced: their organisation, weapons and equipment, tactics and logistical support. In Parthia, logistics in general were neglected. Kings issued a summons to their lords to muster their retainers and rendezvous at an assigned place prior to marching off to war. It was left to individual lords to organise supplies for their men, which invariably resulted in troops living off the proceeds of plunder, either that or starve. Ideally, each man rode off to war with two-to-four weeks' food in his saddlebags and an equivalent amount of fodder on the camel he shared with other men of his village. But the reality was often very different. But Kewab had been tutored in Dura where every aspect of a campaign was pre-planned, with a special emphasis on logistics. When the army marched it did so with three months' supplies for every soldier, civilian, horse and mule that marched with it. Camels were treated differently as they were hardy, could subsist on meagre fodder and endure long spells without water. To Kewab, warfare became a mathematical equation, a balance sheet of pluses and minuses, and he always made sure his troops had all the advantages before a drop of blood was spilt. And his uncanny ability to put himself in the enemy's position, to be able to see what was happening 'on the other side of the hill', meant the foe would be spilling the majority of blood when battle was joined.

'Our dispositions make no sense,' complained Castus, staring at the Roman army deploying on the vast meadow to the east of Kayseri.

'They make perfect sense,' I snapped.

I turned my attention to the dead volcano and wondered if it and the terrain to the north had been created by the immortals for a giant who lived on Mount Argaeus. If the monster had sat on the summit and stared north he would have seen a green and fertile land stretching before him, fenced in by low-lying hills and snow-capped mountains in the distance. The lower slopes of the volcano were covered in trees, and at its base was the sprawling city of Kayseri. Mere mortals to the west of the city had planted more trees, but these were laid out in neat lines and rows – vineyards and orchards. To the north of the city, on the great steppe itself, were fields growing barley and wheat, while to the east and northeast were vast meadows where livestock grazed. Today, though, very different beasts occupied them: Roman legions.

By the looks on the faces of Malik, Diana, Gafarn and even General Hovik, I could tell not only Castus was concerned about our dispositions.

'Kewab,' I said, 'please enlighten everyone *again* as to our battle plan.'

Castus regarded the Egyptian coolly. Like many, he had heard much about the man who until recently had been Satrap of Aria and the man who had held Emperor Kujula at bay. But he did not take kindly to Gordyene's army, *his* army, being deployed by Kewab, which entailed it being divided up. Kewab pointed at Kayseri, some two miles to the south, our own camp between it and us.

'Kayseri sits at a crossroads.'

'We are all aware of that,' said Castus tersely.

Kewab had much experience of dealing with truculent kings and merely smiled.

'The northern road leads to Pontus and Galatia; the eastern road to Parthia; the southern road to Cilicia; and the western road all the way to Rome.'

Castus' cheeks were going red with rage.

'King Archelaus will be arriving by that road,' Kewab spun in the saddle and pointed north, 'while our friends from Pontus and Galatia will be appearing from that direction.'

Beyond the Immortals, arrayed in a battle line facing north, there was nothing but empty terrain, along with the odd flock of sheep grazing on the lush grass.

'You will understand our scepticism, satrap,' remarked Gafarn, 'as there appears to be no enemy troops to the north or the west, and yet there are a great many to the east.'

'Seems bloody stupid to me,' said Kalet, who with his senior warlords were getting itchy, seemingly doing nothing while over thirty thousand Romans were deploying some five miles to the east.

'The Romans are a distraction,' announced Kewab.

Castus looked exasperated and even Gafarn was surprised.

'A most potent distraction, satrap,' said Diana.

'Indeed, majesty,' agreed Kewab, 'but a distraction, nevertheless. The enemy knows we regard Rome's legions as fearsome opponents and assumes we would deploy all our foot and horse to face them.'

He held out a hand to me. 'But as King Pacorus illustrated at Carrhae, Roman legions can be contained by the skilful use of horse archers. That is why over thirty thousand horse archers, supported by the camel trains of Dura, Hatra and Gordyene, are currently moving to intercept the Romans.'

'Horse archers will not be able to defeat Roman legions,' snapped Castus.

Kewab nodded. 'But they will stop them and force them to deploy into a square, majesty, giving us time to deal with other threats.'

'What other threats?' asked Malik.

Kewab pointed to the north. 'Those, majesty.'

There was a slight breeze blowing from the north, barely enough to cause our standards to flutter but enough to carry the drums, horns and chants of a large force of troops approaching. Hovik, who had remained silent thus far, knew instantly what it meant and yanked on his horse's reins.

'If you will excuse me, majesty,' he said to Castus, 'I want to see this for myself.'

He galloped off to the Immortals, standing in their well-dressed ranks, the Aorsi deployed on their wings to provide some, albeit dubious, mounted support when the fighting began. The ominous noise to the north was slowly getting louder, causing the horses, long used to the sounds of war, to get fidgety. Malik licked his lips.

'It will be good to avenge Spartacus some more.'

Castus was quiet now, sinking into a sullen silence as he curled a lip at Kewab.

'It won't be long now,' said the Egyptian, peering to the west, to where the Durans and Exiles were arrayed in three lines, the first line consisting of four cohorts, the second and third of three cohorts.

'The enemy is to be congratulated,' he mused, 'coordinating an attack from three directions in no small achievement.'

'Whose side are you on?' hissed Castus.

'The winning one,' replied Kewab.

Castus was seething with anger, but his ire abated somewhat when Hovik returned to report to his king. The general ignored the rest of us as he bowed his head to his lord.

'A large force of enemy troops advancing from the north, majesty, thousands of Gauls and Pontic soldiers. Mostly foot soldiers, though there are well-appointed horsemen among them.'

He cast me a glance. 'I also saw a dragon banner among their standards.'

'Atrax,' hissed Gallia.

'I would advise reinforcing your soldiers with the Vipers and King's Guard, majesty,' Kewab said to Castus. 'I doubt the Aorsi will hold.'

Castus smarted at the insult directed at his allies.

'I am quite capable of issuing my own orders, Egyptian.'

But he nevertheless joined Hovik in riding back to the Immortals, taking the Vipers and King's Guard with him. Both units were equipped with bows, and though the Immortals had scorpions, the Aorsi were equipped with few bows and Gordyene's medium horsemen had none. An additional thousand bows in the hands of expert shots would be a significant force multiplier. A rider arrived from Sporaces to inform me the horse archers had engaged the Romans, buzzing around them like angry hornets, loosing arrows at the now-static legions. Kewab nodded approvingly.

The first part of his plan was working.

To the mix of chanting, drums and horns to the north was added a new sound: the dull roar of troops advancing from the west. We could not see them because in front of the Durans and Exiles was the expanse of vineyards and orchards, through which the enemy would have to move to get to grips with Dura's foot soldiers. Moving through trees, even those arranged in neat lines, breaks up formations and slows down advances. It was an inspired move by Kewab to suggest the Durans and Exiles be deployed back from the orchards, from where the scorpion crews could wreak havoc among troops emerging from the trees.

'King Archelaus and his Cappadocians,' said Kewab, his face lit up by a contented smile.

Gafarn nudged his horse closer to Horns.

'Is your man a commander or sorcerer? How does he get the enemy to dance to his tune?'

'He has a very analytical mind,' I replied, 'he is the most perceptive person I have ever met.'

Gafarn looked at Kewab issuing orders to two of his subordinates who had ridden back from where our horse archers were battling the Romans.

'If I were Phraates, I would not have dismissed him so lightly. I can't imagine he is happy being back at Dura.'

'I intend to address that problem when we get home. For his services to the empire, Kewab deserves to be richly rewarded.'

A roar of war cries erupted just beyond the Durans and Exiles, followed by a succession of cracks as scorpion crews began shooting their weapons. The Cappadocians were exiting the vineyards. And walking straight into a storm of iron-tipped bolts. They would reform at the treeline, bolts piercing bodies and skewering individuals to tree trunks, prior to hurling themselves at Dura's foot soldiers. I laughed and clenched my fist – little did the warriors of King Archelaus know of the calibre of Chrestus' soldiers. The first-line cohorts would not stand to receive the mad rush of warriors goaded to distraction by the scorpions but would rather launch their own charge to draw the sting of the enemy. The Durans and Exiles would rush forward, the front ranks hurling their javelins before drawing their swords and racing at the enemy, using their shields to barge individuals to the ground before closing to stab and thrust with their short swords. Then the rear ranks in each century would hurl their javelins over the heads of their comrades locked in a close-quarter mêlée with the foe, creating further mayhem among the enemy.

We were now fighting three separate battles – to the north, west and east – and nearby two and half thousand cataphracts stood motionless on their horses. The finest horsemen in all Parthia, perhaps in the world, reduced to the role of a reserve along with Kalet's lords, Malik's Agraci and Gallia's Amazons. I looked at Kewab, who was staring south, past our camp staffed by three thousand armed squires, to the locked gates of Kayseri.

Which suddenly opened.

From her vantage point in the palace, positioned higher than the rest of the city, sitting as it did on a rock outcrop, Glaphyra would have had a panoramic view of the battlefield. She would have seen the legions, now stationary, being harassed by swarms of horse archers on all sides. To the north, she would have perhaps been disappointed to see the soldiers of Gordyene already deployed to meet the forces of Galatia and Pontus. And she would be very aware of her son's forces battling the Durans and Exiles immediately east of the sprawling orchards and vineyards and getting nowhere. She would have also noted the thousands of horsemen standing idle north of the great Parthian camp, many of them in shining armour, their horses similarly attired.

Kewab had pre-empted her thoughts, though, and when the great wooden gates opened, and hundreds of horsemen streamed out of the city, he sent a rider to Herneus and Azad to convey his compliments and request they deal with the city garrison.

He then turned to Malik. 'If you would accompany the cataphracts, majesty, I believe the day will be ours.'

'You too,' I said to Kalet.

He flashed a smile. 'I thought you would never ask.'

Two thousand cataphracts began to move towards the hundreds of horsemen coming from the city, the ground beginning to tremble as hundreds of iron-shod horses carrying big men in scale armour broke into a canter, each hundred-man company arrange in two ranks and deployed in a wedge formation. If a bird was flying overhead it would see twenty wedges bearing down on the foe, akin to steel teeth ready to chew the enemy into pieces. Behind them rode Dura's lords and Malik's Agraci, a rabble in comparison but hardy warriors used to the cut-and-thrust of close-quarter combat. Five hundred cataphracts did not move: Hatra's Royal Bodyguard, staffed by nobles, the sons of nobles and those who had distinguished themselves on the battlefield, an élite force lavishly equipped, riding Hatra's famed pure white horses. They stayed to defend their king and queen.

Five thousand Parthian and Agraci horsemen thundered towards the stream of riders coming from the city, which halted and formed into line to meet the cataphracts. They carried round wooden shields faced with hide sporting interlinked swastika motifs, their blue banners emblazoned with an apricot – the symbol of Kayseri. Each man wore a heavy mail shirt, an open-faced helmet, and was equipped with a lance and sword. There were also horse archers among them, which were deployed ahead of the mounted spearmen, so they could shoot at the oncoming cataphracts and destroy the momentum of their charge. But the arrows merely bounced off the scale armour worn by both rider and his mount, scattering the horse archers and leaving the mounted spearmen to receive the full force of two thousand charging cataphracts.

We were now engaging the enemy in four separate clashes on the battlefield. I had never seen such a thing and could only marvel at Kewab's foresight and ability to place himself in the minds of enemy commanders. But he was not infallible.

'We have guests,' remarked Gafarn without a trace of irony.

'Naked men, highborn.'

Klietas was pointing at a mixed force of horsemen and men on foot around half a mile away, but his eyes had been drawn to those running, who like their hooved animals among them were naked.

'Gauls,' said Gallia, pulling her bow from its case. 'Amazons, face right.'

Zenobia repeated the order and within seconds a hundred riders had turned their horses to face the Galatian horde racing towards us. Each woman strung an arrow in her bowstring and waited for the order to charge. I too pulled my bow from its case and nocked an arrow in the bowstring, as the Royal Bodyguard's signallers blew their trumpets. As one they closed around their king and queen, and the Amazons.

'Straight into them,' Gafarn shouted to the bodyguard's commander, who nodded, spoke to his subordinate, the officer relaying the order to the signallers. Gafarn, the best shot in the Parthian Empire, nocked an arrow in his bowstring.

'Stay close,' he told Diana, who likewise was holding a nocked bow.

The Gauls were closing fast, screaming war cries, the naked ones issuing blood-curdling howls.

'They are drugged,' Gallia shouted, 'one arrow will not be enough. Have a care.'

The cataphracts broke into a gallop and lowered their long lances moments before they crashed into the enemy riders, who appeared to be Gaul noblemen, judging by their burnished helmets, round shields, expensive mail armour and the longswords at their hips. They were also armed with spears but the *kontus* carried by the cataphracts was longer, thicker and far deadlier. The first contact unhorsed around two hundred Gauls, *kontus* points being driven through armour and torsos with ease. The second cataphract rank killed a further two hundred, more Gauls being thrown to the ground as their horses reared up on their hind legs before bolting away from the steel-clad monsters. For a moment, I thought we would not need our arrows as the cataphracts went to work with their axes and maces, Gauls striking back in a swirling mêlée but finding it difficult to penetrate Parthian scale and tubular armour.

But then the 'naked swords' were among us.

The majority were armed with two-hand axes and hammers, though a few carried longswords. Their hair arranged in spikes, having been washed in lime water to make it malleable, their eyes blood-shot and bulging, they literally threw themselves at the nearest foe. Hollering and screeching, they hacked at horses with their axes and war hammers. I saw one launch himself at a cataphract, landing behind the royal guardsman and instantly grabbing his helmet to yank it off. I aimed my arrow and shot it into the Gaul's back, which had no effect on him whatsoever.

'Again,' shouted Gallia, putting another arrow in his back, the cataphract desperately trying to free himself of the wild beast behind him that had pulled his helmet half off. Then the headgear was flung aside and the cataphract screamed. The Gaul, two arrows in his back, was biting off the man's ear!

I shot two arrows into him, Gallia two more and Klietas added a fifth. The Gaul shuddered, went limp and slipped off the horse. The cataphract, clutching at his ear, blood covering his hand and tubular arm armour, turned his horse and retreated from the fray.

A naked sword swung his axe at a horse's chest, causing the severely wounded beast to collapse on the ground, pinning its Amazon rider to the ground. The Gaul pounced on the helpless female, brought his axe down on her helmet to crush the side of the headgear and her skull. He continued to chop at the bloody head with frenzy, laughing manically as he did so. It took three arrows to kill him.

The naked warriors were intoxicated with *soma*, a hallucinogenic drink derived from the *haoma* plant, the juice from which was extracted by pressing the stalk and then being strained though sheep's wool. Called the 'elixir of immortality', it gave those who imbibed it great strength, as well as reducing them to a state of frenzy. Perhaps in such a state of delirium they were able to converse with Camulus. More likely their senses were grossly distorted by drinking large quantities of *soma*.

A naked Gaul pulled an Amazon from her saddle and caved in her chest with a war hammer, the woman gurgling helplessly as her ribcage was reduced to splinters. The Gaul raised his gore-covered hammer in the air and hollered a war cry, turned and was disembowelled when I slashed my *spatha* across his belly. He dropped the hammer, peered down at his entrails tumbling from his stomach and laughed, before crumbling to the ground.

I stayed close to Gallia, my wife shooting arrow after arrow at any naked Gaul she spotted, Klietas, alarmed that it took more than one arrow to even fell these naked warriors, shooting rapidly at targets. A Gaul jumped on the back of Gallia's horse and for a moment I had visions of my wife's ears decorating the soil of Cappadocia. But instantly, and in a move born of decades fighting in the saddle, she pulled her dagger from its sheath, turned the blade in her hand so it faced backwards, and rammed it hard into the Gauls right eye socket. It was enough to cause him to fall from her horse, allowing me to hack down with my sword to cut deep into the side of his neck. A huge fountain of blood spurted upwards from the wound and he collapsed on to his knees, before falling face-first on the grass.

To the frenzied clatter of weapons clashing and the howls of the naked Gauls was added a new sound: the rumble of horse's hooves. I saw spear points, red tunics and the blessed sight of a red banner sporting a silver lion emblem – Gordyene's medium horsemen. The wall of mounted spearmen skewered or rode over any naked Gaul in their way, not even men inebriated on *soma* able to withstand being trampled underfoot by many horses. The din of battle suddenly stopped, the mounted Gauls beating a hasty retreat with the appearance of fresh enemy horsemen, abandoning their frenzied companions to Parthian arrows, swords, spears, axes and maces.

I looked around at the scene of carnage, my heart pounding in my chest and my tunic soaked with sweat. Klietas, one of his quivers empty, was desperately searching for Haya among the exhausted Amazons, alarm etched on his face when he looked at the dead women on the ground, all having suffered dreadful chest and head wounds. Gallia was mercifully unhurt, along with Zenobia and Minu, and Klietas gave a huge sigh of relief when Haya removed her helmet and beamed at him.

It was Hovik who had ridden at the head of the Castus' medium horsemen, the general reporting to Gafarn and me while Hatra's Royal Bodyguard once again formed a cordon around their king and queen.

'We detected a group of horse and foot sweeping around our flank and heading your way, majesty,' he told us. 'The king ordered me to lend what assistance I could.'

'It is very welcome,' said Gafarn.

Hovik stared at dead naked men all around.

'This is a strange land.'

'How goes the battle?' I asked.

'The enemy is falling back in some disarray,' he reported, 'their waves breaking on the unbreakable wall of Immortals.'

'What of the traitor Atrax?' asked Gallia.

'I have no information as to whether he lives or is dead, majesty,' said Hovik.

'It does not matter.'

I turned and was relieved to see Kewab safe and unhurt, though his quiver was almost empty.

'Atrax is merely a landless wanderer,' he continued, 'I suspect King Polemon will grow tired of him and his followers and eject them from Pontus.'

'He will find no sanctuary wherever he goes,' said Gallia ominously.

Karys was dead.

An enemy slingshot that had struck him in the face to kill him instantly had severed another link to Nergal and Praxima. Strange to say, despite our victory, the loss of Nergal's former general made the defeat of the enemy insignificant to me. Besides, the triumph was not mine but Kewab's, whose name would surely now be elevated to sit among the great commanders of history. That night, as the dead were collected, honoured and cremated on vast pyres, for our victory had not been bloodless, I remembered the comrades I had lost over the years: Castus, Cannicus, Domitus, Drenis, Vagharsh, Kronos, Marcus Sutonius, Spandarat, Thumelicus, Silaces, Nergal and Praxima. To those could be added countless more I had marched and fought beside. All now dead. Tears streamed down my cheeks. Gallia comforted me.

'I have lived too long,' I said to her. 'I swore I had done with war, but here I am, staring at the burning bodies of more fine men and women who will never see old age. And for what? Nothing.'

She linked her arm in mine. 'You are here because you honoured the pledge you made to protect Media, as did Gafarn and Diana. It is no fault of yours, or theirs, that Spartacus deceived you.'

Her words did nothing to rid me of the nausea I felt, which was not caused by the sweet, sickly smell of burning flesh. All my life I had comforted myself with the conviction that when I drew my sword, it was for the right reasons. But Spartacus had turned me into nothing more than a bandit at worst, and a debt collector at best. So much for honour! The only crumb of comfort was that in the morning we could commence our march back to Parthia.

Chapter 17

I may have wished to march back to Parthia but Castus had other ideas. Far from being happy that we had won a great victory and inflicted a large number of casualties on the enemy, he was like a boar with a toothache when we convened in his tent for a council of war just after breakfast the next day. Gafarn and Diana, looking tired and pale, embraced Gallia and then me, the old, kind Diana having mercifully returned to replace the angry, vindictive woman of late. There were ten of us at the table, Kewab having led the horse archers out of camp early to harry the Romans who were expected to withdraw back to Syria or Cilicia, or wherever they had come from. Karys was dead, of course, though his passing was met with curt words from Castus.

'Men die in battle, it is the nature of things.'

It would be another hot day, though there was a slight breeze to provide a modicum of comfort and blow away the stench of mass cremation that had taken place outside our camp. Muster rolls had been compiled and officers had made their reports, which had been collated so the commanding generals of each army could report on losses.

'A thousand dead and half that wounded,' said Herneus.

'Seven hundred dead, more or less the same number wounded,' reported Hovik.

'Twelve hundred dead, three hundred wounded,' stated Chrestus.

'A hundred of my warriors were slain,' Malik told us.

'Do we have any estimates concerning enemy casualties?' I asked, stretching out my tired limbs.

'At least ten times our own,' gloated Castus, 'perhaps more.'

Chrestus nodded. 'The orchards and vineyards are choked with Cappadocian dead, and they lost more in the initial clash with my boys.'

'I would say five thousand Pontic and Galatian troops were killed by the Immortals and our horsemen,' opined Hovik.

'Lord Orobaz estimates the horse archers killed ten thousand Romans,' reported Herneus.

'I find that hard to believe,' I said. 'But even half that figure would be a significant achievement. In any case, the Romans will wish to withdraw now they have failed to link up with their allies, leaving us free to escape from Cappadocia.'

Castus and Haytham stared at me with disbelieving eyes.

'Escape? Victors do not escape,' Castus informed me, 'not with unfinished business to settle.'

'What unfinished business?' I demanded to know.

'The not-so-small matter of nineteen thousand talents of gold,' replied Haytham.

Gafarn gave a disapproving frown and Diana shook her head.

'There is not that much gold in the city,' I sighed, 'it was just a ruse to delay us here.'

'How unfortunate for Kayseri,' said Castus.

'We want the head of that bitch Glaphyra,' spat Haytham.

'We have had a lucky escape, Castus,' said Gafarn, 'thanks in no small part to Satrap Kewab. We are in enemy territory and the longer we remain here, the more vulnerable we become, notwithstanding our victory.'

'There are still Roman legions intact and nearby,' I reminded him.

But the King of Gordyene merely stood and marched from his own tent, Haytham trailing after him.

'Hovik,' called Castus.

The general, embarrassed, bowed to us and hurried from the tent.

'What now?' asked an exasperated Diana.

We discovered soon enough. With the Romans having retired back to their camp five miles to the east where they were contained by a ring of horse archers, and the disappearance of the forces of Cappadocia, Pontus and Galatia, our scouts being sent far and wide to ensure they did not return undiscovered, Castus was free to implement his plan. He detailed half the Immortals to chop down every tree in the vineyards and orchards near the city, a wanton act of destruction that showed his immaturity and petulance. However, at least Hovik had the timber collected and used to make scaling ladders for any assault on the city. The other half of the Immortals, plus Spadines' Aorsi, collected the enemy dead and dumped them at the foot of the wall that surrounded Kayseri. This required groups of Immortals adopting a *testudo* formation to allow them to get close to the city wall, without being exposed to enemy slingers and archers. Hovik deployed horse archers near the walls to provide covering volleys as the foot soldiers carried out their grisly task. It was both unnecessary and unbecoming conduct of a Parthian king, but Castus and Haytham were in their element, egged on by Spadines, who unfortunately had survived the battle unscathed. While the ghastly business was being undertaken, arrows were shot into the city with messages attached, stating simply:

King Castus demands his outstanding nineteen thousand talents of gold

The ploy worked.

After three days, when the first visible signs of decay began to manifest themselves among the heaps of dead around Kayseri – bloated abdomens, blood bubbles forming around the nostrils, and the first whiff of the odour of putrefaction – a message reached Castus that the gold would be paid.

I was in one of the hospital tents when he appeared, waving a piece of papyrus in the air. Sophus, his leather jerkin splattered with blood following an amputation of a lower leg that had turned gangrenous, eyed the young king warily. He had taken off the leg but the soldier had died from loss of blood anyway, which had annoyed my physician intensely, though in truth the soldier had suffered a head wound as well as having his ankle splintered by a slingshot. His mood was dark and his temper short when Castus breezed in.

'You see,' he said, thrusting the note at me, 'it did not take much to make that bitch see the error of her ways. She has agreed to pay me what I am owed. A few thousand corpses dumped at her feet soon shattered her resistance.'

'It was your idea to heap dead bodies around Kayseri?'

Castus was taken aback by the sharp tone in Sophus' voice and turned his blue eyes on the curly haired Greek.

'Who are you?'

'This is Sophus,' I interjected, 'the head of my army's medical corps.'

'Attend to matters that concern you, physician,' sneered Castus.

'Oh, but it does concern me,' replied Sophus, 'me and the thousands of others who inhabit this camp.'

'In what way?' demanded Castus.

Sophus' eyes bored into him.

'When life leaves a person, it is not the only thing that departs his body. After around five days, the putrid gases that have built up inside the cadaver escape into the air. Fluids begin to drain from every orifice, especially the nose and mouth. By this time, insects will be feasting on the rotting corpse. The putrid gases are also pestilential, which means they can infect the living, not only the citizens inside Kayseri, but also those in the path of the winds that carry them.'

'As soon as I am paid, we will depart,' said Castus, his face showing alarm.

'Do you know why Greek city states never had kings?' said Sophus.

Castus gave him a bewildered look.

'It is because experience and wisdom are considered more important in Greece than accident of birth.'

'Thank you, Sophus,' I interrupted. 'Congratulations, Castus, and if I could ask you to expedite the transfer of the gold from the city to your carts, we can be on our way back to Parthia.'

Castus' eyes narrowed. 'You have a sharp tongue, Greek. You should be careful, one day it might talk your head off your shoulders.'

He spun on his heels and stomped from the tent.

'Alas for Gordyene,' remarked Sophus.

'Also for you if you talk to him like that again,' I cautioned.

'I thank the gods, majesty, you are unlike other kings.'

'In what way?'

'Most rulers are boorish brutes, who if they had not been born into nobility would invariably be thieves, murderers, cheats and beggars.'

He stopped and tilted his head.

'Which is what most kings are, cloaked as they are in this mystical aura called nobility.'

'I'll take that as a compliment.'

One of Dura's soldiers appeared at the entrance to the tent, screwed up his nose at the odour of vomit, faeces, urine and sweat, saw me and marched over. He snapped to attention and bowed his head, handing me a rolled papyrus scroll with a red wax seal.

'This morning is a time for correspondence, it seems,' said Sophus, noticing the seal of the Governor of Syria.

'Cicero,' he muttered.

I broke the seal and read the Greek words. It was indeed from Cicero, who requested a meeting with me that afternoon, declaring he would come unarmed to our camp, 'if your majesty deems fit to receive me'. I thanked Sophus and left the tent.

'I meant what I said about leaving this area, majesty,' said the physician, 'unless you wish to return to Dura with half your army dead.'

I raised my hand in acknowledgement and hastened back to my tent, accepting the acclaim of legionaries going about their business. How simple and straightforward was the life of a common soldier, and how I envied them. Not for them the machinations of politics and intrigues, or the game of kings and empires. A pain suddenly shot through my leg, causing me to stumble. The soldier who had delivered the letter instinctively grabbed my arm.

'Are your hurt, majesty?'

'No, just old.'

'Do you wish me to send for a cart?'

The final ignominy.

'No, I will manage.'

We lessened the pace to save my embarrassment. I should have really ridden to the hospital tents with an escort, but I found such gestures ostentatious, especially when the destination was relatively close. Back at my tent I penned a reply to Cicero and invited him to my quarters, giving the note to Sporaces and ordering him to ride to the Roman camp with an escort of horse archers. The Romans were content to stay inside their encampment, at least for the time being.

'They will be expecting you,' I told him.

The Syrian governor was all politeness and deference after he had been shown into my tent, a guard of honour of Exiles forming a corridor outside through which he walked. Gallia was on an extended patrol with the Amazons, which was fortunate, as her prickly temper when it came to Romans would only complicate matters. I also did not alert Gafarn or Castus to the governor's arrival. Klietas had arranged two couches in the reception area and served us wine, the northerly breeze making the interior of the tent pleasant, though it was still warm. The governor still resembled one of Rsan's clerks with his receding hair and narrow face, though his mind was as sharp as an ukku blade. His red boots, purple stripe on his tunic and expensive blue cloak fastened to his left shoulder by means of a gold broach indicated his wealth and position. But he was quietly spoken and most reasonable in all his arguments – the consummate diplomat.

'First of all, majesty, may I congratulate you on your inspired tactics during the recent engagement. A most instructive battle.'

'They were not my tactics, governor,' I informed him, 'but those of Satrap Kewab, who until recently was keeping the Kushans at bay in the east.'

'And have the Kushans been dealt with, majesty?' he enquired innocently.

'They have,' I lied.

'Please convey my compliments to the satrap.'

'How may I help you, governor?'

His high forehead creased. 'I am here at the behest of the rulers of Pontus, Galatia and Cappadocia, majesty, who are most unhappy that their kingdoms have been invaded by a foreign foe.'

I smiled. He said nothing of Octavian, but it was his master in Rome he was representing, not some minor kings who could all be replaced with relative ease. Nevertheless, I had always found Cicero good company, so I joined him in the verbal dance.

'Believe me, governor, I am as eager to be away from here as my enemies are to see the back of me.'

'Such a blatant act of aggression on the part of King Spartacus cannot go unanswered, majesty. However, as the King of Gordyene fell at Corum, I believe we can reach an agreement that avoids a general conflict between Rome and Parthia.'

I placed my silver chalice on the low-lying table beside me, Klietas topping it up.

'What sort of agreement?'

He too put down his chalice, placing a hand over it when Klietas made to top it up.

'If you agree to withdraw from Cappadocia immediately, majesty, I believe Augustus can be persuaded not to launch a campaign against Parthia. None of us want that.'

'You have that right,' I agreed. 'But who is Augustus?'

'Ah, of course, you will not have heard. The Senate has granted Octavian the title Augustus…'

'Meaning "serene",' I interrupted.

He nodded. 'In recognition for his services, the Senate has agreed that Caesar will hold high office for life.'

'Caesar?'

'Octavian, that is Augustus, was the nephew of Julius Caesar, a great military and political leader. Much like yourself, King Pacorus. He took the name Caesar out of respect for his assassinated uncle.'

'You flatter me, governor.'

He leaned back on his couch. I liked to think he was at ease in my company. He had, after all, visited Dura to attend the wedding of Eszter and Dalir.

'The death of King Spartacus will, I believe, lead to a lessening of tensions between Parthia and Rome's allies in these parts.'

I thought of the hot-headed Castus but said nothing.

'That being the case, I think if the new King of Gordyene pays a fine to Rome, this campaign can be quietly consigned to the annals of history.'

'What sort of fine?'

He raised his chalice and took a dainty sip of wine.

'Shall we say twenty thousand talents of gold?'

I roared with laughter, causing Klietas to jump. It was Roman pragmatism at its best and was also a delicious irony. Just at the moment when Castus received his gold, it would be taken off him. I could only applaud Cicero's ingenuity.

'May I take it you are not averse to the idea of a fine, majesty.'

I wiped my moist eyes with a cloth.

'You can indeed.'

We talked for around an hour, about Eszter and Dalir, about Byrd and Malik, and our hopes that the peace between Rome and Parthia would last. He said little about Octavian, now Augustus, and I did not mention Phraates once. That made for a pleasant conversation, and in any case, I did not wish the Romans to know of my displeasure concerning the high king.

'You wish the gold to be returned to Kayseri?' I asked.

'Absolutely not, majesty. It will be transported to Rome. Raising, equipping and maintaining in the field seven legions plus auxiliaries is an expensive business.'

A few moments ago, Cappadocia was Rome's ally; now it had become a mere client kingdom.

'If the gold can be delivered to our camp, majesty, I can guarantee your march from Cappadocia will be uninterrupted.'

Castus was apoplectic.

After salivating over the huge amount of gold that was transported from the city just after dawn on carts pulled by oxen – nearly six hundred tons of the precious metal, a quantity neither I nor Gallia, Gafarn of Diana had ever seen, I informed him it would be delivered to the Romans. He had deployed the Immortals in front of Kayseri, and the King's Guard and Vipers closed up on either side of the carts as soon as they were out of arrow and slingshot range, heading for camp. With Gallia and the Amazons, I barred their path, Castus and Haytham initially thinking we had come to admire the gold and congratulate him.

'Greetings,' he beamed, the sound of hooves behind us alerting me to the arrival of Gafarn and Diana who I had invited to attend. I had informed them earlier of the meeting with Cicero and the agreement I had brokered, though I did not know what they thought of it. Gallia knew, of course, and agreed we had to return to Parthia without delay, if only to be away from the nauseating stench that now filled the air as thousands of corpses spewed putrid gasses into the air.

He raged with fury when I informed him of the agreement I had arranged with Cicero.

'How dare you make decisions of my behalf,' he roared. 'Dura has no jurisdiction here.'

'Neither does Gordyene,' I advised him, 'and may I remind you that there are still seven understrength Roman legions nearby.'

He flicked a hand at me. 'We have nearly sixty thousand soldiers, enough to deal with a rabble of worsted Romans.'

'How blind are you, Castus? Do you not realise that we are in Roman territory, and even if we destroy the Romans in that camp, there will be another one hundred thousand bearing down on us when Augustus declares war on Parthia?'

'Who is Augustus?' asked Gafarn.

'Octavian,' I snapped. 'He's changed his name.'

'I have often thought about changing my name,' waxed Gafarn, 'to something refined, Greek, perhaps. Menedaius is a fine name, don't you think?'

'Not now Gafarn,' I pleaded.

'You must surrender the gold, grandson,' said Diana firmly. 'This campaign has been a costly mistake. We have already lost your father and I have no desire to see more members of my family die for no reason.'

Whatever he thought of me, Castus, and Haytham for that matter, had great respect for their grandparents. It had been Gafarn and Diana who had raised Spartacus and he in turn had never wavered in his love for them. He had made sure his sons likewise showed respect to the rulers of Hatra. And perhaps Castus was thinking like a king for once, for Hatra was too powerful an ally to ignore. His eyes darted between his grandparents and me, behind him a long line of carts filled with treasure.

'And if you want gold,' continued Diana, 'don't forget the amount promised your father by King Artaxias of Armenia, which is now owed to you.'

'There is an old saying, Castus,' said Gafarn. 'What you have never had, you never miss.'

It seemed as though the whole world was holding its breath while Castus made his decision. But eventually, sullenly, he agreed to surrender the gold to the Romans. Being unable to witness the sight himself, he ordered Shamshir to carry out the deed, the commander of his King's Guard instructing the carts be smashed and the oxen to be butchered when they reached the Roman camp, or so Cicero informed me the next day when I received a missive from him stating he and the rest of the Romans would be marching south immediately.

We passed the abandoned camp on our way back to Parthia, the air becoming fresher and sweeter as we left the rancid stench of Kayseri. Castus and his brother stayed away from me and declared they and Gordyene's army would be building its own camp each night, separate from the one occupied by the soldiers of Hatra and Dura. It was all very childish, but I kept reminding myself that Castus was still young and inexperienced, and he had just surrendered six hundred tons of gold.

As the days passed, he deliberately increased the pace of his army's rate of advance, which resulted in a substantial gap developing between the armies of Dura and Hatra and his own. I sent Kewab ahead to stress the inadvisability of dividing our combined forces, but to no avail. Eventually, when a thirty-mile gap existed between the two forces, I met with Gafarn and Diana to decide on strategy.

Though summer was coming to an end, the evenings were still warm and pleasant, the air clean and fresh as it blew in from the high ranges of the Taurus Mountains to the east. We were approaching the Cappadocian town of Melitene, which lies in a fertile plain watered by the River Tohma, one of the tributaries of the Euphrates. Melitene, though now small and somewhat neglected, occupied an important position astride the old Persian Royal Road, and marked the spot where the army would divide.

I rubbed my leg and reclined on the couch as Gafarn and Diana made themselves comfortable on the couches arranged for them, Klietas once more becoming a wine pourer for my guests. It had been a hot and dusty day marching through the valleys of eastern Cappadocia and my whole body ached.

'The old wound?' asked Gafarn.

'The old wound.'

Diana gave me a sympathetic smile. 'Poor Pacorus.'

Despite the ache, I was pleased there was no longer any bitterness between her and me.

'I have a favour to ask,' I said to them. 'Tomorrow, I want you to ride ahead to link up with Castus. As the army of Hatra is all horsemen, you should be able to reach Castus by late afternoon.'

'Eager to be rid of us?' grinned Gafarn.

'Eager for you to restrain your grandson,' I replied.

'Pacorus thinks Castus will wait until we have diverted south to head for Dura, before doubling back to reap vengeance on Cappadocia,' said Gallia.

'Just to prove a point,' I said.

'Which is what?' asked Gafarn.

'That Gordyene answers to no one, least of all Dura,' I answered.

Diana stared into her chalice of wine and shook her head.

'He has inherited his father's rage against the world. I fear the loss of Spartacus and Rasha will only feed his bitterness and anger.'

'That is why you two must act as a restraining influence on him,' I told her. 'Besides, at Melitene we would be parting company anyway. I ask you to journey with Castus at least to the headwaters of the Tigris and convince him not to do anything rash.'

'Define "rash",' queried Gafarn.

'Planning a new campaign against Pontus and Cappadocia next year,' I said. 'He still commands a powerful army and his Aorsi allies will be more than willing to join him if they think there is prospect of loot to be won. But such an action will unleash a war between Parthia and Rome, something I am desirous to avoid at all costs.'

'As are we, Pacorus' said Diana. 'Forty-five years ago, we rode from the Silarus Valley, the Romans breathing down our necks. In the intervening years we have defeated numerous Roman invasions, and now we have fought them to a standstill and achieved a hard-won peace. The last thing I want is to give them a pretext for launching a fresh invasion of Parthia.'

'We will rein in Castus, Pacorus, have no fear,' promised Gafarn.

So it was. The morning cool after a cloudless night, we embraced them both as the horsemen of Hatra, their carts and camels rode from camp. The Royal Bodyguard of our oldest friends sat waiting on their white steeds, every *kontus* flying a red pennant emblazoned with a white horse's head. Malik kissed Diana on the cheek and hugged Gafarn, genuinely sorry to see them go. Over the years he had formed a strong bond with the couple that had raised the man who had married his sister and made her the queen of a foreign land. He had felt Rasha's death deeply, as had we all. And like all of us, as he got older he felt each loss he suffered more keenly.

We watched them ride from camp in silence, Herneus bowing his head as he passed us, leading over fifteen thousand horsemen east to link up with Castus. Our road led south and then east, crossing the Euphrates to head into Hatran territory and follow the mighty river until we reached Dura. With Shamash's blessing we should see the city again in less than a month. In my eagerness to restrain Castus and avoid a conflict with Rome, I had forgotten about the enemy.

But the enemy had not forgotten about us.

Chapter 18

The nights suddenly turned cool, occasioning individuals to wrap themselves in cloaks when the sun had dropped below the western horizon. A constant light breeze from the north added to the chill, and though the days were largely sunny and bright, it was clear autumn was on its way. The days were uneventful, the army quitting camp just after dawn and adopting its usual marching formation: Talib and his scouts riding far ahead; a screen of horse archers riding ahead of the vanguard, which comprised a mixed force of horse and foot; the command group, which include myself and Gallia, the Amazons, Chrestus, Azad and Sporaces, plus Kalet and Malik, and a century commanded by the redoubtable Bullus; the cataphracts and their squires; the main body of the Exiles and Durans marching six abreast; the baggage and camel train; a strong rearguard of horse archers; and flank guards comprising horse archers. The army was on half-rations, the campaign having lasted longer than anticipated, though at least the horses, mules and camels had enjoyed rich grazing lands and had not suffered unduly.

It had rained the day before, though not enough to soften the ground only cool the air. The sounds of horses chomping on bits, the dull thuds of hooves on ground and behind the crump of thousands of hobnailed boots tramping the earth filled me with reassurance. I looked up at the craggy ridgeline on both sides of the valley we were entering and shook my head.

'Is your leg playing up?' asked Gallia.

'Mm? No, I was just thinking about the last time I was in Cappadocia, when the Romans captured me. It is not a happy memory.'

'How long ago was that, lord?' asked Kalet behind me.

'Over four decades. We lost many good men during that campaign, including my mentor, Bozan, the father of Vata.'

I turned to look at Kalet, Kewab, Chrestus and Azad, only to see a row of blank faces. I doubt they had even heard of Bozan and my boyhood friend Vata. Just another reminder of how old I was. I decided to reminisce some more.

'Nergal, that is King Nergal, was just an ordinary horse archer at the time and Gafarn was my slave.'

'King Gafarn, highborn?' Klietas was astounded.

'That's right, King Gafarn. We were all slaves after our capture, so you could say we were reborn after being guests of the Romans.'

'Do you hate the Romans, highborn, for what they did to you?'

'Not at all,' I told him. 'You should never hate your enemies, Klietas, because it clouds your judgement, and if your judgement is clouded it inhibits your chances of bettering them.'

'Fog.'

I heard Chrestus' voice and saw the mist beginning to envelop us. Like a phantom, it had appeared without warning, but in retrospect it was entirely predictable. The combination of a light night-time breeze, a clear night sky, recent rainfall and a cool morning temperature created the ideal conditions for valley fog. And then the fog was all around us, visibility was down to around twenty paces and it suddenly felt very cold. But as we plodded forward, I realised it was not cold that I was experiencing, rather apprehension. A chill ran down my spine and I instinctively pulled my bow from its case and nocked an arrow in the bowstring.

'Ready,' hissed Gallia.

Behind us came the sound of scraping as swords were pulled from scabbards. I could no longer hear the sound of marching foot soldiers or the jangling of saddlery. I tugged on Horns' reins to halt him, everyone else doing likewise, knowing that something was wrong. There was silence, but it was a calm laced with threat. Horns, sensing my concern, grunted and flicked his ears. I patted his neck.

'Easy, boy.'

Everyone was peering into the white mist, straining to identify something, anything, but saw no movement or shapes. Gallia spun in the saddle and drew back her bowstring when she heard individuals running, she and the other Amazons relaxing when a transverse crest appear out of the fog. Centurion Bullus deployed his men in two files either side of our mounted party, his men facing outwards to form a shield wall.

'You suspect trouble, Bullus?' I asked.

'I can smell it a mile off, majesty.'

His men shouldered their javelins, ready to launch them at the enemy. But there was no sound of anyone approaching: no curses from men tripping on stones or tufts of grass. Nothing. A horse whinnied, another backed away from … from what?

And then they came at us.

The Romans called the wild frontal attacks launched by the Gauls the *furor Celtica*, but these Gauls approached stealthily, treading carefully to get as close as possible without alerting us to their presence. And they were far removed from the 'naked swords' and ordinary warriors commanded by Amyntas. These were nobles in red, blue and green tunics, wearing leather armour cuirasses and colourful wool leggings. The majority carried longswords in addition to their round shields and cone helmets decorated with horsetails and feathers. A few carried spears, one of which thudded into an Amazon to announce the beginning of the battle.

'There!' screamed Minu, shooting her arrow at the horde of dark shapes emerging from the mist.

There was a groan when her arrow found flesh and then a mighty roar as the Gauls ran at us. Multiple hisses signalled the release of bowstrings, but the Gauls were close and holding their shields in front of them in anticipation of the volley, the one volley they knew would be shot before they got close to the women warriors of Queen Gallia.

To run straight into Bullus' legionaries.

The Gauls had planned their ambush well, infiltrating into the valley and waiting until it filled with fog, no doubt advised on the weather conditions in this particular spot by their Cappadocian allies. But they had not factored in that the King and Queen of Dura would also be protected by a century of their foot soldiers led by a veteran centurion. Nevertheless, as more and more Gauls came rushing from the mist, it became apparent that the century was heavily outnumbered.

I released my bowstring at a Gaul about to swing his sword at a legionary, the arrow striking him in the shoulder, penetrating his leather armour to knock him to the ground. The legionary leapt forward, stabbed the point of his *gladius* hard into his face, and then pulled back. Another Gaul jumped over his prostrate companion, hollering a war cry, his sword held high so he could chop it down on the legionary. Klietas put an arrow into his eye socket and I put another one into his chest, which stopped him dead.

The legionaries were acting as a breakwater, halting the onrushing Gauls to allow us to shoot our arrows. But Bullus had only a hundred men – a reinforced century – whereas the Gauls numbered hundreds.

'Hold them!' shouted Bullus, dozens of Gauls chopping and slashing at the thin line of legionaries with their swords, deflecting *gladius* thrusts with their shields.

More Gauls came from the mist, these armed with spears that they threw at the riders behind our foot soldiers. Most missed but high-pitched squeals signalled that some hit Amazons, who tumbled from their horses, mounts also being struck and felled.

A legionary went down under the blows of two or more enemy swords. Into the gap raced the Gauls who had felled him. Arrows killed two but the third plunged his sword into the belly of an Amazon and dragged her from the saddle. Malik rode forward and slashed down hard with his sword with a sideways blow that almost took the Gaul's head off.

I shot arrow after arrow at any targets that presented themselves – and there were a lot of targets. A legionary was cut down. I killed his slayer. Haya's horse collapsed, its belly opened by a spear thrust.

'Haya!' screamed Klietas, jumping down from his own horse and racing over to where a leering Gaul was about to disembowel his beloved. I tried to shoot the Gaul but in a flash Klietas leapt on his back, dagger in hand, and began stabbing at the man's neck again and again. I saw a fountain of blood and the Gaul go down, Haya jumping to her feet to shoot another Gaul bearing down on Klietas with a war hammer. The Gaul stopped, an arrow in his chest, but continued to stagger forward, gripping his hammer with both hands to bludgeon my squire to death. Klietas spun and slashed his dagger across his throat, showering him with more enemy blood and killing the Gaul.

The mist was still thick as the battle degenerated into a series of isolated fights, Bullus trying to retain some sort of order among his men but failing. Half of them were dead or wounded; the rest were clustered around Gallia and myself, both of us running short of arrows. Chrestus was on his feet, shield in one hand, *gladius* in the other, cutting down Gauls with aplomb as he stood in the rapidly dwindling circle of legionaries. Sporaces and Kewab were loosing arrows like men possessed, some striking faces and chests, others glancing off shields and helmets. Azad, on his feet after his horse was cut down by two Gauls, gripped his sword with both hands to parry the strike of an enemy longsword, defeating the blow before replying with his own downward strike, which cut through the enemy sword. The Gaul, perplexed why this should happen, stared incredulously at his broken weapon, before dying when Azad thrust his ukku blade through his chest.

'Dismount, dismount!' I shouted, aware that we were literally sitting targets as the circle of Gauls around us thickened and the number of Amazons was whittled down.

Without hesitation everyone slid off their horses' backs, sheltering behind perhaps sixty legionaries. All except Kalet. He shouted abuse at the Gauls as he rode forward to slash at them with his sword. But his decision to leave the circle made him suddenly isolated, and he was immediately surrounded by a host of enemies. He cut down one, a second and a third, Gallia frantically shooting arrows at those Gauls near him in a vain attempt to save his life. But he was dragged from the saddle and disappeared from view, his Gaul killers howling with delight at his bloody demise.

'He's mine.'

My anguish over the death of Kalet was interrupted by the loud voice of King Amyntas, two-handed war hammer in hand, who pushed aside one of his lords to face me. Or would have done had not Bullus been between us. He was as big and loud as ever, ginger hair showing beneath his helmet sporting eagle wings, his eyes bulging with rage. His was hammer was smeared with blood, as was his scale armour.

'Just you and me,' he roared. 'Here. Now.'

I gently laid a hand on Bullus' broad shoulders.

'This one's mine, centurion.'

I stepped out from behind him, *spatha* in hand, the sound of men and women dying and the clash of weapons clashing slowly fading as both sides drew breath after the frenzied outburst of bloodletting. Dead Amazons and their horses lay all around, those beasts still living, including Horns, having been released to escape the horror. I prayed to Shamash that my horse, a gift from Silaces, still lived in the mist that showed no signs of budging. But the ring of dead Gauls that surrounded us dwarfed our own losses. Our arrows had reaped a rich harvest, the short swords of Bullus and his men having added to the number of enemy dead. I heard muffled shouts, horns being sounded and drums being beaten and surmised the whole army was under attack.

'Your life ends now,' shouted Amyntas, pointing his hammer at me.

He was bigger than me, stronger than me, younger than me and fitter than me. Apart from that we were evenly matched.

'Don't do it, majesty,' pleaded Chrestus, weighing up each opponent and coming down on the side of the big Gaul.

'Sometimes, Chrestus,' I told him, 'the life of one man can save many.'

I walked forward, skirting a dead Gaul with hideous facial wounds, and stepped over a slain legionary whose head had been crushed by a war hammer, perhaps the one carried by Amyntas, which would soon be wielded against me. I glanced behind at a worried Gallia, her face enclosed by the cheek guards of her helmet. Amyntas was waving his hammer around, displaying a handling dexterity that was intended to intimidate me. It worked. I suddenly felt very old and uncertain, though knew I could not back down. Amyntas roared with glee at the prospect of slaying me, but fell silent when two of his burly warlords rushed forward, grabbed his arms and hauled him back.

His face went red with rage. 'Release, release me at once. I will have your heads for this, you maggots, you traitorous bastards.'

But they did not let go and suddenly a horn sounded and the Gauls began to withdraw. I looked behind at a line of confused but grateful legionaries and a beaming Gallia.

'What in the name of Shamash?' I muttered.

Then I heard the sound of boots pounding the earth and knew our salvation was at hand. Out of the mist, which was finally dissipating, came Lucius Varsas at the head of what appeared to be a full cohort of Exiles, its centurions immediately deployed their men around our bedraggled group. Lucius searched me out, stood to attention before me and saluted.

'You are a sight for sore eyes,' I told him, throwing my arms around him in a gesture of familiarity that took him by surprise, prompting him to become as stiff as a stone statue. I released him.

Chrestus came forward. 'How fares the rest of the army?'

'As far as I can tell, sir, bearing in mind the lack of visibility, it remains untouched.'

'Untouched?' I said.

'A clever ruse by the enemy, majesty,' said Lucius. 'In the mist the enemy made a lot of noise but did not attack us or, as far as I can tell, any other part of the army save your segment. But they made a lot of noise, banged many drums and blew many horns to keep us rooted to the spot.'

'Clever,' said Kewab admiringly. 'The Gauls, having lost many men at Corum and Kayseri, knew they would fare poorly in a battle against Dura's army, so they used the weather to mask their approach and probable weak numbers in their aim to kill the king. No offence, majesty.'

'They nearly succeeded,' I said. 'I doubt I would have lasted long against that big brute.'

'You should let me take some horsemen and hunt him down, majesty,' said Sporaces.

'An excellent idea,' agreed Chrestus.

I discounted the notion. 'No, our main aim, our only aim, is to get back to Dura as quickly as possible and draw a line under this sorry, irrelevant campaign.'

'Pacorus!'

I heard the alarm in Gallia's voice and turned to see Zenobia collapse into my wife's arms. I rushed over as she comforted the commander of the Amazons, whose left side was soaked in blood. An enemy blade, perhaps a spear point, had obviously grievously wounded her. Her face was pale, her breathing shallow and a knot tightened in my stomach. I had seen too many similar wounds and knew it was a mortal one. I knelt beside Zenobia and held her hand, Gallia cradling her head.

'Water,' I shouted.

Klietas thrust a water bottle into my hand. I held the opening to Zenobia's mouth so she could take a couple of sips. She did not speak but her brown eyes were filed with gratitude. Gallia gently stroked her hair as the commander of the Amazons stared into the sky, which was now clearing as the sun burnt away the last vestiges of the mist, to reveal a vivid blue dotted with small white, puffy clouds.

'Shamash bless you, Zenobia.' I said softly as life left her and her soul departed to join the immortals in the afterlife.

Gallia closed her eyes and for a long time she and I remained by Zenobia's side. She had carried my banner for many years, like the griffin statue at the Palmyrene Gate becoming a permanent fixture of the army. She had never married, and as far as I knew had never even had a suitor, dedicating her life to the Amazons and Kingdom of Dura. It was a cruel fate to end her life in some nameless valley in Cappadocia, far from her home. But at least she died surrounded by her comrades and comforted in her final moments by her king and queen.

The whole army stood to attention later as the bodies of Zenobia, Kalet and the others who had fallen fighting the Gauls were cremated on a great pyre. Gallia told me that the Gauls regarded the head as the source of life, emotions and the soul, and that he who captured the head of an enemy attained the strength of the fallen enemy. So I ordered Chrestus to organise the beheading of every dead Gaul, the trophies arranged around our fallen on the pyre before it was set alight. As the flames took hold of the great pile of wood and began to consume the bodies, I closed my eyes and prayed to Shamash that he would accept our offerings and welcome the souls of Dura's dead into heaven.

Seven days later we entered Hatran territory, crossing the Euphrates a hundred miles north of Zeugma and marching along the eastern bank of the great waterway. After the heat of summer it was now low and slow moving, which matched our spirits. The army marched each day and built a camp at night, officers, men and civilians going about their duties as they had done that day, the day before and would so on the morrow. But there was no elation that accompanied a winning campaign, no boasting at night around campfires and no smiles on the faces of soldiers who had tasted victory. Only a determination to be as professional as possible, to ensure standards did not slip and the army marched back to Dura in the same manner as it had left. But everyone knew that when it did return there would be no new silver disc to decorate the Staff of Victory, for this was one campaign no one would choose to remember.

When we first saw the yellow walls of Dura and the Citadel, the black pall that hung over the army was banished. The Durans and Exiles once more had a spring in their step and the spirits of the horsemen rose. Azad ordered the cataphracts to don their armour and Chrestus commanded that the red and white plumes that had been purchased prior to the visit of Phraates to Dura, adorn the helmets of legionaries. Every *kontus* was decorated with a white pennant with a red griffin motif when the cataphracts rode through the Palmyrene Gate, cheering crowds on both sides of the road that led to the Citadel throwing flowers to create a carpet of foliage on which we rode. We waved back at the people, Minu behind us, promoted to command the Amazons, carrying my banner that fluttered in the breeze.

In the Citadel, Rsan, Almas and Aaron waited in line at the foot of the palace steps, while at the top of them stood Eszter and Dalir, both looking royal in fine silk robes and expensive footwear. They both smiled at us and then looked for Kalet among the other riders entering the courtyard.

The pall of blackness suddenly returned.

Chapter 19

Disbelief first gripped Eszter and Dalir when they were told Kalet was dead. They initially found it difficult to comprehend the larger-than-life figure who had become a legend among Dura's people was no longer alive. Dalir, true to form, told me he was glad his father had died with a sword in his hand rather than ending his days as a weak, feeble individual confined to his bed. Eszter was more emotional, breaking down and sobbing in her mother's arms. As I watched her crumble, I cursed the memory of Spartacus, the man who had tricked me into joining his war of profit and plunder, which had turned to dust in our hands.

Malik, having lost over three hundred of his best warriors, some of them close friends, prepared to return to Palmyra. Like me he was old now, his hair heavily laced with grey and his tattooed faced criss-crossed by worry lines. He seemed to have visibly aged during the campaign, his eyes world-weary, and his slim frame now having a gaunt look. He delayed in Dura only to pay his respects to Dalir and Eszter. Though we were all sad, I reflected on how times had changed for the better. There was a time when the idea of one of Dura's desert lords being embraced by an Agraci king would have been unthinkable, treasonous even. That era had been consigned to history, for which I gave thanks to Shamash.

The day after our return we said our farewells to Malik. We clasped forearms and he embraced Gallia and Eszter and put a fatherly arm around Dalir.

'Jamal will be glad to see you, my friend,' I told him.

'It is time Riad led the Agraci to war,' he replied, hauling himself into the saddle. 'I am too old to be riding to the ends of the earth.'

'Me, too,' I agreed.

'That big Gaul would have killed you. You know that.'

I nodded.

'You are too old for brawling, Pacorus. Take my advice, stay at home from now on.'

'I will heed your advice, my friend.'

He raised a hand to us, turned his horse and trotted from the courtyard, his Agraci bodyguard following. When he had gone I walked back into the palace and called Klietas to the terrace, slumping into my chair beneath the awning and putting my feet on the footstool. I had derided Phraates and other kings for owning such ostentatious items, but I had to admit they were excellent for relaxing. Ashk fussed over me like a mother hen, pouring fruit juice into a silver goblet and enquiring if I required food.

'No, you may go.'

He bowed and departed, passing Klietas who hurried on to the terrace. He stood before me and bowed his head.

'Highborn?'

I poured him a drink and offered him the goblet.

'Here.'

'Thank you, highborn.'

'Two things, Klietas. First, stop calling me and the queen "highborn", we find it embarrassing and frankly ridiculous. Second, I am releasing you from my service.'

He looked distressed. His jaw dropped, and misery filled his eyes. I rose from the chair to face him.

'Now before you start babbling about how you have let me down, I want to show you something.'

I took his elbow and led him to the stone balustrade. Below were the blue waters of the Euphrates. I pointed to the east.

'What do you see?'

He focused hard on the barren landscape.

'Nothing, high…, majesty.'

'Now look to the south and tell me what you see.'

He turned his eyes away from the desert across the river to the extensive palm groves and fields on the western bank of the river, extending as far as the eye could see.

'Palms, fields and livestock, majesty.'

I slapped him on the back.

'Exactly, Klietas. People far more qualified and talented than me have made the desert bloom. Where before there was rock and sand, there is now greenery and prosperity. And not just around the city. Thanks to the tireless efforts of the army's engineers over the years, and not a little investment, the land inland from the river for a distance of over two hundred miles is now blooming.

'Dura needs farmers, Klietas, not squires or soldiers.'

I walked back to my chair and eased myself into it.

'That being the case, I am buying you a plot of land to farm, along with animals and everything else to get you started. It is a reward for saving my life.'

His face lit up. 'You are most generous, highborn.'

I rolled my eyes. 'Find yourself a wife and have lots of sons who will carry on your line and work the land when you are gone.'

He raised his goblet and toasted me, grinning like an idiot.

'I will ask Haya to marry me, highborn.'

'Majesty, Klietas, majesty. But Haya is not for you, I'm sad to say.'

His smile disappeared.

'She is promised to another?'

The distraught visage returned.

'No, but I fear she is not the settling down type. She is an Amazon, Klietas, a skilled killer who would be horrified by the prospect of doing whatever a farmer's wife does.'

'If I become rich I can buy her fine jewellery and build her a big house.'

His naivety was touching.

'Cast your mind back to your expedition to Zeugma. Haya killed Cookes?'

'Cookes?'

'The fat governor.'

'Yes, majesty,' he beamed with pride.

'And you have seen Haya fight on the battlefield?'

'Yes, majesty.'

'And have you seen her look?'

'Look, majesty?'

'The look of glee in her eyes when she shoots down an enemy with her bow, the expression of satisfaction and pride at the sight of a foe dying by her hand. I've seen it many times in many eyes. Many soldiers do not enjoy killing but take pride in their profession and kill because they have to, because it is expected of them. Haya enjoys it. For her and others, war is an addiction they cannot do without.'

I looked at him and knew my words were wasted. He was in love with the girl and no amount of reasoning would change that. I threw up my arms.

'But feel free to ask her to be your wife anyway. Neither the queen nor I will stand in your way. But before you do, turn your mind to your farm.'

After having a word with Almas, I found Klietas a nice plot of land around ten miles south of the city, which was part of the royal estates used for horse breeding. It was near the river and nourished by a new canal that had been constructed to bring water from the Euphrates and take it inland up to ten miles. Almas informed me there was already a mud-brick hut in situ, along with animal pens, which would save Klietas valuable time. To aid him in his enterprise, I ordered the treasury to purchase a pair of oxen, which my former squire would use to plough his land more easily, as well as rent out to other farmers when his own land was tilled and seeded. It was a large plot of land so Klietas would need hired hands to assist him, so I ordered the treasury to make funds available to pay hired labour during the first three years of Klietas' endeavour. Finally, I asked Almas to keep an eye on him and let me know if he got into financial difficulties.

Life returned to normality, which meant attending weekly council meetings. Formerly I had found them tedious, albeit necessary, but as the years passed I took comfort in their unrushed certainty and attention to the minutiae that was essential to the smooth running of the kingdom. For reasons of courtesy and as thanks for their services while we had been away, I asked Dalir and Eszter to continue to sit in on those meetings. I also asked Kewab to attend, partly because I wished him to be involved in the affairs of the kingdom, and partly because I enjoyed his company. As a result, the meeting room in the Headquarters Building was rather crowded, though mercifully the fierce heat of summer was now but a memory.

Rsan, pleased and relieved to see his king and queen safely returned to the city, was nevertheless perturbed concerning the first item on the agenda, as was Aaron who pushed the papyrus sheet he and his friend had been studying sideways to his deputy Ira. The cunning and clever accountant studied the words before looking up. I nodded to him to indicate he should begin the meeting.

'Your siege engines have been impounded, majesty.'

'Impounded?' I said. 'By whom?'

'By King Castus of Gordyene, majesty. He is demanding thirty talents of gold before they are released.'

'Little bastard,' seethed Chrestus, 'he should have his arse tanned for his insolence.'

Everyone nodded in agreement, even Kewab who was usually diplomacy personified. Castus was obviously still resentful over losing twenty thousand talents of gold and was making it clear he blamed me. A ton of gold was not an insignificant sum.

'Write back and say Dura will pay the gold,' I said.

'What?' Chrestus was not amused. 'That would set a bad precedent, majesty. You should demand your own property back, and if you don't get it, make clear you will take it back by force.'

'Blackmail should not be encouraged, majesty,' agreed Rsan.

'It would send a bad signal, Pacorus,' said Gallia.

I reached over to take the water jug and poured myself a cup of the liquid, taking a sip. I looked at all the faces at the table and smiled.

'I am old now, and the benefit of age, one of the few, is wisdom. Or at least, experience. Castus is still sulking over the gold he was forced to surrender in Cappadocia, forced to do so by myself. It is an unhappy coincidence that Dura's siege engines were despatched to Vanadzor to prevent them being used in Pontus. That was also my responsibility.'

'That was a sound military decision,' said Kewab.

'Well, it has resulted in the current, unfortunate situation. It seems we have three choices. We can refuse to pay the gold, we can pay it, or,' I glanced at the crop-haired Chrestus, 'next year we can march against Gordyene to reclaim our siege engines.'

Ira raised his stylus.

'Yes, Ira?' I said.

'Forgive me, majesty, but having talked with General Varsas, I believe that these engines are made of wood.'

'Wood is their main component, yes.'

He smiled with satisfaction. 'Dura has an abundance of timber growing along the Euphrates, majesty. Could not the army build some more engines?'

Chrestus sighed with frustration.

'Perhaps you could enlighten Ira on why we want the engines back, Chrestus.'

The general's eyes bored into the pale Jew.

'If Gordyene has siege engines, then it can reduce the Armenian capital to ashes, Sinope too if Castus has a mind to return to Pontus.'

Ira was not convinced. 'Surely, King Castus can also build his own siege engines. I assume Gordyene has trees?'

'Order the gold to be despatched immediately,' I told Aaron. 'Chrestus, order Sporaces to ride north with two thousand horse archers to escort my siege engines back to Dura. And you are right, Ira, Gordyene might build its own engines. But Castus has to pay for a large army, which makes heavy demands on his treasury. Getting our engines back will delay the manufacture of his own engines, should he decided to invest in a siege train and hire personnel capable of operating it.'

'He is like a child who has a new toy,' commented Gallia derisively.

'Or we could march with whole army and array it before the walls of Vanadzor,' said Chrestus casually.

'You would like that,' I replied. 'But I remember a time when High King Orodes did the same thing, in an attempt to rein in another king of Gordyene by the name of Surena. That ended in a great battle in which Surena was killed. I have no desire to see history repeat itself.'

I saw Eszter nodding at Dalir, who cleared his throat.

'You have something to add, Dalir?' I asked.

'We will pay the gold, lord,' he said, to everyone's surprise.

'High King Phraates gave us fifty talents of gold for a wedding gift,' said Eszter, 'most of which remains unused.'

'It is what my father would have wanted, lord,' stated Dalir.

'We accept your generosity, Prince Dalir,' smiled Aaron, relieved that the kingdom's treasury would be spared having to pay Castus.

I was about to object but Gallia caught my eye and shook her head. Dalir and Eszter obviously wanted to make the gesture and it would have been churlish of me to refuse. Perhaps in doing so it meant something positive would come of the campaign that had cost Kalet's life.

The rest of the meeting was far more agreeable. Ira reported record yields of barley and wheat following the harvest, which I congratulated Almas for. It was his foresight and energy in overseeing the building of the kingdom's irrigation system that was responsible for the great crop surplus enjoyed by the kingdom. Farmers paid their taxes in produce, which the treasury then sold abroad through foreign agents in the city, most going to Media. The agents paid gold on behalf of their lords, which went into the treasury's coffers.

Ira also reported an increase in traffic on the Silk Road, camel caravans travelling east and west stopping off at Dura before journeying on to Egypt or back to the east. Each caravan paid dues to camp in the caravan park to the north of the city, and the guards and cameleers visited the city to spend their wages on drink, whores or food, all of which benefited Aaron's coffers.

But my treasurer had the eyes of a hawk and the mind of an elephant, the large beasts that the rulers of the empire's eastern kingdoms used in their armies, which I was reliably informed had memories to rival that of the most intelligent Greek. At the end of the meeting I asked of there if there was any other business, expecting no one to speak. But Aaron raised a hand.

'Just one small matter, majesty.'

He held out his hand to Ira, who handed him a papyrus scroll. Aaron unrolled it and perused its contents.

'This is a list of items to be purchased for your former squire, a young man by the name of Klietas. Let's see. Two oxen, seeds to sow his land, a large area of land by all accounts, which the treasury is also to purchase, along with ploughs, tools, ropes, and so forth. Finally, the treasury is to make available an interest-free loan to this Klietas, which equates to a gift.'

He shook his grey-haired head. 'It amounts to a major outlay, majesty.'

'It is an investment, Aaron,' I told him.

'In a young man who has no collateral, little experience and has no sons to assist him on his farm?'

'No, Aaron, in the future of the kingdom. Until now Dura has been a kingdom organised for war, the treasury's income being primarily directed to the upkeep and enlargement of the army. That army has, over the decades, marched thousands of miles in the service of the empire, winning great victories but also incurring considerable costs.'

'Indeed,' said Aaron without thinking.

'The same army that has allowed you and your family to live in peace and security,' growled Chrestus.

'The point is,' I continued, eager to avoid a confrontation between the pair, 'I want Dura to be a centre of agriculture as well as a staging post on the Silk Road. Men such as Klietas will build the future of the kingdom, while the army will continue to provide its security. As for Klietas himself, he saved my life and I consider a few seeds and a couple of oxen a small price to pay for my life.'

Aaron, long used to knowing when to concede an argument, rolled up the scroll and handed it back to Ira.

'I shall see to the matter personally, majesty.'

After the meeting, I rode down to the Palmyrene Gate and left Horns at the gatehouse before walking up the steps in one of the towers flanking the entrance. I emerged from a small door beneath the fighting platform above, smiling when I saw the stone griffin standing on its base above the gates, staring west unblinking, towards the legionary camp half a mile away and the desert beyond. I dismissed the two guards standing sentry over the griffin, as I liked to be alone in its company, purely for sentimental reasons. After I had stroked one of the statues legs, I leaned back against the plinth it sat on and surveyed my kingdom. To the west was the road to Palmyra, the dusty track filled with camel caravans as far as the eye could see. Behind me was my city and the Citadel, the pleasing aroma of spices being sold in the markets drifting to my nostrils, a city filled with thriving, healthy people protected by an army that was rated by friend and foe alike as a truly formidable instrument. To the south was a great band of green, now extending from the river inland to a distance of ten miles. When I first came to Dura only a thin strip of palm trees hugging the river provided any colour, the rest was a great expanse of yellow, sun-blasted dirt, an abode of snakes, scorpions and Agraci raiders. Now the Agraci were friends and allies and the waters of the Euphrates were used to turn desert into fertile land.

'I thought I would find you here.'

'It's my favourite spot.'

'Congratulations on extricating yourself from Cappadocia, son of Hatra, that was no mean feat, though why one tasked with defending the Parthian Empire found himself in Roman lands remains a mystery. A trip down memory lane, perhaps?'

I did not turn to face her. Hearing her voice was enough.

'I was tricked into participating.'

'The great King of Dura, famous lord of war, tricked? What is the world coming to? Did not Claudia explain to you the legend of Gordis and what happens to rulers of Gordyene who stray from their domains?'

'Spartacus was family.'

A mocking cackle. 'He was not. He was the son of a foreign slave whose memory you have grown ridiculously sentimentally attached to. So much so that it has clouded your judgement. Things will be better now that his son has joined him in the afterlife.'

'Castus might cause trouble.'

'Castus is a mere shadow of his father,' she replied, 'more interested in money than settling scores, as you have discovered.'

'What scores?' I asked.

She sighed. 'Now that his father is dead, the Armenians will renege on their agreement to pay Gordyene gold.'

'Which will lead to war between the two.'

Another cackle. 'Wars are expensive, son of Hatra. Castus is more devious than his father and will find other ways of exhorting gold from the Armenians. Talking of gold, I see you are lavishing it on that illiterate farm boy you rescued in Media.'

'I don't want him to be a soldier. Soil is easier to wash off than blood.'

She laughed mockingly. 'Even after all these years, you are still a sentimental fool, taking pity on the world's waifs and strays and seeing value in the most worthless of individuals. I think that is why the gods love you, son of Hatra, because they take pity on the hopelessness of your causes. And give you great gifts, of course.'

Now it was my turn to mock. 'What gifts? Everything I have done, everything I have achieved, has been through my own efforts.'

'Of course, calm down. How is your Egyptian doing?'

'Kewab? Fine.' I grew alarmed. 'What do you know? Is he in danger?'

'No more than you or I. Well, you, anyway. It was his plan that rescued you from the witch at Kayseri, was it not?'

'Glaphyra? She is a wily opponent and her plan nearly succeeded. I will not deny it was Kewab's battle plan that saved us.'

'How strange that he should suddenly pitch up at Dura all those years ago, a foreigner in a foreign land who just happened to join your army. Who then went on to rise through the ranks, who saved the eastern half of the empire from collapse and returned to save your hide in Cappadocia. Coincidence, son of Hatra? And, of course, there is the greatest gift of all, who will tidy up your loose ends.'

'Who?' I demanded to know, turning to see only thin air.

Epilogue

Gallia had always loved Dura, ever since the first time she had seen its yellow stone walls all those years ago. Even before she entered the city she had fallen in love with it, its stout fortifications, the strong, square towers spaced along the perimeter wall, and the mighty Citadel, the brooding stronghold that was higher than any other part of Dura. In the long years since she had arrived her affection for the city had never dimmed. She had held it against Roman legions and rebel Parthians, had welcomed kings, princes and a king of kings to its Citadel, and had raised three daughters in its palace. And it was the only place she could truly call home. Even before she met Pacorus, the dashing, romantic prince from a far-off place she had never heard of over forty years ago, she had never felt at ease in the Senones heartland. No, that is wrong. She had been made to feel unwelcome by her father, King Ambiorix, who had resented her since her birth. Her mother had given her life but had paid with her own life, making her father bitter and resentful against her, culminating in him selling her to a rich Roman, the owner of a gladiator school in the city of Capua.

When she came to Dura she was an outcast, apart from the world, and so naturally took to a city full of outcasts and the unwanted, a place set apart from the rest of the Parthian Empire by the River Euphrates. Everyone had told her when she had lived for a brief time in Hatra that civilisation ended on the eastern bank of the Euphrates, beyond which was barbarism and chaos. But to her, it seemed the gods had fated her to live among the barbarians and chaos, and she in turn felt an immediate affection for the people of Dura. She felt at home and at ease in the city and its wild, untamed hinterland, which she and Pacorus set about making in their image.

Now the city and the kingdom prospered, succeeding beyond their wildest dreams, benefiting from the Silk Road coursing through it and the establishment of dozens of settlements in the desert south of the city, made possible by peace with the Agraci. Now the city teemed with shopkeepers, entertainers, painters, scribes, metalworkers, lawyers, farmers and priests. In the centre of the city, betraying its Greek origins, was the *agora*, meaning 'open place of assembly', which was in reality an open-air marketplace. It was the beating heart of the city, the abode of confectioners, vintners, fishmongers, dressmakers, cloth merchants, shoemakers, jewellers, potters, and sellers of leather goods. Everything could be purchased in Dura's *agora*, everything except slaves.

The whole world was plagued by the spectre of slavery. Even Hatra, where Gafarn and Diana ruled, possessed thousands of slaves. Tradition had such an iron grip on that kingdom that her friends could not even banish slaves from their own palace. Every city in the Parthian Empire was infested with slaves – except Dura. Slaves accompanied the trade caravans, of course, but they were always quartered in the caravan park outside the city, and it was forbidden to bring slaves into the city itself. There were servants in the homes of the nobility, and they were probably beaten and abused like their servile counterparts in other cities. In this, Parthia was no different from Rome. But Dura *was* different. It was a place where slaves fled to and were given sanctuary, safe in the knowledge that their former masters and mistresses would not dare to pursue them to the kingdom where King Pacorus and his fearsome wife lived. Cruel tongues talked of Dura's army being a force of slaves and they did nothing to contradict the rumours. The 'army of slaves' had never been defeated on the battlefield and with each victory its reputation had grown, until it had become a legend. Even the recent campaign, abortive though it may have been, had increased its aura of invincibility, for it should have been annihilated outside the walls of Kayseri, surrounded as it was on all sides. But it had triumphed and marched back to Dura intact. But there had been casualties.

As Gallia trotted into the city, she cast a glance at Minu beside her. The new commander of the Amazons was remote, withdrawn. She had survived the battle in the fog but had taken several blows to her body that had ripped her mail shirt and bruised her torso. She thought nothing of it, and in the mourning for Zenobia and the thirty other Amazons who had fallen, forgot about her battered body. But two days after the fight she began bleeding heavily. Sophus did everything possible to save her unborn child but failed. Talib tried to comfort her and reassure her they would have other children. But she had lost her first child and blamed King Amyntas of Galatia. She wanted revenge upon him, upon anyone allied with him.

They rode into the small courtyard to the rear of The Sanctuary, two stable hands, both female, taking their horses to the stalls. Formerly, the stables had housed the horses of rich clients come to taste the delights of the most famous brothel in Dura, the establishment where Roxanne, later Queen of Sakastan, had plied her trade. Now Amazons guarded every entrance and men were forbidden to enter the place where women had formerly been reduced to slavery, becoming the playthings of men.

The two Amazons standing either side of the door that led from the stables to The Sanctuary bowed, one knocking on the door behind her. Moments later, the door opened and a handsome woman with emerald green eyes and thick, golden hair stood in the doorway.

She smiled and bowed to Gallia, her tall, slender frame hidden by the black robes she always wore.

'Welcome, majesty, everything is ready for your inspection.'

She was unlike any Scythian Sister Gallia had ever seen, and that included her own daughter. But Claudia had told her she was the best at her craft, which she had been teaching those chosen to continue the war started by Spartacus.

But which she would finish.

Historical notes

The Roman client kingdoms adjacent to the northwestern border of the Parthian Empire were once forces to be reckoned with in their own right, and their rich and bloody stories could fill several historical volumes. But by the time 'Lord of War'– around 26BC – they were shadows of their former selves.

Pontus, first formed as a kingdom in the aftermath of the breakup of the empire of Alexander the Great, was first ruled by Mithridates, the son of a Persian satrap servicing one of Alexander's former generals (Antigonus), between 302BC and 296BC. At first, Pontus had friendly relations with Rome, but this all changed with the accession to power of Mithridates VI. He came to power in 120BC and ruled for nearly 60 years, during which he methodically conquered neighbouring kingdoms in a rapid war of aggression. He cut a swathe of destruction in the area that resembles modern-day Turkey, slaughtering up to 80,000 Roman citizens in the process. Such atrocities could not go unpunished, though Rome's retribution was slow in coming due to wars in Africa, Germany and internal political disorder. Eventually, however, in 63BC, following the military victory of Pompey and the death of Mithridates, Pontus was annexed as a Roman province.

King Polemon, who featured in 'Sons of the Citadel' and features in 'Lord of War', earned the gratitude of Mark Antony when he accompanied the *triumvir* during his ill-fated invasion of Parthia in 36BC. Polemon was captured by the Parthians and ransomed. No doubt chastened by the experience, he was careful not to fully commit himself and his kingdom to Antony's war with Octavian. After Actium (31BC), the new undisputed Roman ruler curtailed Polemon's power, though he was allowed to remain in control of

Pontus. He worked hard to prove his allegiance to Octavian, which reaped rewards as by 26BC he was recognised as a friend and ally of Augustus.

The kingdom of Galatia was something of an anomaly in ancient Asia, being occupied by Gauls in the 3rd century BC, hence the name Galatia, or 'Gallia of the East'. The Gauls had migrated east from their homeland in the 4th century BC, eventually settling in modern-day central Turkey. There were three tribes – the Tectosages, the Tolistbobolii and the Trocmi – the kingdom they founded being originally ruled by a national council, but later united under a king. By the time of 'Lord of War' that king was Amyntas, who like his predecessors was largely pro-Roman. Galatia was organized as a Roman client kingdom by Pompey in 64BC, recognizing Deiotarus as the official Galatian King.

Amyntas, a chief of the Trocmi tribe, was the son of King Brogitarix, King of Galatia. He was obviously a man of dubious morals as he deserted Brutus and Cassius on the eve of the Battle of Philipp (42BC) to join Mark Antony. This won him the favour of Cleopatra's lover, who made him King of Cappadocia in 37BC. Gratitude seemed to be in short supply, however, when Amyntas deserted Mark Antony on the eve of Actium, which ensured he remained King of Galatia after Antony's defeat.

Cappadocia derives from the Persian word *Katpatuka*, meaning 'land of the well-bred horses', and that land was under Persian rule for 200 years, thereafter becoming part of the empire of Alexander the Great. Following the Macedonian's death it fell to the dynasty of Ariarathes in 323BC, whose family would rule Cappadocia until 93BC, fomenting friendly relations with Rome. However, during the period of civil strife in Rome at the end of the republic, Cappadocia, like many kingdoms in modern-day Turkey, changed allegiances with alarming regularity. For example, the kingdom supported Pompey against Caesar, switching sides following Caesar's victory at Pharsalus (48BC). In the civil war between Mark Antony and Octavian and Caesar's assassins, Cappadocia initially supported Cassius and Brutus, before changing sides to pledge allegiance to Antony following the defeat and deaths of the assassins. His defeat at Actium left Cappadocia no choice but to swear fealty to the new master of the Roman world: Octavian, who was happy to leave the realm as an independent kingdom in return for its continuing loyalty.

The King of Cappadocia in 'Lord of War' is Archelaus, who was installed as ruler by Mark Antony around 36BC. He was one of the few eastern kings who actually stuck by Antony, fighting beside him at the Battle of Actium. Surprisingly, this seems to have had little effect on his position as King of Cappadocia, Augustus allegedly happy for him to continue as ruler of the kingdom, probably due to his pro-Roman and anti-Parthian views. As such, he was a valuable ally on the eastern frontier.

Made in the USA
Las Vegas, NV
25 April 2024